The Queen's Handmaid

Also by Tracy L. Higley

Garden of Madness

Isle of Shadows

So Shines the Night

City on Fire: A Novel of Pompeii

Pyramid of Secrets (available in e-book only)

"I love Tracy Higley's novels. Meticulously-researched, spell-bindingly written with luscious prose and compelling and complex characters, each one is a treasure. Higley knows her history, but more importantly, she knows just how to capture the struggles and questions of the human heart—yesterday and today."

—Tosca Lee, *New York Times* best-selling author of *Havah: The Story of Eve* and the Books of Mortals series

Garden of Madness

"Readers will find much to enjoy here: fine writing, suspense, mystery, faith, love, and a new look at an old story."

—*Publishers Weekly*

"The author's insights into a woman's inner strengths . . . will leave readers rejoicing."

—*Romantic Times* Book Reviews, 4½ stars, Top Pick!

"Mystical as the Seven Wonders, exotic as the Hanging Gardens. Higley has outdone herself with this exquisite story of intrigue, elegantly told and rich with all the flavors of ancient Babylon. Simply magnificent."

—Tosca Lee, *New York Times* best-selling author of *Havah: The Story of Eve* and the Books of Mortals series

"Even more riveting than the historical background is the mystery that Higley creates as the backdrop to her exploration of the ancient world . . . Readers will not be satisfied until they have discovered the truth along with Tiamat."

—Dr. Shannon Rogers Flynt, Assistant Professor, Department of Classics, Samford University

Acclaim for Tracy L. Higley

City on Fire, previously released as *Pompeii*

"Higley's Pompeii ignites with riveting and compelling characters. No one unleashes the secrets of history with a masterful hand the way Higley does! Authentic and powerful, [*City on Fire*] is a fiery tale of a city lost to the power of Vesuvius. I simply could not read fast enough!"

—RONIE KENDIG, AUTHOR OF THE
DISCARDED HEROES SERIES

"[*City on Fire*] is a richly detailed story of powerful redemption and raw courage. Higley takes readers right to the foot of the legendary volcano, Vesuvius, and spins her tale under the shadow of certain disaster."

—GINGER GARRETT, AUTHOR OF
WOLVES AMONG US

"Higley brings Pompeii to life again in this exhilarating tale of love and adventure. The story was so enthralling to me—I want to read it again!"

—ELIZABETH GODDARD, AUTHOR OF
THE CAMERA NEVER LIES

So Shines the Night

"Higley proves once again that she has a great talent for historical fiction. It is easy to get lost in the ancient world with Daria during her adventures. The story is so well detailed and the struggles between different faiths and cultures is exceptionally illustrated. Daria characterizes all one would hope for in a strong, brave woman of faith."

—*ROMANTIC TIMES* BOOK REVIEWS,
4-STAR REVIEW

The Queen's Handmaid

Tracy L. Higley

THOMAS NELSON
Since 1798

NASHVILLE   DALLAS   MEXICO CITY   RIO DE JANEIRO

Published in Nashville, Tennessee, by Thomas Nelson. Thomas Nelson is a registered trademark of Thomas Nelson, Inc.

Thomas Nelson, Inc., titles may be purchased in bulk for educational, business, fund-raising, or sales promotional use. For information, please e-mail SpecialMarkets@ThomasNelson.com.

Publisher's Note: This novel is a work of fiction. Names, characters, places, and incidents are either products of the author's imagination or used fictitiously. All characters are fictional, and any similarity to people living or dead is purely coincidental.

Library of Congress Cataloging-in-Publication Data

Higley, T. L.

   The Queen's handmaid / Tracy L. Higley.

      pages cm.

   Summary: "From the servant halls of Cleopatra; Egyptian palace to the courts of Herod the Great, Lydia will serve two queens to see prophecy fulfilled. Alexandria, Egypt, BC. Orphaned at birth, Lydia was raised as a servant in Cleopatra's palace, working hard to please while keeping everyone at arm's length. She's been rejected and left with a broken heart too many times in her short life. But then her dying mentor entrusts her with secret writings of the prophet Daniel and charges her to deliver this; vital information to those watching for the promised King of Israel. Lydia must leave the nearest thing she had to family and flee to Jerusalem. Once in the Holy City, she attaches herself to the newly appointed king, Herod the Great, as handmaid to Queen Mariamme. Trapped among the scheming women of Herod; political family; his sister, his wife, and their mothers; and forced to serve in the palace to protect her treasure, Lydia must deliver the scrolls before dark forces warring against the truth destroy all hope of the coming Messiah"— Provided by publisher.

   ISBN 978-1-4016-8684-0 (pbk.)

   1. Queens—Fiction. 2. Slaves—Fiction. 3. Egypt—Fiction. I. Title.

   PS3608.I375Q44 2014

   813'.6—dc23   2013037409

Printed in the United States of America

14 15 16 17 18 RRD 5 4 3 2 1

For Steve Laube
In gratitude for nearly a decade
of unwavering support,
wise guidance, and genuine friendship

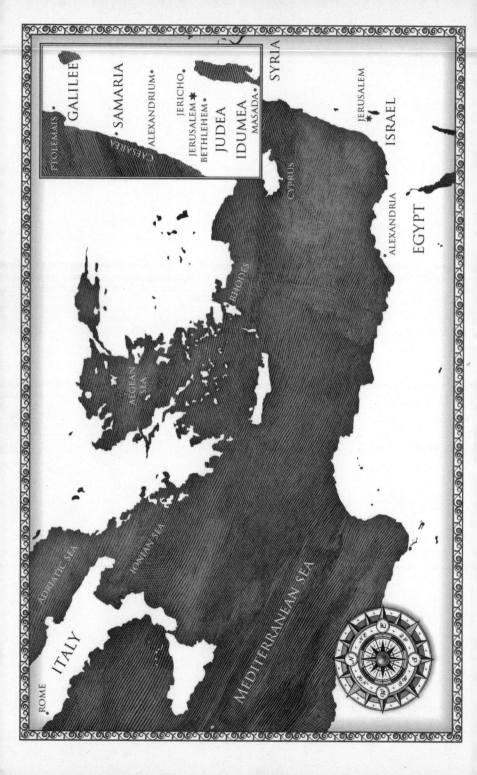

THE HASMONEAN DYNASTY

(Also known as the Maccabeans)

Not a complete family chart—only characters referenced in the book or familiar from the New Testament

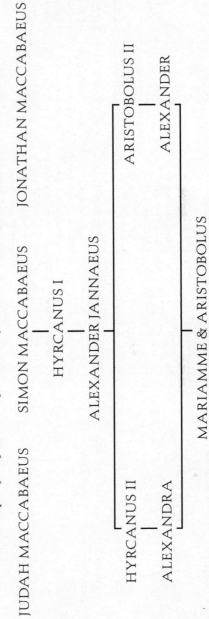

JUDAH MACCABAEUS

SIMON MACCABAEUS

JONATHAN MACCABAEUS

HYRCANUS I

ALEXANDER JANNAEUS

HYRCANUS II
ALEXANDRA

ARISTOBOLUS II
ALEXANDER

MARIAMME & ARISTOBOLUS

HEROD'S FAMILY

Not a complete family chart—only characters referenced in the book or familiar from the New Testament

Antipater II

Phasael — Joseph — Herod the Great — Pheroras — Salome

Salome

Berenice
(daughter of Salome:
married Herod's son
Aristobolus; mother
of Herodias)

Children of Herod the Great:

Antipater
(mother: Doris)

Alexander
(mother: Mariamme I)

Aristobolus
(mother: Mariamme I)

Philip the Tetrarch
(mother: Cleopatra of Jerusalem)
Eventually married his
neice Salome who danced for
Herod Antipas; mentioned
in Luke 3:1

Herod Antipas
(mother: Malthake)
Ruled Galilee & Perea; Married
his brother Philip's wife
Herodias (she was the daughter
of Herod the Great's sister Salome
and his son Aristobolus)
Executed John the Baptist;
Pilate sent Jesus to him after
Jesus was arrested.

Archelaus
(mother: Malthake)
ruled Judea &
Samaria - Mt 2:22

Herod-Philip
(mother: Mariamme II)
first husband of Herodias
and father of Salome
who danced for
Herod Antipas

Descendants of Aristobolus:

Herod Agrippa I
arrested Peter; died of worms -
Acts 12 and 23

Bernice
listens to Paul in Acts 25,
with her brother Agrippa II

Agrippa II
listens to Paul in Acts 25

Drusilla
married to Roman
prosecutor of Judea, Felix,
listened at Paul's trial in Acts 24

One

Alexandria, Egypt
January, 39 BC

Lydia detached herself from the surge of chaos in the palace kitchens and slipped along the shadowed corridor, to a door in the south wall where a few coins would finally find their way into her palm. If she was not caught.

The shouts had come thirty minutes earlier. The Idumean governor of the north-country province of Israel was navigating his ship into the royal port. Slaves assigned to watch the darkening harbor scuttled back to the palace.

In the kitchens, Banafrit was barking commands at her frantic staff, her voice a whip-crack over slaves and servants alike who scurried to do her bidding. But Lydia's presence was neither needed nor expected there, and her secret errand would not wait. She risked a beating, or worse, but it was not the first time.

From somewhere in the cavernous palace came a haunting melody plucked on lyre strings, but the gray walls of the darkened corridor tunneled away from the sound to the south wall. Lydia

1

sped forward on sure feet, sandals scuffing the stone floors. She could navigate these halls in darkness, and often did, to be alone with her thoughts.

The blue glaze of the jug she carried was smooth, but her fingers instinctively sought out imperfections, any trapped air or roughened clay that would render the piece less valued. A figure in the narrow doorway ahead shifted, the moonlight outlining wide shoulders and brawny arms.

At his sudden appearance, her back stiffened.

"You are late." He spoke in a whisper. The light behind him left his features undefined, but the voice was familiar.

In the harbor beyond, the eerie sound of a cat yowling for its next meal raised the hair on Lydia's arms. "I had difficulty getting away. We have a guest arriving—"

"Yes, Herod. The whole city is aware. But one politicking Arab need not disrupt all of commerce!"

Lydia bit back a sharp reply. Her small jug was hardly the stuff of exotic trade. She held the piece to the moonlight. "I gave this one shaded striations of blues and grays, and you'll see that the neck is quite delicate—"

"Girl, you know I care nothing about beauty." He snorted. "The only beauty I know is the lovely color of the obols your pieces fetch me." He jingled a pouch at her eye level. "Pity you can't work faster. Your work is always in demand."

Lydia handed him the jug and took the pouch from his outstretched hand. "Someday." She shook the coins as he had done. "When I have saved enough of this."

Though at the pace she found time to make pieces, she would be older than Banafrit by the time she broke free of palace service to open her own shop. If she survived that long. "Someday."

He shrugged and disappeared into the night with a disinterested wave and a muttered, "Until next week."

Lydia's free hand lifted of its own accord, as if to bid farewell to the jug that was a part of her, as all her artwork became.

She turned back into the corridor, and a flutter of white caught her eye. Her pulse jumped. "Who is there?"

Silence met her question. She tucked the money pouch with its scant obols under the folds of her outer robes and hurried forward, sliding her fingers along the length of the damp wall. Around the first corner a smoldering torch painted the corridor in a smoky half-light. Her quarry vanished around the next bend, but not before the jade-green robes and pale flesh had given her away. Andromeda.

Had the girl been watching? Seen the transaction in the shadows? Lydia paused in the hall, one hand braced against the wall and the other clutching the meager pouch. Cleopatra's anger knew no limits and was as unpredictable as summer lightning.

The scent of smoke watered Lydia's eyes and a chill breeze snaked through the hall and sputtered the torch, mimicking the beat of her heart. She swallowed against a bitter taste. She was so close to her goal of six hundred obols. She needed only to keep her head down and stay safe from Cleopatra's wrath until she earned a bit more. But if Cleopatra found out . . .

She would not follow Andromeda. Better to tuck the pouch's dismal contents into the carefully concealed pocket of her sleeping mat, in the lower level of the palace she shared with two other servants, than to try to figure out the girl's plan. Lydia passed the smoking torch, rounded the corner hesitantly, but Andromeda was already gone, off to spread gossip, no doubt. The girl was younger even than Lydia, perhaps only fifteen years old, but never missed a chance to outshine her. Lydia escaped to her bedchamber, secreted away the coins in the straw, and hurried to the kitchens to assess the damage.

The palace kitchens bordered a spacious atrium with a central *impluvium* beneath the open sky catching rainwater. Tonight, at the four corners of the *impluvium*, four large bronze pots were suspended by chains over cook fires. The overflowing pots pitched and heaved like ships on tempestuous waves of fire. Heat radiated through the courtyard, barely escaping into the night air. No expense, no effort would be spared to impress Herod. Cleopatra had made her desires clear.

Around the fires, palace staff stumbled, shoved, and shouted. The raised arms of pretty serving girls rushed past with platters of delicacies, and new-muscled boys shouldered amphorae of wine in a parade of luxury marching toward the spread tables.

Lydia weaved through the bedlam to the huge kitchen off the atrium, following the sound of Banafrit's roar of impatience.

"What do I care about such nonsense tonight, girl?"

Lydia hesitated in the doorway, jaw tightening. Andromeda had already found her way to Banafrit, to pour her poison into the woman's ear and try to curry favor. But Banafrit elbowed the girl away, bustling around a table littered with the remains of radish and carrot tips and greens and scowling at the noisy kitchen staff all at once.

The woman's gray-streaked hair was struggling free of its combs, and in the fire-heat, strands plastered her pink cheeks. Flour coated her left eyebrow, and she wiped the back of her hand across her forehead, the tan smudge like a scar.

Blustering as she was, Banafrit was the closest thing to a mother Lydia had ever known, though Lydia would never admit to the woman that she had constructed the role for her. Lydia belonged nowhere, but at least in this kitchen, she was acknowledged.

The older woman eyed Lydia in the door frame, glanced from her to Andromeda, and scowled once more. The younger girl seemed to understand where Banafrit's loyalty lay and slunk off to complain to a servant boy who was always hanging about her.

But it was another who greeted her, rising unsteadily from a chair against the wall. "Lydia, at last." He ringed a table of servants arranging pale-green melons on platters and came forward to greet her.

"Samuel." She held out welcoming hands to her friend. The aging man's usually laugh-crinkled face was somber, his white beard uncombed. "What brings you to the palace on a night such as this?"

"I—I need to speak with you—"

Banafrit waddled between them and swatted at Samuel in a familiar gesture born of years of acquaintance. "Be gone, old man. We've no time for lessons and studies here tonight. Herod will be wanting his food and his comforts, and we've nothing but slow-witted servants and lazy slaves about."

She cast an evil eye over Lydia, though a fondness lay behind her expression. "And you—why is it everyone wants to speak *about* you, *to* you? Haven't you duties of your own tonight? I should think that brat—"

"Cleopatra is readying her son herself this evening." Lydia idly rearranged some pomegranates and green grapes on one of the serving dishes into a more pleasing display, with complementary colors better balanced. "She wanted to remind him of the proper manners before a Jewish Galilean governor."

Samuel grunted. "He's not Jewish. And as for proper manners . . ." He left off, with a glance at the ceiling and a shrug.

Samuel's hostility ran deep. Although he had been born in Susa, in what had once been the Persian Empire, he was intensely loyal to all of Israel, from whence his people had been exiled centuries ago. And Lydia was equally loyal to him. If Banafrit was mother, then Samuel was father. Though it was best to remain independent, to keep some distance. A battle Lydia continually fought.

"Banafrit is right, Samuel. I should make myself available for whatever is needed tonight. Our lessons must wait."

"Hmph, lessons." Banafrit poked a servant girl and handed her the fruit platter. "Why you want to learn to be Jewish from this man, I'll never understand. You're not even a Jew."

Lydia raised her eyebrows. "How do you know?"

Banafrit's glance flicked to Samuel, then away, as though the two held a confidence between them. "I told you I've no time for chatter."

But Samuel grabbed her hands, dwarfing them in his own large grasp. "No lessons tonight, Lydia. There is something important I need to tell you. Something has happened—"

"Ly—di—a!" The screech echoed through the kitchen chamber, familiar enough to freeze every servant and slave at his task.

Cleopatra sailed into the kitchen, raven hair unbound and streaming, dressed only in a white sheath. Her dark eyes were wild with anger or excitement, perhaps both. "There you are! I have been calling for you all over the palace like a peasant woman chasing down a wayward husband! I need you at once. Caesarion has hurt himself, and I am not even *close* to being ready to meet Herod." She gave a glance to Samuel, his hands still wrapped around Lydia's, and frowned. Then she spun and departed, her expectation clear that Lydia would follow on her heels.

Lydia tried to pull her hands from Samuel's grasp, but he held firm. "Not yet, child. I have something vital I must tell you. Something of your future—something that is past the time for telling."

Banafrit's never-ceasing activity stilled.

Lydia bit her lip at the intensity in his eyes. "What do you mean, past the time—?"

"Ly—di—a!"

She snatched her hands from his. "I must go, friend. I will find you later." She fled the kitchen, but his declaration thudded inside her mind like an omen of destiny. Her *future*. And perhaps her past? She wanted to reach back for the knowledge, but it was like grasping at a wave and finding only sea spray. When would she have another chance? The deep ache, with her always and all the more these past months, swelled against her chest, full and yet desolate.

She shook her head against the emotion and crossed the flame-lit kitchen courtyard. Her mistress was already gone. She hurried down the front hall of the palace, up the massive stairs, to the chamber suite of Cleopatra Philopator, reincarnation of Isis, Pharaoh of Egypt.

The white-kilted Egyptian guard nodded at her approach.

She rapped her knuckles twice against the wooden door but did not wait to be invited. Caesarion's wailing penetrated into the hall, and Lydia's instinct propelled her into the room.

"What is it, little cub? What's happened?"

She pulled up short. The boy sat inconsolable in the lap of Andromeda. The girl's green robes were smirched with wetness, and her dark and stringy hair hung over his head.

Andromeda shifted her eyes toward Lydia and gave her a tight smile of challenge. It was no secret that Andromeda sought to replace her in Caesarion's affections. Already the girl cared for Cleopatra's newborn twins. Was that not enough?

The thought of separation from the boy tightened Lydia's throat. She should not have allowed herself to get so close.

But at Lydia's voice, Caesarion struggled free of the younger girl's arms and sped across the chamber, arms high.

Lydia caught him up in her arms. Tears sparkled in his dark lashes and ran rivers wide as the Nile down his cheeks. "Now there, what has happened?"

"I fell." He sniffed and pointed to a scraped knee.

"I was about to dress the wound." Andromeda's voice was buttery soft for Cleopatra's benefit.

Lydia set the boy down again. At seven years old, he was too big to carry. She needed to get Andromeda out before she mentioned what she had seen in the corridor. With a nod toward the girl, she said, "That will be all. I'm sure Banafrit needs your service downstairs."

Andromeda narrowed her eyes, glanced at Cleopatra on the far side of the chamber, oblivious in her wardrobe preparations, then strolled from the room.

For all the frenzied commotion of the lower-staff level, Cleopatra's multiroomed chamber was an oasis of peaceful luxury, with flaming braziers scattered against the walls warming the rooms and heavy tapestries at the windows to block the winter chill. The rooms were spacious and high ceilinged, the walls frescoed in golds and reds by the best Alexandrian artists.

Cleopatra herself was a thing of beauty, draping herself in her signature eclectic mix of jewel-like Roman purples and crisp

Greek whites, with the Egyptian's cropped black wig, striped *nemes* head cloth, and rearing gold cobra shimmering at her forehead. Indeed, the meeting of these two leaders was a blend of nearly all the world—the Greek pharaoh of Egypt now sought by Rome meeting the Arab governor of a Hebrew province.

Caesarion was still crying, and Lydia dropped to the floor beside a warm brazier and pulled him to her. "Let us look at this knee. There, now that is nothing. Look. A scrape, and only a little blood clings to it. How shall you be a fine Egyptian soldier if you wail over such a small wound?"

He snuggled closer to her, head on her shoulder, and she sang softly to him, a favorite tune that always calmed his restlessness. Her voice carried, pure and gentle, across the chamber.

"I swear by the gods, Lydia, that voice of yours could charm a monster." Cleopatra laughed coldly and inclined her head toward Caesarion. "Or a monstrous child."

Cleopatra still fussed with the purple-edged toga she was arranging, and Lydia left the boy to cross the room and help. With deft fingers she draped the toga in the Roman fashion, tucked the ends snugly against Cleopatra's slim figure, and turned the woman toward the bronze.

Cleopatra surveyed herself and smiled. "Yes, as usual, everything you touch grows more beautiful, does it not? How could we possibly manage here without you?"

The compliment should have warmed Lydia, but she knew better than to believe it was born of affection. Cleopatra never allowed anyone to feel secure. Though only ten years older than Lydia, since Caesarion's birth, Lydia had seen her order the murders of both a younger brother and sister. And her second brother's death—

Lydia tried to refuse the memory, the soul-suffocating memory that crouched in waiting if she was not diligent in breathing it away. Cleopatra had followed in her father's royal footsteps, having watched him order the execution of her older sister, Berenice, while Cleopatra was still a girl.

Lydia returned to Caesarion, still cradling his knee, and pulled him to herself.

Cleopatra turned to her, eyed the two on the floor, and tilted her head. "You always find a way to look prettier than your station should allow, don't you? Is that one of my dresses you have pilfered?" Her mood had turned sour suddenly, as it often did.

"What? No!" Lydia smoothed the white linen sheath dress embroidered with delicate threads of blue. "No, I sewed this myself."

"Hmm. Well, you look too elegant to be a servant. I am sick of you and your ideas. Perhaps it's that troublemaker you spend time with, Samuel. I've been meaning to get rid of him. He's far too old to do much good at the Museum any longer."

Lydia opened her mouth, but there was nothing to be said. Better to ignore the threat and pray it was spoken without much thought.

Cleopatra observed herself in the bronze once more. "Well, this should be good enough to win Herod as a friend."

Friend? As the only living Ptolemy left, besides her son, she was a shrewd and wary ruler and no friend to anyone. Not even Marc Antony, who had fallen victim to her charms two years ago, after the assassination of his mentor and her lover, Julius Caesar. She had nothing left of Caesar but his son, and she had quickly understood the need to ingratiate herself to the next man in line to rule all of Rome. Antony's twins had been born to Cleopatra a few months ago, and she had only grown more paranoid since.

The queen floated from the room on a wave of perfume, leaving Lydia hugging Caesarion all the more fiercely, the younger brother she would never have.

Often as a child she had pretended that she was a princess too. Stolen from her parents who even now searched the world for her. But such dreams were remnants of childhood, and there was nothing, no one, that was truly hers. No one to whom she belonged.

She buried her face in Caesarion's sweet-smelling hair.

It was best to keep some distance.

Two

Where would she find Samuel when Lydia finally got free from the demands of Cleopatra, to hear his important news? She would make her appearance with Caesarion as brief as possible and be on her way.

The magnificent central courtyard of the palace, so recently a storm of preparation, was silent save for two huge braziers flanking the reflecting pool, their massive fires devouring dried dung chips and heating the chilly courtyard. Lydia entered from the south hallway, Caesarion in tow, and slowed to a stop under the columned portico.

Cleopatra stood with her back to them, regal at the head of the stone pool, head high. Waiting. On either side of the queen, bare-chested Egyptian guards like sentinel sphinxes rested easy hands on sickle swords.

And then in a moment, the governor of Galilee swept into the courtyard, his retinue in his wake. Dressed in a tunic the color of mustard seed and a white robe tossed casually over his shoulders, Herod had the dark skin and oiled curls of his Arabic heritage, but the bearing of a Greek. He did not lower his head in respect to Cleopatra. At this, Lydia sucked in a small breath. The queen would not be pleased.

But Cleopatra was holding out her hands as if Herod were an old friend come to visit. "At last we meet." The honeyed tone was one she reserved for manipulation. "How is it such a great friend of my Antony could go all this time unknown to me?"

Herod gave a lift of the eyebrow and a small smile at the gracious greeting. He took her hand, brought it to his lips, and brushed her hand with the briefest of kisses. "My lady. It is indeed an honor to meet the woman who has so recently claimed the heart of one of my oldest friends."

Lydia ducked her head to hide a smile. Already the two were sparring—Cleopatra claiming Marc Antony as her own possession, and Herod reminding the queen that the two men had been friends for fifteen years, while Antony's dalliance with Cleopatra only went back two.

"How fortunate for me that you chose to make a stop here on your way to Rome." Cleopatra extended a hand to a three-sided placement of cushioned couches. "Please, I hope you will not find our Alexandrian winter too cold for dining outdoors?"

Herod eyed the couches, then the braziers, and smiled. "The heat of the fire is almost unnecessary within the warmth of your hospitality."

A chill breeze lifted Lydia's hair and chased it around her face. At her side, Caesarion fidgeted and tugged on her hand. "I want to go to Mother."

Lydia felt his restlessness. The hieroglyphic-carved column was cold, and she wanted to move as well—off to find Samuel and hear this mysterious message about her past and her future.

She pulled Caesarion forward, past the reflecting pool with its water black under the night sky and white lotus flowers straining at the edges as though wishing to break free. In the darkened portico surrounding the massive courtyard, several dozen servants loitered in silence, waiting to be summoned, the whites of their eyes like the lotus flowers. The occasional *scritch* of sandal or whispered word betrayed their watching presence. In a palace, even the staff schemed in alliances and competed for positions. Conspiracy was not just for royalty. Lydia glanced along the wings. Was Samuel among them?

Cleopatra and Herod settled themselves onto opposing couches, a table laden with Banafrit's efforts spread between them—flatbread and dates, sycamore figs and almonds, and filled cups of wine. Several young women clustered onto the couches around Herod and two guards stood behind. Cleopatra's guards likewise circled to her back. The braziers on either side blurred the air with heat.

Lydia hesitated at the perimeter of the couches and waited for Cleopatra to acknowledge their presence.

"And who is this, my lady?" Herod's gaze traveled the length of Lydia, then rested on Caesarion. "Dressed as a little Roman?"

Cleopatra waved them forward, and Lydia prodded the boy to take a step.

"This is Ptolemy Caesar, Herod. My son and coregent of Egypt, and son of Julius Caesar. We call him Caesarion."

"Hmm, yes. 'Little Caesar,' is it?" Herod shrugged. "Or so they say."

Cleopatra pulled Caesarion to herself, pinning him under one arm on the couch beside her. Julius Caesar had been officially deified by the Roman Republic two years ago, and Herod's casual reference was nearly blasphemy. Or would have been, had either of them been Roman.

Lydia stepped back. Could she make her escape now?

"And his nurse, I take it?" Herod's gaze was on her again.

"Yes, sit, Lydia." Cleopatra jabbed a finger at an adjoining couch. "You may take the boy in a few minutes."

Lydia suppressed an exasperated sigh. Cleopatra needed her son as a prop, but it should only last a few minutes before she tired of his restiveness and sent him off. Lydia sat at the edge of the couch, fingers tapping against the fabric. As much as she wanted to find Samuel, Cleopatra's mood was dangerous, and it would not be prudent to cross her tonight, not after the hostility and desperation she'd shown in her chamber.

"And what of Antony's brats? I am surprised you have not displayed them tonight."

Lydia cringed at the harsh reference.

Cleopatra seemed unfazed. "So, you go to Rome to throw your lot in with those who would rule. It seems that Octavian, Antony, and Lepidus have formed quite the solid threesome, have they not? And you hope they will support you against those who would prefer to see a Jew on the throne of Judea?"

Herod draped an arm around one of the women who lounged at his side. He was perhaps a few years older than Cleopatra, in his early thirties, and still exceedingly handsome, with an athletic build and the sensuous features of his heritage—warm, dark eyes and full lips. "I look forward to meeting Octavian." He reached for a cup of wine and raised it to her. "As I have anticipated meeting you."

"I fear you will not find Octavian so easily won over as my Marc Antony."

Lydia watched Cleopatra's eyes, the calculations that spun like a Persian astronomer studying the night. She lifted her own eyes to the black dome. A star tracked silver across the expanse. Tonight, even the heavens were restless.

Caesarion pulled away from his mother and crawled onto Lydia's couch, tucking his warm body against hers. She squeezed him to herself in silent acknowledgment of their shared discomfort.

The queen did not appear to notice, but Herod's gaze followed the boy and then strayed to her once more, lingering. "Your boy seems enamored of his nurse."

Cleopatra sipped at her wine. "Are not all boys? Soon enough he will share the throne in more than name and need the strong arm of a pharaoh. Let him have his affections now."

Herod was still appraising Lydia. "Yes, well, his affections have found a worthy home."

At this, Cleopatra turned a fiery eye on Lydia. "Perhaps it is time to send these two on their way." She nodded toward Herod's reclining women, then gave him a sultry smile. "And others as well. I should think two rulers would have much to discuss, in private."

Herod leaned forward and tapped his empty cup twice on the cedarwood table. "And I say it is time for more wine."

Cleopatra's eyes were like ice now at Herod's decided lack of awe in her presence.

As if she had anticipated his need, Andromeda was within the square of couches in an instant, amphora in hand.

How did the girl always present herself at the right moment? She was so focused on pleasing people, would do or say whatever might gain their favor. In this, Lydia had to admit she recognized a bit of herself.

Andromeda still wore the jade-green robe Lydia had glimpsed in the corridors after selling her jug. Would she choose this moment to report Lydia's moneymaking scheme?

"And yet another beauty." Herod took the cup from Andromeda's hand, letting his fingers brush hers. "I should have visited Alexandria years ago."

"Ah, we would have entertained you well, yes, Andromeda?" Cleopatra lifted her chin to the girl. "Tell Herod how well we entertain those who make a stop in our fair land."

Andromeda gave Herod a sly smile, almost flirtatious. "The queen is most generous to all her visitors. In fact, it would seem that any head of state who enters her palace also enters her bed."

Lydia sucked in a breath, shot a glance at Cleopatra. Was the girl only ingratiating herself to Herod, or did she purposely seek to humiliate Cleopatra?

The queen's expression darkened. She pulled herself upright on the couch.

Even Herod's perennially charming smile slipped. He cleared his throat and set the wine on the table.

Cleopatra signaled one of the guards behind her with a flick of her finger. "Take her."

The guard circled the couch in a moment and grabbed Andromeda. The amphora dropped to the mosaic floor and cracked. Wine spattered the stones.

Lydia pulled Caesarion backward.

But Cleopatra's wrath had been building all night, born of tension over Herod's visit and perhaps her own scheming plan for Judea.

"Kill her."

Lydia gasped, sat forward. "My lady!" She thrust Caesarion to the edge of the couch. "Think of your son."

Cleopatra turned cold eyes on her. "It is my *son* I am thinking of, girl. How will he learn to rule Egypt well, except to see the strength of his mother?"

Lydia half turned to Andromeda. The girl's eyes were wild with panic, and she struggled uselessly in the soldier's grip. He reached for a short sword on his belt.

Lydia clapped her hand over Caesarion's eyes. The boy whimpered but did not pull away.

A slight gurgle was the only sound Andromeda made before she fell, and her blood mingled with the spilled wine, seeping between the mosaics.

Bile rose in Lydia's throat. She released Caesarion and fell to the stones beside Andromeda. The light was already going out of the girl's eyes. Lydia smoothed her hair with a shaky hand. Andromeda's body twitched once and was still.

Had the braziers eaten all the air in the courtyard, suffocating them all? Lydia struggled to take a breath, her chest constricted, her limbs trembling.

Herod lifted her to her feet and guided her back to the couch to fall beside Caesarion. She rocked the boy against her chest, as much to comfort him as herself.

Cleopatra's gaze found hers and held. "This is what happens to servants who displease me, son." Though she addressed the boy, the words were clearly for Lydia, there was no doubt.

Neither did she doubt that Andromeda's fate would eventually be her own.

How much longer could she fashion pots in stolen moments,

secreting away a few obols at a time, hoping to one day get free? Cleopatra's jealousy spiraled faster than Lydia could spin pots.

She must find out what Samuel had kept hidden about her family.

And then she must leave the palace and find wherever it was she truly belonged.

Three

The palace halls were in an uproar.

Lydia pushed past clusters of servant girls, yapping like hens in a yard, and threaded through enough low-ranking guards to quell a riot.

Andromeda's execution had fired panic in the chest of every servant. The girl's virtues were praised, her shortcomings forgotten.

Cleopatra's patience with her son's whimpering ran out while Andromeda's blood still ran along the stones, and Lydia had fled with the boy, tucked him into his bed with a kiss and a whispered promise to return later, then hurried to the kitchens to seek Banafrit.

Lydia breached the smoky room as the older woman snapped a thin reed against the bare legs of a servant. "Quit your gossip now, girl, and tend the lamps!"

Banafrit's voice was pitched high and strained, the only evidence that the courtyard execution had affected her. Cleopatra valued the cook's skills highly, but the respect did not go both ways. The whipped girl ran past the kitchen slaves bent over their tables. Banafrit turned on Lydia with a scowl.

"I should think you would be hiding yourself in your chamber by now. Haven't seen enough for one night, have we?"

"I must find Samuel. Did he come back here to wait for me?"

"Pah!" Banafrit waved a meaty hand and shoved past Lydia to poke a servant at the cook fire. "I've no idea where the man keeps himself. Why ask me? Isn't he about his prayers or some such thing at this hour?"

Of course. She had lost track of the time. But surely he would be finished at the synagogue soon. He had seemed as eager to speak with her as she with him.

Lydia retraced her steps through the halls and avoided the questions tossed at her by servants curious to hear an eyewitness account of Andromeda. She squeezed up the narrow stairwell from the servants' level, then took the wide steps at the back of the palace to the expansive second level and along the greenery-covered balcony. She crossed to its end, where it overlooked the city, only one story above the street level, down the length of Soma Street, to the Museum and Library of Alexandria.

From here she could see if Samuel returned to the palace from the stately synagogue of the numerous and respected Jews in the city. The night winds rocked boats in the harbor, slapping waves against their hulls, and across the half-moon of harbor water, high above the promontory, the bronze-reflected fires of Alexandria's famed lighthouse sent a warning message across the sea to distant ships.

Lydia stood at the half wall and watched the street for the shiny pate of Samuel as he hurried back from his prayers. Torches bobbed through alleys and the wide Soma Street, reflecting from the abundance of white marble buildings. The streets, like the harbor, led away to unknown destinations. Lydia had never been more than an hour's walk from the palace. How many distant places the world contained.

She had been to the synagogue with Samuel often, taking in the lessons of the Jews' One God, so different from the magical and mysterious Egyptian gods and the lecherous and angry Greek pantheon. The beauty of all of it interested her in an academic way, though she did not identify herself with any of them religiously since she did not belong to any of them.

Her coloring seemed to indicate both Greek and Egyptian bloodlines, so perhaps she was a mongrel—like the Greek-Egyptian god Serapis, manufactured by the Greek Ptolemies to unify their Egyptian realm.

There! There was Samuel. The fringed linen *tallit* he wore for prayers draped his shoulders and he bent, muttering to himself, but she would know that hunched walk from any distance, any height.

She ran past the potted junipers to the balcony entrance and then was down the staircase before Samuel had a chance to reach the palace arch. Her sandals slapped a rhythm on the stones as she ran, and she breathed a prayer of thanks that he was still at the base of the outer stairs when she caught him.

"Samuel!" Her whisper sounded harsh, seemed to echo against the relentless waves of the harbor.

He jerked his head toward her, his eyes large. "What has happened? Have they found you?"

"What?" Lydia followed his gaze left and right. "Who?"

"You are frightened." He took her elbow, then led her from the open staircase, past one of the sphinxes that guarded the stairs to the stone wall along the harbor.

She took a deep breath to control her voice. "Have you heard what she has done?"

At Samuel's confused look, Lydia spilled the wretched tale.

"I must get out of this palace, Samuel. I know I shall be next. If you could see the way she looks at me—"

His fingers on her arm were like ice. "Why? Why should she look at you as any sort of threat?"

"I—I do not think she is threatened—only . . ." It seemed laughable to say the queen of Egypt should be jealous of her son's nurse, so Lydia left off and shook her head. "She has executed her own family to protect her power. My death would not even give her pause."

But he was distracted, her teacher, looking out over the water as if searching for a ship or one of those distant ports. "Yes. Yes, I think it is best that you go."

"But I have not saved enough for a shop yet. I cannot support myself." She shook his arm to regain his attention. "You said earlier that you needed to tell me something. Something about my family. Please, if I have a connection somewhere—anywhere— you must tell me so I can fall upon their mercy."

"Family? What did I say of family?" His eyes had gone dark again.

Lydia leaned against the cold stone, suddenly tired and chilled. "You said it was something of my past. And my future."

"Yes. Hmm, I suppose it is your family. Your *true* family."

She bit her lip against the strange fear his words brought and tasted the sea and the salt in the air.

"Lydia, you must hear me carefully." He held her forearms in his own cold grasp. "We may not have much time. I have reason to think that secrets I have kept for too long are coming to light. Secrets I should have told you years ago, before there was such danger."

Lydia's heart stuttered, but she did not pull away from his grasp. "Samuel, you are frightening me."

"Yes, it is right to be frightened, to be careful. But you must listen." He stared into her eyes, as though waiting.

She nodded, returned the intensity of his gaze.

"I have taught you and trained you in the ways of the Law and the Prophets for several years now, as I have many others in my lifetime. But you are the first one I trust, though you cannot seem to trust others yourself. But perhaps it was meant to be this way, that it would be you . . ." His look had drifted, his words fading as if he spoke only to himself.

Lydia squeezed his arms.

"And anyway," he resumed as if he had not lost his place, "a woman would be far less suspected."

"Suspected? Of what? Please, Samuel, you are making no sense!"

Footsteps echoed along the harbor wall, and Samuel sucked in a breath and pulled her into a huddle against the wall. A dockworker, late to his night duties, strolled past and nodded a greeting.

Samuel's grasp around her shoulders relaxed only a notch. "I have no children, Lydia. You know this. And I should have. It was my duty and yet Abigail, she never conceived, and I gave up questioning God. And perhaps I gave up even the belief that it mattered if there was a son to inherit my calling and my duties, may HaShem forgive me."

His words were coming in a rush now, and though she understood little, she would not stop him.

"When Abigail first sought you out, began to teach you her skill with the wheel, I thought she had only found the daughter we did not have, to pass on her potter's art. But these last few years, I believed you could also be the son—" He shook his head violently, as if to dislodge unwanted memories.

"Twelve generations, Lydia. For twelve generations, from father to son the charge has been passed down, a sacred trust and duty not to be forgotten. And for much of that time, all was well. But then, when they were lost and my grandfather came to Alexandria as he was instructed, we lost touch with the others. And it all became like some nursery tale, the stuff of legend. Until tonight." At this, he shuddered, and his eyes took on that hunted look once more.

She stroked his arms, as though to warm him. "Samuel, you must give me more details. I am not—"

"You are the one, Lydia." His voice quivered. "After all this time and among all those scattered to search, you must be the one to return them."

"Lydia!"

The sharp voice rang across the harbor wall, and both Lydia and Samuel startled and drew back.

"Lydia, you are wanted in the palace!" One of Cleopatra's guards leaned over the wall. How had he thought to search for her out here?

Once again she would be pulled from Samuel before she made sense of his cryptic words. She bent her neck to meet the guard's call. "What does she need? Is it Caesarion? Is he still afraid?"

The guard straightened and turned away, but not before she heard his answer.

"Not the queen. It is Herod who summons you."

≈

"What do you know of Judea, little Lydia?"

The governor sprawled upon a green-cushioned lounge in the opulent chamber Cleopatra had assigned. On either side of the couch, narrow windows taller than a man afforded a view of the marble city and the lofty lighthouse, and the gold silks that hung at the windows rippled in the night breeze like the skirts of a palace dancer. All of it—the glittering gold-painted frescoes and the colorful glazed pottery—was familiar since Lydia herself had been tasked with crafting the room into a beauty the governor would appreciate. But tonight the chamber was cold, too cold, and only a small brazier had been lit.

Lydia stood a few steps inside the door, hands fisted at her sides and heart racing. "I know a bit of Judean history, my lord. My . . . my friend Samuel, he is a Jew, though he has lived in Alexandria all his life and his family came from Susa." She did not add that even after three hundred years of foreign rule by Seleucids, Greeks, and now Parthians, Samuel still called his homeland Persia. "But he has taught me of the Jewish holy books and the Jewish God and—" She bit back her rambling at the impatient wave of Herod's hand.

"Religion, bah. I am talking about leadership. Politics."

She swallowed against the dryness in her throat. "Samuel has taught me of King David, of his royal line." No, this was the wrong thing to say to an Idumean, not of Jewish birth, who had been chosen to rule.

Herod swung his legs over the side of the couch and leaned

his forearms on his knees. A nearby servant girl started forward as if to help him to his feet, though why a man not yet thirty-five needed assistance to stand, Lydia could not see. Herod ignored the girl and remained seated, eyes on Lydia.

"And what of my grandfather, Antipater, king of the Jews? Did your Samuel teach you of him?"

"No. I am sorry." Lydia flexed her tight fingers, grown numb in the cold room and under scrutiny.

"All that brutal business with the Maccabees years ago?"

At the familiar reference, she nodded. Scraps of knowledge from Samuel there.

"Yes, well, the Maccabees freed Judea from the Seleucids and set up their Hasmonean dynasty. The Jews took over my Idumea and forced the Idumeans to convert, and nothing has been simple for my family since, though we have learned to make Rome our friend. Only a few years ago, Cleopatra's dead lover, Julius Caesar, made my father chief procurator of Judea. Father gave my brother the prefecture of Jerusalem and myself the governorship of Galilee. Ever been to Galilee, Lydia?"

Why was he asking her these questions? Her stomach roiled with the memory of Andromeda. Did Cleopatra lurk somewhere in the shadows of the room, listening for Lydia to misspeak? She shook her head. "I have never left Alexandria."

Herod got to his feet, unassisted despite the attendant's lurch forward, and ambled to the window. He slid the silk aside with one finger and leaned against the open edge, his gaze lifting to the street of grand marble temples and, farther down, the Museum and the Library.

"Galilee is a region of dusty rocks and dustier people. A people with more sheep than wits."

"Is your father not dead? Why retain the governorship of a region you seem to despise?"

Herod turned slowly, a smile creeping across his thick features.

Lydia studied the woven carpet beneath her feet. She had said too much.

"You see, that is why I have called you here. I saw it in you, down there in the courtyard. Bold enough to challenge Cleopatra. And now I see a quick mind—one familiar with the Jews."

"My apologies, my lord. I spoke—"

"No, no." Herod waved a hand and strolled toward her, his charming smile still fixed. "So you know a bit about politics after all. My father was assassinated three years ago. And that Jewish fox Antigonus was made High Priest by the interfering Parthians—yes, it is all quite a mess."

He was in front of her now and lifted a stray hair away from her face.

She recoiled at the touch.

"But you know what I want, I imagine. Don't you, Lydia?" His voice was low, conspiratorial.

Lydia pulled back farther. Her legs trembled under her, and she fought to keep her voice solid. "I should think you want to be king."

He leaned in, his lips at her ear, his voice a whisper. "Exactly."

With that he spun and returned to the couch, dropping to the position of ease where she had found him upon entering.

"I am on my way to Rome to gain Antony's support. And his ally Octavian, I should hope. When I return to Judea it will be in war against Antigonus. And when I have taken Judea as my own, I will also take the High Priest's daughter as my own. Do you know of my betrothed, Lydia?"

She shook her head. Samuel's teaching only extended so far.

"Mariamme is the granddaughter of Israel's High Priest and a Hasmonean—a direct descendant of those popular Maccabees and both branches of Hasmoneans. When we marry, it will unite my kingship with the royal and priestly blood, and the Jews will have all they could hope for—a king who has become part of their precious noble families, who will rule them with all the intelligence gained from a Greek upbringing in a cosmopolitan world." He patted the cushion at his side. "Come, sit. Tell me how old you are."

She paused only long enough to take a deep breath, then crossed the room to sit on the edge of his couch. "I am eighteen."

"Yes, I guessed it—the same age as my Mariamme. We have been betrothed two years."

And they were not yet married? But perhaps he was waiting until he had been made king.

Herod ran a finger along the fabric across her upper arm. "You will be good for her, I believe."

"My lord?"

"For Mariamme. She has your beauty, but she does not have your strength, your confidence. She needs someone to encourage her in that regard. A lady to wait upon her, one who has seen what it looks like for a woman to be a queen."

A coldness stole over Lydia's limbs, climbed down into her belly. She met Herod's gaze for the first time since seating herself beside him. The mustard-yellow tunic gave his skin a sickly pallor, despite his famed charm. "You want me to be lady's maid to your wife?"

He smiled and shrugged one shoulder. "Why not?"

As if to punctuate the strange response, the door flung open.

Herod's two guards dove forward, short swords drawn, then fell back at the figure in the doorway.

Cleopatra.

Her gaze traveled the room, took in the two on the couch as though it were not strange to see Lydia with the Idumean governor, and passed to the open window. "You shall catch a fever, Herod, if you do not light more fires. Shall I send for tapestries to block the night air?"

Herod smiled. "You forget I am from the desert, my queen. Your moist sea air is like a balmy breeze."

"And my son's nursemaid? Is she also a fresh breeze?"

He laughed, the low laugh of one engaged in a match of manipulation, and got to his feet.

The couch shifted without his weight, and Lydia put out a hand to steady herself.

"She is indeed. We were just discussing the good she could do in Judea."

"Judea!" Cleopatra's hard glare shot to Lydia.

Herod folded his arms and inclined his head to study Cleopatra. "Yes, I should think at his age, you would be eager to pass the young Caesarion from his nurse to a tutor. Since he is coregent of Egypt, that is." He swept a hand toward Lydia. "And I could make much better use of her in Judea, as lady's maid to my betrothed wife."

Cleopatra advanced on Lydia, her hand raised. "Why, you scheming little—"

Herod took two quick steps and caught her wrist. "Careful, my lady. I should hate to report to Antony that his latest lover seems never in control of her temper. Not such a good quality for a ruler, would you say?"

Lydia's breath shallowed but she did not speak. How could it be that she was being defended by Herod? What strange turn of the stars had positioned a servant girl of little worth between two powerful rulers?

Cleopatra dropped her hand, but her eyes spit fire at Lydia. "Very well. She is nothing to me. Easily replaced. As easily as that whining Andromeda." She lifted her chin and narrowed her eyes. "You think you are so special, with all your talent for beauty and art. But you are nothing. Palace servants are as numerous as palace rats, and you have no more idea of where you came from than a common vermin in the cellars."

Lydia rose to her feet, the condemnation echoing in her ears, echoing through the hollow parts of her as if she were no more than a used-up, dry husk.

"I have tried . . . tried to be of value to you . . . to help . . ." Her chest shook.

"Ha! Do you think you are the only one who can sing a pretty tune or sculpt a pretty pot? There are girls lined up to take your place. So go! Go with him!"

Everyone—first Samuel, then Herod, and now Cleopatra— seemed to wish Lydia out of Egypt. But it was the only home she'd ever known. She had sworn by her independence, by her refusal to need anyone. But how could she leave Caesarion? Samuel?

Herod patted her head as though she were a favorite pet. "There now, it is settled. I am pleased—"

"No." The word bubbled up from her chest unexpectedly.

Both rulers eyed her in surprise, as if they had already forgotten her presence or perhaps her ability to have an opinion of her own.

"No, I have no desire to leave Alexandria."

Cleopatra chuckled. "You don't seem to understand. I have no desire for you to remain."

The fear, the cold fear of being ripped from the cobbled-together family she had created for herself, drove the words from her mind to her lips and into the air before she could stop them. Despite Andromeda, or perhaps *because* of her hideous unde-served death, Lydia spoke aloud what lay hidden in her heart.

She stepped forward, hands tight at her sides. "Who will know which of the plants in your chamber must be kept well watered and which to keep dry? Who will remember which robes and jewels you wore for each city appearance and how to arrange the striped *nemes* and gold uraeus so they frame your face in a way both feminine and regal? Who will help you fool your visitors into believing that it is *you* who knows how to spread a banquet table or furnish a room with luxury?"

Pathetic, all of it, and yet she kept on spewing, as if she could prove her worth with such a list. "And who, my lady, will sing your boy to sleep when he wakes up screaming nightmares of his mur-derous mother?"

Oh, this last—this last she should not have said. Even Herod seemed to take a step backward, to abandon her there on the field of battle.

Lydia had proven nothing, had won nothing. Only lashed out in pain, the desperate act of a condemned woman.

And she saw her condemnation in Cleopatra's eyes, though the queen held her tongue. Her lips remained sealed, her jaw tight.

Lydia was empty now, empty like that dry husk waiting to be blown away in the hot wind of Cleopatra's wrath.

"That will be all for tonight, Lydia. I have business to discuss with our new friend. If it should please you to give us privacy, that is."

The sarcasm cut as sharply as any rebuke, but it was only the dull leading edge of what was to come.

Lydia bent her head to Herod, then to the queen, and pushed toward the door. As she passed Cleopatra, she could almost feel the cold radiating from the woman's body.

Lydia reached the hallway alive, which seemed no small miracle.

Andromeda had spoken out of a naive foolishness and had her throat slit for the indiscretion. What would Cleopatra do with a servant whose condemnation had been calculated with intent?

Lydia hurried toward the steps, her hand stealing to her throat to feel the reassuring though unsteady leaping of her pulse.

Whatever was to come, nothing would be the same.

Four

Cleopatra watched with satisfaction as Lydia fled into the hall. The girl's petite features and slight stature brought to mind a colorful butterfly. Indeed, she had been fluttering around the royal family for years now. If the girl weren't such a favorite with Caesarion, Cleopatra would have rid the palace of her after Ptolemy's death.

She slammed the door on the girl's flight, then turned in one smooth motion to smile at Herod. "I am surprised." She crossed to a small table along the wall, set with a jug of wine and a platter of Alexandria's finest cheeses. "I should not have thought you a man to waste your time on servant girls." She tossed a coy smile over her shoulder. "Especially when there are women of more— consequence—who might claim your attention."

Herod was at her side in a moment and took the cup of wine she had poured for herself. "And you are indeed a woman of consequence."

Were his words flattery or mockery? She studied the fine lines at the corners of his eyes, the long lashes. The full lips as he brought the cup to his mouth. She could not read him, and it was unnerving.

She poured another cup and raised it to his. "To our mutual concerns."

Herod eyed her over his cup. He had a way of holding one's gaze for a moment longer than appropriate, then looking away with a smile, perhaps of amusement or perhaps simply pleasure. He crossed the room to the low couch. "Have we mutual concerns?"

"But of course." She joined him on the couch, sliding too close. He smelled of all parts of the world: deserts sands and Eastern spices and even the flora of his hilly Galilee. His powerful blending of Eastern and Greek influences made him more like her than any man she'd been with, and the attraction was too potent. She pulled away, tried to focus on her objective. "I remember your father well."

He chuckled. "I should think so. Without his help, Caesar would never have had the armies of Mithridates, nor the Nabateans, to give him success here in Alexandria."

She sipped her wine. "Hmm, yes, well, the Nabateans are no friends to either of us now, I hear."

Herod's eyes flickered in surprise. "Your sources keep you well informed. I have only just come from Malik in Petra. I offered even to leave my nephew as security against my requests for soldiers and funds, but the Parthians got to him first, and he had me dismissed as a common enemy."

She tsked and shook her head. "Unthinkable. Was not your mother a noblewoman in Petra?"

Herod's fingers tightened around his cup. "I spent the better part of my childhood there, in protection against my father's enemies in Judea."

Cleopatra hid a smile. Men were out of balance when their precious pride was wounded, and she liked it that way. "Well, he is no ally of mine either, I can assure you."

Herod leaned on one elbow along the couch, distancing himself from her. "And that is saying something, as you are a woman adept at gaining allies."

She gave him a quick, half-amused smile. "There have been some who found it advantageous to ally with me, yes."

"Come, don't be modest. You are something of a legend in Rome. The way you charmed your way into Julius Caesar's heart within hours of his landing on your shores. You put all your hopes into Caesar, I suppose? Thought perhaps your son would take the throne of Egypt and then be handed Rome as his birthright as well?"

Cleopatra stood and strolled to the wine again but, noticing the shakiness of her hand as she lifted the jug, she thought better of it and took a bit of cheese instead. She kept her back to Herod. This interaction was not proceeding well. She was accustomed to gaining the upper hand from the start of the conversation. The room was chilly, and she crossed to the single burning brazier, lifted the leather-wrapped rod with the torch end in the fire, and used it to light two more braziers. The delay gave her time to consider her next words.

"There was none more saddened than I by the brutal slaying of Caesar. His death was a loss to Rome, and to all the world."

"Yes, no doubt Antony said much the same thing when he found himself in your bed soon after."

"Two years!" She turned on Herod, the poker solid and hot in her hand. "It was two years before Antony . . . won my affection away from the memories!"

His smile spoke more than words. He had bested her by wounding *her* pride—a point scored on his side now. They were too evenly matched for comfort.

He stood and came to her, took the rod from her hand, replaced it on the edge of the brazier, but did not release her hand. "What is it you want, Queen of Egypt?"

It was time to take back the power.

She stepped closer to him, until the fullness of her diaphanous linen dress brushed his robes. "I want us to find a way to work for each other's benefit, of course."

He touched her lips with his forefinger. "And what would such an effort look like?"

She smiled under his touch. "Your support against our mutual enemies—Malik and the Nabateans. My support of you with Antony."

"Hmm. Perhaps for that support I would do better gaining the favor of one of Antony's *wives*."

She laughed. "Antony's marriages mean nothing. His latest wife is a step toward power, nothing more. It is I, and our precious twins, who hold sway over his heart."

Herod said nothing, and she flicked a glance at the guards at his door. "Perhaps we could consummate our . . . agreement without an audience?"

With a cool smile, he ran his finger along her jawline, down to the pulse of her throat, then turned his head slowly to the guards and motioned with his chin. "Wait outside until the queen is ready to leave."

At their exit, Cleopatra focused on her power, her control. She would not allow him mastery of this night. She breathed a prayer to Mother Isis, Queen of Heaven.

He turned back to her with an appraisal that was too cold. Too condescending. "It seems to me, my queen, that you have little to offer and much to gain by all your alliances."

She drew back, muscles tightening. "Egypt has more grain than Rome will—"

"But Rome has Egypt." He shrugged. "Rome has Egypt, and Antony has you, and even your people resent three hundred years of Greek Ptolemies on the throne since Alexander gave them up."

She was shaking now, with rage and something worse: fear. But she would not surrender so easily. She pulled him to herself, to the other side of the room, toward the bed surrounded by tightly woven tapestries and piled high with cushions. "Come, Herod, you know there is more at stake. I have Antony's allegiance, and you would do well to make me your friend—"

Herod yanked her to his chest, his breath hot on her neck.

She could feel the pounding of both their hearts between them.

He inclined his head toward the bed. "And what allegiance of Antony's would I have, should I take his place there?"

She tangled both hands in his wavy hair and pulled his mouth to hers. No man had ever refused her, and this grasping governor of an uncivilized province would not be the first.

He returned her kiss, but his was a kiss of anger, of hatred, of punishment. He wrenched her hands from his head, then pulled away, wiping his mouth with the back of his hand.

"I will give you ships for Rome"—she was grasping now, and hated herself for it—"you can enjoy the winter here in Alexandria— it is no time for sailing—and in the spring Antony will hear only good reports—"

"Stop!" His chest was heaving, but not from anger nor repressed desire. No, he was laughing. Laughing! "Antony will hear reports, yes. But they will not be pleasant to his ears."

He mocked her? He dared to mock the Queen of the Two Lands of Upper and Lower Egypt?

His refusal was like a plunge into the cold harbor waters, and it left her pulsing with fury. In this very room she had seduced Gaius Julius Caesar, the most powerful man in Rome. And this upstart Idumean who could not even gain the kingship of a tiny province would laugh at her?

She grabbed the nearest thing, a gracefully painted pot—one of that worthless Lydia's creations—and heaved it at his head with a curse.

He dodged it easily and the pot smashed on the floor.

The guards were through the door in an instant.

"Ah yes, good." Herod waved them in. "Please see the queen safely back to her chambers. We have nothing more to discuss."

She resisted the urge to spit upon him as she passed. It would only make her seem weak. Instead, she stalked down the hall with his guards trailing.

No, she would find better ways to punish Herod. He could not be allowed to go to Rome with his poisonous words for Antony. She had seen already how Rome reacted to her alliance with Caesar. She could afford no ill will there. She must destroy him.

Inside her own chamber, she slammed the door on his guards and collapsed against it.

It would be a delicate business to destroy one of Antony's closest friends without incurring her lover's wrath.

But she had not ruled Egypt alone for nearly twelve years without learning how to make convenient deaths appear as accidents.

Five

Lydia pulled her mantle tighter around her shoulders. The weight of the woolen fabric she had chosen from the merchant who brought his goods directly to the palace served her well on cool nights, but even its heavy warmth could not calm her shaking chills.

Plunged into the dark labyrinth of the city streets, instead of watching it from a balcony above, one lost the perspective of all roads leading to distant places and the awe of grand old marble buildings. Here there was nothing but the stink of garbage and waste, the nighttime rattling of beggars searching for food in alleys, and stray cats prowling docks for the leavings of fishermen.

Why had Samuel not waited for her at the palace after they had been interrupted a second time? But she had searched and questioned, and no one had seen him. Now she scuttled through empty streets, away from the palace looming at her back, toward the nearby Delta—one of the five sectors of the city and the one dominated by Jewish people.

Samuel lived above a weaver's shop, but its shutters were closed to traffic at this late hour. She had been here many times, learning pottery at the hands of Samuel's wife. Until Abigail was taken from her, as those Lydia loved tended to be. Someday she would have a home of her own, and she would make it as lovely and inviting for those who belonged to her as Abigail had. But tonight, no lamplight glowed from the window above the weaver's shop.

Lydia paused in the street, eyeing Samuel's windows. If not here, then where? Would he be asleep when he had seemed so intent on speaking with her?

Another chill, this one full of evil omens, shuddered through her. She took the outer staircase to the second level, knocked only once while calling his name, and entered.

Moonlight filtered through the open window and fell upon a room in disarray.

She had taken her lessons in the palace of late. Had he let his possessions come to this?

A low moan at her right startled her.

"Thanks be to HaShem, He has brought you in time."

"Samuel?"

"The lamp—in the back room."

She dodged the obstacles strewn across the floor to reach the small doorway at the back of the room, where a faint light signaled a lamp still burning. She found the lamp on the floor, quickly trimmed the wick, and refilled its oil from a tiny jug, then hurried back to the front.

Samuel lay on his side, on a mat near the wall, half curled into himself.

"You are hurt!" She ran to tend him but tripped over a fallen chair. A broken spindle scraped her leg as she fell. She cried out and braced a hand against the floor to protect the lamp. Her hand fell upon something soft, and she rolled, still holding the lamp aloft.

A man! She gasped in horror and pulled backward, waving the lamp over the prone form.

"He is dead." Samuel's voice was a croak from the mat. "I killed him."

"Samuel! What has happened here?"

"They found me. I found it, but somehow, so soon, they found me."

More cryptic words. She crawled to his side, set the lamp at his head, and examined him with a frantic eye. "Where are you hurt? Tell me what he has done to you."

"Not this one. I got to him first. There was another."

The mat on which Samuel lay had been ripped open. A jagged tear or perhaps a knife cut rent it from top to bottom, and the straw that spilled from it was stained red.

"You are bleeding!" She rolled him gently to his back and gasped at the wound. A gash through his tunic, across his chest, and down to his belly.

"He must have thought I kept it hidden under here." Samuel coughed, then moaned with the pain. "He searched everywhere else."

"Don't speak. I must get something to bind the wound—"

He caught her arm before she moved to search. "You must listen, Lydia. It can wait no longer."

"It can wait until we have stopped the bleeding and found a physician!"

"No." His grip on her arm was strong, given his condition. He would bleed faster if she wrestled with him.

"Say it then, Samuel. Say what you must and then let me help you."

"I . . . I have been training you these years with a purpose, Lydia."

He wheezed with the effort, and she sat beside him, stroked the tousled hair from his forehead. A bit of blood specked his white beard and brought tears to her eyes.

"I have learned much from you, Samuel, and been grateful for all you have taught—"

"Yes, you have been a good student. But I have not taught you everything. You know the writings of the Prophets?"

She nodded. His people's prophets had been largely misunderstood and tormented in their time, but their writings were sacred and she had learned of them.

"There is a group, for many generations, who have guarded a secret. Scrolls of the prophet Daniel, not to be opened until the fullness of time."

She knitted her brows. She knew of no such writings. "Where are these scrolls?"

He gave his head a slight shake. "First, you must understand that what is written is sealed until that time, and we must only do our duty to keep it guarded, to keep it ready."

"We?"

"This group—in the days of Daniel, in Babylon after the Medes and Persians came—a sect whom Daniel trained in the ways of the One God. To these he entrusted the sealed writings. Their descendants kept the scrolls hidden, guarded, cherished. Waiting. My grandfather was one of these, the Chakkiym."

"Kahk—?"

He nodded. "Say 'Kahk-keem.' Yes. Aramaic. It was my

grandfather and his fellow Chakkiym who lost the scrolls, to their great devastation. Each of them was assigned a different part of the world, a different path to follow, to hunt for the stolen scrolls."

He paused, breathing hard. A trembling hand fluttered near the wound, as if he wished to press away the pain.

Lydia's heart pounded and she searched nearby for something to bind his chest.

But he was not finished. "Should any of them succeed in finding the scrolls, they had instructions on how to return them to the Chakkiym in Persia. My grandfather was sent here, to Alexandria, to search. At his death he passed his duty to my father, who passed it to me."

"I do not understand, Samuel. What is it that these scrolls say?" A basket of clothing had been upended in the corner, but his grip on her hand did not allow her to retrieve anything there to wrap around his wound.

"We do not know. Only Daniel knew. And the angel who gave him the words to write—and instructed him to seal them. And the Holy One." His words were growing more labored. "We only know the writings shall become vital at the end of days when Messiah will rise. Must be kept safe until then. A task in which we failed."

"Is this why you were attacked? Someone was looking for the scrolls? Here?"

He gripped her hand in a spasm of pain.

"Please, Samuel. Allow me to find a physician! I fear—"

His hand clenched around hers with greater strength. "You cannot leave me without hearing it all. And he may return."

"Speak quickly then, friend, I beg you." Her tears were flowing now, and she pulled the mantle from her shoulders and began to wrap it around his chest and belly, lifting his arms and rolling him as he spoke.

"No son to take up my duties. Trained many boys over the years, but none gained my confidence. The Holy One did not give me ease about any of them. Only you. You who cause everyone to rely upon you even as you refuse to need anyone yourself. Only about you did He say, 'This one, Samuel ben Eliezar. This is the one.' So you see, it is your destiny."

A shudder ran through Lydia. "You want me to find the scrolls?"

"No, Lydia. I want you to return them to the Chakkiym."

Her skin prickled. Samuel's hand shook within hers.

"You have found them?"

He closed his eyes, a slow smile softening his features.

"Samuel! Stay with me. You have found the scrolls? Where?" She finished her binding and tucked the end of her mantle securely.

"If I live to see dawn you shall have that story. But now is the time to speak of what is next. You must know there are enemies. I sent Isaac—you remember Isaac from the synagogue? Sent him to Jerusalem, to look for the one who was to be waiting." He paused for breath.

She held her tongue. It was useless to beg him to let her go. Better to let him finish his tale.

"All of us, all the ones spread across the world to search, we knew that if we should find the scrolls, there would always be a man in Jerusalem waiting. Waiting on the steps of the Temple, on the day of Yom HaKippurim, wearing a red-striped tallit with red and blue corded tassels. Say it after me, Lydia. Say how you will know him."

It was unreal, what he was asking of her, but she repeated the words to keep his story flowing. "On the steps of the Temple on Yom HaKippurim, red-striped tallit."

"Red and blue—"

"With red and blue corded tassels."

"So many generations had passed. How to be certain the charge had been passed down in Jerusalem as well? I sent Isaac. Not with the scrolls. Only with questions."

"And what did he find?"

Samuel closed his eyes again, this time with a look of pain. "He did not return. Only these"—he jutted his chin toward the dead body behind her—"only these have come. If Isaac found the one waiting at the Temple, he must have also found our enemies."

"Is that all of your story? May I go for the physician now?"

"Lydia! I must be certain you understand how important this is. How important *you* are." He somehow found the strength to roll to his side and prop himself on an elbow to draw his face closer to hers. He cradled her cheek with his palm. "You will hold the sealed scrolls in your hand, and their destiny is your destiny. You have been chosen and marked for this purpose. Lydia, the battle will be physical"—he put a hand to his wound—"but spiritual as well. Powers of darkness will come against you, desperate to thwart the coming of the Messiah. But I promise you will be protected."

The declaration seemed to cost him strength. He fell back onto the ripped mat and blood-soaked straw with a gasp.

Tears clouded Lydia's eyes and she held his hand as it slipped from her cheek and kissed the palm. She could not lose him, not Samuel.

She bent to kiss his forehead. "Tell me what I need to know, then," she whispered.

"Back there." Only his eyes moved in the direction of the back of the room. "Under the large amphora that lies broken in the corner. There is a box under the floorboard. Bring it."

She scrambled to her feet and hurried to the corner. A chink between boards was the only hint that something might be secreted beneath. She used a shard of the broken pottery to pry the board loose. It splintered and popped, and she reached a hand into the dark alcove and felt her fingers brush the top of a dusty box, narrow and long as her forearm. A moment later she was at Samuel's side.

"Open it." His voice was weakening. There was little time left. "Tell no one, Lydia. You understand? You must never tell anyone what you hold."

Inside lay three wax-sealed scrolls of deerskin, their edges crumbling but otherwise intact. She lifted them carefully and nodded to Samuel. Underneath was a necklace—an engraved pendant on a finely wrought gold chain. She set the scrolls aside, took up the necklace with one finger, and held it to the lamplight. "What is this, Samuel?"

He did not answer.

"Samuel!" She patted his cheek gently, then harder. "Samuel!"

His eyes fluttered and his unfocused gaze finally settled on the necklace. "You found it."

She dropped the chain back into the box, set all of it aside, and got to her knees. "All of that can wait. I am going to fetch—"

"It was your mother's." His voice had softened to a dreamy, half-awake murmur. "She brought it from Cyprus."

"What? The necklace?"

His lips were moving, and Lydia had to bend to catch the words. "She was very beautiful. Like you. I promised I would give it to you someday. But it was too dangerous. Too dangerous for you to ever know."

"Samuel, you knew my mother? You know who I am?" The strength went out of her limbs and astonishment drove away all other thoughts. Not stolen away, then, as in her childhood fancies. Given up, abandoned. "Why did you never—?"

"You must let yourself love, Lydia. Despite what we have done. Let yourself need others."

"Samuel, my mother—"

But he was sucking in a great, gasping breath, his eyes suddenly large and unseeing, as though he stared past the roof, past the stars even, to something unknown. "Yes, Lord!" The words were nearly a shout, so strange after the weakening of his voice.

And then his body seemed to collapse, to deflate, and he fell back against the mat, still and unbreathing.

No. No, it was not happening. Could not happen.

This man, this mentor and teacher and friend, was the only father she had known.

"Samuel!" She shook his shoulders, bent an ear to his chest, put her fingers to his lips to check for breath.

Nothing.

"No!" The word erupted like a scream, and she dug her fingers into his shoulders once more. "Do not leave me alone!"

She had never said the words, never told him.

"I love you!" She bent her tear-streaked face to his, pressed her wet cheek to his bearded one, called the words into his ear as if they could follow him to wherever he had gone. "I love you, Samuel."

Her body shook now, trembled with grief and fear, with a shock like a limb had been torn from her body. Her fingers dug into the loose straw that lay under them, and she grabbed up handfuls of the bloodstained bedding, lifted it to her head, and released it to fall over her hair and her shoulders like ashes of mourning. It settled in her hair and stuck to her tears and her lips and she did not care. Again and again she released the bloody straw over her head. Let Samuel's attacker return and take her too.

She had spent her life alone, abandoned by her parents like some unwanted rubbish, unworthy of love.

Yet she had always had Samuel.

No longer. Now she was truly alone.

Alone with a destiny she neither wanted nor understood.

Finally, cradling the scrolls and with the strange necklace wound around her fingers, Lydia lay beside the still-warm body of Samuel and fell into an exhausted sleep.

Six

Somewhere in the early morning hours, Lydia crawled from the torn sleeping mat in Samuel's house, past the body of his enemy and hers, and forced her numb legs to stand.

The lamp had long since gone out, and in the half-light of dawn, she found the slender wooden box and replaced the three deerskin scrolls with icy fingers.

The necklace she lifted over her head and let it settle around her throat, the pendant dangling to hide under her robe.

And then she left.

Stumbling down the outer staircase with the box, she looked neither right nor left, though Samuel would have wanted her to be wary.

With the box tucked under her arm and her mantle missing, still wrapped around Samuel's body, she felt exposed and vulnerable, and too stunned to care.

It would be a stormy day from the looks of the low-hanging clouds that churned above like gray woolen tunics in dirty wash water.

She plodded toward the palace, with only a few stray thoughts of what might come next. Samuel was dead, and Andromeda was dead. She had this strange box worth killing over, and even Cleopatra surely wanted to see Lydia's throat slit, for reasons more sound than stolen writings and a secret order.

The docks were quieter than usual, perhaps because of the weather. Lydia avoided the street-side palace entrance and arch and chose to trudge around the perimeter to the harbor entrance of the palace, where her arrival might go unseen.

At the base of the wide stone steps leading down to the harbor, near the colossal sphinx where Samuel had first begun to speak of her new destiny, a well-dressed man argued with a cluster of sailors, his upraised arm punctuating angry words she could not make out from this distance.

Herod?

She drew closer, slowed, and listened.

He was trying to arrange passage out of Alexandria. These sailors were part of the crew that had brought him. Didn't he arrive on his own grand ship as she had imagined? The sailors were refusing to put out to sea so quickly.

"You are a madman to ask us to sail in this weather!" The brawny sailor wore no shirt in spite of the chill. "And we have only just arrived. No time to make repairs, to reload cargo that would make the trip to Rome worthwhile!"

Herod's back was to Lydia and his next words were lost to her, but it was clear he was angry.

The sailor waved a dismissive hand. "Go to the lighthouse, then. Ask the Keeper to arrange passage for you. She has connections and boats of her own." He and his companions returned to their rigging.

At this, Herod shot a glance at the pinnacle of the lighthouse, its night fires burning still in the gloom of the morning, then stalked away in the direction of the Pharos.

In that moment, Lydia saw with clarity what must happen next.

She must leave with Herod.

She pushed away the panic that the thought of sailing brought, for with the certainty flowed something else, an icy surge through her veins that lifted her chin and tightened her arm around the wooden box and propelled her toward the palace steps. Anger.

None of this should have happened. If Andromeda had kept quiet, perhaps Lydia would not have spoken so foolishly. If Samuel had let the secret writings be the stuff of family lore and legend, he would not lay cold in his house.

She stalked across the outer courtyard, past the line of carved, fat-bottomed columns whose lotus flower capitals still lay in darkness far above.

If Cleopatra was not such a monster, Lydia would not be running toward a civil war.

But no, it did little good to blame. For if she were merely running, she could run anywhere.

It was the box under her arm that drove her east, toward the homeland Samuel had never seen, toward a man in a red-striped tallit.

Only a few servants crisscrossed halls and courtyard at this hour—secret liaisons, and those tasked with the nightly maintenance of the fires and the early morning food preparation. Banafrit would still be in bed, as would Caesarion. But Lydia would not leave without saying good-bye to these two.

At the thought of leaving Caesarion, her heart lurched against her chest. No choice. She had no choice. If she stayed for his sake, she would share Andromeda's fate and be no more good to him than if she ran.

How long did she have before Herod secured passage out of Alexandria? It must not have gone well for him after she left him with Cleopatra in his chamber last night. Sailors preferred to put out early. Would he wait until tomorrow, or did Cleopatra's wrath burn as brightly toward him as it did toward Lydia herself?

In the room she shared with five other servant girls, now sleeping, Lydia quietly threw her belongings into a stained sack used for carrying clothes for washing in the basins near the kitchens. She had few items that concerned her—some spare tunics, a few tiny scrolls Samuel had given her during their lessons, which she put into the box with the others. A few tools and brushes for her pottery. Only a single mantle besides the one she'd left with Samuel, and this she would wear. She reached under her sleeping mat, to the carefully concealed pocket she'd sewn there, and found the pouch of money. Was it only last night she had tucked it away, worrying about Andromeda spilling her secret?

The money she placed under the scrolls, then positioned the box at the bottom of the sack under the rest, flung the mantle around her shoulders, and gave a glance of good-bye to the room.

It had been home for nearly eighteen years, and she would not miss it for a day. How could a person not belong in the only place she ever lived?

With the sack in stiff fingers, she slid from the room, toward the larger chamber off the kitchens that Banafrit's status afforded her.

The woman's snoring covered the sound of Lydia's entrance, and she stood over Banafrit for several moments, letting the memories wash over her. She had never been what one might call "mothering," but at least Banafrit had given her a place here as a child and duties to occupy her time and make her useful. It had been a gift, though until this moment, Lydia had not felt truly grateful. She wished she could take Banafrit with her, but if Lydia stole her favorite cook, Cleopatra would certainly hunt her down.

She rested the sack on the floor beside Banafrit's mat and dropped to her knees. "Banafrit." She whispered the name and gently shook the large woman's arm.

"Wh-what is it? Have they found her?" Banafrit shot up, clutched Lydia's shoulder.

"No, no, shh." Lydia smiled and took Banafrit's hand in her own.

"Child, you're alive." Banafrit dragged her into an uncharacteristic embrace. "She had guards searching for you. I thought . . . I thought . . ."

No time to waste, then. Even if Herod's hasty departure were not her only chance to provide for herself and fulfill Samuel's instructions, staying in the palace was impossible.

Banafrit's glance, misty and dark, shifted to the sack, then back to Lydia. "Where will you go?"

Lydia shook her head. "It is best if you can say you do not know. But I will be safe."

"I have family in the city—"

"No, Banafrit. I am leaving Egypt."

Another embrace, this one bringing fresh tears to Lydia. Were they not all spent over Samuel's body? She would not tell the woman of Samuel. Let her learn of it later, when Lydia was gone.

"Send word if you can," the older woman whispered.

Lydia nodded, though they both knew it was impossible.

"I must say good-bye to Caesarion."

Banafrit gave her a sad smile and touched her cheek. They both knew how difficult the next good-bye would be.

"Watch over him for me, Banafrit. Find another to love him well."

"I will. I promise."

One more embrace and Lydia was gone, drifting through the quiet halls once more, to the narrow stairs at the back of the palace, then along the corridor to the nursery.

She took a great chance. Caesarion's door was always protected at night, and if Cleopatra already had guards looking for her . . .

But as she hoped, it was Panhsj who stood sentry this morning. Panhsj, who always had a self-conscious smile and a nod for Lydia, who smiled at the honey cakes she secretly brought him as his duty ended each morning.

He had no smile for her today, only a look of alarm at her approach. "She—"

Lydia held up a hand. "I know. She is not inside, is she?"

He shook his head but glanced beyond Lydia to the empty hall, his jaw tight.

"I must go in, only for a few moments, Panhsj."

He stepped aside at once, even opened the door for her. "Listen for my voice." He pulled the door gently closed. "I will warn you if she comes."

Dear Panhsj. Why did everyone suddenly seem so precious this morning?

She slipped to the boy's bedside, watched his gentle breathing, the way his wavy light-brown hair fell across the cushions under his head.

For all Samuel's teaching of his One God, she had never

offered a prayer to Him, but she prayed now, that his God would give her the strength to leave this boy she loved so dearly.

Yes, loved, and that was her failure.

"Caesarion." As she had done with Banafrit, she bent over his prone form and touched his arm.

He blinked sleepy eyes and smiled at her, then closed his eyes again.

"Caesarion, you must wake up. I need to tell you a secret."

At this, his eyes fluttered open. The boy loved games. "What secret, Lydia?"

She drew him into her arms, his body still warm and heavy with sleep. "I am going on a secret journey. But you must tell no one that I have left."

He pulled away. "I want to come!"

"No, no, this journey is only for me. I need you to stay here and keep my secret safe. Can you do that?"

"When will you return?"

Like a blow to the chest, his question stole her breath.

"I . . . I am not sure, Caesarion. But it is time for you to have a tutor, perhaps. Someone who will teach you wonderful—"

"I don't want a tutor!" His arms wrapped around her, hugging fiercely. "I want to go on a journey with you!"

She panted with the effort to stay strong, to stay upright and do what she must.

"I know. I know. But I will think of you often and you will think of me, and in that way we will still be together until I return." Hollow, foolish words.

How had she let this happen? How had she let herself get so close? First Samuel, now the boy. Like the ripping of two limbs from her body, and she would never be whole again.

More tears, like a flood, like an anointing over the boy, and at her tears he seemed to sense the finality of the good-bye. His own eyes filled and his chin trembled. At his cries, a sob tore from her chest and she clutched him to herself.

Her body felt so heavy, so unbearably heavy, as if she were weighted to this time and place and this boy with iron chains.

She pulled away, tried to loosen the chains, but he clung to her, weeping.

"Lydia, no, no, no. Do not leave me." His fingers tore at her clothes.

Just like Samuel. Just like the words she had screamed out to the old man as he lay dying. As he was taken from her, just as Caesarion now must be.

She was going to be sick. Her stomach roiled and rebelled, but she had not eaten in many hours.

Fingers twined with his, kisses on his wet cheeks and his soft hair, wrenching sobs she fought to keep silent.

She would return. Somehow, someday—she swore by all the gods she knew—she would find her way back to this boy.

And then she tucked him into bed one last time, took up her dirty sack, and fled.

≈

The tiny island known as Pharos at the end of the breakwater held little besides the majestic Lighthouse of Alexandria and the Temple of Isis. Jutting into the center of Alexandria's double harbors, it signaled incoming ships that they neared land, and its soaring flame was said to be visible for three hundred *stadium* out to sea. Herodotus had claimed it in his writings four hundred years ago as one of the Seven Wonders of the World.

Lydia reached the square base of the lighthouse as the sun struggled to break, pinkish-gold, through the heavy clouds. She craned her neck to gaze all the way to the top. Her lungs burned and she pressed a hand against a cramp in her side. She had been running too long.

Running with her heavy sack, though it was lighter now than when she left the palace. After her good-byes there, she had one more task—another early-morning flight through the streets to the synagogue, where she found some of Samuel's friends at morning prayers and told them of the night's happenings. She made it through the telling without tears. Perhaps they were all spent at last. The distraught men tore at their clothes as was their custom. Who would pay for Samuel's burial? They were poor scholars, all of them. She had pressed her pouch of money into one of their palms, shook her head at the objections, and run for the lighthouse.

Truly, she arrived here with little more than this assignment Samuel had given.

Was she too late?

A half-dozen boats bobbed along this side of the harbor, all of them empty.

But no, Herod was here, striding from the double doors at the base of the lighthouse, his retinue of slave girls and attendant boys hurrying behind. And two others: the Lighthouse Keeper and her husband. Lydia had never met them, only seen the woman, Sophia, and her Bellus, a retired Roman soldier, from a distance. They were friends of Samuel's, and of some of the other Jews at the synagogue, like Sosigenes who was also a Museum scholar. There had been a time, many years ago, when Sophia had been Cleopatra's tutor. But the two had parted ways.

Perhaps around the time Cleopatra started murdering her siblings.

Lydia stood alone at the end of the narrow land bridge, and the emerging group slowed as one when she was noted.

Herod's gaze flicked over her in confusion, then recognition. But it was Sophia who strode forward, hands extended. "One of Samuel's students, am I right?"

Lydia tried to smile. "Yes. Lydia."

The woman caught her hands and squeezed.

Her warmth seeped into Lydia's hands and into her soul, giving her courage. She looked to Herod. "Do you still want me, to serve your wife?"

Herod narrowed his eyes. "I am not certain if the spirit I witnessed last night would be an inspiration or a bad example to my Mariamme."

Lydia lifted her chin. "Is the Lady Mariamme a woman like Cleopatra?"

Herod chuckled and glanced at his companions. "Your point is well taken. I should think I am in little danger. But what of you? Is your queen not searching for another throat to slit?"

"She is."

Herod's gaze flicked toward the palace. "Ah, I see. One more victory for me, should I take you along."

"I will serve you well, you have my word."

Sophia moved to place her arm around Lydia's shivering frame, a gesture of such kindness, it felt as if they were old friends. "She is a good girl, Herod. Smart and dependable. You would do well to have her in your palace."

Herod's slow smile revealed his pleasure at Sophia's reference. He had no palace yet, this money-strapped Galilean governor with an eye on the kingship.

Bellus was smiling at Sophia. "You'd do well to heed my wife, Herod. Smartest woman I know."

"Very well. One more aboard." He waved his attendants toward a merchant ship secured to the dock, then gave his thanks to Sophia and Bellus and followed.

Sophia released Lydia but turned to her. "I do not know what has happened, but I know Samuel trusts you. So I will tell you this—be strong, and brave, and smart. And believe all that your mentor has told you."

Sophia glanced at Bellus, who smiled at her as if she were a queen herself, then back to Lydia. "In a world supposedly run by men, I can tell you that this advice has always served me well. You are all these things and more, I can see. May the One God hold you in His hand."

Lydia caught up Sophia's hand in her own and squeezed. The woman had placed more value on her in a fleeting moment than Cleopatra had in so many years. "Thank you."

Sophia smiled and inclined her head toward the ship. "Go. Your future awaits."

The sun had disappeared into the thick clouds by the time Lydia descended into the belly of the ship. She fought back the unreasoning panic. She had not been on a ship in more than seven years, not since that awful day. She took her place beside one of Herod's servant boys who introduced himself cheerily as David.

The pitch and rock of the ship as it cleared the harbor and took to the open sea triggered not only sheer terror but waves of nausea. Thankfully, her belly was still empty.

Empty like the rest of her, for she was leaving everything that had ever been important on the disappearing shores of Egypt.

Seven

Lydia sought the rail of the ship soon after they cleared the Alexandrian harbor. Here on the open sea, she was safely out of Cleopatra's reach. And the hold below deck already stank of the ship's previous journey and whatever cargo—alive or rotting, human or beast—it had once held. The wind caught her hair and the city disappeared into the fog. Besides Caesarion, and perhaps Banafrit, there was nothing, no one, who would miss her there for long. She looked northwest, toward Rome, and tried not to think of capsizing.

Twenty days.

Twenty days on board and they would reach that near-fabled city that sought to rival Alexandria in architecture and learning, but was filled with a warring class of men who understood little of Greek learning, Egyptian beauty, or Persian elegance.

At least, that was what Samuel had taught her.

Little wonder that Herod should seek out the patronage of Marc Antony and his troops to aid his bid for power in Judea. Where else but Rome would one go for military strength? Would

Antony come through for Herod when they reached the famed city? And then they would go on to Judea, where she could rid herself of the scrolls and figure out how to get back to Egypt while keeping safe from Cleopatra.

The boy, David, joined her at the rail and wrapped knobby hands around the cold metal. He was a boy becoming a man, perhaps twelve, with all the lanky awkwardness of his age—limbs grown longer than accustomed and a voice that pitched as erratically as the boat's heave and plunge over waves. He said nothing, only smiled, then ducked his head when she smiled in return.

She watched the churning clouds on the horizon, a swirl of more hues of gray than she'd ever created on a palette. "Have you been with Herod long?"

"Almost three years." He cleared his throat. "Since just before we were forced to flee Jerusalem."

"And your parents, are they in service with the tetrarch as well?"

David drew himself upright and squared his shoulders. "My father raises sheep in Galilee. It is a poor living, and it was necessary for me to help with the family income."

The words were delivered without resentment, but so young? He had known a bit of loneliness himself, then.

"Tell me of Jerusalem, David. I have never seen that part of the world." Only through the eyes of Samuel and his teachings, but he had never seen the land of his fathers either.

"It is the City of God." The simple statement was delivered with quiet passion.

The ship surged over a peaking wave and Lydia gripped the rail, sucking in a terrified breath. "And . . . and does Herod also worship the Jews' One God?"

David huffed, then glanced over his shoulder at the sailors

shouting instructions about the mast to each other. "Herod worships himself alone. Yet he would be king over our people."

"I know little of Judean politics."

David turned and leaned his back against the rail, elbows propped, as if to appear unconcerned at the increasing waves. "It is complicated, and yet it is simple." His voice had taken on the cadence of a rabbi in Samuel's synagogue.

Lydia would have smiled, had she not been so focused on the waves.

"Antigonus has been king over Judea for many years and Hyrcanus has been High Priest. They are both Hasmoneans—direct descendants of the Maccabees who freed us more than a hundred years ago. When the Parthians invaded last year from the East, they supported Antigonus because he hates Rome as they do. They exiled the High Priest Hyrcanus to Babylon and cut off his ears."

Lydia grimaced. The practice of mutilation was a common one. A man thus maimed could not serve in an official role. Still, it turned her stomach to think of it. Or was it the sway of the boat? She was feeling rather ill.

David was not finished with his brief history lesson. "The Parthians supported Antigonus and declared him both king and High Priest. But Herod's father, Antipater, was supported by Rome, so the Romans put *him* in charge of Judea. He claims kingship, so there is civil war in Judea. Herod fled Jerusalem under attack by Antigonus. He hopes to bring back troops from Rome to establish his family's rule."

So, Jewish Antigonus and the Parthians against the Roman-backed Herod. Surely there was much more to all of it, but at least she understood why they undertook this trip to Rome.

As if an omen, lightning streaked across the horizon, piercing the sea like a spear thrown from heaven. A heavy crack of thunder snapped on its heels.

David eyed the swirling clouds. "We'd better go below."

Lydia nodded in relief.

The other twenty or so who traveled with Herod were scattered across the large bowel of the ship, some seated on benches, others with their backs against the inner hull. Herod himself reclined on a low couch, attended by the same girl, Riva, who had been beside him in Cleopatra's courtyard—a sharp-featured beauty a few years older than Lydia who followed Lydia's entrance with David with narrowed eyes and tight lips.

Over the course of the long day, David tried to distract her from her nausea with tales of each of their shipmates—some slaves, some servants, and several advisers. But the variable swells and valleys that rocked the ship united them all—tetrarch and slave alike bent over pots to empty their bellies.

The day wore on, with the stench of salt and seawater, vomit and smoking oil, building in the hold. Waves crashed against the hull, and those below edged inward, as if the center were safe. In the oily torchlight, sweat-sheened faces, tinged green, shone in a ring of fear.

Two days later no one had eaten. Sailors cursed and screamed above deck. Servants cried and Herod whined. They lay half prostrate in a heap, often thrown against each other intimately. Lydia's clammy skin crawled at the human touch and she tasted nothing but salt.

They would not reach Rome. Not in this weather. Already word had leaked downward from the crew that they had been blown off course in an easterly direction and now hoped only to find land somewhere before the ship was torn to pieces. Cargo was jettisoned, two sailors were swept off the deck by waves, and all but one of the torches in the hold were extinguished.

Herod's favorite servant girl, Riva, mopped his sweaty brow, but she looked as though she would soon be unconscious.

In the belly of the ship, Lydia lost her sense of time and place, tumbled backward into the black memory that always sucked away breath and hope, the cold and slimy pressure of river water wrapped around her little-girl body. She tore herself from the memory, back to the present, but it offered little hope.

She sat upon the sack that contained Samuel's precious scrolls, but what good would it do anyone at the bottom of the sea? She would fail in the last task he had given, the only way that remained to honor his memory, to deliver these scrolls. Lydia owed him that much and more, and yet she would fail.

On the fourth day out from Alexandria, David began to sing.

It was a quiet, mournful tune in the language of his people. Lydia clung to the sweet, high voice and the words she did not understand, as if they were an anchor. She curled into a ball on the sticky floor, her possessions tucked against her belly, closed her eyes to all but the sound of his voice, and wished for death.

On the fifth day, they made landfall.

Herod's entourage stumbled onto the deck and then to the dock—blinking in the light, filthy and stinking, clutching at rails, at ropes, at each other.

The island of Rhodes. A long way from Rome but solid ground.

The boat-strewn port hugged the edge of a jewel-like sea—sapphire and turquoise and diamond. The famed colossal bronze statue lay fallow beside the harbor, broken at the knees for nearly two hundred years, a greenish shadow against the white stones of the harbor streets.

The ship had limped into port, wind-torn and leaking. It would not put out again anytime soon. Herod was once again a refugee, without funds or army and now without a means to secure either one.

The group found shelter in a dimly lit tavern while Herod sought out friends. From what Lydia heard, the man had friends everywhere. She had seen little of his reputed charm, save the one night in Cleopatra's courtyard, but the days at sea had not been a good indication of anyone's character.

They washed, were given bread and wine, and reclined on benches and couches for several contented hours. When Herod returned it was with good news. He had already convinced supporters in Rhodes to raise the money to build him a ship that would take them to Rome. In the meantime, they would be housed by one of the leading citizens of Rhodes and treated well.

Lydia sighed and turned her head toward the tavern wall. She had set out for Jerusalem by way of Rome, learned that Jerusalem was held by Herod's enemies, detoured to Rhodes, and now would have to await the building of a new ship. The errand Samuel had given seemed as far as the horizon, and just as unreachable.

Would she be in Jerusalem by autumn, when the day of Yom HaKippurim would allow her to finally deliver the scrolls?

Eight

Lydia stood with David at the rail, watching the warm, sun-washed shores of Rome sharpen across an expanse as smooth as blue-green glass. The weather for sailing in the month of April was far better than January had been, and the months spent on the island of Rhodes had strengthened them all for the journey. But their earlier passage from Alexandria had heightened Lydia's great fear of ships, and she rose every day to eye the horizon with anxiety.

"And what shall Rome bring to us, do you think?"

David snorted. "Harder work, I imagine." He ran a hand through his sun-lightened brown hair and laughed. "We have all grown quite spoiled, I fear." He jutted his chin across the deck where Herod lounged in luxury, his servant girls attending. "And none more spoiled than Riva."

As if she heard her name even from this distance, the girl looked up with a sly smile and, with a swing of her head, swept her hair over one shoulder. She never missed an opportunity to be at Herod's side, making herself essential—more often at night than during the day.

Herod was a man aware of his own allure, and he enjoyed making Lydia uncomfortable with the brush of a shoulder or touch of a hand on her arm. Always their conversation was about Mariamme, how Lydia would serve her well when they finally reached Judea and rescued her and his family from the fortress where they held off Antigonus's men. Riva had hovered around their exchanges, narrow-eyed and suspicious. Did she wish Herod to herself, or was it Lydia's future position with Mariamme that caused her envy?

Riva had proven no friend to Lydia in these last months, taking every opportunity to criticize her to Herod, but the girl was much like Andromeda, and the likeness somehow softened Lydia's heart toward her.

But David, dear David . . . She had tried with all her strength to resist his friendship. He was like young Caesarion and wise teacher Samuel, both of whom she missed desperately, rolled into one. Friendship with David was far too easy, and therefore far too dangerous. She fought a losing battle. Already she relied on him; already she needed him more than he needed her.

They put into port a half day's journey southwest of Rome and switched to a barge that carried them the fifteen miles up the River Tiberis, which flowed through the heart of Rome. Every one of them clutched the rails now, watching the wonders of Rome revealed.

David had warned her, though he had never seen Rome, only garnered stories from every source he could. The city was a forest of columns, a sea of tenements. It was pocked with vast expanses of open forums and stadiums. It could swallow a person whole.

She had a task awaiting her in Jerusalem, but somehow it seemed she would fall into Rome and never emerge.

As if he understood her concern, David patted her shoulder as the barge's ropes were thrown to the quay and dockworkers hauled it forward to tie off on the iron cleat. The brotherly gesture compressed the air in her chest. She must not get too close to yet another who could be snatched away.

A small crowd had gathered on the dock, and it gave way to a man striding through it with confidence, an easy smile, and an upraised hand.

From the prow of the barge, Herod shouted his greeting. "Antony, my friend! It is good to see your face!"

Marc Antony grinned. "What a time you had getting here, eh? Well, come ashore and let us show you how Rome treats its guests."

Lydia gathered up the sack that had been her constant companion since leaving Alexandria and filed behind David and the others to disembark. She wore the pendant at all times, now strung on a leather cord beneath her tunic, and the box of scrolls weighted the bottom of the sack, pulling the fabric taut in her hands.

Three months since she left Alexandria. Five months remaining to reach Jerusalem, still held by Herod's enemy Antigonus, before Yom HaKippurim, the Day of Atonement.

The feeling that Rome would devour her followed her from the barge, along the planking, to the waiting crowd, like a needling prick at her thoughts.

"I hope you like it here." Riva's voice at her shoulder was unfriendly. She pushed past Lydia, narrow hips swaying as she caught up with Herod.

How long would it take Herod to convince Mark Antony to lend troops for the war against Antigonus? Lydia needed to get out of Rome before Riva's unfounded jealousy did more damage.

The procession climbed from the murky River Tiberis toward the tree-lined summit of one of Rome's seven hills, the Palatine. Marc Antony, as expansive and outgoing as Lydia remembered from his time in Egypt, ordered a wide litter for himself and Herod to be transported up the cobbled road. Lydia and the others followed, trailing between lofty umbrella pines that sharpened the air with their spicy scent, welcome after the stench of sea travel.

Lydia took in every detail of the city as they climbed. The immense Roman Forum stretched at the base of the hill on their left, its lofty temple columns and administrative buildings peeking white from between the pines, visible even from this distance. In the valley to their right, an elongated oval stadium matched the length of the Palatine. Would they see chariot races even tonight, be able to witness the action from this height?

But it was the hill itself that demanded attention, with its magnificent white-stoned estates spread under the cloudless blue sky, housing the elite of Roman society. The breeze on the hill contained no whiff of city odors. Lydia lifted her head to the dark wings of a bird, wheeling lazily over a two-storied estate, and despite all, she smiled.

Laughter rang out from the litter ahead, and the eight straight-backed litter bearers slowed as one. The curtains were thrust aside and Herod's head appeared.

"Riva!" He scanned the cluster of those following the litter until he found the girl, already hurrying forward. "Come."

Riva bumped a shoulder against Lydia's arm as she passed, then tossed a superior smile over her shoulder. The dark-skinned men who bore the litter lowered it nearly to the ground, and Riva climbed onto the cushioned bench, disappearing from view. Now heavier with three occupants, the men grunted and heaved as one as they lifted the litter to their shoulders and continued.

The procession wound past several estates and stopped at a midsized house with two stories and a peristyled garden in front, its portico columns circled with glossy vines.

Inside, the staff was taken to separate men's and women's quarters, given jugs of water with which to wash, loaves of hard bread, and mats where they might rest. When the room was empty, Lydia took care to hide the scrolls in an unused urn in the corner.

They were all to be included in the reception Marc Antony had planned for his younger friend that evening. Where Herod was all quiet, Eastern intensity and studied charm, Antony was the hard-drinking reprobate who loved to spend money on a party.

The reception proved to rival any Cleopatra had given, if not in scale at least in quality. Lydia hovered with a few other servants near the frescoed wall of the large dining hall. Others of the party—Herod's advisers, plus Riva and a few other women—reclined on three couches set around a massive square table.

The reds and yellows of the fresco at Lydia's back were warm and inviting, and the spread of food magnificent. Plump green olives and creamy white cheeses, jeweled cups of wine and steaming platters of roasted pheasant. Her mouth watered at the delectable scent of the meat. There had been no cooked foods aboard the ship from Rhodes. She must be content to wait, though Riva's hard smile as she tore apart of bit of seasoned meat made the delay grueling.

Herod reclined on the couch opposite Antony and stuffed his mouth with a large grape, chewing while speaking. "So when am I to meet the young man who so captured Julius Caesar's affections that it gained him a fortune, a claim to power, and an enemy as formidable as you?"

Antony's face darkened briefly. "Octavian and I have come to an agreement. There is no enmity here."

"Ha!" Herod spit the grape seed to the mosaic floor. "You have, what, twenty years on the boy? And yet all I hear in Judea is Octavian, Octavian." His voice was mocking. "Octavian adopted by Caesar and named heir in his will. Octavian forces Marc Antony to flee to Gaul. Octavian made senator, given *imperium*, given a consularship—"

"Enough!" Antony slapped the table.

Lydia jumped and her shoulder struck the wall.

His usual good humor seemed spent. "Our alliance with Lepidus has made the Second Triumvirate official—something Caesar never had. There are plenty of Roman holdings for the three of us. Lepidus has Africa, the East is mine. I am content to leave Italia and its neighbors to Octavian."

"Hmm." Herod's gaze grew hard and calculating, as she had seen in his sparring with Cleopatra. "It is that very East I have come to speak with you about."

Antony raised a hand and shook his head. "Later. Tonight is for enjoyment only." He waved in a group from the doorway, where they had apparently been waiting for a signal.

Musicians with drums, lyres, double-reed mouth pipes, and a large cithara filed in with solemnity, set up quickly in the front of the room, and began to play a slow and steady drumbeat accompanying a minor-keyed tune.

But it was the man who entered at the start of the music who captured Lydia's attention. Tall and narrowly built, with a straight Roman nose and full lips. Expressive eyes that roamed the room grazed her quickly, then returned for a second look. She swallowed against the sudden dryness in her throat and looked away.

A slave paused in front of Lydia with a platter of fruits, but she shook her head at the offer and returned her attention to the new arrival. Without looking, she could feel that Riva's gaze turned that way as well.

"Ah, here he is." Antony grinned and nodded toward Herod. "Our premier poet, Lucius Varius Rufus."

Lucius Varius Rufus. Lydia repeated the name in her mind and it echoed against her heart.

"You will love this, Herod. Nothing like it in your dusty Galilee, I am quite certain. My wife adores him."

Herod frowned. "Your wife? I didn't want to mention her. I was told that Fulvia—"

"Fulvia is dead. Yes." Antony's casual attention on the poet seemed strained. "I have remarried. Octavia."

"Ho!" Herod's sharp laugh overmatched the music. "Octavian has given you his sister! And where is the lovely Octavia tonight if her favorite poet is here?"

"She is unwell, I fear. And her favorite handmaid has recently run off, leaving her with no one to dress her. You will meet her tomorrow. When you meet her brother."

Herod smiled appreciatively and raised his cup to Antony. "I have underestimated you, my old friend. Alliance, indeed!"

Antony said nothing, and the poet began his recitation.

The words poured from him, lovely and heart-wrenching and lyrical. The lines seemed torn from an epic poem praising the hard-won battles of Rome in a far-off land—couplets that transformed bloodshed and war into something both tragic and beautiful.

Lydia leaned into the recitation, heart racing and lips parted. She had been in Cleopatra's palace all her life, and yet this night, with its sensual food and smoking torches and the plaintive cry of the cithara's strings, all as a backdrop to the enrapturing voice of Lucius Varius Rufus, was like nothing she had experienced.

When it ended, Lydia breathed again.

Others in the room snapped fingers and thumbs in approval, and Antony called out, "When are you going to write such a poem about *my* victories, boy?"

The poet lifted his chin and returned Antony's casual look with one far more intense. "When you achieve a victory worth immortalizing, my lord."

A nervous laughter circled the room, but Antony apparently chose to ignore the slight and dismissed the man with an incline of his head.

But instead of departing, the poet circled the perimeter of the room toward the back.

Lydia watched him come, palms flat against her thighs. Where was he going?

And then he was there at her side. She kept her gaze trained on the nobility on the couches but could feel him studying her.

When he spoke, his voice was low in her ear, as if they were the only two in the room. "I believe of all those present, you were the only one truly listening."

She took a shallow breath. "It . . . it was so beautiful."

"You are very beautiful."

She looked up at him, and his gaze was traveling over her as it had done when he first entered the room, not a crude leer as she had seen on the faces of many men in Cleopatra's palace. More like the appreciative touch she would give an especially fine piece of pottery. Like the cool water poured over her after their long journey.

She laughed, a clipped, nervous sound, then lowered her head. The room had grown warm with torches and food and bodies, and her tunic felt damp against her back.

A moment later they were no longer alone.

Riva clutched his arm. "Your poetry has everyone inspired. What was your name again?"

He dipped his head. "I would be pleased to have you call me Varius."

He did not owe Riva any courtesy—an artist of his standing speaking with a foreign servant. He did himself credit to treat her thus.

Riva's gaze shot to Lydia and soured. "But why do you hover at the wall with the slaves? You must join us on the couches."

Varius glanced at Lydia, his expression surprised at Riva's false identification of her as a slave.

Riva leaned in before Lydia could correct the insult. "I have just been speaking to Herod about you."

Lydia's stomach twisted.

"Antony's new wife, Octavia, is in need of a handmaid, as her last one has gotten herself with child." Riva laughed, including Varius in the joke. "She must have pleased Antony more than she pleased his wife." Her cunning look returned to Lydia. "Herod seems to agree that the gift of a new handmaid would garner much of Antony's favor." She smiled, a false smile of friendship. "Since you are so highly regarded as a lady's maid, that is."

She took Varius's arm and pulled him toward the couch she had shared with Herod. "Just be certain you focus on pleasing *Octavia*." Her laughter trailed behind, and Varius followed her to the couch like an obedient pet.

Once seated, however, his gaze strayed more than once to where Lydia braced herself against the back wall.

Rome had its attractions, to be sure.

Would Samuel understand if she were to find herself needed, wanted, here in the majestic city of the seven hills?

Nine

"May I brush out your hair, mistress?" Lydia fiddled with ivory combs scattered across a black-veined marble table beside Octavia's gridded window.

True to her word, Riva convinced Herod that Marc Antony would be pleased if his new wife was attended by Lydia, at least while the entourage stayed in Rome. She must make certain it was no longer. The woman seemed very difficult to please.

Octavia sighed and did not stir from where she reclined on a cushioned couch. Her black hair, thick with curls and unbound, tangled about her head like a thicket. "Perhaps I should make a sacrifice."

Lydia crossed to the couch, knelt beside it, and attempted to unravel her knotted hair. Octavia didn't resist.

"Yes, mistress, a temple visit might be just the thing to cheer you."

How many times had Lydia seen Cleopatra carried in her litter to the Temple of Isis when she was distraught over some matter of state? Although Octavia's sadness seemed born of something far more personal.

"Cheer me?" Octavia turned her head from Lydia. "What purpose is there in being cheered?"

"For your children, mistress, if not for yourself. Would not Marc Antony be pleased to see his children—?"

Octavia snorted and swung her legs over the side of the couch. "Marc Antony? Foolish girl. They are not his children."

Lydia rocked back on her heels, comb suspended. The rumors here in Rome of Antony's wanton behavior with women had been more than rumors in Alexandria—Lydia had witnessed his meeting with Cleopatra two years ago, and the precious twins who were the result, even while he was known to be married to Fulvia. But to hear that Octavia had also been unfaithful—it was not proper, even for a Roman woman.

Octavia crossed to the marble table and retrieved a small comb to secure her hair.

Lydia scrambled to join her, took the comb, and expertly twisted half of Octavia's hair atop her head in the Roman style, then secured it with the comb.

"Antony is my second husband. We have been married less than a year. My brother gave me to him after his third wife, Fulvia, died. I bore the three children to Marcellus."

Second husband, fourth wife. Roman marriage alliances worked much as Ptolemaic, then. Octavia did not look older than thirty years, and yet there was an air of resignation about her, the knowledge that her life had been chosen for her without her consent.

"Not that I believe he is truly my husband." Octavia fluttered her hand with a practiced nonchalance. "While in Rome he attends my handmaidens, and while in Egypt—" She turned on Lydia and clutched her arm. "Tell me of the queen Cleopatra. Is she so much more beautiful than I?"

Lydia clasped her hand over Octavia's. "Shall we go to a temple?"

Octavia allowed herself to be led but did not forget her question. "She is powerful. Perhaps that is what he sees in her—all that power. It is said she would kill any person who stood against her for the throne, her own family, even. Is this true?"

They passed from Octavia's private chamber into the wide peristyle that surrounded Marc Antony's leafy courtyard.

"She is very determined to lead Egypt well."

Octavia gave her a half smile. "You are loyal to your former mistress. I admire that. And already I can see why she chose you to serve her personally. You are like clean air in this stale place."

"I would see you happy, my lady."

Octavia's gaze drifted to the courtyard, torch lit in the darkness but deserted. "You are good to wish it."

The commendation warmed her. For the long months in Rhodes and aboard ship, Lydia had not been needed by anyone. Feeling worthless these months had worn her spirit raw, and she welcomed Octavia's appreciation of her skills.

"But my happiness matters little. Perhaps soon it will be of no consequence at all."

Lydia glanced sideways at the woman. What did such hopeless words mean?

A thick-necked slave stood at the entrance to the home, head lowered and hands clasped. He had an Egyptian look about him and the connection made her smile, but he did not smile in return. Lydia whispered to him of his mistress's desire to visit the nearest temple, and he disappeared without a word into the darkness beyond the front door.

"Is it far, my lady? Will they bring a chariot or a litter, or will you walk?"

"The Temple of Cybele is here on the Palatine, but he will bring a litter all the same. Antony would not appreciate his wife walking the streets at night."

Octavia insisted that Lydia remain with her, and so she followed the litter away from the house, as she had followed Herod's entrance that afternoon. It was strange, this feeling of having been passed from Cleopatra's children, to Herod's future wife, to Marc Antony's second. But it would not be permanent. How long must they remain in Rome before Herod would have the promises he needed and they could sail again? In the meantime, she would do her best to make herself useful here in Rome.

Perhaps learn some poetry.

The Temple of Cybele sat high on the western slope of the Palatine Hill, overlooking the Circus Maximus and opposite the Temple of Ceres on the Aventine Hill beyond. They took a long flight of steps upward to her altar, at the foot of the statue of Cybele, with her crown and two chained lions. The temple was as lofty as Egyptian temples, if not as beautiful.

Where Egyptian architecture was voluptuous curves, Roman was straight lines. The lotus-flowered capitals atop fat-bellied columns in Egypt, carved in deep relief with the wondrous colors of the hieroglyphic language, were replaced with fluted white marble, capped with austere scrolls that seemed to frown down upon Lydia as they wandered into the first court.

But any temple at night, with its shadows weaving between columns and reaching out from hidden recesses, had a beauty that was, at best, sinister. Lydia followed in Octavia's wake toward an open-air altar already glowing with embers. From the warm shadows of the portico, a priestly whispered chant seemed to reach out and surround them. The smell of burning flesh and smoke and incense burned her eyes.

"Do you feel it, Lydia? The darkness? Always darkness. This shall perhaps be my final sacrifice."

"You will disavow the goddess, my lady?"

"She has disavowed me." Octavia's face was like stone. "I can only pray that other gods will accept my soul."

Lydia sucked in a breath. The woman's sadness ran dangerously deep, a heaviness of the heart that transferred to Lydia. Could she somehow help this woman at the end of herself?

Lydia stood unmoving through the rites, through the water poured over Octavia's outstretched hands, through the slit throat of the glassy-eyed, unsuspecting bird and its blood dripping into a golden bowl. Cybele was "Great Mother," conscripted from the Greeks, and her worship was more restrained and refined than that of Isis. The way she leashed the lions showed a control over nature that contrasted with the Egyptians' more rapturous oneness with it.

When Octavia began to chant the prayers in a low monotone, Lydia compared the words to Isis's prayers, and even those of Samuel's God. *"Hear, O Israel, the Lord is our God, the Lord is One . . ."*

She had avoided Cleopatra's religious rites for years, in deference to Samuel and his disapproval of all other gods—his insistence that they were false and their worship angered the One God. What would Samuel think of her eagerness to please the Idumean Herod with his Greek ways, or of her desire to be needed by this Roman consul's wife?

And which worship was right? With all these different deities, was it even possible to know the gods at all? Perhaps there really was only One, and He had somehow been fragmented into many.

Would someday people return to the worship of only One? She must ask David about it.

The hour was late when they returned, and after the day of travel and all she had seen of Rome, a bed would be most welcome. She had been handed to Octavia after the meal and not been shown where she would sleep. Should she ask her temporary mistress?

But in the courtyard, the sound of laughter, low and feminine, drifted from between the darkened ferns. Riva.

An encounter with the Judean girl was always unpleasant, but Riva would know where she was to bed down.

"My lady." Lydia slowed Octavia's walk along the peristyle. "May I attend you in a few minutes to prepare you for the night? I have a question for one of my fellow travelers."

Octavia still moved with the quiet hush of the temple. She lifted one shoulder slightly. "Do not tarry long."

Lydia bowed her head. "Yes, mistress."

The laughter had ceased when they entered the house, but Lydia circled the courtyard, passing along the columned walkway to where the ferns and palms grew thick in a private bower.

"Lydia." Riva's voice emerged from the darkness, her face half-hidden, half-glowing in reflected torchlight. "You are wandering late."

Riva was not alone. The poet Varius leaned one shoulder against the wall at her side, his ruby-red tunic matching the deep-red paint, and the white of his toga in stark contrast.

"I accompanied Octavia to the Temple of Cybele."

"Ah, always faithful, our Lydia."

The condescension brought a flush to her cheeks. Did Varius see it in the darkness?

A slave hurried along the walkway toward them, one of their

own brought from Judea. "Riva!" His voice was sharp with reprimand. "Herod is calling for you."

Riva's face went dark for a passing moment, then cleared, the
look replaced with a false smile. "Then I must leave him to you,
Lydia." She ran a hand along Varius's arm, and her smile for him
was most sincere. "Do not forget me by tomorrow."

Varius bowed once. "Impossible, I assure you."

Riva was gone a moment later, her hair swinging behind her
shoulders as she walked. Lydia had forgotten to ask her about
where they were to sleep. And it would appear Riva did not have
to concern herself with the question.

She swallowed once, twice, and did not turn to face Varius,
who stood silent behind her.

"Perhaps you would like to walk around the courtyard?"

No. *Yes.*

He held a hand to her as she joined him. "Honey cake? Riva
brought it to me from the kitchens, but I have had enough."

Lydia took the sticky golden morsel from his hand and tasted
a small bite. "Thank you."

"Of course. Besides"—he smiled and cocked his head as they
walked—"now that you are here, I have all the sweetness I need."

She tried to smile at the words, but they fluttered in her chest
and stole her breath. She finished the honey cake and licked her
fingers. What clever thing would Riva say at such a moment? Or
perhaps Riva was beautiful enough that she did not need words
to charm.

"I . . . I enjoyed your poetry." Had she told him that already?
Stupid girl.

But he smiled and bowed his head at the compliment as
though it were the first time he'd heard it. "I am afraid my

comments afterward to Marc Antony were less well received. I should stick to my recitations, perhaps."

"Oh no, I admired that as well! The way you are unafraid to speak your mind, even if it causes others to think less of you—" What was she saying? She licked sticky fingers again, more to quiet her mouth than because of remaining honey.

Varius chuckled. "Yes, that has always been a fault, I fear. One of these days it will probably earn me a dagger in the belly. Or worse, they will nail me to one of their infernal Roman crosses."

It might be true, but still she admired him. The artist within her connected with his creativity, but she would never have his boldness.

They had come full circle around the courtyard now, but Varius continued as though he did not wish to end their conversation. She should return to Octavia. Already Lydia had been too long, and the woman's desperation frightened her. She followed Varius, only a step behind.

He slowed until she caught up with him. "And while I seem to often enrage those around me, I should think everyone finds you quite pleasing."

She smiled and shrugged. "Riva is the one whom everyone—"

"That is not what I meant." His gaze drifted to where Riva had disappeared into the shadows. "Riva is entertaining, perhaps, but she is like a vapor." He circled Lydia's arm with cool fingers and squeezed. "There is something far more—solid—about you."

Lydia laughed, the tight anxiety in her chest loosening a bit, in spite of his touch on her arm. "Solid. Yes, that is what every woman wants to be called."

Varius slowed and turned her to face him. "No, do not tell me I have offended even you with my words." His look on her was dark, intense, and his voice melodic. He smelled of something she did not recognize. Ink, perhaps? It was a good smell.

She shook her head. "No. No offense."

He smiled. "Ah, good. I should not wish to think—"

"Lydia!"

She jerked her head toward the sharp voice.

"My lady, I . . . I was coming soon—"

"I am tired and wish to sleep and yet have no one to wait on me. I was forced to search for someone." Her attention rested on Varius. "It seems you are otherwise occupied."

"No, Varius was only—"

Octavia waved a hand. "Do you think I concern myself with the affairs of plebeians and servants? The details are nothing to me. I only know Herod recommended you as the girl who would serve his betrothed wife. I shall have to tell him you seem fit only to serve children."

It should not have troubled her, this censure from a Roman noblewoman who had little to do with Lydia's life or her future, and yet the feeling of having displeased Octavia, of being seen as unfit, worthless—it was like the floor of the courtyard falling open beneath her. Like the wide-eyed surprise of the bird on the temple altar earlier as its throat was cut, the sharp shock of being nothing more than a means to an end.

She wished to redeem herself in Octavia's eyes, convince her to stay silent with Herod. But at the lifeless look in the woman's eyes, Lydia pushed away the selfish thought and instead touched Octavia's arm with a gentle but affectionate pressure.

"How may I please you, mistress?"

The question hung unanswered in the humid courtyard air, and it seemed the question she had been asking all her life.

Ten

Lydia spent the next morning and afternoon making drastic changes to Octavia's bedchamber and praying that the woman would be pleased rather than angry at her presumption.

The room was in urgent need of freshening. How long had Octavia's former handmaid been missing? If the rumors of the girl's dalliance with Marc Antony were true, perhaps she was not focused overmuch on pleasing Octavia even while she remained.

Lydia removed the heavy drapery at the windows, had it taken to the courtyard and the dust beaten from it by a slave. Octavia's gauzy dresses were washed and hung in the sunlight to dry, then arranged on hooks in the wall. Floors and walls were scrubbed of accumulated soot, wicks trimmed in lamps, and vases of fresh flowers brought from the gardens.

"Lydia, you have worked some magic."

Lydia's heart thudded at Octavia's sudden appearance, but she smiled a nervous welcome at the woman's return from a meeting with Herod and Antony.

Octavia took in the chamber. "While I have been watching over Rome, it appears you have been watching over me."

"It would seem too long since anyone had, mistress."

Octavia closed her eyes briefly. "Yes, you could say that." The words seemed to reach into that place of sadness again, but then she blinked and tried to smile. "All of this restored beauty puts me in mind for some new pleasures." She crossed to a table, fished through the contents of a small wooden box, then turned to Lydia with a handful of coins. "Here, take these. I want you to go to the market and make some purchases for me."

Lydia let her drop the coins into her palm but shook her head. "I have not left this house since arriving, my lady. I would not know where—"

Octavia waved a hand. "It doesn't matter how long it takes you. There is time to get lost and explore the city if you like. Here, I shall make you a list."

"I . . . I should not wish to leave you, if you are still feeling the darkness, my lady."

Octavia sighed. "Just to hear your concern lifts my spirits, Lydia. Perhaps you can convince me that there is value still in this life. But not today."

Minutes later, armed with nothing more than a scrap of papyrus scrawled with Octavia's demands and a pouch of heavy coins, Lydia crossed the courtyard, biting her lip.

The freedom to explore Rome was a wondrous gift, but she would prefer to watch over Octavia. And Lydia had no idea where to begin, nor what areas would be unsafe to roam.

"Stealing away for a secret tryst, are we?"

Lydia peered around a leafy palm to the voice hidden in the shadows.

Varius appeared, his teasing smile falling on her.

"What? No! No ... I ... Octavia asked me to make some purchases for her." Why did she always sound like a child when she spoke with him?

Varius emerged from the portico and drew closer. "She has come to rely on you thoroughly, I see. And so soon. But I am not surprised. You have that effect on people everywhere, I would guess."

Lydia ducked her head and toyed with the silk pouch.

"Where is the slave she has tasked to accompany you? Surely you are not going alone?"

A slave. That would have been a logical request.

At her hesitation, Varius took her arm in his. "Your humble servant, then, my lady."

"No ... no, thank you, Varius. That is not necessary."

But Varius would not be dissuaded. He insisted first on a walk under the lofty pines of the Palatine to look over the Circus Maximus in the valley below.

He drew close, so her gaze traveled the length of his raised arm to where he pointed. "There at the end is where the chariots emerge." His voice was low, a murmur against her ear, as if the telling were a secret. "It is the most thrilling thing you could imagine. All those thousands in the seats, screaming for their favorites."

He lowered his arm and shifted to stand almost behind her, his hand resting lightly on her hip. "Close your eyes. I will help you see it."

She obeyed, and his lyrical voice filled her senses.

"It is like a festival and a banquet and a war, melded into one great spectacle of glorious color and heat. The deafening crush of the crowd, a sea of white togas striped in all the colors of the Republic, raised fists, perfumed air, the sand churning under chariot wheels, black horses sheened with sweat, and the walls and wheels of golden chariots glinting like a dozen eyes in the bright, bright sun."

Lydia inhaled deeply, the sharp scent of the pines mixing with the imagined smell of sweat and glory, raising the hair on her arms.

Varius still whispered in her ear. "There is blood and beauty, death and victory, all of it in one place, in one day, for everyone to feel. You would weep and you would laugh to see it, Lydia."

She nearly did both with only the imagining.

"Come." Varius woke her from his spell and pulled her away from the lip of the hill. "It grows late and the sun will be falling into the west before your purchases are made."

She turned from the Circus Maximus, not a little breathless. If the chariot-racing stadium was such as he described, what must the famed theaters built for gladiator fights and the battles of wild beasts be like? Would she be in Rome long enough to witness such?

On the other side of the Palatine Hill, the valley below held the magnificent Forum, the heart of Rome. It stretched into the distance like a city unto itself, and they paused before descending for Varius to point out its highlights—the Via Sacra winding through basilicas and the Temple of Vesta, the Curia Julia where the Senate would meet once the building was finished.

"They've been at it for years now, but it was Julius Caesar who began the project, and it seems to have fallen off since his death. Perhaps the new Caesar will finish it. Or perhaps when he has his way, there will be no need for a Senate at all."

"If the Curia is not finished, where do they meet now?" Octavia had mentioned that the Senate would convene to vote on Herod's request. Would it be somewhere below?

"In the Theatre of Pompey, some distance from here. It's a magnificent theater, with a large quadriporticus behind for strolling and shopping before and after the dramas, and there is a curia in the rear where the Senate meets." Varius led her down the path toward the Forum. "It was on those steps where Julius Caesar met his end."

They descended the path, then the steps that led into the Forum as the sun also lowered behind the western end of the Forum, bathing the white marble forest in a pinkish hue. She hurried Varius along, concerned about the setting sun and Octavia left so long alone. But she wished to linger, to take in every moment of it—the way the stones felt under her feet, the breeze that went from cool and feathery on the hill to warm and humid as they descended, the light falling on Varius's dark hair and handsome features.

The Forum still boasted crowds, and they jostled through, Varius pulling her along to make her purchases. She sniffed the perfumes in tiny amphorae he waved under her nose before making her choice, tasted the olives he bought and placed into her mouth.

Near the western end of the Forum, the Curia Julia's marble went from pink to gold, blinding the eyes. They turned to face the length they had traversed. It had grown cooler, and Lydia rubbed her arms to fight the chill.

Varius circled her shoulders with his arm and pulled her against the heat of his body, saying nothing.

She was content to experience this moment, bathed in gold itself, this sense of belonging, of being important to someone—a man—in a way she had never felt.

Except Samuel.

A stab of something—guilt?—lessened the warmth in her heart. She pushed it away.

Varius pointed to a raised platform nearby. "The Rostra. Where speakers spout their rhetoric. It's where Marc Antony gave his funeral speech for Julius Caesar. Got the Roman mob so whipped up, they burned down the homes of Brutus and Cassius and chased them from the city."

Was there a note of jealousy in Varius's voice at the effectiveness of Marc Antony's recitations?

"And just a couple of years ago, when Marc Antony had finally had enough of Cicero's meddling, he had the man killed and then hung his severed head and right hand there on the Rostra."

Lydia shuddered. "His right hand?"

Varius smiled. "To signify his pen and the words it had produced, I suppose. It was not enough for Antony's last wife, Fulvia, though. She came and pulled out his tongue, then jabbed it repeatedly with her hairpin to condemn his speeches as well." He shrugged. "Perhaps I shall suffer a similar fate."

Lydia forced her gaze from the gruesome memories of the platform and lifted it to the Palatine. The Forum lay in gloomy dusk. "It is time for me to return."

They talked little on the walk back. Lydia's heart was full of the closeness of Varius, but her mind churned with the symbols of death and violence she had seen today. What kind of city was this Rome, so intent on power and strength to find its place in the world?

Varius left her outside Antony's home, perhaps reluctant to be seen with her.

She delivered the purchases to Octavia, who thankfully was in the bedchamber of her youngest, stroking the sleeping child's hair with a peaceful, if somber, expression.

In the days to follow, Varius seemed to frequent the house more than expected for a poet, and he often took a turn around the courtyard with Lydia in the evenings. On the night of their fifth day in Rome, he left her with a kiss on the hand and a warm good night.

She walked slowly to the room she shared with the other female servants of Herod's party.

Near the door, she heard loud voices and slowed. Riva's voice she recognized, but not the other—a man's. Was Riva so bold as to entertain a man in the shared chamber? Should Lydia confront her or slink away to return later?

"I have nothing, I tell you!" Riva's words were edged with fear.

Lydia drew closer to the door, leaned around the frame. A brawny man dressed in a dark tunic had his back to her, but Riva's white face and wide eyes matched the fear in her voice. Was that a dagger in his hand?

He reached for a bedding mat and slashed it open.

A memory surfaced—Samuel's rooms, torn apart by someone searching for the scrolls.

The man had Riva pinned against the back wall.

Lydia turned and fled to the front of the house, where a slave always guarded the door.

"Please, come quickly!" She stumbled into the hall and grabbed at the arm of the bare-chested slave. "A servant girl is being attacked!"

Eleven

The brutish slave who always guarded the door, with his short sword strapped to his waist, shook off Lydia's grasp as though she were an insect. "Servant girls—bah! What is that to me?"

Lydia balled her fists. "He . . . he is stealing from the household. Searching through belongings for anything of value!"

At this, the slave's jaw tightened, bulging the veins in his neck. "Where?"

Lydia turned and fled toward the shared room. Riva's cries sounded through the hall as they approached.

"Where are they?" The intruder was still firing questions at Riva. "Tell me and live. I know you brought them from Alexandria!"

From behind her, the slave barreled past and into the room without pause. Lydia hovered at the door frame.

The intruder spun, Riva in his grasp and the dagger at her throat. The girl's eyes bulged like a fish in the market and her lips were drawn back over her teeth.

The room was in chaos—belongings flung aside and bedding torn.

Lydia's glance darted to the corner where she'd secreted the scrolls. The urn looked undisturbed. For now.

"I care not what you do with the girl." The slave's voice was the growl of a predator. "But you are not leaving this room alive." The sword had found its way into the slave's hand and he half crouched, his stance wide and ready.

Riva's attacker seemed to realize the pointlessness of his hold on the girl and cast her aside into the disarray of the room. Riva scrambled backward until she slammed against the side wall, and her hands worried at the plaster behind her as though she would push her way through. Her skin was plaster-pale already, her hair disheveled.

The two men faced off, but the slave had been bred and trained to defend the household, and his sword was longer than the thief's dagger. It was only a moment before the slave's sword punctured the black tunic at gut level. The trespasser doubled over the sword and grabbed at the blade as if to pull it from his belly. The slave held the sword as the man fell, freeing it from his body.

Riva launched herself from the wall and ran for the door. Pushing past Lydia, she shot her a look as black as death itself and kept running.

It had happened so quickly. And the aftermath was quick as well. The slave hoisted the dead man over one shoulder and carried him out without a glance at Lydia, nor a concern for the blood on the floor or the contents of the room.

She dared not check on the scrolls yet. Someone else could appear.

But the words of Riva's attacker burned through her mind. *"I know you brought them from Alexandria."* What would anyone think

Riva had brought? Something worth crossing the sea? Something worth killing for?

A shudder ran through her, a delayed shock at the attack, perhaps. Or an omen for the future.

As a substitute for checking the scrolls, Lydia pulled the necklace from under her tunic and ran a light finger over the embossed surface of the pendant.

David skidded into the room. "Lydia!" He sped to her and took her shoulders in his hands. "Are you hurt? I heard—"

She released the pendant and patted one of his hands. "I am well, David. He—it was Riva he attacked." But had he been alone? Was there another, waiting to strike again? And what would Riva do if she realized the attack was meant for Lydia?

David spun a circle in the room, surveying the disorder. His brows knit together.

"He was searching for something."

Lydia swallowed, the action an effort. Oh, what a relief it would be to tell David of the scrolls, of the task Samuel had given her. Perhaps she could even pass the task to him. With his Jewish blood and his ties to Judea, he should be the one to deliver the scrolls to the Temple steps.

She spread shaky palms. "Whatever it was, he did not find it."

David's gaze fell on her pendant. His lips parted and he took a quick step toward her. "What is this?" He lifted it from her chest.

She pulled it from his grasp and took a step backward. "It is nothing. Just something Samuel gave me."

But at his wide-eyed look, she paused before secreting it beneath her tunic again. "Why? Do you know what it means?"

He took a breath, paused, and exhaled again. "I . . . I don't know what it means, but the symbol: it is Hasmonean. It is Jewish."

"Samuel gave me the necklace just before he died." She turned away, started straightening sleeping mats into orderly rows. "He said it belonged to my mother."

"Your mother! I thought you had no idea who your parents were."

She kicked some loose straw that had spilled from a gashed-open mat to the pool of blood. "I don't. And he told me nothing more. Only that my mother gave him the necklace for me, before she gave me up."

"Lydia, do you know what this means?"

She picked up a bundle of another servant girl's clothing and replaced it on the girl's mat.

David grabbed her hands and squeezed, waiting for her to meet his look. The silence of the room closed in around them.

"Lydia, you belong to the House of Israel."

Her mouth went dry and her hands trembled in his.

"Yes, Lydia. If this pendant was your mother's, then it could only mean she was a Jewess. And therefore, so are you."

You belong . . .

A people. A place.

"But why—why would Samuel not tell me of my parentage?"

"Perhaps because he understood what it means to be Jewish." David's sad smile made him look wise beyond his age. "The conquest by Rome is only the most recent for our people. When Julius Caesar's ally Pompey began his siege against Jerusalem, my father was only a boy, but he remembers it well. Twelve thousand Jews killed, and our king and High Priest stripped of his throne to become a client kingdom of Rome. But we are accustomed to such."

Lydia nodded. "Samuel taught me of your people's exile in the lands of Persia."

"Yes, Babylon and Assyria, Ptolemies and Seleucids—there has been very little time of peace for our people. We are hated in our own lands and hated wherever we travel. This is why Samuel would not tell Cleopatra of your parents. You are a Jew. That is enough."

"But someday that will change?" Because of her scrolls, burning in their hidden place in the corner?

"Oh yes." David's face glowed. "Yes, one day our Messiah-king will come and rescue us. And I believe it will be soon."

"Samuel seemed to think so as well."

David sat straighter. "It must be soon. With Gentile dogs on the throne, surely HaShem will not tarry. Perhaps we have mishandled our affairs as a people in the past, but at least it was *Jews* who were our kings."

"And yet you serve Herod."

He grinned. "To be close, Lydia. To be close to the action when it happens. When our people rise up against Rome and throw off the yoke forever. Surely this is the fullness of time!"

The fullness of time. Samuel had used such a phrase when he spoke of the scrolls and their importance to his people. A flutter of something tickled her belly—apprehension, excitement.

Destiny?

She had given too little thought of late to the task given by Samuel. Was it as important as he had said that she deliver his scrolls to the Chakkiym who watched for this Messiah?

Was this why Samuel had been so intent on training her in the ways of his One God? If so, could He also be *her* God? Could she belong to Him?

She had no time to think on the significance. One of Herod's advisers poked his head through the door. "Herod is about to leave for the Senate meeting. All staff in the courtyard."

David released her hands and they headed for the door. It pained her to leave the room in such a state, but there would be time after Herod's grand departure to return and repair.

To return and to think.

The combined staff of Herod and Marc Antony were arranged in two parallel lines running through the courtyard into the front hall and out the door to the graveled garden beyond. The lines buzzed with the murmurs of dozens of people, the words jumbled and confused.

Lydia assumed a place at the end of the line, tried to calm her features and shaking limbs into serenity. The faces of the stiff-backed staff in the line across from her blurred in her vision.

Antony and Herod emerged, talking and laughing between them, and paraded through the channel, without a real glance at anyone. A chill breeze blew through behind them, as if it would sweep them into the tumult of Rome.

"Not to worry, my friend." Antony slapped Herod's shoulder. "No one has forgotten your father's favors toward Caesar years ago. Nor who is more capable of rule."

"Yes, well." Herod looked worried despite Antony's instruction. "Antigonus has that cursed Hasmonean blood, which makes him favored by the Jews regardless of ability."

And then they were gone, passing out of earshot and then out of the house.

Lydia exhaled, her shoulders dropping with the weight of Riva's attack and David's revelation.

Riva was at her side a moment later, breathing on her neck. The girl's dress was torn and her hair still tousled, but the perfume she wore bespoke elegance. Like the scent Lydia had purchased for Octavia in the Forum market.

"This was your doing, little Egyptian."

Lydia leaned away, studied Riva's pinched expression. "My doing?"

"Do not think I am a fool. That brute was looking for *you*. He thought I was you. Said you had taken something from Alexandria and he wanted it back. I should have known you were a thief."

David crowded in between them. "Lydia is no thief!"

Riva scowled. "No? Do not be so sure, boy. And you"— she pinched Lydia's arm—"do not be so certain you will serve Herod's new wife. That is a position best left to someone more qualified."

Bitter words burned in Lydia's throat, but Riva's revelation distracted her. Was this the intruder who had killed Samuel? The second man in Alexandria? She scowled at the thought. His death at the hand of the slave had been too quick, then. He should have suffered as Samuel had.

~

Herod and Antony returned in high spirits, talking of the speeches given by the professional orators Antony had hired to endorse Herod and degrade Antigonus, that conspirator with the Parthians, archenemies of Rome.

The vote had been unanimous, apparently. Not only troops to take on Antigonus, but the unexpected conferring of a new title for Herod: "King of the Jews." Though from the good-natured teasing Lydia overheard, she doubted the title was much of a surprise to either man.

But as evening approached, there would be no avoiding Riva in the shared room. Lydia lingered in the darkness of the courtyard before bedding down, delaying the confrontation.

"There she is again, pretty as the spirit of a goddess in moon-light."

Lydia smiled and sighed.

Varius was beside her at the central fountain in a moment. He rested a light hand on her shoulder. "So glad I found you before it was too late."

"Too late?"

"To see the reflection of the moon in your eyes."

His words should have brought her pleasure. Perhaps they did. But the events and discoveries of the day had been too much. She wanted only to be alone with her thoughts.

She smiled at him. "Perhaps tomorrow night. I need to attend Octavia."

A flicker of annoyance crossed his face, but then his pleasant look returned. "Tomorrow, then. I shall look forward to it."

She should go to Octavia but lingered instead in the court-yard, her thoughts tumbling like water over rocks. Such conflicting emotions she had experienced in the past few days. The warm connection to Octavia, however formal. The fluttery attraction to Varius, with his eloquent words and cool touch. All reasons to stay here in Rome. And yet, the strange and wonderful feeling of David's assurance that her pendant meant she had a place to call home.

But even more than this newfound personal connection to Judea, Lydia had something precious to her people—*her people*—secreted in the corner. Though they had not claimed her, they needed her. What was she doing, making herself needed here in Rome?

Perhaps this time she would not try so hard to keep herself apart, to make herself important to someone without letting herself need them in return. The desperation to belong and to be important was a selfish and petty thing she had seen in Riva's eyes. Lydia would not be that person any longer.

She had undertaken Samuel's mission out of loyalty to her mentor. But something was changing. The charge he had given her was becoming *her* mission.

Could she let go of her vow to return to Egypt? She would go to Jerusalem, no matter the cost. Learn more of the Jews' One God. Find the Chakkiym and deliver the prized scrolls. Samuel had devoted his life to protecting them. She would do nothing less.

And with the decision, she felt a solidity, a peace, and a strange sort of tethering—as though a rope had been tied round her waist, anchored far away on the steps of the Temple of Jerusalem. Pulling her gently, but irrevocably, toward home.

"Have you tired of me as well, Lydia?" Octavia's flat voice emerged from the shadows. "Your thoughts are only for the poet, I suppose. But why should I be surprised?"

Twelve

The stricken look of guilt and regret in the girl's eyes pricked Octavia with a bit of compassion. She huffed and waved a hand.

"Don't go to tears over it, girl. Simply come to my chamber. It grows late."

"Yes, mistress."

Octavia walked slowly to her chamber, feeling the hem of her dress trail across the mosaic of the courtyard and the scrape of her sandals across the stone pavers of the shadowy peristyle. It was a trick she had practiced of late—this deliberate movement and heightened sensitivity. At times it seemed the only thing between her and the numbing darkness. Since Claudia Minor's birth three months ago, Octavia had been unable to lift the curtain of sadness that seemed to weight every new day.

She went through the motions of preparing for bed, allowing Lydia to remove her dress and sandals, to slip the gold bands from her arms and remove her beaded earrings. She sighed as Lydia unfastened her hair and let the unruly curls fall about her shoulders. The girl had a gentle touch. Already Lydia had found time to arrange Octavia's scattered jewelry into a pleasing arrangement, and there was a vase of fresh white roses on the entry table that had not been there earlier.

"You will come in the morning, first thing, Lydia." Octavia slipped into her bed, and Lydia smoothed the bedcovering over her.

"Yes, mistress."

But morning came too early, the sky still dark in the east, and Octavia kicked at the coverings that had tangled about her feet as she struggled through the night. What kept her from sleep? Was it the same cold deadness she had felt in her spirit these last months?

No, there was a fear there, a whisper of fear that must be rooted out.

It had begun when that Arab-turned-Jew had arrived, his charming smile and winning manner making him an instant favorite in the house.

What had she to fear from Herod of Judea?

Not him, perhaps, but the damage he could wreak on the uneasy alliance between her brother and her husband.

The alliance supposedly sealed and ensured with the gift of Octavia herself.

She had no illusions that a mere marriage was enough to keep Marc Antony and Octavian from tearing each other apart, and if this Herod, with whatever demands and requests he had brought, became a source of contention between them, she would pay the price. She was aligned with both of them now, and the victory of one over the other made her a loser either way. She and her children by another man—a man who had opposed Julius Caesar, the single uniting loyalty between her brother and husband.

She waited at the window for dawn to arrive, watching the

sky through the wooden grid of diamonds as the sun lifted over the seven hills of Rome.

"You have been waiting for me, my lady." Lydia's voice at the door held apology and perhaps a bit of fear.

Octavia shrugged and pulled away from the window. "I could not sleep. But now that you are here, I need you to dress me well." She straightened her back. "I have a meeting to attend."

Lydia's deft skill with her hair resulted in a prettier style than the banished handmaid Caelia had ever accomplished, and the girl found new ways to drape fabric around her body in a manner adequately modest yet alluringly feminine.

Octavia examined herself in the blurry bronze. "Yes, that is good. I must remind them all that I am more than a shipment of grain or a camel load of gold and spices."

"My lady?"

Octavia laughed, quick and humorless. "You would not understand, I am afraid. Servant girls are the most necessary part of a Roman household. Wives, on the other hand, have only one purpose—as a bribe to keep powerful men from destroying each other."

Lydia blinked at the harsh statement and lifted her eyebrows.

"Do not look so surprised, my girl. You have spent too much time in the palace of a woman who stands in defiance of her place in the world. Here in Rome, it is the men who wield the power."

"I think perhaps you are wrong, my lady. For a woman to be used thus—as the glue that will hold two mighty men together—she must command great influence indeed."

Octavia flexed her shoulders and tugged a final adjustment to her dress. "I pray to Cybele that you are right, Lydia. For today there will be three of them, and it may fall to me to be that very glue."

Neither Antony nor his charismatic young friend Herod were to be found when Octavia emerged from her chamber, and she arranged her own transportation to the house of her brother.

When the slaves lowered the litter for her to step to Octavian's graveled garden, her brother emerged, a slight scowl on his youthful face. At only twenty-four, he had already grown accustomed to the mantle of his adopted father Julius Caesar's money and power, and the legions of loyal soldiers at his disposal made it impossible for any rival to dismiss him because of his age.

"Expecting someone else, brother?" She smiled sweetly, though he was certain to catch the acid beneath her honeyed tone.

Octavian looked over her shoulder, through his front gardens and beyond. "This Herod I have heard so much about—I would have thought you would still be at home, hanging on every delightful word that fell from his lips."

She kissed both of her brother's cheeks, an obligatory peck that he did not return. "You know you are the only one whose company I find anything but tedious, Octavian."

"Caesar. It is four years now I have been telling you that my name is Caesar."

She exhaled and tilted her head. "Little brother, I am not one of your generals." She waved a hand and pushed past him into the house. "Besides, how can I keep up with your name? It changes as often as the seasons. What is it now, Gaius Julius Caesar Divi Filius? Ridiculous."

He followed at her heels. "Ridiculous that after my adopted father's deification, I should also be called Son of the Divine?"

The anger that sparked in his voice did not suit her purposes. She stroked his arm and smiled. "Show me the new frescoes in the *triclinium* while we wait for the others."

Octavian's wife, Scribonia, lay across a couch in the dining chamber, morose and petulant as always.

"Scribonia is feeling ill these days." Octavian seemed to feel the need to excuse her natural state of unpleasantness. "The pregnancy, no doubt."

She gave her sister-in-law a smile, called from a false place within her. Scribonia was five years older than Octavian—*Caesar*—and it was no secret that she had been forced to divorce her husband and marry Octavian for political alliance. In the outrageously tangled web that was Roman politics, Scribonia's sister's husband, Sextus, was the son of Pompey and a man both Octavian and Marc Antony were working hard to court, since Sextus had taken control of the straits of Sicily and begun blocking grain ships sailing for Rome.

And as if the intrigue weren't complicated enough, Scribonia had no love for Marc Antony, since it was his late wife Fulvia's daughter, Clodia, whom Octavian divorced to marry her.

Disgusting, all of it, and barely worth keeping track of. When the histories were written of this great Roman Republic, would they tell of all the women whose lives were upended and twisted like trees in a hurricane, traded and bartered like coin in the marketplace?

And yet, perhaps what the servant girl Lydia had said was true. Power was yet in her hands.

She dutifully admired the freshly frescoed walls, then followed her brother to the receiving room. Thankfully, Scribonia did not join them. She would be no help in keeping peace.

They did not have long to wait. Marc Antony and Herod breezed into the receiving room ahead of the servant who tried to announce them. Antony was all smiles and warm embraces for Octavian, a show for Herod.

"What an honor"—the dark-skinned Herod bowed to both men—"to be received so well by the two greatest men of the Republic."

Octavian laughed, pleased at the flattery. "Let us not forget Lepidus."

Herod shrugged a narrow shoulder and smiled, a sly smile of conspiracy over the missing third of the Triumvirate. "Africa is a long way off."

The three sat, and Octavian spread his hands. "But you have recently come from the coast of that great continent, Herod. Tell me of Cleopatra. Is she as beguiling as ever?" He gave a slant-eyed look at Marc Antony. "Were you able to resist her charms, as both my father, the Divine Julius, and our own Antony here were never able to do?"

Octavia exhaled heavily, her annoyance loud enough that the three men were forced to acknowledge her presence. Must they talk about her husband's lover with her in the room? Cleopatra's twins were born to Marc Antony before Octavia had a chance to bear him any children of her own.

Herod laughed, but it was a nervous laugh of discomfort, and his look darted warily between the two men. "She is well, Caesar, and sends her great affection."

Antony crossed one leg over the other and folded his arms. "Let us leave off talk of Egypt. It is Judea that concerns us today. Judea and that young upstart Antigonus, who has only added to our Parthian problem by aligning with them."

Octavian leaned forward, his gaze taking Herod's measure. "Yes, the Judean problem. The little region continues to plague. But Antony tells me that you, dear Herod, are the solution."

The meeting continued for some time with Octavia as

spectator for the most part. Each time the exchange between her husband and brother grew testy, she interjected a soothing flattery, an inane observation, a timely reminder. And as the conversation continued, it became clear that Herod's charm had won him yet another supporter in her brother. She breathed her relief. Thanks to Herod's wit and her shrewdness, there would be no falling out today.

She was more than glue. She was the oil that could keep the gears of Rome running. Perhaps unseen and unappreciated, but valuable nonetheless.

And when the histories of the Republic were written, perhaps there would be a line or two about her.

Thirteen

Your visit with your brother went well, I trust, mistress."

Octavia sailed in, unwound the blue *stola* from her shoulders, and flung it across the bed. "Excellent. Your Herod will get all he needs from Rome. And Antony still serves as a lubricant between Herod and my brother, rather than an irritant."

The political machinations of Egypt and of Rome held little interest for Lydia, but it was good to see Octavia's spirits lifted. She took up the blue stola from the bed and hung it with others of its kind.

"But I received some disturbing news in the courtyard, I am afraid." Octavia dropped a ruby necklace to her dressing table. "What do you know of this piece?"

Lydia frowned. "You wore it two nights ago, I believe. Nothing more."

"It was handed to me by Herod's girl, Riva. She claims she took it from you. That you stole it."

"What?" Lydia's breath shallowed.

"The truth, Lydia. That is all I require."

She hesitated. "I do not know the truth, my lady. Only suspicion and guesses, and it does not seem right—"

"I am not giving you a choice. I will hear your suspicion and guesses, if that is all you have."

Lydia ran a hand through her hair, tangling it in the curls at her neck. "Riva has taken a dislike to me. I don't know why. I think perhaps she covets the position of handmaid to Herod's future wife, which he has promised to me."

Promised was perhaps too strong a word. Even now, Herod might have already agreed to leave her behind.

"I would guess she is jealous of nearly everything about you, Lydia." She waved a hand. "But go on."

Lydia lifted her palms and shrugged. "I can only assume that she stole the necklace herself, to make her accusation."

Octavia nodded and seemed satisfied. She turned to her dressing table and laid the ruby necklace across it. "All the more reason for you to rid yourself of that awful Jewish lot—or whatever it is that Herod calls himself—and stay with me."

Lydia's heart raced against this news. "You flatter me, my lady—"

"I know you will object. But I have decided."

Lydia raised pleading eyes.

"I must keep you near, to keep the darkness at bay." She inhaled deeply. "And I will give you a good life. No troubling with a husband or ruining your body with children."

These assurances only frightened Lydia further. She had no wish to be alone forever. She dropped to her knees and clutched Octavia's hands. "Please, my lady."

Octavia's eyebrows lifted, but she returned Lydia's handclasp.

"Please, you must know that serving you these last few days

has been my pleasure—more pleasure than I ever had serving Cleopatra, I assure you."

At this, the corner of Octavia's lip tugged into a pleased smile.

"But, my lady, I must go to Judea. I beg you to let me go."

"I need you, Lydia."

"You will find another. I know you will. Find someone old and ugly and kind—someone Antony would not even notice."

Octavia laughed. "Good advice."

Lydia smiled with her. "Please understand that it is only my duty to Judea that takes me from you. I am so grateful for your trust in me."

"Duty?"

"I cannot explain. But there is someone in Jerusalem I must see. It is where my mother was born."

"Ah, family." At this Octavia pulled her hands from Lydia's grasp and turned away once more. "Family means something very different to Roman nobles than it does to the plebs and servant class, I've found. You all know loyalty, where we know only treachery."

"But you are smart, my lady. You will protect yourself and your children."

Octavia seemed lost to her thoughts for a moment, but then nodded. "Yes. Yes, I will." She lifted the ruby once more, draped its gold chain across her hand. "And you must fulfill your duty to your family as well." She opened Lydia's palm, pressed the cool ruby against it, and closed Lydia's fingers over the stone. "Perhaps this will help."

"My lady—I cannot—"

"Yes, you can." She smiled conspiratorially. "You should have seen Riva's face when I insisted that you had not stolen it—that I gave it to you as a gift."

Lydia pressed her lips together, fighting a grin.

Octavia patted her cheek. "I was in a dark place when you arrived, Lydia. It is different now. This is the only way I can thank you."

"You found the strength within yourself, mistress. It was not I."

"But it was you who showed me that the strength was there to be found." Octavia gave Lydia a quick embrace, then pulled away, eyes shining.

Lydia swallowed against the sudden emotion that tightened her throat. Another good-bye.

"Now go, Lydia." Octavia smiled. "Judea—and your family—awaits."

Fourteen

L ydia! Tie that flap down!"

Riva's shrill voice matched the whistle of hot wind tearing through the encampment tent, ripping at any vulnerability.

She did not need Riva's instruction. Her hands were already straining at the leathers that laced the tent corners. The thin strips were a futile match for the desert that baked them dry and brittle, as it did the nerves of every member of Herod's staff. The leather bit into her hands, already cracked and bleeding. She breathed a curse at this place forsaken by all the gods.

Did the soldiers, whose tents ringed this one, feel the attack by heat as furious as any enemy troops?

They worked at a feverish pace, each of them, inside Herod's massive command tent. He had gone out to meet Silo and could return at any moment, for the meeting that would be the culmination of the four brutal months since they had landed at Ptolemais, far north of this desert wasteland.

David hauled tables and couches from the loaded wagons they had brought south through the mouth of the tent where other servants relieved him and moved them into place. Riva and the women scurried in and out carrying amphorae of wine and water, baskets of breads and cheeses, olives and dates—all the stores that remained since their march began. Lydia focused on hanging the curtains to divide private from public areas inside the tent and unrolling woven carpets in a pointless attempt to block the sand.

Yes, the sand. It was everywhere. In the eyes, the ears, the mouth. Caked under fingernails and crusted on eyelashes. When they had first landed near Galilee and traveled through mountain passes and along verdant streams, the country had seemed more beautiful than even her native Alexandria. But here on the border between Judea and Idumea—the region of Herod's birth—the relentless white-hot sky seared the spirit into something harder than any pot she'd ever fired. Perhaps it explained Herod's seemingly indestructible nature. But at least they traveled on land, not another frightful ship.

"They are coming!" David's voice shot through a gap in the tent flap along with a slice of sunlight. He dropped the flap at once, an ineffective barrier.

Lydia's heart hammered. The tent preparations were unfinished. She looped the gauzy curtain's purple embroidery over the bone hook extending from the upper tent seam and hurried with the others to stand outside the tent. She held a palm above her brow and peered across the endless orange-beige to where tiny explosions of sand and the occasional flare of sunlight on metal signaled an approach.

Herod had arrived at last with Silo, the Roman general ordered by Marc Antony to help Herod liberate Judea from the hands of the Parthian-sympathizer Antigonus.

They came from the east, with the cerulean-blue Salt Sea stretched out like a dead thing, broad and flat at their backs. Silo's legions marched in the shadow of the lone mountain that held the reason for their coming.

Masada.

Lydia's gaze strayed to the plateau atop the massif's blood-red cliffs. From this distance it was impossible to see a single living soul, nor the defenses that made Masada the safest fortress that could hold the women of Herod's family—his mother, his sister, and Mariamme, his betrothed.

But below it was a simple matter to see the spread forces of Antigonus, who had been laying siege to Masada for nearly a year. Herod's tent was pitched at a careful distance from the Jewish troops, and the ragtag army of soldiers Herod had raised in Galilee camped behind them. When their ship landed in Ptolemais and they learned that Rome had not yet rescued Masada, Herod once again used his connections and support to rally together a willing band. In spite of his non-Jewish lineage, many powerful Jews were attracted to his cause. Some had suffered atrocities under Antigonus, and many saw the Jewish king's alliance with the Parthians as betrayal.

They marched with him south along the coast, skirting Samaria, and took the critical seaport of Jaffa in Judea, then passed through Herod's Idumea and subdued resistance there. Turning east they marched for Masada. Word came that Silo's forces were coming down from Jerusalem as well but had been ambushed by Jewish nationalists, supporters of Antigonus.

Herod sent troops to join the Romans and put down the nationalists. It had been a long and uncertain four months, with Herod leading the troops and his staff still traveling with him. But now at last, the Roman legions would join with Herod's, and they would take Masada.

Lydia flexed her shoulders and dropped her hand. David had shouted his warning too far in advance. In the desert you could see a fire ant crawling across the horizon, and they would all surely turn to stone if they waited in this heat. Waves of it blurred the legions into a mass of iron and leather, the troops advancing like a horde of insects themselves, with helmets plumed in red to match the cliffs of Masada.

"I will be finishing in the tent." She escaped the heat and continued her preparations, but the reinforcements arrived sooner than she thought possible.

Herod and Silo swept into the tent with a haze of grit clinging to them. "Water, girl." Herod waved a hand at her, his voice etched with sand.

Silo sank to a couch, dropped his head back onto its rolled arm, and began unfastening the leather across his chest. "Tell me again why this land means more to you than a hill of dung."

Herod swung on him, but Lydia placed the cup of tepid water into his hand before he could answer. In the enforced pause he seemed to collect himself. "You forget I was raised in a place much like this, Silo. Have you been privileged to see the Nabatean kingdom? To walk in the shadow of Petra's magnificently carved cliffs?"

Silo grunted. "Give me the hills of Rome any day."

"Or the hills of Jerusalem?"

Lydia crossed the tent to give water to Silo. He accepted the cup, his eyes narrowing at Herod's insinuation.

"Do not lay the blame for Ventidius's actions at my feet."

Lydia moved to continue with the curtains. Several other

servants worked inside the tent as well. The two powerful men took no more notice of them than if they were deaf and mute. Little wonder servants sometimes knew more than the royals and heads of state whom they served. Lydia sat cross-legged with the tent fabric warming her back, stitching repairs into a leaf-green curtain's hem and listening.

"Ventidius?" Herod was saying. "Tell me, is it only your general who has Antigonus's coin lining his purse? Do not be modest, Silo. You can take a bribe as well as Ventidius."

Silo fluttered a nonchalant hand and closed his eyes.

Herod strode to the couch and kicked at the man's leg where it draped to the floor.

Silo shot up, scowling. "Do not forget who is the conqueror and who is the vassal, Herod."

"And you should not forget who is the close friend of Marc Antony and has the favor of Caesar Octavian and the Roman Senate. The same Rome who ordered your legions to relieve my family." He jabbed a thumb toward the unseen plateau hovering above their tent. "They have sent word that they are nearly dead of thirst up there. If the recent rains hadn't added to the cisterns, their blood would be on your hands."

Silo took a long drag from the water in his cup. A silent taunt but still effective.

Herod whirled away toward Lydia.

She bent her head to her stitching, forgotten in the heat of the conversation. The closer they had come to Masada, the more anxious Herod had grown. The charming politician of Rome had become the forlorn husband-to-be, desperate to see his beloved. The transformation had surprised Lydia.

Herod folded his arms and studied the pattern of one of her

elaborately embroidered curtains already hung, his gaze tracing the leafy detail as though it contained a map of battle strategy. The design seemed to calm him, thankfully.

"It is time to get them down from there, Silo. Time to bring the battle to Antigonus. I ran like a whipped dog a year ago, but I return with the strength of Galilean supporters at my back and the might of Rome at my side." He turned to the general. "Masada is their last stronghold here in the south. We take this, and the Parthian-lover will have little but Jerusalem. The city will easily fall into our hands."

Lydia met David's gaze where he worked setting up food stores. His face lit with subdued excitement and he nodded once, a tiny movement, to acknowledge that he had heard. The boy wanted nothing more than to go to Jerusalem.

She shared his enthusiasm. These months of traveling the land around the capital city, with Samuel's scrolls still in her sack and her mother's mysterious pendant around her neck, had only strengthened Lydia's desire to see Jerusalem, fulfill her destiny, and perhaps even find out who she was. Rome was a memory, and she had determined to leave off thoughts of love and focus on her work and her task.

She had plied David with questions continually about the history and prophecy of the land of Israel, especially those given by the prophet Daniel, from his place in the empires of Babylon and Persia. More important, she grew every day in her understanding of the One God who claimed Israel as His treasured possession and perhaps would one day claim her, if she would please Him by fulfilling her task. Only one month remained until the Day of Atonement, Yom HaKippurim. Would they all be safe inside the city by then?

"How many are up there?" Silo had joined Herod at a wooden table, and the two bent over a piece of Egyptian papyrus.

"My brother Joseph has about two hundred men. They tried to escape to Petra a few months ago, but Antigonus's men held them off, so Joseph and his men are still there. And about five hundred women."

"Five hundred!" Silo's eyes widened. "By Jupiter, man, what did you need with five hundred women up there?"

Herod's voice was tinged with amusement. "I took them from Antigonus when I fled Jerusalem. They were to be part of his payment to the Parthian king Orodes in exchange for his throne."

Silo barked a laugh and clapped Herod on the back, hostilities apparently forgotten. "That must have incensed the old goat, eh?"

Herod shrugged a shoulder in false modesty. "The Parthians used it as an excuse to start looting Jerusalem."

Silo shook his head. "When are these Jews going to realize their foolish insistence on retaining their independence is suicidal?" He jabbed a finger at the spread papyrus. "So. Five hundred women."

"Only three of any importance, however." Herod's gaze lifted toward the front of the tent, as though he could already see them descending in safety. "My mother, Cypros. My sister, Salome, and Mariamme, my betrothed wife." He shrugged. "And I suppose that witch Alexandra, Mariamme's mother, ought to be saved if possible."

Silo nodded. "Four, then, among five hundred. Though if the battle goes to the heights, the trouble will be finding the correct four. Women all look alike to me."

"If the battle goes to the heights." Lydia spread another carpet, lifted two table legs to unroll it farther, then the other two. Were

her hands trembling? She had not feared the encounter in Jaffa, nor the skirmishes in Idumea. Why now, for the first time, was the thought of battle frightening?

Because it was the true beginning. The start of Herod's war on Antigonus. There would be no retreat. If they were defeated here at the foot of Masada, the Judean troops would annihilate them down to the last slave. How long would it take their blood to evaporate in this heat? How long until the scrolls would lie buried forever under drifting sand?

She shook off the black thoughts. Death and chaos might reign outside, but inside the tent she would create beauty and order, and with it bring peace to at least her small part of the huge and terrifying world.

And indeed, outside the tent when the sun rose the next morning, red and angry on the far side of Masada, death was on the horizon with it.

The hostile forces clashed early. Untrained Galileans and well-disciplined Romans fought side by side, advancing against the entrenched troops of Antigonus, whose long siege, if Fortuna blessed, had perhaps weakened their resilience.

Lydia watched from the front of Herod's tent, the rest of the staff ranged across the sand with her. The battle made allies of them all, and even Riva stood in companionable silence beside Lydia.

Or perhaps Riva's silence was born of something else. Herod's attention toward her had decreased the nearer they came to Masada, and it was Mariamme's name that was often on his lips.

The clang of sword on sword reverberated across the desert, but the cursed sand obscured their view. Even here, far from the fighting, all smelled of sand and sweat and blood. Lydia forced her hands to her sides, but they were back at her waist in a moment—tight, grasping fingers that flinched with each battle cry. She tasted nothing but salt, and could not remember when last she ate.

"They are pushing forward!" David's voice held the excitement of a boy who wished to be on the front lines.

How could he possibly know? Lydia stifled an irritated reply. They were all on edge. No need to take it out on him. She had barely slept last night, and her fatigued senses were tighter than the tent lacings.

But then she *could* see. Could see that David was wrong.

Soldiers were crisscrossing up the red cliff, taking one of the three winding paths that led to the plateau. It was too soon for it to be Herod's men or Roman legionaries taking the fortress. The Judeans had sent soldiers upward, no doubt to put an end finally to those who had forestalled them for a year. Could they hold out long enough?

Already, the desert was littered with carnage. Impossible to tell who had lost more. The battle spread wide along the base of Masada, condensed to a funnel, then spread wide again.

The sun rose, hot and deadly, and with it a scorching wind, tangling Lydia's hair. She dashed it away from her eyes and mouth. Behind them the tent flaps snapped in the wind, sharp cracks that echoed the battle sounds.

What was happening? The sand and the sun conspired to keep them all in uncertainty. Lydia ran to one of the wagons and climbed atop its bed. Would the height provide a better vantage point?

The Judeans had advanced. They had pushed much farther from the cliff's base than their camp. They were closing the gap. If they swarmed forward, taking the plain, how long until they reached Herod's camp to ensure no survivors?

Lydia clutched the wagon's splintered front bench, a wave of dizziness like the undulation of desert heat roaring from her toes to her head.

Would it end here? Before Jerusalem? Before she learned of her mother and delivered Samuel's scrolls? Her fear of failure somehow matched her fear of death. It was like sailing across the sea to reach a destination and instead falling off the horizon into nothing. She felt as though she were falling now, pitching forward into obscurity and nothingness. Her vision spotted with the blackness of it.

"Lydia!"

David's voice sounded far off, concerned. Had the battle reached them so soon?

It was not enemy soldiers, but the desert that rose up to meet her—hard-packed sand that had been trying to kill them all since they began this ill-fated journey.

Fifteen

Shouts and running footsteps. The brutal clang of pikes against shields. War cries sounding from a thousand angry throats.

Lydia blinked and shot up from where she lay.

"Whoa, slow down." David's worried face hovered. His hands pushed her shoulders gently back to the cushion.

"Have they broken through?"

David nodded. "It is over."

She struggled against him. "We must run!"

His brow furrowed, then cleared. "No, Herod's troops have broken through to the base of the fortress. A contingent climbs now with supplies. The rest of the men are returning to camp."

The sounds of battle outside the tent—they were victory cries, the pounding of weaponry in jubilation.

She sighed and relaxed against Herod's couch. Then glanced at her surroundings. "David, let me stand!" Herod would return any moment. It would not do for him to find her lounging. "I am fine."

Indeed, it was only a moment after she stood at David's side before Herod strode into his tent, flinging armor from his body.

He lifted his head to his staff, assembling quickly in a line that cut through the middle of the space.

"Pack everything at once. We are going up."

The line broke, and the tent so recently assembled was again torn apart, deflating like a burst wineskin, and packed into wagons and carts.

It took the better part of an hour to trek the switchback path up the red cliff to the fortress. Herod rode his own horse, its hooves picking over the loose gravel with care, as though he wanted to ride onto the plateau as a conquering general. His personal staff followed at an appropriate distance on foot. Three or four of the women climbed behind Lydia, with Riva trailing, her expression glum.

Three women, Herod had said. Three women he cared about. Salome and Cypros, his sister and mother. And Mariamme.

Lydia's heart pounded with the exertion of the climb, and something more. She had come a long way to serve Mariamme. Would the woman be a tyrant like Cleopatra? As gentle as Octavia? Herod clearly cared for her, but he had said little of her character. He did not seem to think highly of her mother, Alexandra.

From the height of the cliff the desert stretched to the edges of the horizon, with only rock formations and the Salt Sea to break its silent desolation. They marched without speaking, each lost to his own thoughts.

But just before breaching the top of the winding path, a shout of welcome rang out and a single man rushed from the lip of the plateau.

Herod swung from his horse, arms outstretched. "Joseph! How glad I am to see your ugly face!"

The two embraced, Joseph pulled Herod upward, and a servant caught the reins of Herod's horse. They followed.

Chaos reigned on the top of Masada.

Everywhere men barked commands. Women scattered and clustered, some holding babies, others with bulging pouches. And the noise! How had they not heard this cacophony as they climbed? The hot wind that threatened to send them all over the edge must have torn it from them and flung it skyward, for here among the rock-built ramparts the chatter bounced and echoed and deafened.

Lydia pushed forward into the enclosure only because others waited on the narrow path behind. Others jostled and edged around her.

Herod was following his brother Joseph, and where Herod went, his staff followed, so they all walked forward to a large building, crudely constructed from peach-colored stone and mud-brick, near the point of the elongated plateau.

A guard at the door stepped aside for Herod, but the newly titled king of Judea hesitated, glanced back at his staff. Was it a nervous insecurity in his expression?

"You"—he waved a finger in Lydia's direction—"the girl from Egypt. Lydia. Come."

She broke from the others with only a glance at David. Herod ducked under the lintel to enter the building and she followed.

The interior was dimly lit, and it took a moment to make out the figures of two women, one standing and the other seated.

The woman standing, perhaps about forty years old, sneered at him. "Well, Herod, another few days and we would have shriveled like field grass and blown off the plateau."

But Herod's attention was on the woman still sitting, hands resting in her lap and gaze cast downward. She wore a simple tunic with a light mantle the color of sapphires across her shoulders and a matching blue head covering. When she raised her head, it was Lydia's face she focused on, not Herod's.

So innocent. Somehow, in all these months, Lydia had conjured an image of a woman as sophisticated as Cleopatra, hardened to a polished edge by the intricacies of political life.

But Mariamme's lightly freckled skin and wide blue-green eyes held nothing of hardness. Lydia had heard from the staff that Mariamme was a singular beauty, and they had not exaggerated. But the girl had a sweet perfection that went beyond physical beauty, an inner sadness that provoked a strange feeling of protectiveness in Lydia.

"Mariamme, my beloved." Herod was at her feet, kneeling, grasping her hands.

She allowed his touch but did not seem to welcome it. Her gaze was still upon Lydia, and in that tiny slice of a moment as their eyes connected, it was as if the girl opened her heart for Lydia to read, shared all the secrets that perhaps her mother did not even know.

An invisible thread of connection tugged at Lydia and she smiled, offering her friendship in that instant, seeing the answering smile from Mariamme as it was accepted.

Herod was glancing back at Lydia, tracing Mariamme's attention. "Yes, yes, the girl. I have brought you Cleopatra's finest handmaid, my love. Fit for a queen, she is. Served in the grand palace of Egypt for years, and prized for her way with children. And she is an artisan of some sort—I cannot remember—"

Mariamme rose, the movement smooth and elegant. She took a step toward Lydia, hands outstretched.

Lydia met her halfway, returning the handclasp.

"Thank you, Herod. I am certain she will serve me well." Mariamme's voice was serene, like cool water, and quiet.

Herod scrambled to his feet and circled to stand before her again.

Lydia took a step backward to allow the two to reunite.

Herod took Mariamme by the shoulders. "Our time is nearly come, my love."

Alexandra cleared her throat and Herod dropped his hands, but not before flinging a withering glance in her direction.

"We have only to take Jerusalem now. And after this victory they will be at the gates to welcome us, I have no doubt. And then we will be married and you shall sit upon the throne of Judea as my queen."

Alexandra snorted. "She is a queen with or without you, Herod. Her Hasmonean blood makes her queen, while your blood is as common as—"

"Silence, woman!" Herod's hiss of a command held venom. "I have been granted kingship by right of descent from my father, Antipater, have been declared so by the Senate of Rome, and have earned it on the battlefield. Let me not hear your insults again."

Alexandra's gaze rolled to the ceiling, but she held her tongue.

Herod turned back to Mariamme, his hands taking hers once more. "It is time, my love. Time to reclaim Jerusalem."

≈

Accommodations at the Masada fortress were better than the desert tents, but not much. The sun beat as mercilessly and the wind tore at everything without respite. Lydia assisted Mariamme in packing her things, but there was little to be done in that regard. Instead, it was the supplies for feeding the soldiers and women that required the most work, and Lydia left

Mariamme the second morning to help, if only to speed them all toward Jerusalem.

She paused at the entrance of the large stone building where the provisions were housed and the men ate their meals. A dozen soldiers and a few women packed the room, lining crates with straw. One man, also dressed as a soldier, stood apart with a critical eye and hands on his hips. She crossed the room to him.

His glance flicked at her and then back to his workers. "Do not tell me those women are insisting on a finer meal *today* when we are trying—"

"I am here to help."

He looked her up and down. "Help with what, little girl? Have those arms ever carried anything heavier than a platter of figs or an ivory comb?"

She frowned. "Have I somehow offended you before we've even met?"

He gave a patronizing little laugh and bowed. "My apologies, my lady. I am Simon. It is my job to get every worthless scrap off this plateau, down to the desert, and to the walls of Jerusalem. It is your job, I understand, to keep one woman pretty."

"Ah, I see. It is not *me* you dislike, but only my position."

He blinked and scowled. "I did not say I dislike you."

It was Lydia's turn to laugh, and when she did Simon looked at her once more, this time with more interest.

He was an attractive man, though perhaps ten years older than she. Tall, but with a lean build, skin a bit darker than the average Jew, and wavy dark hair in need of a trim. A day's worth of stubble clung to his sharp jawline and dark shadows sagged beneath his eyes. Had he slept since they arrived?

"I am Lydia. The princess Mariamme has no need of me at the moment, and I came to see if I could be useful to you."

"The *princess*? I see the would-be king Herod has you trained already."

"I spoke of Mariamme's Hasmonean descent, not her marriage to Herod. But you are part of his troops. Do you not support his kingship? Believe that the Parthian influence must be removed from your land?"

In response, Simon berated a passing slave girl for moving too slowly.

The girl jumped at his harsh rebuke, glanced at Lydia with tear-filled eyes, then ran.

Simon watched her go, then cleared his throat. "I am accustomed to commanding soldiers. I forget how delicately women must be handled."

Lydia straightened. "You'll find me able to take instruction, and to give it. Give me something to do or to oversee. Perhaps you could rest awhile."

"Ha!" Simon jabbed a thumb toward the soldiers packing crates. "And you think my men would take orders from a pretty young girl?"

"Perhaps not, when they are accustomed to . . . you."

He turned on her, arms crossed. "I don't know where you've come from, little Lydia, but clearly you do not know much of this world. Nothing is as simple as you seem to think. Perhaps you should run back to your princess and see if she needs her feet washed or a cup lifted to her lips."

His condescension stung, but she only nodded and pointed to one of the soldiers. "And you should tell your men that amphorae packed so closely will expand in the heat as we travel and arrive cracked and empty." She smiled. "But since that is your job, I'm certain you already knew that."

She turned and strolled from the building but could feel his gaze on her back.

Indeed, over the next few days of frantic preparations, as everyone worked to pack crates and saddlebags, to load animals and small wagons, Lydia felt Simon's glance turn toward her more than once, though she could not understand why. He had made his disdain for her, for Mariamme, and even somehow for Herod, very clear.

It took days to ready the hundreds of people and their belongings, to bury the dead on the battlefield, and to break down the soldiers' camps—both Roman and Galilean. No one seemed sorrowful to leave the fortress they had feared would be their tomb, and Herod was heard declaring more than once that enlarging and improving the fortress, even building a palace up here, would be the first of his many planned building projects when he had secured his kingship.

When at last the thousands set out for Jerusalem, David calculated for Lydia that only a week remained until the Day of Atonement, Yom HaKippurim.

"Already you are becoming a Jew, Lydia." He grinned and pointed north across the desert. "Only a Jew would be eager to see such a day in the City of God."

She had told him nothing of her task, and he never asked about the wooden box that weighted the bottom of her sack of belongings.

Days of walking, nights of sleeping under the cold stars, more walking. From the pit of the Salt Sea to the heights of the city, it seemed they had walked not only northward but a mile upward.

The march gave Lydia little time to spend with Mariamme, who rode in a roofed chariot with her mother and her younger brother, Aristobulus, bouncing over the rutted ground until her teeth must have rattled. Lydia was glad to walk.

Herod instructed his brother Joseph to keep a close watch on Mariamme's brother, Aristobulus, to be certain he didn't slip away to join Antigonus's ranks, then chose to ride with his own mother and sister. He was clearly devoted to both. Along the way the story was whispered more than once of the night they had all escaped from Jerusalem a year earlier, when one of the loaded wagons, in which his mother was traveling, overturned. Herod thought Cypros had been killed, and in the misery of his nighttime flight and the loss of his mother, he nearly ended his own life.

Of Herod's sister, Lydia had yet seen little. Salome was like a mountain cat—dark and sleek, moving unseen in the shadows. Her presence seemed to be felt everywhere and yet she appeared nowhere.

On the fourth day, Simon appeared at her side, though he did not look at her or speak to her, only kept walking. She left him to his silence for as long as she could, but if he did not wish to speak to her, why did he walk with her?

When she could tolerate the strangeness no longer, she thought of a question. "What do you know of Salome, Herod's sister?"

If he thought it odd that she spoke to him, he showed no sign. Only rolled his shoulders as if the topic were uncomfortable. "She is a frightful woman. Makes no pretense that the Idumeans' forced conversion to Judaism has touched her personally. She worships the idols of her Nabatean mother, with all their oracles and divination and darkness." He glanced across to her. "Keep your distance from her, Lydia."

"I appreciate your concern."

He huffed. "You are clearly young and ignorant. I was only making a point—"

"Then I apologize for mistaking a soldier's orders for a friend's concern."

This time the sound was more of a growl. "You have a way of twisting my words—"

"So then we *are* friends?"

His shoulders and head dropped, as though she had bested him in a wrestling match, but he laughed. "I am not a man whose friendship is typically sought."

"No? I am surprised."

He did not look at her, but by the amused set of his jaw, he knew she was teasing.

And why did she try to provoke him?

Perhaps because he was the most interesting man she'd met since Varius. He was as different from the poet as a man could be, but still interesting. Even if he saw her as nothing more than a spoiled child with the pampered life of a royal handmaid.

"You are eager to see your Jerusalem, I suppose?"

"See her *free*, if that is what you mean." Simon's subtly traitorous words were delivered quietly, with rancor.

"But you fight for Herod."

"I fight for Israel." His face was set toward the north. "For the land. The possession of HaShem."

"Is your family there?"

At his long silence, she regretted her prying.

"My family did not survive the first part of the civil war between Herod and Antigonus, before Herod fled. I left three years ago to join Herod's ranks."

His tone did not invite further questions, but she could surmise some of the answers. The pain ran deep beneath the words—a vulnerability born of loss she well understood—one that drove him to the life he had chosen.

"What's this, Captain?" Another soldier, middle-aged, jostled a shoulder against Simon's. "Found a woman at last who does not flee like a frightened gazelle when the jackal roars?"

Simon smacked the back of the other man's head. "Mind your own men, Jonah. They're as undisciplined as a flock of sheep."

Jonah laughed and leaned forward to wink at Lydia. "Be careful of this one, girl. He bites."

When he moved on, Simon shrugged. "Jonah is right, I suppose. But perhaps we have all grown unfit for the company of women. Such is the life of a soldier."

Lydia did not argue. But Simon was not as disagreeable as he seemed to think. His passion for Israel reminded her of Samuel, and there was a hint of humor under the gruffness.

They reached the outskirts of Jerusalem within a week, set up camp in the hills west of the city. Herod now had the city isolated—surrounded by his troops and his allies in Samaria with its large Greek population in the north—and cut off from the sea. But it would be the third siege on the city in less than twenty-five years, and Herod was reluctant to subject those he hoped to soon rule to such devastation. Instead, he declared to his family and advisers that he would take the city with the force of his magnanimous personality alone.

Lydia was serving breakfast in Mariamme's tent when this announcement was made. A few exchanged looks that signaled the doubt of everyone but Herod that his plan would be effective.

But Lydia was making plans of her own. This close to the

city, and only two days until Yom HaKippurim. She would be on the steps of the Temple with her wooden box whether Herod had taken the city or not.

She had only to find a way in.

≈

In the half darkness of early morning, Lydia took up her sack, crept out of her tent, and followed the scouts and soldiers Herod sent toward the city as ambassadors to the people.

She had emptied all but the wooden box from the canvas and wore it knotted across her chest, the box bouncing at her hip as she hurried along the edge of a wide valley toward the city. When the sun rose behind Herod's camp and slid along the rocky valley and hills, she joined a cluster of people at one of the massive gates, which was being opened just as she reached it.

She had little difficulty blending into the crowd. One woman could do little harm, after all. And those who guarded the gate had their attention on the soldiers she had followed.

Herod's emissaries had already begun shouting their message to anyone who would listen. "Herod comes for the good of the people and the safety of Jerusalem!"

The heads of all at the gate turned toward the speaker.

"Tell your families, your friends. Herod has no desire for vengeance, nor to cause harm to those inside the wall. He offers forgiveness to all his opponents, including the unlawful Antigonus!"

Those around her wore guarded expressions, suspicious.

"No harm will come to the city. Open the gates to Herod and welcome him as your savior. He brings the blessing and prosperity of Rome with him!"

Perhaps this mention of Rome was overmuch. Backs were

turned, and not a few men spat in the direction of the soldier who spoke. He did not let up, however. As the crowds moved in and out of the city, the message was repeated. How many other city gates had soldiers delivering messages? Would word reach Antigonus that Herod was attempting a coup from within?

Indeed, word was spreading quickly. It followed her like a flame lit at the end of a cord, burning its way through the city as she hurried along cramped streets strung with bright-colored clothes hanging in the sun and crowded with children and donkeys and women. An air of tension pervaded the streets. No doubt the people were well aware of the massed Roman legions outside their walls and the traitorous Jews at their flanks.

Lydia moved toward the highest building she could see. Would it not be their Temple?

Soldiers stalked the streets, shouting at the people to return to their homes. "Close your ears to the lies of the pretender!" One soldier glared down on Lydia as he passed. "He is no Jew, and no royal blood flows through his veins. The king's nephew, held hostage by the Idumean, has more royal blood than Herod!"

It took Lydia a moment to work out this claim in her mind. Mariamme's father was brother to Antigonus, which meant that her younger brother was the nephew of Antigonus and had a more legitimate claim to the Judean throne than Herod. Perhaps that was why Herod kept the boy so close.

Riots were breaking out in the streets. The citizens of Jerusalem did not seem to favor being forced into their houses on a solemn day of such religious importance. Lydia skirted several small mobs being chased down by soldiers and kept her focus on the great white-and-gold building above that must surely be her destination. She allowed herself only quick looks. It was better to keep her eyes trained downward to the street, to appear to be hurrying home.

But the Temple was still a good distance off when her chest began to constrict with fear that she would not make it. The crowds were thinning, the streets emptying.

She reached the outer court of the Temple, still so far from the steps where she would meet the Chakkiym, and she was met instead with the lowered pike of a guard.

"No one in the Temple courts this morning. Orders of the king."

She sucked in a breath. "Please—I must—there is someone I must meet." The box at her hip felt heavy, accusing.

"Get to your home, woman." His eyes narrowed as he took in her clothing. She had not thought to don a head covering such as the Jewish women wore. "Where is your husband?"

She took a step backward, glanced left and right. Was there no other way into the courtyard?

The soldier called to another, "Do you know this woman?"

Was every woman of the city known? Was she so conspicuous?

She scuttled backward, clutching the sack knotted around her neck to her chest.

An hour later, head pounding and heart brittle enough to shatter to a thousand pieces, she retraced her steps through the now-deserted streets to the gate on the west side of the city. She had found no way in, and she had found no Chakkiym.

At the edge of the camp, the sun highlighted the silhouette of one man on a ridge. She was nearly upon him before she realized it was Simon. His eyes were accusing and his face grim. "Where have you been?"

Had he noticed her absence? Or was he only curious to see her returning from the direction of the city?

"I . . . I wanted to get a closer look at Jerusalem."

"Foolish girl! Could you not wait until Herod has beaten the people into submission?"

Again, the hatred for Herod, whom he claimed to serve. "I do not understand you, Simon. What do you want to see happen here?"

He took a step closer, his eyes on fire with the heat of his words. "I want a free Israel, as every Jew does."

She caught her breath at the intensity. The poet Varius had the same passion, but it was only for battle-glory and adventure. This fervor in Simon's eyes was something deeper, more substantial, something he felt with his heart and his soul and his whole being.

"But a free Israel is not to be today." He took her arm, as if to drag her back into the camp.

She yanked her arm from his grasp. "I am not one of your soldiers, Simon. You do not command me."

"I am not trying to command you! I'm trying to protect you. As any man would."

"I do not need a protector. And I sometimes wonder if you *are* a man—since you have the head and the manners of a bull!"

They were crossing through the tents now, and he stalked away without a word.

Near the command tent, Herod and Silo were shouting at each other, ringed by Roman legionaries and Herod's top men.

"We have no provisions!" Silo's face was red with rage. "You cannot expect us to winter here." He jabbed a thumb toward the city. "The Parthians have left almost nothing behind."

"You forget how much support I have here." Herod extended his arms, as if to take in all of his friends in Samaria, in Galilee, in Idumea. "I'll have ample supplies sent down to Jericho, which will serve as the winter supply depot. Settle your men in the region. I'll send Joseph to Idumea with a couple thousand infantry and cavalry as well." He pointed to Simon passing by. "And I'll give you my best man to manage the supplies in Jericho. He kept everyone from starving for more than two years at Masada. You'll have no trouble there." He turned a greedy eye on Jerusalem. "If they are too foolish to see what is in store for them, then I will take the rest of their country apart, one piece at a time, and return when we are strong enough to take the city by force."

Silo threw his hands skyward as though there was no reasoning with the man, then whirled away toward his men.

Mariamme had appeared outside her tent and stood behind Herod. Her voice was low, barely loud enough for Lydia to make out the words. "And where shall we go, Herod? My mother and brother and I? Shall we live in soldiers' tents until you have gained the victory?"

The question was asked without rancor, but it seemed to cut at Herod. He spun and took Mariamme's hands. "No, my love. You shall spend the winter in the finest quarters I can find. But not here. In Samaria. You shall be safe in Samaria."

Mariamme sighed and nodded, then turned away. Was she as eager to return to her native Jerusalem as Lydia was to see it for the first time?

It did not appear that either of them would see their wishes fulfilled. They would go to Samaria, and Simon would go to Jericho. A strange feeling of deflated hope settled in her chest with both of these facts.

As the sun set on the Day of Atonement, Lydia sat on the ground, her back to her tent and the sack in her lap.

Somewhere in the city, a man in a red-striped tallit with red and blue corded tassels waited for her on the Temple steps, watched and hoped for the precious scrolls to be delivered. Did he sense that this year was different? That this year, the lost scrolls waited just outside the city wall, in the hands of a nobody, a servant girl who had failed at the only task of true importance she had ever been given?

Sixteen

The Jericho winter makes a soldier grow soft.

Simon shifted sore muscles against his horse and led the three servants who accompanied him on a slow route through the capital of Samaria, to the outskirts where Herod's lavish family home housed the four battling royal women.

His discomfort stemmed from both the bumpy journey and the thought of what lay ahead.

The busy year in Jericho's winter palace, hiring staff and securing supplies in preparation for Herod's successful campaign, had evaporated like mist. But the effect of the mild weather and the comfortable accommodations was a long way from a soldier's life. Would he even have the skill to fight again, if called?

Herod's estate clung to a small hill, nothing as grand as Jericho but still flaunting wealth. Simon left his horse with the servants, took only the single item he had been charged to bring, and wandered through the front courtyard.

There was no protection at all in the front of the house. Where were the guards and watchmen who should have been posted to keep the women safe?

Despite his reluctance to engage with the royal family, Simon's pulse quickened over the one woman he would not be sorry to encounter. When the troops pulled back from Jerusalem a year ago, scattering to the corners of Judea, the handmaid Lydia had come with Mariamme. Would she still be here?

He did not have long to wonder.

A woman bent over a patch of flowers in the front garden, her back to him, but he knew her immediately. He scraped a sandal across the stone paving and cleared his throat.

She startled and whirled. At the sight of him, her lips parted and a flush pinked her cheeks. She took a step closer, one hand extended.

Simon nodded in greeting, noting the flush with a suppressed smile.

"What are you doing here?" She clutched a handful of stems at her side, the yellow-eyed centers grinning up at him.

So. She remembered.

He held up the scroll he had retrieved from his pack. "A message for the royal women. From Herod."

Lydia glanced to his hand, then back to his face. "Is he in Jericho, then? Is the fighting over?"

She was largely unchanged—still delicate in stature with the olive complexion of a mixed heritage, her long dark hair unbound around her shoulders like an Egyptian. But even in her few words, it was clear she had grown in spirit. More subdued, perhaps. Less of a child.

"Yes to the first question. And he hopes to report the end of the war soon. But not yet."

She looked to the scroll again, as though she would ask what else it contained, but then straightened and smiled. "You have come a long way. You must be tired. Please, come inside and let me serve you."

The kindness washed over him like a balm. His staff in Jericho, just as his soldiers on Masada, treated him with fearful deference and kept their distance. His brief moments with Lydia had lived in his memory for just this reason—she seemed to see him in a softer light. Was he truly the man she saw, or would she treat even an enemy with such generosity?

He allowed himself to be led indoors, following on her heels like a pet. "I should deliver the letter."

She continued toward the back of the house. "They do not even know you are here. Your letter can wait until you have at least taken some water."

Had his soldier's training fallen away so completely that he now took orders from a woman? What was it about this girl? She was nothing like Levana.

At the thought of Levana it was as if a door slammed in his heart. He would not go there again.

In the kitchens, she placed him at a table with the firmness of a mother, then brought more than water. He ate the bread and cheese and fruit with the hunger of a starving man.

"Do you miss the fighting?" She lowered herself to a chair across from his. "Your duties this past year have been quite different, I would guess. And you have been far from the front lines where you seemed committed to do some good."

He chewed a bit of crust and swallowed, his heart ragged with memories, not only of four years ago, but of all he had seen on his journey northward to this house of luxury.

He placed his palms flat on the table and studied her eyes. "There is a desperation in the people, Lydia. It grows every year, every month. They are hungry and weary of war. They are weary of waiting for the promise and many are giving up hope."

"The promise?"

He balled his hands into fists. "I forget that you are not one of us. The promise of the Messiah, who will end all of this and bring redemption to the land."

At the declaration, her head dropped and then she looked away. When her gaze returned to his, it was cloudy and sorrowful. "What can be done?"

He jabbed a finger at the plate of food. "Something more than living like this while the people starve."

Her gaze fell away again.

He reached a hand across the table and covered hers. Her skin was warm and soft under his touch. "I am sorry. I did not mean to accuse. It is not your fault."

What would Jonah say, to hear him apologizing to a servant girl?

As if she read his thoughts, she pulled her hand from his. "What do you hear of your friend—Jonah, was it? Does he still fight for Herod's kingship?"

"I told you once, Lydia. We do not fight for Herod. We fight for a free Israel." The old anger had risen in an instant, the surge of blood that would serve in battle. Perhaps he was not such a palace pet as he feared.

"Jonah too, then? He joined Herod only to get close to the enemy?"

Was that condemnation in her tone? He pushed away from the table and circled to stand before her.

She studied him, not with accusation but with anxiety. Did

she fear for him? He bent to one knee, bringing his face to the level of hers, and peered back at those lovely dark eyes. "We had no choice. Do you not see that? We have tried to fight them, to fight them all, and the wars have ravaged our land, destroyed our people. Those of us who are willing to be seen as traitors are quietly finding a better way. We will rot the enemy from the inside out."

She reached across the narrow space between them and touched his jaw, touched the place where an old battle scar furrowed the skin. "And what if you do not survive the rottenness yourself?"

He sucked in a breath at her touch, reached for her hand, and returned it to her lap. "A small price to pay for the vindication of those we have loved and lost."

"Lydia?" A young man's voice called into the kitchen, followed by his body. "Have you seen—? Oh, there you are."

Lydia jumped to her feet, backed away from where Simon still knelt before her.

Aristobulus was much changed. Simon eyed the boy's muscular frame as he pulled himself to his feet. Good. They needed him strong for the days to come.

"I heard there was a messenger." Aristobulus glanced to Lydia, then returned Simon's appraisal with a bit of suspicion. Perhaps even jealousy? "Herod sent *you*?"

Lydia frowned. "Yes, Simon—I did not think to ask. Why didn't Herod send a servant with his letter?" Her eyes widened a bit. "Is there danger here? Is he worried for us?"

How much should he say? "Herod sent me to assess the holdings here in Samaria. In case supplies are needed."

Aristobulus strode across the kitchen and thrust out a waiting hand with the brashness of a youth training to be a king. "I will take your letter, soldier."

When the boy had gone, Simon turned to Lydia, trying to avoid those eyes. "I cannot stay long. I am expected back in Jericho immediately."

She nodded but grasped his hand once more. "Be safe, Simon."

Yes. Safety. But it was not the battlefield he feared. It was this one girl, who was threatening to crumble four years' worth of cultivated indifference to the world of home and family and anything that involved his heart.

He could not afford to let that happen. Not when they were so close.

≈

Mariamme reached an arm across the silky fabric of the red cushion and yanked a few grapes from an overripe cluster on a gold tray. They went soft between her fingers, and she tossed them back to the platter.

"You are peevish this morning, Mariamme. Have an orange if the grapes do not please you." Her mother chewed slowly, her dark eyes lowered. Servants crossed behind her, carrying and settling more trays of food before the women, pouring wine.

Herod had spared no expense in settling his women in the lavish family home his father had built in Samaria. Though himself a Greek-lover, the house was built in the style of a Roman villa, with a large frescoed *triclinium* for dining, its three sumptuous couches arranged around a brazier. With only a small, high window on one wall, the brazier's flames lit the room and chased off the autumn chill.

Mariamme propped herself on one elbow and scowled over

the brazier. She rarely confronted Alexandra, but her mother's indifference today left her restless and irritated. "It is the Day of Atonement, Mother. A day of fasting." She spread a hand toward the heavy-laden tables. "And you prepare the most lavish of meals. Have you forgotten what it is to be a Jew?"

Alexandra's lips thinned to a tight slash. "How dare you, girl? Everything I have done has been for my people." A slave bent to place honey cakes on her platter and she shoved him away. "Even now, with your Herod wandering the countryside for the past year, trying to grasp the kingdom with his greedy Idumean fingers, I am here—planning, directing—"

"Manipulating."

Alexandra's eyes were dead cold. She smoothed back her still-black hair, worn loose in the Roman fashion. "Call it what you will. My father was High Priest of Judea for nearly all my life, before that traitor Antigonus had him exiled to Babylon. I know where power lies and how to command it." She reached for a jeweled cup and raised it to Mariamme. "You'll see me in Hades before I let both the High Priesthood and the kingship be stolen from our family."

Mariamme's stomach churned, though she had eaten no food since Yom HaKippurim had begun at last sunset. "Then why do you insist on this alliance with Herod? Can you not see that my brother—"

"Your brother is too young." Her mother's words were clipped, rushed.

Mariamme would not be dismissed so quickly. "He is fourteen. Perhaps not old enough for the High Priesthood, but the people would soon serve him as king. The Pharisees would back him."

Alexandra swung her legs from the cushion and sat upright. "You *will* marry Herod, Mariamme. I am tired of this argument."

"And I am tired of being no more than a coin in a nasty bit of bartering!" She flung out a hand and flipped the tray of warm grapes. It clattered to the mosaic floor, the grapes smashed beneath it.

Her mother's brows rose at the uncharacteristic outburst.

Mariamme sank against the cushions, already spent by the argument. But the truth must be spoken. "He frightens me, Mother. Do you not see it?"

She shrugged. "He has the way of a king about him. They are all power-hungry tyrants, else they would not be kings." She leaned forward with a sly smile. "And I may be your mother, Mariamme, but we are both women. Do not try to tell me that all that strength, all that cunning charm, does not fire your blood just a bit, eh?"

Mariamme would not acknowledge the innuendo. Nor the stab of fear that her mother's comment was perhaps a truth better left concealed. She despised the way Herod made her feel—both repulsed and drawn at once. What kind of woman did that make her?

Herod had already divorced his first wife—a commoner by the name of Doris—and cast aside their son, to be free to make this alliance with her family. He had no scruples, no morals. But if the divorce did not concern her mother, something else must. "That business in Galilee in the spring—do you not remember his face when he told of it? He lay right there"—Mariamme pointed to Alexandra's couch—"and told of the Galilean nationalists he slaughtered, his men lowering cages to where they hid in cliff-side caves, dragging them out, forcing some to leap to their deaths."

How many nights had she lain awake, thinking of those poor Jews clinging to the sides of cliffs? And of Herod's nonchalant amusement as he told the story? Yes, her hatred of Herod ran as deep as his own ambition.

Alexandra sighed, as though Mariamme were a child afraid of nothing more than imagined fiends.

"Mother, he laughed when he told of that father of seven who stood at the cave's mouth, called his children one by one and killed each of them, then killed his wife and himself rather than to fall into the hands of an imposter king who is not a Jew—"

"Enough!" Alexandra shot to her feet and circled the couches. She sank a knee into the cushion beside Mariamme and grabbed her wrist.

Mariamme half turned and lay prostrate under her mother's wrath. Her heart raced but she met Alexandra's glare with hostility of her own. How she longed to fling Alexandra from her, to push back against the force that had always been too strong for her.

"You are a foolish girl, Mariamme. You do not understand the way of things. We are a small piece of the world here in Judea—a tasty morsel being fought over by the two mongrels of Parthia and Rome." She shook Mariamme's arm, her lip curled. "Rome will win, there can be no doubt. My father, Hyrcanus, understood that, and he made sure that when Rome put Herod's father, Antipater, on the throne of Judea, he made himself a friend to the man. With Antipater dead these five years, of course Rome's favor has fallen on his son, Herod."

She loosed her grip on Mariamme's wrist and stood. "And I am my father's daughter. Where he befriended Antipater, I befriend Herod. You *will* be his wife, and together you will rule Judea." Her voice turned to pleading. "Do you not see, Mariamme? We are not aligning ourselves with Herod. You, my daughter, will be queen.

A Hasmonean will still retain the throne. Herod is aligning himself with *us*."

Mariamme half raised herself from the couch, her arms still propped behind. "Then it is *you* who is the fool, Mother. Rome will never see me as anything but Herod's wife and Ari as a yapping dog."

Alexandra's face slap was swift and unexpected.

Mariamme fell backward, hand against her stinging cheek, breathing hard.

Alexandra's eyes were aflame. "The boy will be king someday, have no doubt. But we must bide our time. And you must do your duty to bridge the gap."

Mariamme turned away. The argument was useless, but still she rebelled. How could she marry a man such as Herod? Give him children? She tried to stifle the shudder that passed through her body. Mother would only see it as weakness.

"And do not underestimate Salome, my girl. She gains some kind of power from her wicked spells and idolatrous worship of her pagan gods. Sometimes I believe she has the very demons ready to do her bidding."

A voice at the doorway drew them both. "My lady?"

Alexandra sighed at the servant girl's interruption. "Yes? What is it?"

A shrieking sound echoed through the courtyard beyond the doorway.

"What in heaven—?" Alexandra's hands went to her hips.

"That is what I was coming to tell you." The girl inclined her head toward the courtyard. "Salome is searching for you and in a singular rant. She has heard that you turned away the silk merchant without letting her make a purchase."

"Ach! The greedy little hyena would have us all eating cattle feed for the sake of her wardrobe. Run off, girl, and tell her I've gone out. I can't abide dealing with her this morning." Alexandra rubbed at her temples. "I have a headache."

"Yes, my lady."

The girl passed another on her way out. Aristobulus, her dear younger brother.

At fourteen, he was quickly becoming a man, though the famed beauty of his childhood still rested on his perfect features. Tawny hair, deep-set brown eyes, and full lips. Every young girl who set eyes on him fell in love, and every old woman wanted him for a pet.

He lingered in the doorway, his gaze scanning his mother standing over his sister.

Alexandra's arms widened to an open embrace. "My son. Come. Have something to eat."

Aristobulus's gaze shifted to Mariamme, the question in his eyes obvious. Was it not a day of fasting?

Mariamme gave him a small nod and a tiny shrug of one shoulder, and he shook his head and sighed. Despite their five-year age difference, they were always able to communicate with few words. Perhaps it was all the hours spent together, hiding from their mother's moods. No sister and brother could be closer.

"No, thank you, Mother." Aristobulus leaned against the doorway. "I am not hungry."

Alexandra gave an exasperated snort. "You and your sister. Two of a kind."

He would not even mention the day. Aristobulus was no stronger than she when it came to confronting Alexandra.

Ari handed their mother a sealed scroll. "A letter, Mother.

Just arrived with a soldier from Jericho—Herod's new favorite, Simon."

"Jericho!" Alexandra tore at the waxy seal. "What is he doing there?"

Mariamme's pulse hammered in her throat. Herod sent letters only when there was significant progress in his battle against Antigonus. And to send Simon—did it mean Herod was coming to claim his bride? "Read it aloud, Mother."

She waved a hand in Mariamme's direction, her attention already fixed on the letter, scanning its lines as though she would lift only the critical content from the papyrus. A moment later she raised stricken eyes and nodded. "He begins with greetings for all of us. Cypros and Salome first, of course. That man has an unnatural affection for his mother and sister—"

"The letter, Mother!"

She shrugged. "He greets me, then you and your brother. Then tells of his progress since he visited here in the spring. 'Antony sent two legions and a thousand cavalry to my aid in Galilee under that snake of a general Macherus. We were to assault Jerusalem together. Macherus thought himself worthy of a bribe by Antigonus instead, but Antigonus refused him. Macherus returned to me, slaughtering every Jew he met along the way, including many of my own supporters.'"

Mariamme gasped. These Romans were dogs, as Mother had said.

Alexandra continued reading. "'Your husband's brother Antigonus is a fool, but nevertheless the people favor him too well because of his lineage. Even the Pharisees have joined with their rival Sadducees to back him. With your father Hyrcanus in Babylon, all the hopes of the people are focused on him. And so it is time for Rome to make good on her promise to make me king.'"

This would be it, then. The news worth writing about. Mariamme hardened herself for whatever was to come.

Alexandra lowered herself to a couch, her finger running over the lines.

"'I left Joseph in Judea with orders not to quarrel with Macherus while I myself pushed forward to Syria to intercept Antony where he was fighting the Parthians. He finally made good on the troops he should have given a year ago, and the general Sosius and I traveled south with legions. It was here in Antioch that I had a most terrible dream, my love.'" Alexandra stumbled over the word and lifted her eyes to Mariamme.

Herod's letter had been written to her mother, as was proper, but clearly he had Mariamme in mind as he penned it, accidentally addressing her. The oft-repeated endearment was always delivered with a sickening flattery. Why, when she had given him no encouragement, did he seem to dote on her?

"Continue, Mother."

"'A terrible dream. You know how I am severely troubled by them at times, and how the gods seem to speak to me through them. I dreamed that my brother was dead. I will not horrify you with the details of the dream, but the next day when I awoke, I learned that Joseph had disregarded my instructions and led troops against Antigonus. He is dead, my love. His head flaunted in grotesque display before the people, even when our brother Pheroras offered to redeem it.'"

Mariamme closed her eyes, heart heavy. She had spent a year in the fortress of Masada with Joseph and his men there in protection. He had been a decent man.

"'That is not the worst of it, I fear. News of his death spread quickly. The nationalists have tasted blood and want more. Revolts are flaring all over the lands we hold in Galilee and Idumea. Prominent supporters are being drowned in the sea. I must urge you to take care there in Samaria, for I believe Antigonus's general—the brute Pappas who severed the head of my brother with his own sword—is on his way to take Samaria as well.'"

Alexandra's voice faltered, the only sign that Herod's news struck fear into her as it did Mariamme.

"'As for myself, there is nothing for me but to push forward despite the coming winter rains. We have marched to Jericho, and from here will advance on Pappas's troops. But you must be strong, all of you gentle and dear women of my heart, and keep yourselves safe until he is dealt with. We have the might of Rome behind us now, and we cannot fail. I shall see us all in the palace of Jerusalem by spring, I have no doubt.'"

Alexandra let the letter flutter to the cushion.

Mariamme snatched it up, searched its lines for anything more. But there was nothing.

Her mother and brother drifted from the room, lost to their own thoughts, it seemed. Lydia appeared soon after and began clearing the uneaten food. Her hands shook. Had she heard the news directly from Simon?

The girl had become indispensable here in Samaria. What would she have done without Lydia when Herod's sister, Salome, needled her with cruel remarks, or Mother chastised her for being too cold, too quiet, too everything?

Yes, the gift of her handmaid was the only good thing Herod had ever done for her. Lydia knew when to speak and when to be silent, and everywhere she moved she left some touch of beauty in her wake. In the year they'd been together, Lydia had grown in confidence and in talent. Often Mariamme envied the girl's freedom. No one would force her into a marriage of alliance. But Lydia had been morose all day. It could not be the words of the letter that left her sad.

"It seems we are to be attacked, Lydia."

The girl's gaze flicked sideways, then back to her work. "Bad news, then, my lady?"

"Perhaps you had an omen. You have been so glum today."

"It is Yom HaKippurim, my lady. A day to reflect on one's guilt."

Mariamme tilted her head and examined Lydia. "But you are Egyptian. What do you care about a Judean holiday?"

Lydia swept crumbs into the palm of her hand and deposited them on a tray. "I have reason to believe my mother was Jewish."

Mariamme sat upright. "Reason to believe? Do you not know who your mother was?"

Lydia shook her head but continued her clearing of utensils.

"Well then, I shall consider you my Jewish sister." How had she never heard this? "Perhaps we should go to synagogue together for the closing prayers today. It is a good day to pray. We are in need of both forgiveness and protection."

"Yes, my lady."

Perhaps HaShem heard their prayers, for as the autumn leaves fell and the winter rains descended, the nationalist Pappas's army was besieged by the Roman Macherus's legions and never came closer than a Roman mile from the Herodian family home where the women waited daily in anxious expectation of attack. The news came sporadically—Herod had defeated rebels in Galilee in a night attack; he had been wounded in Jericho. The story came of a house collapsing only minutes after Herod and his prominent guests had left, a good omen in Herod's mind. Then a series of savage raids in which Herod captured five towns and put more than two thousand captives to the sword in vengeance for his brother's death. He was gaining support; his ranks were swelling with those who hated Antigonus and those who would throw their allegiance behind whomever was succeeding.

And success was being parceled out to Herod. After an ambush set like highway robbers, Pappas's nationalist force was annihilated and Pappas himself killed, his head cut off and sent to Pheroras in just recompense for their brother Joseph's death. It had been a massively bloody battle, and only a blizzard prevented Herod from turning at once on Jerusalem, where Antigonus was nearly ready to surrender.

Herod had predicted they would be in Jerusalem by spring, and when the countryside greened with new growth and the damp air freshened with the scent of almond blossoms, another letter arrived with news that was expected.

The women gathered in the columned courtyard to hear it, and Mariamme listened to the reading with head high. She would not cry, not let her mother see the terror the words brought. It was her familial duty.

Herod's troops had been besieging Jerusalem for a month. He was confident the city would soon be his. As a show of confidence, he was coming to Samaria. Their five-year betrothal would finally be consummated. The wedding would show the entire country that he was to be their new king, married to the Hasmonean princess who united both lines of the feuding brothers in her blood.

Mariamme put a hand to a green-and-gold-painted column

to steady the dizziness that swept her vision and tumbled in her head. She felt like she was falling from the blood-red cliffs of Masada, still in the air, still intact, but watching the merciless ground rush up to claim her.

"Prepare," his letter instructed the four women living in constant hostility.

"I am coming for my wife."

Seventeen

It must be today.

Lydia tightened the leather straps that held the precious scrolls to her chest, then shrugged into a stained tunic. She threw a mantle of drab brown around her shoulders and over her hair. Would she blend into the terrified city? One more girl combing the bloodied streets in search of crumbs for her family?

Herod had taken Mariamme for his wife in Samaria, but he had brought them all here to Jerusalem, including his sister, Salome, and her new handmaid, Riva, to watch the siege that he and the Roman commander Sosius directed from their encampment outside the northern walls. Herod boasted that he attacked the city from the north where it was unprotected by ravines, in the same manner as Pompey some twenty-five years earlier. He would be equally successful, he declared.

Lydia slipped from the tent before Mariamme awoke and called for her. David had his instructions and would provide her excuse. He had protested when she whispered her plan to "see the fighting firsthand" the night before.

"They say the city will fall tomorrow, Lydia! After five months of siege, why must you get closer *now*?"

Did she still not trust him with her secret? Had he not proven himself in nearly three years? He was a man of fifteen now, the uneven voice and gangly frame swallowed by depth and muscles. And she was a woman of twenty-one. Still with no husband or children.

"Do not press me, David." She turned away, disappeared into the tent where she slept on a mat outside Mariamme's enclosure when Herod was in the field.

This morning she ran, half bent, with darting glances between the shadows of the encampment. It was all so reminiscent of the first Yom HaKippurim in Judea, two years ago, when she had failed to reach the Temple.

She would not fail again.

It was a gift of Samuel's God that Herod would take the city today, the Day of Atonement. She would follow on the heels of his soldiers, all the way to the Temple steps where she would finally be delivered of the scrolls that burned the flesh of her chest with their unknown messages of the future.

Once clear of the camp, it was all open field. Every tree for miles had been savaged to erect siege towers or bundled into fascines—the large rolls of logs bridging ditches so battering rams could roll ever closer to the crumbling walls that Herod's father, Antipater, raised years ago.

The second, outer wall had fallen soon after Herod returned from Samaria, gleefully announcing his marriage to the Hasmonean princess, as if the wedding would convince the Jews within the city that he was their legitimate king. Perhaps some who had been on the fence fell to his side, but the Nationalist party dug in their heels, screaming that the Arab pig would never have their throne.

Another few weeks and the first wall fell. But still the Temple and the Upper City held out, determined never to yield.

Lydia drew up to get her bearings. The palace-fortress of Baris at the northwest corner of the Temple poked from the collapsed wall, dark stones streaked with mildewed age. Did Antigonus watch from the upper windows? Curse the sun as it leaped from the horizon on what could be his last day?

The fighting would be bloodiest near the Temple. She could follow the troops over the wall, directly into the worst of it. Or she could circle and slip through the streets, with more time for strategy and caution. Approach the Temple from the south.

Yes, the streets.

She did not have long to wait. The sun poured an east-west path of gold across the city. The ragtag Herodian soldiers screamed a war cry and swelled over the earthworks to scale the walls. Sosius's legions followed, red-plumed helmets glinting cold and silver in the morning sun.

The clash of swords and shrieks of defiance rang across the ramps. The pounding throb of thousands of feet on stone and earth. The acrid odor of tar fires.

Head down and arms wrapped round her middle, Lydia scuttled behind the soldiers. She slid down a shallow ravine on the inside of the wall, hit bottom too hard, and fell forward into the dirt.

No time to check for scrapes and bruises. She scrambled to her feet, wiped her sweaty hands against her tunic, and picked her way up the rocky incline into a street to the west of the Temple area.

But the narrow streets were no safer. Already the legionaries swarmed the streets, hacking at any who appeared defiant.

Lydia kept to the mud-brick walls, still shaded and cold. There were no open doors, no calls of welcome. But locked doors could not withstand the smash of a *pilum*'s shaft or the kick of a hobnailed boot.

She hid behind pottery, dodged into alleys, huddled against doorways.

She had been a fool to come the long way around to the Temple. Better to have pushed through the melee and been done with it. Her mind shrieked at her to turn back, but her feet did not obey.

The butchery advanced through the streets and houses, a steady drumbeat of death punctuated with screams of terror like cymbal clangs.

The maze of streets confused and disoriented her. Lydia broke through to a small square and flung herself toward the rising sun.

Everywhere, people ran and people screamed. Some bloody already, lurching and clutching at walls, searching for home and safety.

A woman ran past, about Lydia's age, one cheek slashed from lip to eye. Her gaze tumbled over Lydia without comprehension, without reason. Lydia gasped with pity.

The siege fires were everywhere now. Smoke snaked upward from the city in a hundred columns of death, lives and homes reduced to ash. It burned her eyes and clogged her throat.

Still, she followed the walls, hands worrying the stones she passed until her skin was roughed and cracked. The cry of a baby, unnaturally cut short, chilled the blood in her veins. In the next street, a wagon rolled across the stones, its bed in flames but wheels grinding onward, oblivious to its fate.

Perhaps she was no better than the wagon. Still pushing toward the Temple, unknowing that she was already as good as dead.

And the Chakkiym she was to meet on the steps of the Temple? If he were as loyal to Israel as Samuel was, would he not be defying the foreigners even now? Would he stand defenseless on the steps, waiting for her, while all around him his brothers fell to Roman swords?

The certainty that he was already dead was like a stone in her chest.

Why had she come? Three years she had been trying to rid herself of Samuel's unwanted charge. Last year in Samaria, on the Day of Atonement, she had felt her failure keenly, even though there was no way she could have made the journey to Jerusalem alone. But this year was no better. If the Chakkiym was not already dead, surely she soon would be herself.

The fighting grew fiercer the nearer she came to the Temple area. Its enclosure walls hid an enormous courtyard. The Temple itself soared above the walls, its face set toward the east. Sunlight glanced off gold and Lydia blinked against the glare, raised a hand to her brow.

Bodies were everywhere. Romans, Jews, and Herod's men alike littered the paving around the Temple walls. Blood pooled in cracks, ran like liquid mortar in tracks around the flat-hewn stones. Bashed heads, gored chests, lopped limbs. Lydia braced a hand against a nearby wall. She forced her gaze to the hills above the city, breathed through her mouth with deliberate measure. She could not afford to be sick.

Even if she could force her way through to the Temple steps, she would be cut down where she stood.

The Temple steps. Did Samuel mean the outer steps that led to the gate of the Temple enclosure? Or the steps of the Temple itself, somewhere beyond those walls? How had she not considered this question until now?

She climbed the hill beside the Temple for a better view. The battle had an ebb and flow, and Lydia watched the tide from halfway up the Mount of Olives, her back to the gnarly trunk of an olive tree that had already been ancient when the Roman Pompey attacked more than two decades ago. She leaned her head against its sun-warmed strength and tried to calm her panicked heart.

Olive trees were notoriously long-lived. How many battles had this one witnessed, here above the Temple? Had it seen the Temple desecrated by the Seleucid king's offering of pigs over a century ago and cheered Judah Maccabee as he led his revolt? Three hundred years ago, when Alexander the Great conquered most of the world, had it mourned for the fall of Jerusalem? Nearly six hundred years ago, when Nebuchadnezzar had destroyed Solomon's Temple and carried away the best of Israel to Babylon, had this olive tree weathered even that? The history of Israel was a history of war, Samuel had taught her. Forever and always the enemies of Israel sought to control, suppress, annihilate. And yet she remained.

And one day, Israel's Messiah would appear and set all things right.

Lydia put a hand to her chest for the thousandth time since she left the military camp, felt the outline of the scrolls strapped against her skin.

The battle tide had taken its final turn. The cries of defiance were fading. The Roman ranks spread like a red stain across the plain around the Temple, up the steps and beyond the wall. From her perch on the hillside, Lydia could see into the massive courtyard within the enclosure, clogged with the bodies of the fallen.

She trudged downward, her feet and heart heavy. Somewhere among that carnage she would find one Jew with a red-striped tallit, corded in red and blue. There was little sense in searching, but she must. She owed it to Samuel.

The Romans were lining up in ranks by the time she reached the outskirts of the Temple area and sneaked along the edge of the battle site. Herod was not to be seen, but Sosius stalked back and forth in front of his legion, his face sheened with sweat and a purple-red slash of crusted blood across his left upper arm.

A commotion behind Lydia—the buzz of a crowd moving as a unit—pushed her toward the Temple's outer wall.

A group of men, dressed in the fine robes of nobility and heads held high, strode across the paving stones from the direction of the palace-fortress of Baris. They seemed to form a circle as they moved, with one man enclosed within. Lydia stood on her toes, craned her neck for a better look.

But in a moment the central figure's identity became clear. In a rush that defied the imperious dignity of his escort, he broke from the circle, ran forward, and threw himself at the feet of Sosius, clutching the general's boots, forehead to the stones.

Antigonus. It could be no other.

The king who had so long defied Herod's attempt to take the kingdom Rome had already granted to him looked no fiercer than a common shepherd facing a mountain lion.

Sosius laughed. He *laughed*. Kicked out at Antigonus's face.

The defeated king kept his head to the ground, no doubt waiting for the blow that would sever the head from his body.

"Whom do we have here?" Sosius's voice rang over the massed troops, the bloodied bodies, the walls and stones of the Temple of the One God. "This must be *Antigone*, eh?"

As one, the legions laughed with him. Sosius's use of the female version of the king's name was a deliberate insult, though if Antigonus felt the slur, he showed no sign.

Sosius jutted his chin toward a centurion. "Chain him. We'll let Antony decide what to do with him." He toed Antigonus's shoulder. "Perhaps you'll get to see Rome, Jew. Antony loves a good triumph, complete with a parade of prisoners."

Lydia found a spot on the ground, empty of body or blood, and waited. Cross-legged, back to the outer Temple wall, head bent, while Roman corpses were carted off for cremation and Jewish bodies were looted for what little they had.

She could see the outer steps. A half-dozen bodies were strewn across them, hands reaching for the Temple gate, blood congealing in the sun as it passed overhead. None of them wore the sign of the Chakkiym.

When the steps were in shadow and the crowds dispersed, she crept along the outer wall, through the open gate, and into the inner courtyard.

She kept her eyes half closed to the slaughter, slitted only enough to pick her way around the fallen. If all was as it should be, would she even be permitted here? She wandered past the stone pool and the square altar, toward the steps at the base of the Temple building itself.

Bodies, yes. But no Chakkiym.

What did it mean?

Had his striped tallit been lost in the battle? Or perhaps he never came, frightened by the fighting.

Perhaps he did not exist, was only a passed-down legend clung to by old men in exile.

She pressed a hand against her chest again. But these, the scrolls, they were real. Not legend.

She sat again in the shadow of a column until the sun set once more on the Day of Atonement. No sacrifices had been offered. No High Priest to atone for the people's sin, to release the scape-goat into the wilderness.

What would Simon think of today's victory when he heard of it in Jericho? It had been a year since she had seen him in Samaria, but she often wondered about the soldier who seemed too angry to be serving the foreign governor whom Rome had declared king. Did he still dream of a free Israel? Still rebuff everyone with his brash arrogance?

Lydia lifted her head to where the roofline of Antigonus's palace could be seen beyond the Temple walls.

It was to be her new home. Herod already had plans to renovate and expand the fortress, as he seemed to have for all of Judea.

She would serve the queen within those walls, a few minutes' walk from the Temple steps.

"Next year in Jerusalem."

It was the line spoken at the end of every Yom HaKippurim service by Jews scattered around the world, separated from their homeland.

Well, she had been *this year* in Jerusalem. But little good it had done.

It grew dark and even more unsafe to find her way back to the camp. Lydia rose from the ground and began the long walk back, the scrolls as cold and stiff against her chest as her rigid limbs and her aching heart.

Eighteen

The plan was foolish from the start, and Lydia should have declined.

But Alexandra's demands on Mariamme became her daughter's begging request of Lydia. In the cloying darkness of the predawn, she scurried at the tail end of the little group of four, through the underground tunnels and passageways of the palace.

In spite of her large belly, Mariamme led them all on swift feet as though she spent all of her days traversing these tunnels. It was Lydia who liked to wander in quiet places to think. Had Mariamme practiced an escape? Alexandra followed, then Aristobulus, head and shoulders above the women.

Lydia kept close behind the brother in the darkness. He had become a well-built, exceptionally handsome man of seventeen, one who had carved a place in Lydia's heart, just as David had, despite her resistance. Their early-morning flight had everything to do with the hopes of a mother and daughter resting on his shoulders. The invitation to Egypt must be acted upon swiftly, if they were to have help. Lydia feared for him, for the risk he took and the danger it entailed.

But more than the foolishness of this plan and the likelihood that they would all be caught, the pressure of the day bore down on her from beyond the stone walls. Yet another Yom HaKippurim had begun at sunset. When the day grew light, despite her hopelessness about the reason, Lydia had somewhere she needed to be. She had strapped the scrolls to her chest with their yearly bindings before leaving her chamber this morning. They itched against her skin in silent reminder. But her loyalty to Mariamme and Aristobulus would not allow her to abandon them.

The four reached the stable at the edge of the palace. Open to the north, the sky beyond was still snagged with a thousand cold stars like needle pricks in a dark canvas. A sudden snort and stamp of horses met their arrival. A single small torch bobbed in the open air beyond the stable and poked light between stalls, falling in splinters on dirty yellow straw and the glistening hides of horses.

"There he is." Mariamme's whisper was sharp, strained.

The torch became a man, rough-hewn like a stableman, with hair as matted as the straw. "Got 'em right here, my lady."

He waved the torch in the direction of the grassy area beyond the stable. The outline of a wagon sprang into relief. And in the bed, two coffins. As arranged.

At the sight of the crude wooden boxes, Aristobulus sucked in a breath and squared his shoulders.

His mother cut off his protestation. "We'll be fine, Ari. It won't be long. We'll clear the city walls within minutes, and within an hour it will be safe to emerge." She grabbed at his arm. "Then to

Egypt! You have been invited by Marc Antony himself. Surely he will be swayed to our cause!"

Mariamme clutched his other arm. "Please, brother. I know it is a shameful thing for HaShem's High Priest to be carted from the city like something unclean. But Mother is right. Cleopatra's hatred for Herod surpasses even my own, I believe. She will convince Antony that you should be more than High Priest. You should be king."

At the mention of Egypt, Lydia's heart pounded an irregular beat. A longing that was physical wrapped around her and squeezed. Almost five years. Could she not slip out of the city and make the journey home with them? Would Caesarion recognize her, even remember her? He would be twelve now—the age of David when they first met in Alexandria. Becoming a man, like David and Ari. She swallowed against the tightness in her throat and focused on the task.

"It will be light soon." She extended an arm to the wagon. "We should make ready."

Aristobulus shook off his sister's and mother's grasping hands. "All I have seen of Cleopatra's actions since Herod took the throne tells me she wants only to restore her Ptolemaic kingdom of old—including Syria and every bit of Judea. Look at all she has convinced Antony to grant her already—the rights to collect bitumen tar from the Salt Sea, the date-palms and balsam of Jericho—"

"The wealth of Judea, yes." Mariamme's voice was earnest, and she lifted her pleading eyes to her brother. "Antony appeases his Eastern plaything with our wealth. But not our *land*, Ari. The land of Israel is our own, always. Antony sees that. He knows it must be this way."

Lydia eyed the lightening sky. They must be off before there were questions. Herod had kept Alexandra under guard since she began actively seeking the help of Cleopatra and her influence over Antony. If the guard discovered the woman's absence—

"My lord"—she touched Ari's arm and felt the tension—"the day will soon be upon us."

He turned an affectionate eye on her. "Lydia understands, don't you, Lydia? Cleopatra is no friend to Israel."

She did not answer, could not, for the conflicting emotions that warred with logic.

Mariamme's plea to her younger brother was silent now, just a tearful biting of her lip. She kept one hand on her swollen belly, as if to remind him that more Hasmoneans were to come, that he must do this for the sake of their family, if not their nation.

Aristobulus smiled sadly and touched Mariamme's reddish-brown hair, a gesture that spoke of nostalgia and a profound sadness at their parting. He blinked away the emotion and dropped his hand.

They were a matched pair in age to David and her, these two. While she had spent the years attending to Mariamme, David had served the brother. It was David who had helped them get past Alexandra's guard and even now did his best to delay their discovery.

She felt Ari's repugnance. To crawl alive into a coffin somehow seemed a worse fate than simply hiding under woven blankets or within a chicken cage. But it was their best chance. Few Jews would insist the coffins be opened for examination upon leaving the city.

Alexandra had been subdued since slipping from her chamber, but she climbed into her box with her usual muttering venom. "The filthy Idumean thinks he can control my family. We shall see. We shall see."

Aristobulus took to his coffin without a word, only a final nod to Mariamme.

The driver lowered the lids over both, ran a hand through his greasy hair, and shrugged. "That ought to do it."

Mariamme started forward. "You know where—"

"Aye, mistress. I'll get 'em there."

There had been no good-byes, no embraces.

Lydia stood at Mariamme's side in the cold morning air as the cart rolled into the darkness, with all the hopes of the Hasmonean dynasty interred within.

Mariamme spoke without turning. "You served Cleopatra, Lydia. You've met Marc Antony. Do you think she can convince him?"

Lydia did not answer at once. It was a difficult question. "Your mother's first letter was effective. Cleopatra persuaded Marc Antony to invite Aristobulus to Egypt."

In truth, it had been quite the scandal. Antigonus had been declared both king and High Priest by his supporting Parthians. When Herod took the throne, he would have loved to become High Priest as well. But he was not a Jew. He would never be permitted by the Sanhedrin to take the priestly office. Instead, he recalled the aging Hyrcanus, Mariamme's grandfather, from his exile in Babylon and restored him to his Temple duties. The poor man's mutilated ears prevented him from having the title, so Herod appointed his friend Ananel to be High Priest—a man with no claim to royal blood, who would not be a danger.

In a fury at her son's being passed over, Alexandra wrote a letter to Cleopatra, along with portraits of her son and daughter to show to Marc Antony, urging her to persuade Antony to favor Aristobulus. Such a beautiful person was surely destined for greatness. And perhaps Antony would be interested in Mariamme?

Antony requested that Aristobulus come to Egypt and Herod panicked. The boy was the age Herod had been when Antony first became enamored of him. Would Aristobulus steal the Roman's favor, convince Antony that he should rule Judea?

Herod refused Antony's request. The boy was too popular in the city. It would cause riots if he were to leave. To keep Aristobulus in Judea and away from Antony, Herod made him High Priest, deposing Ananel, who had been appointed for life. His Jewish subjects now hated him all the more.

But their animosity did not extend to Aristobulus. No, everyone loved the boy. And the two women were counting on Antony's agreement in the matter. Three women, if Lydia included herself.

"I still do not know how your mother got that second letter out to Cleopatra while under Herod's strict guard. Sohemus takes his role as captain of Herod's guard very seriously."

Mariamme said nothing.

"But now they are on their way. And she will help you if she finds it in her best interest."

The two turned back toward the stable, Mariamme walking slowly. She had picked up a piece of straw and twisted it in her fingers as she walked.

Lydia glanced again at the purpling sky as they entered the stable. She needed to be on the Temple steps by dawn, fruitless as it might be.

"How has it come to this, Lydia?" They took the silent tunnels slowly now. "My two grandfathers—brothers—squabbling over the throne thirty years ago. Did they not see that their rivalry left a foothold for Roman intervention? Once Rome tasted Judea, how soon it became occupation and then domination. And now—now we have Herod, a king who would murder forty-five Sanhedrin members with all the cold-bloodedness of a lizard."

The Sanhedrin purge after Herod took the throne had been a dreadful thing. Only twenty-six members were spared, those who declared loyalty to Herod. Those who still claimed ties to Antigonus, even though he had been tortured and beheaded by Marc Antony, found themselves with the same fate as their former king.

"You must have faith, my lady. Faith that your One God holds the future of Israel in His hand."

Or perhaps strapped to her chest.

Mariamme sighed. "How oddly you speak, Lydia. After all this time, I still cannot determine whether you think of yourself as a Jew or not."

Lydia's hand strayed to the cord around her neck that hid the pendant under her tunic. "Nor can I."

"But it is the Day of Atonement, and I know you have your strange and secret tradition. I will let you go to it."

A surge of warmth for Mariamme, who had grown so dear to her, brought a smile in the darkness. "Thank you, my lady."

Minutes later Lydia was hurrying out of the south end of the Antonia palace. It had been Baris when Antigonus ruled, but Herod had wisely renamed it during its extensive renovations, and now the royal residence and fortress of Antonia was a grateful salute to the man who had helped Herod gain the throne. The lavish palace was Herod's primary residence, though he had been constructing another in Jericho and was even somehow building something grand on the cliffs of Masada.

In her two years in Jerusalem, Lydia had seen little more

than the palace, which, though staffed with Jewish servants, was entirely Greek in its culture to please its king.

It was still early. There was still time. She wrapped her mantle tightly against the morning chill and headed for the Temple steps for the third year of waiting. Since Rome, she had given up fretting that those who had come after the scrolls and killed Samuel would find her. She was alone in this, for better or worse.

That first Yom HaKippurim, when the smoke rose thick from the city and the bodies lay even thicker in the streets, she had known the Chakkiym would not come. One year ago she had come again. Perhaps a replacement would have been found. But no one had come.

This year she expected nothing.

She reached the outer steps, outside the Temple enclosure walls, and found her usual spot. She still could not be certain if the appointed place was these steps or those within the courtyard, but if she watched every person who came and went, she could not miss him.

The sun rose on another Day of Atonement. Mariamme and her mother had chosen this unlikely day for the escape, for they feared the people's acclaim of Aristobulus during his duties would result in some kind of attack in the crowd, contrived by Herod. But the two would need to be well away before the High Priest was missed.

Mariamme's earlier observation returned to Lydia. Was she a Jew or was she not? The mysterious pendant proved nothing. But if she were a Jew, she would have cause to worry. The One God demanded this yearly sacrifice to atone for the sins of the people. He had many requirements and laws, some of which were in the written Law and some added over time by the Pharisees, who sought to please Him with their whole lives. She could understand this desire. If pleasing God were the goal, then it only made sense to work as hard as one could to please Him better. What would it mean for the High Priest to be missing on this holiest of days?

She longed to close her eyes against the unending flow of people. To examine each one as they passed was exhausting, and the warmth of the early autumn day made her drowsy. An old woman picked her way toward the Temple, leaning heavily on a stick. Her slow, steady tread was like a soft heartbeat, lulling Lydia to sleep.

Would she come every year? Probably. But only out of duty. Not because she believed the Chakkiym would ever appear.

She would be an old woman someday too. Still sitting on these steps, hunched and bent and waiting.

And would that old woman have a family? Anyone who loved her? Or would she still be in service to Mariamme? An aging queen and her aging servant.

Her thoughts strayed to Simon as they often did, despite their short acquaintance. To the fiery national fervor in his eyes and the tight set of his jaw. Since the victory in Jerusalem two years ago, she heard that Herod had made Simon the manager of his newly constructed winter palace in Jericho. No doubt he ran it better than the Jerusalem palace, which always seemed to be lacking something.

From commissary soldier to palace manager, Simon's fortunes were increasing while she remained in the same position of lady's maid to the queen and, at twenty-three, quickly grew too old to be marriageable.

She returned to the palace slowly that night, the weight of the coming years, empty and purposeless, pressing against her lungs as firmly as the undelivered scrolls.

The palace was not a refuge, however. A furtive buzz of servants and angry shouts from the throne room greeted her entrance.

A passing kitchen slave saw her enter and could not wait to share the gossip.

The queen's mother and brother had been caught sneaking from the palace.

And Herod was in a rant.

Lydia ran for the throne room, her heart keeping time with her pounding sandals.

Nineteen

Lydia slid into the crowded throne room and took a quick measure of the uproar. Did Herod know who was involved in the attempted escape?

He paced the head of the room, punctuating angry words with furious gestures. His dark, oiled curls swung with each upraised fist, and torchlight reflected from the gold band across his forehead like a third eye. Salome stood alongside, arms folded over her narrow body and her dark features pulled into a contemptuous scowl.

What Herod's throne room lacked in the colorful carved beauty of Cleopatra's palace, it made up for in severity. He copied the Greek- and Roman-style pillars, with their sharp fluting of marble that shot upward to a lofty ceiling lost in darkness at this hour. On the north side of the chamber, the coppery fabric at open windows snapped in the evening breeze like the crack of a whip over the gathered crowd. Torches blazed at fixed intervals in sockets along the wall, their scarlet flames bending in obeisance to Herod's rage.

Lydia sought out Mariamme, where she stood near the

throne. Best to keep her distance. No need to let Herod put all the faces together of those who had been complicit.

Alexandra was on her knees before Herod. Aristobulus stood straight backed, with all the defiance of a youth before a tyrant. Good man.

"And I must hear it from a eunuch!" Herod's face purpled and he jabbed a forefinger into the wine-colored tunic of a nearby servant.

Mazal, the eunuch who had apparently spoiled their plot, bore a satisfied smirk. He had been a stableman in the palace since Lydia arrived. But there were whispers that he had once been cupbearer to Herod's father, until Antipater was poisoned to death and the pall of suspicion had fallen on Mazal. He had the slight build and unusual height typical to his situation. Perhaps it was his height, but he seemed always to be leaning toward Herod, as though trying to bow and scrape his way back into the family's favor. It would appear he had found a way.

David emerged from the shadows to stand beside her, and she gave him a sideways glance. He was taller than she now, handsome and strong, and his sharp-cut features were fixed, focused on the drama.

She pressed an arm against his, silent communication of the anxiety they must share. Would Herod learn of all who had helped in the botched escape? The salty smell of a fearful crowd invaded her senses. Perhaps they all wondered if blame would fall on the guilty and the innocent.

But Herod's wrath poured toward Mariamme. "You were part of this!"

She shrank away, eyes wide but lips silent, covering her belly with a bare forearm.

Herod stalked at her, closing the gap. "You think *he* should have my place, yes? Rule over Judea?" He leaned in. "Always the Jew, always the Hasmonean, never my wife!" His voice dropped, but the intensity, laced with a note of pain, carried it across the crowd. "Where is your loyalty? Have I not loved you better than anyone?"

She dropped her gaze to his feet, still silent.

"Bah! You and your precious bloodline." He waved a hand at the mother and son, then in the direction of the palace's courtyard beyond the throne room. "Building your ridiculous booths to hide in, still clutching at the traditions of the past, as though something new has not come."

The harvest's Feast of Tabernacles was upon them tomorrow, and all week palace servants had been constructing the traditional stalls to commemorate the booths that had sheltered their people when God had brought them out of slavery in Egypt.

Aristobulus spit at Herod's feet. "Scoff at our customs if you must, Herod. But leave us to them."

Do not go too far, Ari. It is not safe.

Herod's face contorted, but perhaps he sensed that in matters of religion, he was outnumbered even in his own palace. He tried to take Mariamme's arm gently, but she pulled away. He dismissed the crowd with a harsh curse and a rude gesture, and all who had gathered fled the throne room.

Lydia breathed her relief as Mariamme and Alexandra hurried Ari away.

≈

Lydia kept busy with holiday preparations, and when the Feast of Tabernacles drew to a close seven days later, the people of Jerusalem who gathered in the Temple courts for the final sacrifice would never have known what animosity the king bore toward the new High Priest. Smiling and waving at his subjects and surrounded by advisers, Herod entered the Temple enclosure from the palace side, weaving his way through the crowd. A tittering drumbeat from unseen musicians accompanied his entrance.

Lydia assembled with the rest of the palace staff, lined along the outer gate. Riva stood at her side, still trying to gain Herod's attention. Did he still call for the girl, even though his heart seemed only to belong to Mariamme? Lydia did not want to know.

Herod ascended the steps to the first doors to the Temple courts, then turned to smile over the crowd, but their attention had already shifted.

From the south side of the hill, a row of priests in white tunics ascended, appearing over the rise and followed by the High Priest, Aristobulus.

A hush fell over the crowd to see the tall young man. He was already so striking without his robes, but now he was arrayed in the garments of glory and beauty, the pride of Israel. Smiles and wide eyes greeted his appearance. The linen ephod, woven in threads of gold and blue, purple and scarlet, hugged his muscled chest, and the jeweled breastplate with its grid of twelve stones shone with the inner light of emerald and sapphire, diamond and amethyst, turquoise and onyx—twelve stones, each engraved with the name of one of the tribes so the people would ever be before HaShem when the High Priest entered the Holy Place. Beneath the ephod a blue robe hung past his knees, and the tinkling of golden bells stitched to its hem played over the hill.

Lydia's heart soared to see him so exalted. He should have the scrolls. The thought came unbidden, but was it not right? As High Priest and hopefully their future king, would he not be the perfect one to entrust with her secret? The One God she was beginning to know through David's patient teaching had given her two younger brothers to fill the void in her heart left by Caesarion. Was it not fitting that one of them be the answer to her prayers over the scrolls?

The silent awe of the crowd at Aristobulus's resplendence broke, replaced with wild shouts of admiration and upraised arms and fists. The masses parted, allowing him entry through the mob like Moses through the Sea of Reeds. To his credit, Aristobulus accepted their frenzied praise with a mature smile and a dip of his head, and the engraved gold plate fastened to his turbaned mitre winked in the morning light.

Lydia pulled her gaze from Aristobulus to his brother-in-law, the king, still standing upon the steps before the wooden doors with his sister beside him, both with a hatred so pure, it seemed to swallow the light that radiated from the High Priest.

In a flash, the drumbeat sounded more like a funeral dirge. The acrid scent of burning sacrifice coated Lydia's tongue and the pressing flesh of the crowd grew claustrophobic. When Salome leaned to speak into Herod's ear, Lydia could almost hear the hiss of her whispered malice.

Aristobulus's gold-plated mitre and jewels continued to wink over the riot of the crowd, as if passing a traitorous message to those who cheered. On the other side of Herod, Mariamme's gaze went from husband to brother. She saw it too. The dangerous acclaim.

Lydia's pulse skipped over a drumbeat. A darkness fell over the crowd.

No, it only surrounded Salome and Herod, as though they had shadowed in the glory of Ari.

Lydia frowned, glanced left and right to see others' reactions to the strange shifting of light.

But though the crowd watched the royal family, no one seemed to notice anything amiss. She blinked. Was it only a trick of her eyes? And yet, she *felt* the darkness more than she saw it—felt it pressing and growing from the brother and sister, reaching, clawlike, toward Ari.

And in that moment, Salome's gaze jumped to Lydia. The darkness shot into Lydia's eyes and all grew dim. She blinked again, returned Salome's stare, and the strangeness lifted.

"Powers of darkness will come against you . . ."

She had not thought of Samuel's warning in years. She looked to Herod, chilled at the danger to Aristobulus.

But already Herod's expression was clearing. A passive smile fixed itself to his face, no less frightening for its blandness.

What would Alexandra have thought if she had seen all this? She was not present, since Herod had ordered her kept under the guard of Sohemus in the palace since the traitorous attempt to escape to Egypt.

The ceremonies proceeded as planned, closing out the Feast of Tabernacles as the Jews had done for centuries. Herod seemed all good spirits and generosity, and by the next morning proclaimed that the royal staff would head north, down the steep descent to the winter palace of Jericho, some 150 *stadia* from Jerusalem.

The news found Lydia where she worked in the palace courtyard, tending to Mariamme's quilled brushes and ivory combs, and it heated her limbs like the sun blazing from behind a cloud.

Jericho.

How often had she thought of the winter palace? Wondered

how its chief staff member fared in his duties? She took a deep breath at the thought of seeing him again, surprised by a flutter of nerves.

Two days of frantic preparation and they were off—a caravan of over a hundred, including the royal family. Herod seemed eager to prove that Aristobulus's attempt to escape to Egypt was forgotten, that only brotherly love existed between the two, and insisted the young man join them on the holiday.

Horse-drawn chariots, pack-loaded donkeys, and attendant slaves on foot circled the Mount of Olives, and from Lydia's perch in Mariamme's private chariot, the Temple gleamed gold and white in the distance, like the first time Lydia had seen it.

She turned her face toward Jericho, heart beating in anticipation, though they still had hours of dusty travel ahead.

The route took them past Bethany, then descended sharply, bouncing over an arduous yet well-rutted road taken by pilgrims, merchants, and soldiers for centuries. The dramatic change in altitude thinned the vegetation, first to straggly trees, then to nothing but shrubby growth, and finally to only the hardiest of desert succulents. They navigated a narrow pass of red rock and Mariamme mentioned its name—Ascent of Blood.

The road to Jericho was often beset by bandits, and anyone traveling alone took the chance of a beating or worse. Lydia eyed the rocky crevices, searching out the shadows. Chariot wheels crunched over dun-brown dust that rose to coat the skin and invade nostrils and mouth. A bath would be most welcome when they finally reached the palace.

Would she get the chance to wash before greeting the Jericho staff? It had been two years since she had seen him. Perhaps covered in dust and vastly aged, she would not even be recognized.

≈

The Jericho palace appeared as an oasis in the desert, lavishly supplied by the astounding aqueducts Herod had built across the oft-dry Wadi el-Kelt, irrigating the plains around the city into forests of date-palms and balsam plantations.

Lydia had the opportunity to wash, the chance to explore, the time to wonder if she would even find Simon in the vast palace. Finally, hungry and frustrated, she wandered to the kitchen complex, a warren of connected rooms with stores, cook fires, and tables for preparation.

And there he was.

With his back to her she knew him still, in large part because of the clipped Persian accent that attached itself to his barking commands.

"You there!" Simon waved a hand at a passing servant. "Where are you going?"

Lydia drifted to a table along the wall and eavesdropped on the reprimand. In this, he seemed unchanged. Still hounding his inferiors into working harder, faster, and better with the force of his will, uncaring if they rolled their eyes and curled their lips at his back.

She reached for a chunk of goat cheese from a platter on the table, put it to her lips without thought, fingers trembling. Why did her pulse pound at merely having found him in the kitchens? Surely he would not even remember their brief meeting years ago.

As if she had shouted a greeting, or perhaps only sensing her pilfering, Simon whirled on her where she stood near the wall.

He glanced at her face, the cheese in her hand, the platter of delicacies. "Does the royal family require something we have not provided?" The tone was annoyed, almost resentful.

"What? No." Lydia reached to replace the half-eaten cheese, then held it to her side as though he would forget the theft.

"Palace kitchens are not typically frequented by the queen's handmaid."

Lydia swallowed. Heat flooded her face and she cursed the blood in her veins.

The activity in the chamber had slowed, with attention pinned to their conversation. Simon scowled at the entire room, then marched toward her, took her elbow, and kept moving. "Come. There are tables spread in the courtyard."

Lydia dropped the cheese and stumbled after him. She glanced over her shoulder at the staring faces of the kitchen slaves, then pulled her arm from his grasp and followed him to the courtyard.

He stopped beside the fountain and indicated a table set with cooked lentils, flatbreads, and onions. "I trust this will satisfy your appetite?"

She glanced numbly at the food. "Yes, thank you. It looks— the whole palace—looks wonderful." Foolish, childish words.

He bowed his head as though flattered, but the compliment had clearly meant little to him. "Nothing like the splendor of Egypt, I am certain."

So he did remember.

"But then you have been in Jerusalem all these years, I suppose. Perhaps by now the pretty Egyptian who pleases everyone has forgotten her homeland."

"Never!" Lydia drew herself upright, found her courage, and returned his hard glare. "But I have learned what good management looks like, and I wanted only to commend you on your fine work here."

Simon's mouth twitched. "Even if it was accomplished by a man only half human, with the head and manners of a bull?"

Even this he had remembered? He had brushed it off back then, yet he had remembered. The vulnerability she had glimpsed under the harsh exterior had not been an illusion.

She hid a smile and drifted to the fountain to dip her fingers into the cool water. The dust of the journey still seemed to cling to her skin. "I suppose even bulls have their place."

He touched her elbow again, turned her to him. "You are changed, little Egyptian." His gaze roamed her face, her hair, her dress. "Still elegant, still beautiful, but the charms rest more easily on you now. The maturity of a woman who knows herself." He tilted his head and frowned. "You have enchanted the entire palace with your mysteries by this time, I suspect."

The heat rose to her face again, and she looked away from the furrowed brow and the deep eyes that gave away his soul. Looked to his hand, still grasping her arm, and noted disconnectedly how strong and tanned it was.

"I am not as Egyptian as you think."

He dropped his hand. "No? Converted, are you? Like Herod?"

The ridicule had returned. She took a step backward again, her hand pressing the pendant under her robes. "Perhaps I am Jewish."

"Ha! Two years in Jerusalem does not—"

"My mother was Jewish."

Simon circled to stand before her. "Is this true?" His face seemed lit with something—anger? Disbelief?

"I . . . I believe so. I never knew her."

"And you were raised in Egypt, in the palace of the Greek whore."

Lydia flinched at the epithet but nodded.

"So then you have seen the truth since last we met! You have discovered what it is to be Jewish, and you are ready to fight against the Gentile dogs who would steal our land from under our very feet?"

Lydia's breath had shallowed. "I . . . I am only trying to serve my mistress—"

"Bah!" He turned away. "Perhaps you have not changed."

Anger flamed in her chest. "Who are you to criticize my service? You labor here year-round to create luxury for an absent king whom you despise—"

In a move both sudden and unexpected, Simon clapped a hand over her mouth. "Quiet, little Egyptian! Do you want me hanging from the gallows by morning?"

She shook off his hand, stared into his eyes. "Then why do you do it?"

His hands were wrapped around her upper arms and he pulled her close. "I will do whatever I must to see Israel free. There is no greater calling. Would you have me simply wait, year after year, for someone else to rescue our people?"

Year after year. The words echoed in her mind, reverberating against the memories of the years marked waiting at the Temple for the promised Chakkiym.

Had she done enough? If the dying Samuel had slipped the scrolls into the eager hands of Simon instead of her, would he have already accomplished the task?

He shook her slightly. "You see it, don't you, Lydia? The time is drawing near. Our liberation is at hand."

There it was—the intensity she remembered, undimmed by the years that had passed. Her gaze was fixed on his mouth, on the way his lips formed the words, like an orator in the marketplace, passionate and persuasive.

"You know what it is to long for freedom!"

She said nothing, only listened to her heartbeat, then closed her eyes. It was as though there had been something dormant within her since they met—something waiting to be awakened.

The heat between them shifted. The press of his lips against her own was as expected as her next breath. She rose to meet his kiss, joined him in it.

And in the kiss something was unleashed within her that had little to do with the way of a man with a woman, and everything to do with the way of an Israelite passionate for her people and her land. Like the winter rains thundering through a dry wadi, it swept her into something connected, something Jewish, something forbidden.

She was still adrift in a great sea, perhaps, but she was *part* of that sea, a piece of a greater whole, joined to a movement and a cause more important than her own.

Simon pulled away from the kiss, pushed her from him, took a step backward, as if he had shocked even himself with his boldness. He looked at the ground as though shamed.

But Lydia felt no shame.

The churning of her spirit within her was like an answering cry to a shouted invitation.

There would be no waiting another year. No biding her time until the next Day of Atonement. Somewhere in Judea, someone must know of the Chakkiym. Know how to find the one who would take the scrolls and deliver them to those who would use them best.

She would find that person. She would take her destiny and shape it with her own capable hands.

Compelled to seal her decision with an act outside herself, she took three swift steps forward, wrapped her hands around Simon's neck, and kissed him soundly once more, eyes wide open.

And then she ran from the courtyard before he had a chance to recover his voice and deliver the reprimand she did not want to hear.

Twenty

The Jericho palace had enough halls and corridors for Lydia to wander with her thoughts, and she strolled with little awareness. They had been in residence several days, long enough for her to memorize its layout, from the tiny chamber at the end of a corridor in the lowest level, where she slept and kept the scrolls hidden, to the huge stone pool for swimming on the south side of the palace walls. A luxury Herod insisted upon when he rebuilt this palace, proof that he was as modern as any Roman.

She had lived with this family, this strange hybrid of Idumean, Greek, and Jewish, for nearly five years now and had brought her Greek-Egyptian heritage with her. Simon's patriotism showed her that it was time to choose, time to become her true self. Was there a way to learn more about her parents? At least she could learn what it was to be Jewish, not simply from David's lessons and Mariamme's example, but by a studied pursuit. She would find a synagogue when they returned to Jerusalem. Ask questions about the prophecies of Daniel, discover an expert. Someone who knew of the Chakkiym and the lost scrolls.

"Lydia!"

She jerked her head upward at the sudden call.

Mariamme stood against the wall near the end of the corridor, the light from the courtyard beyond outlining her figure and that of another, a man. Mariamme shifted slightly away from her companion.

"My lady." Lydia bowed.

The man kept his gaze on Mariamme. It was Sohemus, captain of Herod's guard. His personal friendship with Herod had earned him the unenviable position of Alexandra's keeper, so he had come to Jericho with the family. He wore the insignia of his position but did not seem engaged in official business at the moment.

"I was just . . . asking Sohemus . . . if he had seen you." Mariamme cleared her throat and pushed away from the wall. "Come, I have a task for you."

Lydia followed, passing Sohemus, who did not move, and giving him a polite smile.

Mariamme led her to a small, windowless chamber off the central courtyard. The room was lit by a single oil lamp on a desk, half blocked by the man who sat before it.

"I have found her, Simon." She entered the room. "Now I have you both."

Simon turned from his scrolls and pens, neatly organized on the desk, then stood.

Lydia hovered in the doorway and did not meet his gaze, which felt a bit cold even from this distance.

"Lydia, I have given Simon instructions about a banquet to be held tomorrow evening. We are going to entertain the finest of the city's nobles in style."

Simon ran a hand through his dark hair. "My lady, it will be very difficult in such a short time—"

Mariamme waved away his protest. "It must be immediate." Her attention drifted to the empty doorway. "My sister-in-law, Salome, is already trying to set herself up here as though she were queen. We must demonstrate that Herod's wife is the true queen."

Lydia bent her head to hide a smile. The words came from Mariamme, but their source was clearly Alexandra.

"Lydia, you must help Simon with the preparations."

Simon started forward. "There is no need, my lady—"

But Mariamme was already pulling Lydia into the room. "Make use of her, Simon. You will find she is a wonder at this sort of thing. Give her a room with tables to adorn, and it will be the most beautiful thing you've ever seen."

"Indeed." Simon's noncommittal word hung in the air as Mariamme departed, leaving them stranded and awkward.

Simon inhaled and lifted his chin. "Shall we get started, then?"

So there was to be no mention of what had transpired between them, only this angry coldness. Perhaps that was for the best.

But if Simon resented Mariamme's dictate that Lydia be involved, he did not show it. Indeed, by the next afternoon she was set up in the central courtyard where the banquet was to be held with everything she had requested. Three slave girls worked at her direction, transforming the courtyard. Crates of fresh fruits weighted the tables, along with heaps of fragrant blooms and bolts of Eastern silks in colors like precious jewels. A wooden-slatted box of ripe peaches warming in the sun gave off a heavenly scent, tempting her to forget her work and bite into the juicy flesh.

When Simon appeared, brow puckered at the chaos of the

overloaded tables, she laughed. "You must wait. It will come together. I promise."

Simon snapped his fingers toward the slave girls, then flicked a hand toward the kitchens. "The girls are needed to prepare food."

They trotted out, giggling, until they passed their scowling superior. The first of them turned as she passed Simon and thrust out her tongue toward his back. He ignored their passing.

Lydia huffed at the reduction of her workforce. "Perhaps I shall retract my promise if I am to have no help!"

"I will help you."

Lydia bit her lip and bent to the flowers. "You are already annoyed that I am involved at all. I do not expect you to attend me like a slave."

He came to stand beside her, reached for a knife, and followed her lead in stripping leaves from the lower stems of the white lilies and setting them aside in a glossy pile. His arm brushed hers and did not move away. "I am not annoyed." The words were given softly, with his attention fixed on the flowers.

Lydia sighed and set her own knife on the table. "Simon, I must apologize for what happened—"

"No. You must not."

"It was only the fierce way you spoke of Israel, of freedom . . . It . . . it made me feel—"

"Well, I shall not apologize. You are a pretty girl, admired by everyone from servant to queen, and I am certain you are accustomed to such bursts of admiration."

Lydia shook her head. "Have you not met Riva? Or Salome?"

Simon let out a hiss of derision. "Riva admires only herself. And Salome? Fancying herself as royalty? You are more of a princess than she will ever be."

Lydia fought the flush that crept across her throat, glad they worked side by side and he could not see her face.

"It is obvious the queen both depends on and is fond of you."

Lydia rubbed a lily petal between two fingers. "You have also gained much since last we met. The new palace is impressive."

"Yes." He laughed, humorless and clipped. "And I am so well loved here."

She turned, still holding the stem, and lifted the bloom to enjoy its scent. "They see only your hardness, Simon." She waved the flower at him until he looked at her. "Perhaps show them less of your thorns."

He smiled and reached for another stalk, his attention on the work. "And more of my petal softness?"

"Do not pretend you have none. I know you better than that."

His hand stilled in mid-reach, then dropped to the table as though he needed it for balance.

Why had she said such a thing? She did not know him.

"And this is perhaps one reason why everyone admires you, Lydia. You see the best in us all." His voice was quiet, the words uttered with a trace of regret.

She gathered a pile of lilies into her arms and carried them to a massive ebony vase at the end of the table, painted in the Greek style with gold-leafed figures chasing around its girth. She slid the blooms one by one into the vase, arranging them asymmetrically. A nearby bowl of lemons and oranges filled the air with a citrusy freshness, but it was still the peaches that tempted her most.

"The queen was right." Simon brought the rest of the lilies. "You have a way with beauty."

"I want the banquet to be perfect for Mariamme."

"You care for her greatly."

Lydia shrugged. "She is a kind and fair mistress."

He handed her new stems, and they worked in tandem to fill the vase. "And the boy you are so friendly with—what is his name?"

"David?" Lydia pushed past Simon to gather the stripped leaves into a pile to be burned. "We have served together for some time now, that is all. It is unwise for staff to form strong attachments, don't you think? Positions are changed, people let go or moved." She unwound a bolt of jade silk, letting the fabric pool on the table. "It only causes problems if people become too connected."

Simon did not answer.

She glanced sideways to find him chuckling.

"I amuse you?"

He shrugged one shoulder. "I have never met a woman so insistent on remaining alone while at the same time drawing everyone so inescapably to herself."

She inhaled, a deep breath to push against the constriction in her chest that was ever present when someone got too close, and grabbed the knife to slash the silk into two equal pieces. "And what about you? Are you still alone? Or have you married since last I saw you?"

"No. I have not married."

She pushed past him, back to the vase. "Why not?"

"Too much to do."

At this, she laughed aloud and the strange tension broke.

He came to stand behind her, watched as she arranged the fabric into a river of jade, flowing around the vase, then scattered a few of the fallen lily petals across the silk.

"Breathtaking."

The word was whispered against the back of her hair, and it raised a chill across her arms. The sun had fallen lower than the rim of the courtyard, and she shivered in the waning afternoon. "I am glad you like it."

"You are cold." His hand rose toward her arm.

"A little." She straightened and reached for the second piece of silk. "But the work will keep me warm."

He stepped to the table to survey the effect, then plucked a peach from the crate. "Your efforts are for Mariamme, I know. But you will make *me* look good in the process, and so I thank you."

She smiled. "You see. You are quite capable of good manners."

He dipped his head and handed her the fruit. "Perhaps I have only had a fine teacher today."

She took the peach from his hand and bit into its softness. She should focus on the great amount of work still to be done, and the banquet only a few hours away. Yes, he could be charming when he wanted to be. But the brusque overseer might have been better. There was something decidedly dangerous about this other Simon.

≈

The tables were laid with gold-plated dishes and jeweled wine cups. Torches blazed at all corners of the courtyard and threw leafy shadows like masks across the faces of the gathered nobles and their wives. In the light of the tiny oil lamps Lydia had scattered through the flowers and fruits and silks, the tables glowed like midnight rainbows.

All was ready and the guests were present. She retreated into the corridor, then up the wide front stairs to the second-floor chambers that ringed the courtyard. Mariamme would need assistance to finish dressing and fasten her necklaces. Lydia had neglected her mistress too long in an effort to perfect the banquet.

She paused on the upper floor to peek over the rail at the scene. Simon was right—she had helped to make his event a success. She smiled and turned to continue to Mariamme, but the voices in the open-doored chamber behind her caught her attention.

"Well, they must be found, that is all there is. If the prophecies hold any truth, the time is soon upon us."

Salome's voice, low and threatening as always.

Then Cypros. "But if the prophecies are true, how can we—?"

"There is always a way, Mother! But we must know what the scrolls say."

Lydia's breath hitched in her chest and she pressed herself against the wall beside the open doorway.

Cypros spoke again. "How can you be so certain they were found? That poor young man—he would have said anything to end his agony. Perhaps it was all a fabrication."

"No. I have been given to know he spoke the truth. He screamed out the name of Samuel ben Eliezar in Alexandria with his dying breath. If this was not truth, why else would both men I sent to retrieve them have disappeared without a word?"

"You and your dark voices—"

"It is those dark voices that will keep your son on the throne, safe from all contenders!"

A chair scraped across the floor.

Lydia took a small step away from the door but she could not flee. Not yet.

"I know the writings are in Egypt. I will do whatever I must to obtain them."

"I still do not understand why these scrolls hold any danger for your brother."

"Argh! If we are to live and rule among these filthy Jews,

Mother, then it behooves you to understand them. Their prophecies speak of a Messiah, a King to rule them forever. And what would happen if these holy writings were brought forth and the people believed them to be written of our boy-priest, Aristobulus?"

Cypros said nothing, but the sound of both women moving across the room filtered to Lydia.

"But the boy will not be a problem for long." Salome was nearly to the door.

Lydia retreated, back toward the steps she had ascended.

The women appeared in the doorway, Salome smiling, a cold smile of satisfaction. "After all, I am my father's daughter."

They passed Lydia in the corridor as if she were not there. When they reached the stairs, her breath expelled in a rush, leaving her chest with a hollow ache.

The scrolls. Could Salome speak of any other than those that were even now secreted in Lydia's own chamber?

But it was the words spoken against Aristobulus that sped her feet toward Mariamme's chamber. The queen must be warned of the danger to her beloved brother. And Lydia could not lose another brother either.

Leodes was missing from Mariamme's doorway. The eunuch who had been her personal protector since they came to Jerusalem never left his post. It could only mean that Mariamme had already gone down to the banquet. She must have found another to attend her while Lydia was preoccupied with the preparations. Lydia hurried back to the courtyard, but the festivities had already begun, and it would not be appropriate for her to approach the king and his wife where they dined.

And there was handsome and open-hearted Aristobulus, ruddy with a bit too much wine already, laughing at the flattery being poured into his ear by a citizen of Jericho on one side and the pleasantries of Herod himself on the other.

Lydia took a breath to steady her racing pulse and nodded to herself. All was well with the royal family, and there would be time to speak to Mariamme when the guests had departed.

She busied herself in the kitchens, not because she was required, but only to distract herself from Salome's strange and frightening revelations. There were platters to be fixed into more pleasing arrangements before they were carried in an endless parade from kitchen to courtyard, and she kept busy as the evening waned. Simon was not to be seen, perhaps for once trusting his kitchen supervisor.

The evening was still warm, and some of the men slipped from the courtyard at Herod's insistence that they experience the pleasures of his new swimming pool. The women gathered in little knots of conversation, and servants moved silently through the tables, gathering the remnants of the meal.

The party atmosphere had quieted when the first scream was heard.

Lydia's stomach lurched at the sound. She had never heard Mariamme lift her voice, but it was most certainly her mistress who screamed and screamed again.

Was the baby come too soon? She had been having some pains of late, and earlier in the pregnancy there had been signs of a possible miscarriage. Lydia dropped the basket of wilted flowers and ran toward the screams, past the clusters of noblewomen who stood with mouths agape.

Through the south entrance, out into the night air. The screams had come from outside.

There, there she was. Near the swimming pool. Not doubled

over with birth pains but huddled against Sohemus, Herod's friend and captain of the guard. Mariamme's face was buried against his chest.

A group of men, several of them dripping from the pool with hastily tied towels at their waists, huddled in a circle, bent over a prone form.

The stars swam in the sky above Lydia's head.

She took two shaky steps forward, leaned against the air that had grown thick enough to clog her throat.

Aristobulus, naked and blue, lay at their feet.

She could not breathe. Could not draw freshness into her lungs. Could not expel the stale air that congealed in her chest like dark blood. A black fuzziness brushed the edges of her vision like vulture wings, and pinpricks of light flashed deep behind her eyes.

Not again.

She was eleven and terrified. Wet and cold and near drowned herself. Screaming and screaming.

Her legs collapsed, too lifeless to hold her upright.

"Lydia."

The ground did not rush up to meet her. Only a pair of solid arms around her middle, the scrape of a stubbled jaw against her cheek, the smell of smoke and spice.

She struggled in his arms. Thrashed out against the slippery Nile reeds that would drag her to the bottom. Gagged on river water.

"Sshh, Lydia, you are safe."

Pressed against him, she beat her fists against Simon's chest, and the air returned to her own. "Not again!" Her body shook with the wet chill, her teeth rattling against her skull.

Simon swept her up and carried her into the palace.

She half sensed the rush of banquet guests past her, the deserted courtyard, the smallness of Simon's private office.

He set her in his chair with a jarring thump, disappeared, returned in a moment with a coarse blanket and wrapped it tightly around her shoulders. "You have had a shock."

Her teeth still tapped a frantic beat and her body convulsed with sobs she could not control. Simon pulled her into an embrace and ran brisk hands across her back to warm her.

"Wh-what happened?"

"I do not know. Apparently there was some horseplay in the pool. Men dunking each other under the water and the like. No one noticed him in trouble."

She shook her head, the motion jerky and stilted. "No. No, it was not an accident."

Simon put two fingers over her mouth and his eyes said enough. *Do not repeat such a thing.*

She shook off his touch and whispered to herself, to the floor, to the gods. "I am a worthless servant. What good have I ever been to anyone?"

Simon clutched at her hands. "Lydia. Lydia, look at me." He sat back into a squat before her chair. "I know you cared greatly for him." His deep, gray-flecked eyes were sad but quizzical. "Or was it someone else? You said 'Not again.' Were you reminded—?"

"It was a long time ago." She brushed the hair from her eyes, from her tear-soaked cheeks.

He nodded, as though the explanation was enough.

It would have to be.

She should have warned Mariamme as soon as she heard Salome plotting.

The shivering returned, along with the suffocating feeling of the weight of river water against her chest.

She had thought to give Ari the scrolls. But now he was gone. And it had been her fault.

Once again it had been her fault.

Twenty-One

Salome should have known they would be forced to return to Jerusalem with the boy's body.

There was no question of Aristobulus being buried anywhere but in the tomb of his fathers, and the preparations for the journey began even before the last banquet guest had departed.

Ah well, the would-be king would not return to his city with the same sort of fanfare under which he had ascended the hill to the Temple the week before.

Salome directed Riva to gather her clothes and jewels for the journey, but only she herself was permitted to pack and store her elements of worship for her patron goddess, Al-Uzzá.

The caravan left the following day, with Mariamme and Alexandra sitting white lipped and silent in the chariot of mourners, the body under wraps and hidden from the sun, pulled behind on a wheeled cart.

Salome rode with Herod and their mother, discussing their next action in tones quiet enough to be mistaken for grief. It was agreed that Ananel should resume his post as High Priest. The people would feel some satisfaction in his restoration.

But the satisfaction she should have felt in having the contender to the throne removed evaporated before the family's seven days of mourning had even ended. A letter arrived, a messenger from Syria with word from the Roman Marc Antony.

Herod was to join him on the battlefield at once, to explain the death of the High Priest in his personal swimming pool.

In their mother's private chamber, Salome paced beside the open window that faced west over the city. Fiery shades of sunset slashed the sky and lit the roofs of houses. Despite the holiday in Jericho, the scrolls were never far from her mind. She must have them, must make them hers to decipher to understand when and where this Messiah would appear. Or perhaps was even now among them. Once she had this knowledge, she could destroy him, and with him, the hope of a thousand zealots who would see the kingdom ripped from her family.

Across the room, Herod crumpled the letter and threw it across the room. "How could he possibly have heard so quickly?"

Salome stopped her pacing and shot her brother a chilly look. "Surely you are not such a fool." She raked a hand through her hair, loosening its tight binding. "It is that simpering wife of yours and her monster of a mother. They are determined to use Cleopatra's hatred to poison your friendship with Antony."

Herod growled low in his throat. "I should have kept that woman under lock and key despite the mourning period. Sohemus would have made certain Alexandra never wrote another letter."

Salome folded her arms. "And your wife? Are you still so blind—?"

"Close your mouth, Salome. You are not to speak of Mariamme."

"Argh!" She turned to Cypros, who reclined quiet but angry on a low couch. "Do you hear him, Mother? Tell your son that he makes a fool of himself for that girl." She turned on him. "Mariamme hates you, Herod. Can you not see—?"

"Enough!" Her brother's face reddened and his fists tightened at his sides. "She is my wife and perhaps mother to the next king of Judea."

"Yes, yes, we all know she will soon place a child in your arms." Cursed, wretched baby that clung to life despite Salome's efforts. "And have you so soon forgotten the son you already have?"

He waved a hand. "Child of my youth. Before I knew what family blood meant to these Jews." He pushed his hair behind his shoulder. "But perhaps you are only jealous, sister. With no child of your own?"

If she could have struck him dead where he stood and still retained her position of power in the palace, Salome would have done it.

"Perhaps I should not have been forced to marry that old goat of an uncle."

Herod scowled. "Joseph is a good man."

"Joseph is an *old* man. I do not know what our father was thinking, marrying me to his brother instead of into the royal Jewish family, as you were."

"Fortunate for me, since you now occupy yourself with keeping *me* on the throne."

The barbed words were undergirded with something like affection, and Salome begrudged him a half smile. "We do know how to get things done."

But Herod had turned serious again, his eyes on the wadded

letter on the floor. "Do you think he has another in mind for the throne?"

Salome chewed her lip. "We must find out what the women have reported to him. Whether he has reason to believe it was anything but an accident."

"Mariamme's seven days of mourning have just ended."

"Then I believe I know where to find her."

The women's baths on the lower level of the Antonia palace were as fine as any in a Roman villa. Salome's hunch had been correct. Mariamme was out of her torn *shiva* robes at last, submerged to her collarbone in the steaming water. Her pale little Egyptian girl sat on the edge of the bath, scooping water and pouring it over the queen's tilted head.

They both turned at Salome's entrance.

She stopped at the entrance to the *calidarium* and leaned against the doorway. Condensation slicked the stone and dripped from the ceiling. She scowled through the steamy air at her sister-in-law. "I hope you are pleased."

Mariamme's head lifted and she blinked. She did not look well. Puffy eyes and an air of fatigue about her.

"What is it, Salome?" Even her voice was weary.

Salome entered the baths, passing the brazier with its heated stones and running a hand along the frescoed wall of soothing blues and greens. "Enjoying your bath while your husband waits for Rome's condemnation?"

At this, Mariamme's eyes flicked open a bit wider, and the servant girl's ladling paused in midair and then resumed.

But before Mariamme framed a defense, the sudden hiss of water poured over the brazier stones drew their attention.

Alexandra.

The queen's mother replaced the jug beside the brazier, slid past Salome to sit on the lip of the bath beside the servant, and crossed one long leg over the other, her widow's robe trailing over the damp floor.

Ah, now Salome had both conspirators together. She should have brought an incantation.

"My daughter is enjoying a bath after a long week, Salome. The heat eases the pain in her back. Late pregnancy can be such a strain, as you know." Alexandra tilted her head. "Or as you've *heard*."

Salome ground her teeth together but would not show her irritation.

She had tried every spell and incantation she could find, pleading with the goddess to give her a girl child. There was no use having a boy—he would never rule. But a girl whom she could marry to Herod's son by the commoner Doris—that would be a marriage to solidify their family's claims to the throne, and Salome's daughter would be queen. Her pleas and spells had been ineffective. At thirty-four she was beginning to despair.

"I am sure your week of mourning your dead brother and son has been most difficult."

Alexandra started up from the bath, hatred burning away the clouded air between them, but a quiet word from Mariamme restrained her. Instead, Alexandra lifted her chin, straightened her shoulder as if *she* were queen, and gave Salome a cold smile. "It would seem you may soon understand Mariamme's pain. The pain of losing a brother."

Salome's muscles tensed and she took two steps forward.

The servant girl stood and stepped between them as if her skinny frame could protect the queen.

"You sent one of your vile letters again, didn't you?" Salome's blood ran hot through her veins, and her fingers itched to strike the smug smile from Alexandra's face. "What false accusations did you feed the Egyptian tramp?"

Mariamme's shoulders lifted above the water, wet hair streaming against her pale skin. Her blue-green eyes were like ice chips above the steam. "False? You dare to deny that you and Herod plotted to murder my brother?"

Salome looked from mother to daughter. What did they know? "Antony will never believe you. He loves Herod."

"Ha!" Alexandra's mockery bounced off the dripping walls and ceiling. "Marc Antony does what is best for himself. If that is Herod as king of Judea, so be it. If not"—her dark eyebrows waggled above narrowed eyes—"then your family's fraudulent reign is finished."

It would serve no purpose to attack Alexandra. But oh, how she wished to place her hands around that wrinkled neck, to push her backward into the bath, to show her exactly how her son had died, lungs gasping, eyes bulging . . .

"Fraudulent reign? Fraudulent! We have fought and scrabbled for everything we have gained in this miserable land, from the day your forefather Jacob stole the birthright from our forefather Esau, to the day your great-grandfather conquered Idumea and put us to the sword if we did not convert. Now at last we are given a chance to govern what should have always been ours, and you dare to call us false? It is you who have worked falsely to push Herod from his rightful throne in favor of Aristobulus!"

Mariamme rose from the water, and the servant wrapped a robe around her dripping body. "And it is you who have plotted to kill him. Do not deny it, Salome." Mariamme inclined her head to the Egyptian girl. "Lydia heard you and Cypros."

Salome focused on the girl for the first time. "Lydia. And I suppose it was Lydia who ensured that your letter would reach her former mistress, Cleopatra?" She peered into the girl's eyes, tried to get the measure of her. She had sensed an unwelcome strength about this girl before. "Perhaps you have been here on Cleopatra's behalf all these years? Spying on us, sending your lies to Egypt?"

Lydia met her gaze. "I am no friend to Cleopatra. And neither do I lie. But I know what I heard."

The impudent little thing. Salome would deal with her later.

Right now there was the more immediate double crisis. Herod's execution might be ordered by Marc Antony, and Mariamme could drop a son into the world at any moment, a son who would be hailed as the logical replacement for both Aristobulus and Herod. And if named king, the boy would have his mother as coregent, with the grandmother backing them both.

And where would that leave Salome?

A direct attack on Mariamme would likely only result in the child's healthy birth. It was too late for another try with her herbs and potions. Besides, the child might be a girl and not named king at all. Better to wait and see before taking the risk.

"My daughter is in need of rest now, Salome." Alexandra put an arm around Mariamme's shoulders. "You will excuse us."

No, she would not excuse them for anything. But she would let them go.

For now.

≈

Salome gripped the rail of her private balcony and watched Herod's entourage roll away from the Antonia palace, north toward Syria and Herod's fate.

There had been no tears at their good-bye. They were not that sort of family. But Herod's nod toward her held all the final words needed. *Watch over my kingdom until I return. Do not let them take it from us.*

Would he return?

She would hope for the best and plan for the worst. Herod's young son, sequestered away with the divorced commoner Doris, would need to be protected. Mariamme's child, if a son, would need to be eliminated.

And Salome needed a daughter.

She turned from the balcony and startled. "Joseph! Why must you always be so quiet, sneaking up on me?"

Her husband leaned over the rail. "Have they gone?"

She shoved past him into her chamber. "He will return. Antony loves him."

"I am to keep guard over the queen while he is away."

Salome whirled on him. "Oh, you will enjoy that, won't you?" At his quick flush, she laughed, though the truth still grated. "I have seen the way you look at her, old man. But Herod might as well have left a eunuch in charge, eh?"

Joseph looked away, focused on her table of goddess-worship accoutrements.

So Herod had left her husband to watch his wife. Not his friend and captain of the guard. Interesting. Had he too seen the exchanged glances between Mariamme and Sohemus? Salome had noticed for months but said nothing. Better to save the information for when it was most useful.

Joseph fiddled with the figurine of Al-Uzzá on her table.

She crossed to him and smacked his hand away.

His shoulders drooped. "Herod believes he will not return."

She straightened her sacred beads and sacrificial knives. "Do not speak foolishness."

"He gave me instructions if he should not."

She turned a wary gaze on him. "What sort of instructions?"

He shook his head. "Sometimes I believe the boy has a madness in him."

Joseph's reference to Herod as a "boy" when her brother was nearly forty only highlighted how very old her husband was.

"He says that if Mariamme is not to belong to him in life, then she is to belong to him in death, and to no one else."

Salome's heart raced. "What are you saying?"

"He gave me orders that if we receive news of his execution, it should be followed swiftly by Mariamme's death."

Oh, this was too delicious.

Salome twirled a knife in her hand. How best to use this information?

If Herod were executed and if Mariamme died before birthing a son, their family's reign through Doris's son was still assured. But it was too many ifs. Herod might still return.

She sighed mournfully. "Poor Mariamme. Herod loves her so dearly and yet she believes that he cares nothing for her."

"How can that be? He is so devoted—"

"She wants more, I suppose. You know these Jews. They are never satisfied with what they have."

Joseph's gaze drifted to the open balcony where Herod had disappeared, but his thoughts seemed elsewhere.

It was enough for now.

"On your way out, husband, tell my maid to fetch me Mariamme's maid, Lydia."

He nodded once and shuffled to the door.

She did not have long to prepare.

She moved on silent feet about the chamber, drawing the heavy drapes at the windows and balcony, assembling her instruments on the marble table near her bedside. All the while communing with the fertility goddess in mind and spirit, seeking Al-Uzzá's dark wisdom and strengthening power.

A voice came from the hall. "You sent for me?"

No address of respect. No "mistress" or "my lady." The girl seemed to think herself equal with the queen by nature of Mariamme's reliance on her.

"Come in, Lydia. Close the door."

The girl hesitated, but what could she do but comply?

With the door shut and no lamps lit, the chamber fell into a weighty darkness, velvety and cool against Salome's skin. Her eyes fluttered briefly and she felt the pleasure of the goddess on her.

"You must find this land strange, Lydia. With its One God and all His many requirements."

The girl stood straight and composed. "I am a long way from home."

"And were you a worshipper of Isis back in Egypt?"

"I . . . I had a variety of religious influences in the palace."

Salome tried to read the level of devotion in the girl's heart. "Hmm. Yes, I'm sure." Strangely, she could see nothing. Did the girl have no faith of any kind? "And since coming to Judea? Have you taken hold of the One God?"

"Was this why you wanted to see me, my lady?"

Salome lowered herself to the chair placed at an angle before her bedside table and ran a light hand over her instruments. "I am only trying to discern where your loyalty lies. I would hate to think you still favored the queen of your youth over the queen you currently serve."

"Mariamme has my full devotion, I assure you."

Salome picked up a hooked blade, squeezed its solid bone handle within her fist, and closed her eyes. Though a physical tool, in the right hands the blade could be used to dig knowledge from the soul of another, or even to hollow out that very soul. She turned it slowly in the air, tiny motions like the scraping of a strigil. She would extract whatever the girl knew, then leave her powerless and open to future probing.

But the blade seemed only capable of chafing the air.

A flicker of fear chased along Salome's veins.

She turned on Lydia, used razor-sharp thoughts to bring all the power the goddess had granted down on the girl, blanketing her with a suffocating darkness.

And then the blanket evaporated like mist.

Confused, she rose from the table and circled the girl. Had she underestimated her? Perhaps she was a sorceress and had brought the power of Isis with her from her ancient temples and pyramids.

Lydia's feet remained fixed, but she followed Salome's slow circle with her gaze, as though perplexed. Her face remained clear, guileless. Not the face of a sorceress wielding power.

"How are you doing this?" Salome's voice came out as a hiss, more frightened than threatening.

"My lady?"

"How are you hindering me?"

The girl frowned—a quick, puzzled look that gave away nothing.

Salome grabbed Lydia's arm. A jolt like summer lightning

shot up her fingers and into her chest. She jerked away. The girl's skin was on fire!

The shock ran through her, down to her feet, and left her woozy. She put one hand out to empty air to steady herself and another to her nauseated belly.

Lydia faced her and her lips were moving.

Salome heard nothing but the *whoosh, whoosh* of blood in her ears. She swayed and thrust one hand between herself and the loathsome girl.

Lydia took a step toward her, hand outstretched like a claw.

Salome scuttled backward, her own hands thrown in front for protection. "Get away!"

It was more than the barred entrance to the girl's soul. There was a power that surrounded the servant, a power Salome had never encountered. She gasped for air, her chest constricting. What god or goddess was this?

And why had she been abandoned by her own? "You are protected. Not from within, from your own doing. From without. Whose power surrounds you?"

But Lydia said nothing.

Al-Uzzá had failed her. Salome had been carried on a wave of energy, buoyed by the goddess's support for so many years, transported toward her goals. But this—this was a different sort of power, and the wave of power collapsed under her, leaving her suffocating in darkness.

She cursed her buckling legs, cursed the stone floor that cracked against her knees, cursed the girl who bent over her, lips still moving in silent incantation.

"Salome? Are you ill?"

No incantation. Only words of pretended concern.

She braced her hands against the floor, knees throbbing and chest heaving. Tears dripped from her eyes, but she would be dead before she let the girl see them.

Lydia leaned forward, her outer robe falling toward the floor and a leather-corded pendant escaping from her tunic. The pendant swung before Salome's eyes.

In the darkness it was difficult to see. Was that—? She grabbed at it.

Lydia pulled back.

But Salome had seen it. A bronze disc with a raised relief.

"Where did you get that?" She peered at the necklace from her place on the floor. "Are you also a thief?"

Lydia's hand circled over it, hiding the pendant. "I will call for the palace physician."

"No." Salome pushed herself to standing. "No, just go." She would not admit that with Lydia's presence removed, her physical symptoms would abate. The servant seemed to have no awareness of her own power.

Indeed, when the door closed behind Lydia, Salome's strength rushed in like a torrent filling an empty cistern.

The goddess was silent, but Salome was not.

In a rage that gave her uncanny sight into every object in the dark room, she hurled pots and overturned furniture and screamed.

She had gone unchallenged for too many years to be overthrown by a servant.

Her list of objectives had a new addition.

Mariamme and her baby must be eliminated, yes. But Lydia of Alexandria must go with them.

Twenty-Two

L ydia laid Mariamme's yellow linen undertunic over a padded couch in the queen's bedchamber to dry. If Mariamme grew much larger, she might no longer fit the tunic.

"There is another here that has a tear, Lydia. Would you see to it?"

Lydia straightened her shoulders with a brief closing of her eyes, then turned to the queen and took the ripped dress from her. Her fingers snagged against the silk. "There seems to be no end to clothing troubles today, my lady." She meant for the words to sound light, but her irritation leaked out.

Mariamme did not seem to notice. She sat at her dressing table, fiddling with her cosmetics. The room was one of elegance and comfort. From the frescoed walls to decorative pottery and luxurious bedcoverings, Lydia had spared no effort in making Mariamme's chamber the finest in the palace.

The brazier in the corner had mercifully died down to embers. The room was overly warm. Without the brazier's light, only a single lamp dispelled the evening gloom. Lydia moved about the chamber, straightening cushions, clearing cups and platters from earlier in the day, running a damp cloth over the marble furniture and bases of the green-and-gold-painted columns. Her stomach churned with an evening meal that did not sit well, and her thoughts were far from her duties.

Their sudden departure from Jericho in the wake of Aristobulus's death—his *murder*—had been necessary but painful, if she were to admit it. While her friendship with David had been a balm since leaving Caesarion in Egypt, the beginning of the friendship with Simon had been something altogether different. The way he comforted her after the drowning . . .

She shook off the dark thoughts and folded the jumble of waiting baby clothes from a woven basket. She was back in Jerusalem now, and if the High Priest's death had done nothing else, it had served to solidify her decision to take the matter of the scrolls into her own hands and find the Chakkiym before the next Yom HaKippurim. Before Salome realized they were hidden in her own palace.

Lydia moved from the baby clothes to examine a new dress that had been sent up for Mariamme earlier in the day. She would add some gold stitching at the shoulders and waist, but the Tyrian purple dye was still so pungent, it watered her eyes.

Salome.

Lydia's shoulders convulsed in a little chill, a reminder of the encounter. She had been nearly oblivious to Salome and her dark obsessions all these years. What bearing did any such thing have on her?

And yet in Salome's chamber, there had been something—a feeling, a pressure—upon her that had been very personal. She had fallen under the scrutiny of Herod's sister in the baths. Salome was angry that Lydia repeated the threat against Aristobulus and helped the women get a letter out of the palace. But the animosity Lydia felt in the woman's chamber was something more.

"You are protected. Not from within. From without."

What did it mean? Was it Samuel's promise that his God would protect her? She had done nothing to earn it, though she was trying to learn and sometimes sent a few coins with David for sacrifice at the Temple, as Samuel had done in Alexandria. At the thought of her old friend, an unexpected jolt of anger coursed through her. Why had he given her this task that seemed to draw darkness to her—forces she did not understand? She needed to get rid of those scrolls.

"Lydia, come and brush my hair. It is nearly time for the dinner."

She took up the brush and ran it through Mariamme's heavy red hair mechanically. The passing chatter of a cluster of servant girls in the hall grated against her nerves.

"You have been quiet tonight, Lydia."

"Apologies, my lady."

Mariamme shook her head slightly under the brush. "No need. I am merely concerned. But then, you have been somber since Jericho."

Images of Aristobulus's blue body floated in her memory.

"We all have."

Mariamme fell silent and her head lowered as if too heavy to hold upright.

Lydia paused in her brushing and put a hand to Mariamme's shoulder. "I am sorry again, my lady. I did not mean to remind you—"

"As if I could forget." Mariamme sniffed, lifted her head, and indicated Lydia should continue brushing. "But I am trying." She half turned with a smile. "I thought perhaps your sadness arose from leaving behind that palace manager—Simon, is it?"

Had Mariamme learned to read her so well? The distance from Jerusalem to Jericho seemed vast and hopeless.

The brush hit a tangle and caught. Lydia jerked it downward.

Mariamme squeaked in protest. "Oh my. I was only teasing, but perhaps there is too much truth." She turned, forcing Lydia to stop brushing. "You know staff liaisons are considered inappropriate. I'm well aware that it goes on all the time downstairs, but it cannot be public." She returned to facing her bronze mirror. "Besides, you are far too valuable as my maidservant to lose you to a foolish flirtation. Are you not happy with me?"

"Of course, my lady. You are very good to me." A coldness had crept through her limbs, despite the warm room.

"And I will keep Salome away from you, I promise. You must not pay any mind to her ravings."

Lydia put her fingertips to the pendant under her tunic. "My lady . . ." She hesitated, her usual reticence to share anything private seizing the words in her throat.

"What is it, Lydia? There is something else tonight, I can feel it."

Lydia rocked on the edge of indecision for the space of two heartbeats. Was it not better to remain silent? A flush of fear swept her. But curiosity won out. She pulled the pendant from under her clothing.

"I have never shown you this. It was . . . it was my mother's, and is all I have of her."

Mariamme smiled, a smile warm with sympathy, and leaned toward the pendant. "You know so little of her, I am glad you have something to—"

The words hung unsaid, and even in the light of the single lamp, the sudden paleness of Mariamme's face was startling. Much like Salome's reaction.

"Where did you get it, Lydia?"

The chill across her skin grew, and the pendant seemed like ice in her fingers. "Salome saw it. She accused me of stealing it. But, as I told you, the pendant was my mother's."

Mariamme was standing now, and she looped a finger around the leather cord, then grabbed Lydia's arm with her other hand and pulled her toward the lamp. She held the pendant closer to her eye.

"It is the same." Her words were a whisper. "I am certain it is the same."

A foreboding hammered in Lydia's chest. "I did not steal it."

Mariamme dropped the necklace and peered into Lydia's eyes. "Of course not." She eyed the silent hallway, then took up Lydia's arm again. "Come. Everyone will have gone down to dinner. Now is the best time."

Lydia followed Mariamme from the chamber. Her eunuch-guard, Leodes, straightened at the door. Eunuchs were standard for the protection of royal women, but gentle, good-humored Leodes was an unlikely choice. Herod's persistent jealousy would not allow for anyone who might tempt Mariamme's affections.

He stepped to Mariamme's side at once.

"We are only going down the hall, Leodes. Stay here at my door."

He smiled and gave a quick nod.

Lydia glided silently behind her mistress, who seemed to take care to stay close to the wall of the corridor and keep her sandals from clacking against the stone floor.

How was it possible she had worn the pendant for all these years, when every day its secret could have been illuminated if only Lydia had shared it with Mariamme? Stupid, foolish girl. And yet, at the same time, had she made a mistake? Revealed too much?

Mariamme paused in the upper corridor, listening. Lydia slowed behind her.

Apparently satisfied, Mariamme continued a few steps and disappeared into a bedchamber.

Alexandra's bedchamber.

Like Mariamme's room, it was lit with only a single lamp while its mistress was gone and was empty of servants. Empty of adornment as well, in sharp contrast to Mariamme's room.

Mariamme crossed the chamber on sure feet, directly to her mother's dressing table. A squat box of cedar sat in its center and she picked up the box, brought it to the lamp on a side table, and set it down. "Come, Lydia. Come closer."

Lydia pressed damp hands against her robes and took a shaky breath.

Mariamme did not seem to notice her discomfort. She was rummaging through her mother's things—mostly jewelry, it would appear. "Here. Here they are."

They?

The queen pulled two objects from the small box and held them to the light. She glanced at Lydia. "What are you still doing over there? Come here."

Lydia crossed the space and willed herself to look at Mariamme's find.

Mariamme placed them both in her own palm, faceup, and pulled Lydia's pendant from under her tunic once more. "You see? They are the same."

Lydia's legs were trembling and her breath came short and shallow. How could this be?

Her own pendant had a loop of iron forged to its metal disc where the leather cord was strung. The two in Mariamme's palm did not. But there was no mistaking the embossed designs. Identical, all three.

"Wh-what are they?" Her voice sounded scraped from within her chest.

Mariamme shook her head. "I don't know. I used to play with Mother's jewelry when I was a young girl and saw them here often. But I never asked." She looked at Lydia's face, then replaced the discs in the box and snapped it closed. "Do not have any fear, Lydia. Obviously you did not steal it, and I will tell no one you have it."

"Salome knows."

Mariamme's brow furrowed. "I will ask my mother about these two."

At Lydia's intake of breath she placed a comforting hand around her arm. "Discreetly. Do not worry. She will not know why I ask."

Voices in the corridor drew their attention.

"I must go to dinner." Mariamme squeezed her arm. "You go to bed. I can get a slave girl to attend me this evening." She moved from the room as quickly as her overburdened belly would allow.

Lydia followed, then nodded to the queen and took the corridor in the opposite direction.

Go to bed? She might never sleep again.

≈

Lydia descended the back stairs of the palace and passed through the kitchens, busy with the serving of the evening meal. A familiar laugh, seductive and playful, came from the corner.

Riva shouldered up to a serving boy, five years her junior at least, laughing at his shy discomfort.

Lydia looked away. Riva made a fool of herself. Did the woman even understand discretion?

On the far side of the kitchens, a narrow set of stone steps climbed to the second level of the palace, and then another to the third. Lydia emerged into the night air and sucked in great gulps of it, as if it would clear the muddle of her mind.

The roofline of the palace stretched ahead of her, a half wall of protection between its floor and the open air. The city of Jerusalem lay at her feet, vast and glittering with yellow torchlight under the colder sparkle of the stars. She walked the edge, listening to the night. In front of the Temple only a few torches flared, and the Mount of Olives was a wavy purple line across the sky.

"Lydia?" A silhouetted figure perched on the half wall shifted toward her.

"David! What are you doing out here?"

He turned back to the city with a shrug. "Nothing."

He had been like this since Jericho. At odds with himself and the world.

Lydia walked to him, stood alongside for a moment, then impulsively climbed to the wall and sat, legs dangling over the edge as his did.

David glanced at her seated position, then up to her face, a glint of his old self in his eyes, but the light soon went out.

They sat in silence except for the lonely roll of cart wheels against stone somewhere below, and the snorts of animals in some distant pen.

"Cold and beautiful, isn't it?" David's voice sounded empty, hopeless.

"Are you still working in the gardens?" She would try to distract him from his dark thoughts.

He snorted. "Pulling weeds and picking flowers like a slave. Is this what I have worked for all these years?"

"Were you so much happier as Aristobulus's manservant?"

"At least I had the respect of those downstairs. But I cannot blame them for tossing me out into the gardens. I did nothing to save him."

Lydia covered David's hand with her own. "You bear no guilt."

She had said nothing to David of what she overheard between Salome and Cypros. He was so angry over what he believed to be an accident. If he knew the truth, there was no telling what he might do. But if anyone bore guilt, it was her.

She braced her hands against the hard stone and studied the tan roofs beneath the black sky. Would not think about blue skin, nor muddy Nile water.

"If they are going to keep me in the gardens, perhaps I should simply go home to Nazareth. Become a shepherd."

"Is that what you want, David?"

"No, it is not what I want! I want to build things."

She narrowed her eyes at him, laughing. "Build things?"

He sighed, as though a secret had been let out. "With stone. I want to build things with stone. I have so many ideas. Drawings—" He broke off and looked away.

"David, do not be ashamed of it! It's a wonderful thing to create something of beauty with your hands."

"Well, it will never happen. I should have been apprenticed years ago. Instead, I am here. And rather than building something that would improve our land, I am serving the man who would consume it for his own pleasure. And wondering if there is to be any justice anywhere, whether we will ever be anything but Roman chattel."

A breeze lifted Lydia's hair and carried the odors of the city with it, animal dung and cooking smoke. Familiar, homey smells and yet here above the city, they were both so far removed from anything like family. They had only each other.

She swung her legs out over the open space, and a desire to tell him secrets of her own built in her heart.

What was happening to her? First her revelation to Mariamme of the pendant, and now the scrolls?

But something was stirring, she could feel it. Her vow in Jericho. The discovery of Alexandra's matching discs, the frightening threats of Salome. A danger, a shift in what was to come. Words invaded her thoughts like a prophecy.

"You will need your friends."

She had long believed herself friendless. Why did she resist opening herself to people? She could never believe anyone truly cared to listen to her thoughts or see her heart. Now, for the second time tonight, she felt the inner push, like someone's hands on her shoulders prodding her over the roof ledge, the terrifying urge to leap.

"There is something I want to tell you."

He was barely listening, his attention on the city below where neither belonged.

"David, it is important."

He turned dull eyes on her.

She clasped his cold hands.

His expression grew troubled. "What is it, Lydia? Has something happened?"

Yes, too many things. Where to start?

She focused on their joined hands. Began with Egypt. With Samuel and his furtive teaching of a young, abandoned servant girl growing up in the palace without a family.

And she told of the night of his death, in halting, emotion-choked words, and of the scrolls, even now hidden in her bed-chamber, that told of a Messiah who would come to reign over Israel forever. Of the Chakkiym, who never appeared on the Day of Atonement, despite her faithful waiting. She told it all, her gaze never leaving their hands.

He did not say a word through the telling.

When she had finished and raised her head, she found him openmouthed, eyes shining with unshed tears. "Lydia." One whispered word, but in it all the hope of a nation.

A chill stole over her, raising the hair on her arms, the back of her neck.

She shook her head. "I do not know why I was chosen to play this role. It would have been better if it had been someone like you—"

"No. No, HaShem, blessed be He, knows exactly whom He chooses and why. This is your destiny, Lydia, from the time Samuel found you and began your teaching. What other Egyptian orphan had such training in the ways of the Jews?"

She pulled her hands from his, suddenly too chilled to remain on the wall, and stood.

"I will help you, Lydia."

She smiled, her own eyes clouding.

He swung his legs over the wall and joined her. "We will find the Chakkiym together. We will deliver the scrolls that will save Israel."

He was so important to her. Too valued. And his youthful

confidence restored some of her own. She took a deep breath and nodded.

The grate of a cart rolling to a stop outside the palace doors drifted up to them. David peered over the edge, then took a step closer to lean farther.

"Isn't that—?" He inclined his head and waved Lydia forward.

A man had alighted from the cart and was directing two slaves to remove crates from the back.

David glanced at her. "Isn't that the manager of the Jericho palace, Simon?"

What? Lydia looked over the edge, heart stuttering.

As though he sensed himself being watched, the man lifted his head toward the roofline.

Even from three stories above, Lydia recognized the angular jaw, the set of his shoulders, the smile. He raised one hand in greeting.

Her own hand rose in response.

Simon had come to Jerusalem.

Twenty-Three

Lydia forced herself to a slow walk from the darkened roof to the street level of the palace. By the time she and David reached the leafy front courtyard, Simon stood inside the atrium, commanding slaves to work faster bringing cases and crates through to the kitchen in the back of the palace.

He stopped in mid-instruction when he saw Lydia and broke into a smile.

Warmth spread through her.

He nodded to them both. "David. Lydia. I trust you are both well."

Lydia crossed the tiled courtyard and clasped his hands. "What are you doing here?"

"I sent for him." Mariamme strolled from the smaller of the palace's two dining chambers. She caught Lydia's eye and winked.

Lydia pulled back from the friendly greeting. Why had the queen said nothing earlier? It was no wonder that Mariamme had given her the mild warning, however, if she knew Simon was already en route from Jericho.

Mariamme gave Simon a polite bow of the head. "Welcome, Simon." She turned to Lydia and David. "When I saw the way Simon ran the palace staff in Jericho, I knew his talents were being wasted in a palace where we only visit. I sent for him to manage the palace here in Jerusalem."

Lydia's pulse settled down to a steadier rhythm and she smiled in agreement. As though the queen needed her approval.

"But I am glad you are both here." Mariamme drifted sideways to a wide bench at the base of a red column and lowered her heavy frame to sitting with a sigh. "I will soon be confined to my bed to await the baby's birth, and then to recover." She rubbed a hand over her belly. "Lydia, I will have little use for you for a while."

Lydia started at the queen's words, feeling a stab at being unneeded.

Mariamme held up a hand. "But I have been thinking. About where you could be even more useful." She raised her gaze to the courtyard and the second-level balconies. "My husband has an insatiable appetite for construction, as you know. But while he erects palaces and walls, aqueducts and harbors, around this land, he has no eye for the refinements of his buildings. This palace has structural beauty, perhaps, but none of the softer side of adornment." She smiled at Lydia. "All but one chamber, that is. My own."

Simon cleared his throat. "I would guess that Lydia had something to do with that?"

Mariamme glanced sideways at him. "You seem to have taken her measure already, Simon, in the short time of your Jericho acquaintance. Yes, you are correct. And so while I am confined to rest, I want you two to work together again, as you did the night of . . . the night of the banquet in Jericho." Her eyes clouded for a moment, but she recovered quickly. "Lydia, you will give Simon your ideas. Simon, whatever Lydia needs, from supplies to slaves, should be arranged."

Lydia glanced at Simon. Would he resent the immediate interference before he'd even settled into his new role? But he was nodding with Mariamme and seemed already to be making mental plans.

"My lady?" Lydia pulled David forward from where he had been hovering behind. "Since our return to Jerusalem, David has been working the gardens. But I think he would be put to much better use working in the palace, overseeing any repairs or renovations in structure. He has a builder's eye and talent." Or at least she assumed he did.

Mariamme did not look at David, almost as if she were unable. He was only two years younger than Aristobulus and had been her brother's manservant. "Whatever you want, Lydia. David, you need not return to the gardens. You will answer to Simon."

"Yes, my lady." His chest puffed out with the eager words.

Mariamme stretched and pressed a hand to her lower back. "And now I believe I am ready for bed." She stood and started toward the wide front staircase, then paused and looked over her shoulder. "Lydia?"

"I am coming, my lady." Apparently Mariamme had forgotten her earlier assurance that she would find a slave to attend her tonight. Lydia gave one backward glance to Simon, who leaned against the trunk of a small palm, watching her exit with a pleased expression. Further conversation would have to wait for morning.

And by the morning she already had a hundred plans for the palace, conceived while she lay awake through half the night, alternating between ideas of paint and fabric, visions of bronze discs and pendants, and thoughts of Simon.

Perhaps he had been awake most of the night as well, for she found him already established in the palace manager's small room off the kitchen, no trace of the servant who had been in the position previously. The small window, cut high in the wall, faced the rising sun and bathed the room in yellow, sparkling off dust motes in the air. Simon's dark hair was mussed as though he had not slept, waves curling at his temples where he had run a hand through.

He turned at her entrance and extended a hand to a chair beside his desk. "Good morning." A tray of soft breads, tan and crusty, and a comb of golden honey sat on the desk, and the room smelled of fresh bread.

She slid into the chair, a bit breathless. "I am excited to work with you. Thank you for being willing."

He raised an eyebrow. "It is probably due to your success with the Jericho banquet that I am here at all, so I should be thanking you."

"I have so many ideas—"

"Ho! Already? Shall I take notes?"

She grinned. "Perhaps you should."

The day passed quickly, filled with strolls around the palace, pointing and exchanging thoughts, then a return to Simon's chamber to sketch out details and make lists. They worked well together, each feeding the other's creativity and organizational skills. Lydia warmed to the task, feeling more useful than she had in months, and Simon hailed her ideas as inspired.

Another day passed as the first, and then another. In the sheer joy of working alongside Simon, doing what she loved, Lydia nearly forgot about the pendant she wore under her tunic and Mariamme's promise to ask her mother about the matching discs in her chamber. Her desire to locate the Chakkiym and rid herself of the scrolls before Salome took any more action against her abated.

Lying on her bed on the third night, she forced her thoughts back to Samuel's task with a twinge of guilt. How could she have let another day pass without moving forward?

But working with Simon had been so . . . lovely. She laughed to herself. Would any other palace staff believe it so? He was passionate and principled, and too often his desire to set things right ruffled feelings. But with her, he was different. He treated her ideas with respect and never directed her actions as though she were his servant.

She rolled over, pulling the bedcovering to her chest in tight fists. It did no good to think these thoughts. She was the queen's principal maidservant, a position coveted by every servant woman in the country. As such, she would serve the queen alone all her days, becoming her most trusted ally. The maidservants of royal women became almost like mothers or sisters to their queens, and their loyalty was never divided. There was no room for men in such a life.

Besides, what was she thinking, even opening herself to the possibility? Had she learned nothing in her twenty-four years? When had there been anything but rejection, abandonment, and good-byes in her life?

She fell asleep still clutching the bedcoverings and vowing to begin her search for the Chakkiym in the morning.

～

"Lydia? Where are you going? You are needed in the main dining room."

Lydia paused in her exit from the palace's front arch and turned to Simon. "I have something I need to do this morning."

He crossed to the massive arch. "In the city?"

"Yes."

At her lack of explanation, he cocked his head. "A secret meeting with a merchant, perhaps? Some young trader who came through the palace and caught your eye?"

He was teasing, but the implication stung. She drew herself upright. "I am going to the synagogue."

Whatever he had been expecting, it must not have been that. His mouth opened slightly and his eyebrows arched. "I did not realize you were so—"

"Jewish?"

He chuckled. "I will go with you. It is past time for me to meet the locals."

Lydia bit her lip. A chance to spend time with Simon outside the prying eyes of the palace, plus the safety of an escort through the city would be a good thing. But how could she freely ask her questions with him around? Ah well, she only intended to search out a few experts this morning, men she could later visit with inquiries.

"But you do not attend the daily prayers. I assumed you had no interest."

His face darkened for a moment. "I have an interest in anything that concerns Israel. But it will not be prayers that throw off the bondage of our oppressors."

Lydia pulled him toward the arch. The Antonia palace was not the place for such talk.

He fell into step beside her in the wide courtyard in front of the palace. The morning was fresh and cold, the winter air free of dampness today and the sun bright on the paving stones. "And what is your errand in the *beit knesset*?"

He used the Hebrew term, even in the midst of the Greek he always used with her. In Egypt, all houses of prayer had used the Greek "synagogue." Here in Judea, Greek was the second language, though the Greek-loving Herod did not want to hear Hebrew or Aramaic in his palace.

"In Egypt I often went to synagogue with an old rabbi friend of mine, Samuel. He instructed me in the Torah. I miss it."

She felt Simon's gaze on her as they walked into the heart of the city. It was an unusual story, she knew. A servant of unknown parentage, living in Egypt, instructed in the Torah, and a woman.

"And did the old men of the synagogues in Alexandria argue like fishwives as they do in Judea?"

She laughed. "Sometimes. But they were often, I don't know, sad, I think. Perhaps they wished they were here in Jerusalem."

"No doubt."

"Do they argue about the interpretation of the Torah?"

Simon shrugged and stepped around a pile of garbage on the corner. "That, and about politics. The Pharisees believe if they keep enough of the Law—and not simply the Torah, but also the oral law of their traditions—they will bring about the redemption of mankind and justice in the land."

"I assume you disagree. But you are not of the Sadducees."

"Why? Because I am not from an aristocratic family? Much too common to be part of the rich elites who would turn us all into Greek speakers?"

Lydia frowned. "Samuel taught me only of these two political divisions of the people. But you seem to be neither."

He grabbed her elbow and turned her to him in the street.

"That is because I am something else, Lydia. Because I believe something else. That the day is coming when it will not be the Pharisees' observance of the Law or the Sadducees' obsession with the Temple and its rites that brings about our redemption."

"What, then?"

He leaned against her ear, still grasping her arm. "We must fight."

Her blood went cold and she pulled back. She had seen enough of battle, both at Masada and when Herod took Jerusalem two years ago, to last a lifetime.

"Do you not see, Lydia? It is the only way to make things right."

Yes, that was his passion, was it not? He was born to be a fighter, whether in the palace or in the streets.

"And now that I am here in Jerusalem, I will join with those who share my zeal to see a free Israel. Nothing else matters until this is accomplished. I have learned that the hard way." He continued down the narrow street, shaded by the tight-fitting houses hugging the gutter.

She watched his back. So that was why he had come. To connect with others of his kind.

Zealot. It was a word she had heard Samuel use, but there had been none in Alexandria. Now she understood. And understood that Simon was not safe.

She hurried to catch up. "And what is it you hope to accomplish?"

"That is why I seek out the others. Until recently, there was a plan in place. Those two feuding brothers, Mariamme's two grandfathers, were each backed by Pharisees or Sadducees. The Pharisees abandoned Hyrcanus, though, and asked Pompey of Rome to intervene and restore the old priesthood. Abolish the kingship of the Hasmoneans. Instead, Pompey defiled the Temple, a judgment on the Sadducees who protect it, and stripped Hyrcanus of all authority, giving it instead to Herod's father."

Lydia huffed. "Poor Hyrcanus. Since his return from Babylon, he wanders without seeming to understand what has happened. And those ears." She shuddered.

"I've seen him, trying in vain to attend in the Temple. I think his mind is retreating from the truth. After he was exiled, Mariamme's uncle Antigonus went after both the kingship and the High Priesthood. It's been a bloody, muddled mess." Simon's hands curled into fists. "The only solution was to restore what the Maccabees gave us when they first revolted—the Hasmoneans."

"Aristobulus."

"Yes, he was to be king. Plans to overthrow Herod were under way. But we did not take enough care, did not realize that Herod would suspect so soon."

He slowed and glanced at Lydia, as if judging her reaction. "But we shall not speak of Aristobulus. I know it saddens you to remember him, and to remember the other one, who came before."

How had Simon come to know her so well, so quickly? She would not speak of that night, thirteen years ago. Not now, nor ever.

They reached the synagogue in time for morning prayers. An old rabbi frowned at Simon's lack of head covering and pulled a spare from some little niche.

Lydia broke away to sit on the women's benches. She soaked in the graying columns and the graying men, missing Samuel with a terrible ache, loving the familiar crinkle of the Torah parchment, the dim and cool interior that felt like a sacred space, even the arguments between the men on interpretation of the Law, arguments that Samuel had explained brought man closer to HaShem as he made an effort to understand His Law. But this morning was different than Alexandria. Was it being in Jerusalem? Being in the city with Simon? Or the scrolls entrusted to her? Whatever the reason, she felt the difference from the teachings of her youth, when she had cared only for the intellectual pursuit of it all.

She had seen that Simon was not devout, that he cared only for the physical, political promises of his God. But did she know the One God any better? She had tried to please Him. Was that the same as *knowing* Him? But who was she to think He would look on her, see her?

I am the One who knows your name.

She sucked in a breath and glanced at Simon across the dim synagogue. The words had seemed almost audible. But his attention was on the teaching. Who had spoken?

I am the One who knows your name.

A warmth bloomed in her chest and diffused to the rest of her body, flushing her skin as though she had been embraced. She studied her hands in her lap and breathed slowly, lifting a part of her heart heavenward as she had never done before. She had wondered often if she had a true name, a name given at birth. Did the One God know this name, as He knew her?

Twenty-Four

Simon watched Lydia's expression, the way she soaked in the teaching, the glow of her eyes as she lifted them in prayer. She was more of Jew than he was. The realization stung.

How had he come so far from the faith of his fathers? He had been a toddler when Pompey brought the blight of Rome to Israel, and somehow the poverty and destruction had wormed themselves into his core, forged him into a man of anger and passion, with no room for quiet faith. And yet there was space, for he felt the lack of it like an empty hole inside.

When the readings and prayers were finished, he took Lydia's arm and guided her into the street. "Come. I have someone I want you to meet."

The home of Jonah and his wife, Esther, lay at the end of a narrow street, its tiny windows opening to a guttered alley. His friend lived in better accommodations in the years he had served in Herod's army.

Lydia hurried beside him. "You know the city already when you have only just arrived?"

"I grew up here." He did not say more, and thankfully she did not ask. The years in Jerusalem, before he pledged himself to the cause, were like another life. Days when he had wanted only to be a merchant, to have a wife and children and a home like Jonah's, however poor.

Jonah welcomed him at the door with a hug to crush the bones, then pulled them both into the house with a yell to Esther.

"He has come again already? Has he brought the supplies?" Esther appeared from a back room with a wide smile for Simon and raised eyebrows at his companion.

Simon gave Esther a little shake of the head, hoping she'd understand that Lydia knew nothing of his secret errands.

Like water gushing from an opened fountain, children poured from behind Esther.

Lydia laughed. "Do you have the whole city's children here?"

Simon pulled Lydia farther into the front room of the sparse house. "Lydia, this is my friend Jonah and his wife, Esther."

Lydia nodded to Jonah. "We met at Masada, I believe."

Jonah slapped Simon on the back and gave him a dramatic wink. "Ah yes. I remember."

"Ignore him, Lydia. It is the lovely Esther I wanted you to meet. She is a potter, like you."

Lydia turned to the woman and met her warm smile with one of her own.

Esther held out her hands in greeting, which Lydia grasped as though desperate for a like-minded friend.

To Simon, it appeared as if two sisters had found each other.

They were enveloped into the unnaturally large family at once, and Simon explained that the children were orphans of the war between Herod and Antigonus, taken in by Jonah and Esther to raise as their own. He fought to keep the fury from his voice. He hoped for a better Israel for these children, and they should not grow up filled with the hatred that had shaped him.

Lydia's eyes widened and she touched the faces and heads of a few of the children closest to her. "But how can you feed so many mouths?"

A boy of about eight tugged on her robe. "Uncle Simon brings us palace food!"

So much for secrecy. Simon glanced at Lydia, tried to judge her reaction.

Her eyes lifted to his in confusion, then understanding. And then a small smile of amusement and even approval that lit a fire in his chest.

Lydia was so kind, so beautiful. She would be a queen's handmaid for many years to come, and he would always be a soldier. But there were days, like today, when he wished they could pretend to be Jonah and Esther, with a house full of children.

They stayed the afternoon, with Jonah reporting on the progress of those who worked in the back alleys and the marketplace to solidify the coming rebellion. They spoke with angry curses of the desperate poverty of the people, with hopeful certainty that a deliverer was on the horizon, with fearful dread at the sense of outrage bubbling over the people like a pot about to boil.

All of this he allowed Lydia to hear, for she must know the state of things for her own protection. But perhaps all of the disheartening news was lost to her, for she and Esther had attached to each other over their shared art and shared hearts.

When the afternoon waned, Lydia leaned over to whisper to Simon. "I should return. Mariamme's birth pains could begin at any time. I do not want to be far when that happens."

They took leave of the huge family, Esther and Lydia hugging with promises of more visits and the children reminding Simon to bring them fruit very soon.

The walk back to the palace was slow and silent. Simon could not say what Lydia was thinking about the poverty-born generosity of his friends, nor the newest subversive activities she had discovered about him. He only knew that seeing her with his friends, with the children, had threatened all the resolve he had brought with him from Jericho.

≈

The baby did not come, not that day or the next, and Lydia kept busy with the palace renovations, checking only occasionally on the queen and being scolded out of the room to return to her work.

A week had passed and she had not gotten a chance to seek out the learned men of the synagogue whom she had identified during her visit, nor had Mariamme mentioned the pendant again. But Esther had come to the palace once, ostensibly to bring pottery that Simon had ordered, but the two women had gotten a chance to sneak away for conversation.

Exhausted from a day of tedious stitching, Lydia sought out the roof again, wrapped in a heavy mantle to ward off the chill. Standing at the roof's edge, she rolled her shoulders and stretched her neck against the tightness that had built there through the day's work.

From this height and in the darkness, only the beauty of the city could be seen. But Simon, and even Esther, had shown her otherwise. The city was suffering an agonizingly slow death, but it would not be defeated without one final fight. And she had a part to play in it, somehow.

It was not David who found her on the roof tonight but Simon. He eased to her side and studied the city in companionable silence. It was like they had known each other for many years, grown comfortable and familiar with each other's unspoken thoughts.

After some minutes he sighed. "We have accomplished a great deal in a short time."

He spoke of the palace project. But the words were true between them as well. A dangerous closeness was developing. Oddly, she no longer felt the suffocating tightness in her chest in his presence.

Dangerous, indeed.

She wrapped the mantle more tightly against the cold.

Seemingly without thought, Simon's arm went around her shoulders and he pulled her to his warmth.

She closed her eyes with the forbidden pleasure of it and dared not move lest he realize what he had done and step away.

A sense of coming home enveloped her. But how could coming home also be so foreign? The tension in her neck and shoulders melted, the frayed and roughened edges of her spirit smoothed. She sighed and allowed her head to rest against his shoulder.

At the small gesture, his arm tightened around her and his face turned downward against the top of her head.

"Well, isn't this interesting."

Lydia jerked away from Simon and whirled.

Riva stood with perfect lips in an amused pout and skinny arms jutting out, hands on her hips. Behind her was her servant boy of the day, following like a pet.

"I had heard you were no longer serving Mariamme. It looks like I've discovered your new master."

Heat raced from Lydia's feet to her hairline, then drained

away. She fought against the pressure in her chest, which, though absent in Simon's embrace, now came rushing back to remind her of why it never paid to get close to someone.

Riva's admiring gaze fell on Simon, as though she would trade her servant boy for the palace manager in a heartbeat. But when she looked at Lydia, it was with only malice.

Riva would tell Mariamme what she had seen.

Of that, Lydia had no doubt.

Twenty-Five

Mariamme could no longer stand the sight of her bed-chamber.

For all its improvements under Lydia's touch, it had still become a prison since she began her confinement. When the crumbs of her late breakfast were cleared and pale sunlight trickled through her window, she rose from the cushioned bed, waved off the slave girl who jumped from her seated place in the corner, and reached for a beige robe to cover her tunic.

"I am only going to take a little walk in the corridor, Despina. No need to raise the alarm."

In truth, she had been thinking of Lydia, and of the strange pendant she wore, hidden under her clothes. It had been days since Mariamme promised her maidservant that she would question her mother.

She took the hall slowly, her eunuch, Leodes, following in her wake. There was no sense in arousing the attention of anyone else who would force her back to that odious bed.

Outside her mother's chamber, Sohemus personally manned

his duty rather than one of his men. She passed him with only a meeting of the eyes, furtive and quick.

Alexandra was finishing her own breakfast when Mariamme wandered into her chamber. The nearly empty, colorless chamber her mother preferred. The contrast with her own was severe.

She looked up from the tray across her bed with surprise. "Mariamme! You should not be—"

"Oh, hush, Mother. I am well enough for a stroll down the hall." She crossed slowly to her mother's dressing table. "Look, I will sit down immediately."

Alexandra's lips puckered. "A little bored, are we?"

"Dreadfully." She reached for the jewelry box, her movement casual, and opened the lid.

"Yes, well, it is only nature's way of preparing you for the biggest battle of your life. You will see. Soon you will be longing for boredom."

Mariamme hooked a finger around a string of ivory beads, lifted them from the box, and draped them around her neck. "Remember when I was a little girl and would beg to wear your jewelry?"

"And now you are to have a child of your own." Alexandra swung her legs over the side of the bed. "Though of course we pray it is not a girl."

A bird chirped outside the window, a single monotone that somehow sounded hopeless rather than cheerful. Mariamme dug deeper in the box until she spotted the bronze discs and pulled them out. "I always wished these had been made into pendants. What are they, Mother?"

Alexandra stood and brought the tray to her dressing table. "You look pale. Are you eating? Have an apple."

Mariamme bit into the fruit obediently, if only to keep her

mother from being distracted by her refusal. The flesh was mushy and tasteless. She held up the discs again, a question in her eyes.

Alexandra took one in her hand and ran a finger over the raised embossing. "It is your great-grandfather's royal seal."

Mariamme pointed to a nearby chair. "Tell me a story, Mother. Relieve my boredom."

Alexandra's eyes narrowed. "And what story would you hear?"

Mariamme palmed the seal and held it to the window's light. "What was he like, Alexander Janneus? And why do you have his seals?"

"He was a hard man, as I remember, but a strong one."

A trait that had passed to his granddaughter.

"He was a conqueror, was he not? Took Gaza? And Egypt?"

Alexandra huffed. "You give him perhaps too much credit. The Gaza victory was a coup—it opened the Great Sea to the Nabatean trade routes and brought great revenue to Judea. And he did do a bit of maneuvering in Egypt. As I remember, he struck a false friendship with Ptolemy, Cleopatra's grandfather, though he was really allying with Ptolemy's mother against him."

Mariamme took another bite of the apple. "What happened?"

"Ptolemy discovered the treachery and there was a brutal slaughter here." She shook her head and inhaled deeply. "Not only troops, but a small village. Ptolemy's soldiers strangled women and children, then boiled their bodies in cauldrons and ate them."

Mariamme set the half-eaten apple aside, barely able to swallow the bite she had taken.

"Alexander Janneus returned to find those treacherous Pharisees aligned against him. Of course the noble families of the Sadducees backed him. It was the start of six years of civil war here."

"And what of Ptolemy?"

Alexandra waved off the Egyptian ruler like a bothersome fly. "Oh, he was dead by the time our civil war ended. His son, Cleopatra's father, was put on the throne of Egypt. And when he saw which way the war here was going, he understood he could not follow in his father's footsteps."

"Alexander took back Judea?"

She came and retrieved the disc from Mariamme's hand. Her eyebrows lifted and she smiled. "Oh yes. And took his revenge. He was a man who knew how to intimidate his enemies." She turned the two discs over in her palm and her voice was gleeful, triumphant. "I was only a little girl, but I remember it well. He had eight hundred rebels brought here to Jerusalem, forced them to watch as their wives and children had their throats cut, and then crucified the lot of them."

She reached for the ivory beads at Mariamme's throat.

Mariamme drew back as if struck.

Alexandra laughed and pinched Mariamme's arm. "Don't be so sensitive, dear. It was war."

"And what of Egypt? Did he take revenge there as well?"

Alexandra shrugged and regained her seat. "There was no point in it. Cleopatra's father, Ptolemy, was ready for an alliance. His brother had been made king of the island of Cyprus, and Ptolemy knew Cyprus was too close to Judea, too tempting with all that lovely wood for shipbuilding. The two men agreed on a marriage treaty. My grandfather gave the king of Cyprus his daughter to wed."

"His daughter!" Mariamme sat up. "I thought he only had two children—your father and uncle."

"Ah yes. You would think that, since all of the history from that point is about those two bickering brothers. But no, I had an aunt as well, married off at a young age to the king of Cyprus."

Mariamme took it all in, tried to fit the pieces together in her mind, drawing the family lines and intersecting them with those of Egypt. So Cleopatra's uncle had been married to Alexandra's aunt. How strange that she had never known this.

"But you have not told me of the seals, Mother."

Alexandra sighed. "Simply a bit of nostalgia, I suppose. My grandfather gave one to each of his children, your grandfather Hyrcanus and his troublesome brother, who was of course your other grandfather. When your father died and my father was exiled, I inherited them both."

"But Hyrcanus has returned from exile. Does he not wish to have it back?"

Alexandra laughed, without humor. "My father's mind did not return with him. He barely remembers what it means to be a priest."

"What about the daughter—your father's sister? Did she receive a seal as well?"

Her mother shrugged and set the seals on the dressing table. "I suppose. I don't remember what came of her after she was married." She clucked her tongue. "But enough of stories. If you are going to give this family an heir, you should return to your rest."

Was she little more than a brood mare? But her thoughts strayed far away, to Egypt. The possible implications of her mother's story were so astounding, she could not take them in.

A figure at the doorway started forward when she turned.

"Joseph."

Salome's husband-uncle had been watching her carefully

since Herod had been called to face Marc Antony in Syria. Herod must have given him the assignment. Hopefully Herod would not return, and old Joseph would forget.

"My lady, I must request that you return to your bedchamber. Your husband has no wish to see you overtired."

She growled. "My husband cares only about the child I carry, Joseph."

The old man shook his gray head, his watery eyes red-rimmed with age. "How can you say that, dear? I have seen the way he dotes on you. Why, he told me himself that he could never bear to be parted from you, in life or in death!"

Behind her, Alexandra's chair scraped the floor and she circled Mariamme. "What is that supposed to mean?"

Joseph's lips parted slightly at Alexandra's approach.

How could the old fool be afraid of her mother when he was married to a witch like Salome?

"I—He gave clear instructions that Mariamme was to be kept safe in her chamber—"

"Yes?" Clearly there was more, and Alexandra was not going to let it go. "And what else?"

"I am certain he will return and all will be well."

"And if he doesn't?"

Mariamme was standing now, a chill of dread seeping into her bones. After all their talk of Egypt, Joseph's strange words reminded her of the Egyptians' old practice.

"He cannot live without Mariamme, he says. Nor can he die without her. She is to join him in death if he does not return."

Mariamme reached for the back of her chair, but her grasping hand found only empty air. A wave of nausea attacked and her legs trembled.

"What?" Alexandra's shriek bounced from the chamber walls.

Mariamme found her chair at last and sank into it, breath coming in short gasps.

The tedium of her confinement evaporated like a mist. All her life she had been watching a violent play from the safety of the audience, but it was as if the play had suddenly shifted and enveloped her, making her part of the drama, part of the danger.

The Egyptians of old, before the Greek Ptolemies had come to rule, would bury wives and slaves with their dead pharaohs.

Images of Egypt, of Lydia and her pendant, of her mother's unknown aunt married off to Cyprus with Alexander Janneus's seal strung as a pendant around her neck, swam and blurred before her eyes.

Her chair lost its solid feeling, turned to water underneath her, and she melted with it toward the floor.

≈

Lydia awoke early, washed at the jug and basin in the corner of the private chamber she had been given as Mariamme's handmaid, and hurried toward the kitchens. She would venture into the city again today, this time alone, to find Rabbi Phineas who had spoken in the synagogue and ask him questions about the prophet Daniel's writings. She dared a short prayer to the One God that Phineas would look favorably on her even though she was a woman and give her something that would help her find the Chakkiym.

The kitchens were buzzing already, the day's cooking well under way. Even with Herod gone, there were always guests, and even when only the four women—Herod's sister and wife and their mothers—were the only diners, a lavish meal would be spread.

Lydia grabbed some bread from a basket on a side table and

glanced around for Simon. She should explain her absence from their morning work.

She found him in his office chamber, bent over his ever-lengthening lists. "Have you need of me right away this morning, Simon?"

He half turned and raised an eyebrow. "Haven't you arranged it so I am always in need of you, Lydia?"

The tone was teasing, but the words inched closer to that dangerous place between them and her heart skipped over a beat or two.

"I am going into the city for a few things again this morning. I will be back before the midday meal."

He frowned but did not press her for details. "Come, I want to show you something first."

In the courtyard, he pointed upward to a stone lintel above one doorway. A hairline crack had appeared, snaking down toward the frame. "Can you use your clays to repair it?"

Lydia stood on her toes for a better look. "I think we would be better served to have David's men shore it up first. Then I can worry about the cosmetic repair."

"Will you see to it right away, then?"

She glanced at him. "I told you, I am going out—"

"How are we supposed to finish this project, Lydia, if you are always running about the city?"

She said nothing, only cocked her head.

A pair of slaves slowed to observe their conversation, then hurried away when Simon scowled their direction.

He sighed, then shook his head. "Perhaps I do not want to share you with the city. At least go and tell David about the door frame before you go. He is in the storerooms, I believe, seeing about some supplies for the kitchen garden."

"I will find him."

She took to the underground storerooms, wandering past several, her thoughts on Simon's outburst. At times he seemed angry with her, but she sensed the anger was born of some frustration. She felt it herself.

Only a few torches were lit and set in sockets at this early hour, and the murky corridors did not allow her to see far.

The sound of footsteps following turned her around. "David?"

But it was not David who rounded the corner to face her.

A flash of apprehension rooted her to the floor. Why would Salome come to the storerooms?

The king's sister walked toward her slowly, her high cheekbones hollow and sculpted in the flickering torchlight.

"Enjoying your freedom, I hear."

"My lady?"

Salome's lips pursed into an amused smile. "Mariamme has given you a reprieve from her constant neediness, and now you spend your time enjoying the company of men."

"I do not—"

"Riva has told me everything, Lydia. Do not deny it."

Riva. Lydia's teeth clenched against the girl's name.

Salome was circling her now, her sandals scraping against the paving stones, eyeing her up and down like a market purchase.

Lydia raised her chin. She did not need to defend herself to Salome.

A draft of cold air from an unknown source slithered around her feet, and the nearest torch flickered and bent.

Salome's scrutiny was more than that of a noble for a wayward slave.

It was there again, the pressure Lydia had felt in Salome's chamber, suffocating and dark.

She was a curiosity to the woman for some reason. What had she done to create such antagonism?

You bear the scrolls.

The words whispered through her from somewhere outside her mind. The same voice she had heard in the synagogue.

Her heart responded with words of its own. *HaShem, protect me.*

The cold air fled, replaced with the warmth of a dozen torches. Or was the warmth only in her own body?

Whether external or not, Salome felt something. Lydia could see it in her eyes.

Her voice hissed through the corridor. "Who are you, little Egyptian?"

"I am no one. But HaShem knows my name."

Salome drew back as though slapped. Then shot toward Lydia with a raised hand and bared teeth.

Lydia took a step away.

Salome did not follow. She leaned forward, but it was as though her forehead were pressed against a wall. She could go no farther.

Lydia fled down the corridor, into a dark storeroom, then turned to face the door.

The room smelled of wine and grain, and she could make out the dusty shapes of pointed-bottom amphorae leaning against the walls and casks of wheat. The taste of grain was on the air.

Salome appeared in the doorway. Her paint-rimmed eyes shone in the half-light.

A spark of memory exploded in Lydia's mind.

Facing Cleopatra's wrath. Running.

She would not run again.

"What do you want from me, Salome?" Her voice sounded strong, confident.

"I want to understand you." She slid one step into the storeroom. Her hands were curled like talons at her sides. "Perhaps I want to destroy you."

"What have I done to anger you so?"

Salome's head tilted, like an animal examining its prey. "You do not yield."

And then, in the space of one heartbeat, Salome flew at her.

Lydia cried out—a cry to the One God for protection.

Salome fell back, panting. "What. Are. You?" The words were weighted with outrage.

Lydia said nothing.

Salome came at her again.

Again, she spoke the Name over the attack, and again the attack failed.

This time Salome pressed her back against the far wall, her eyes unnaturally wide.

"Lydia?"

Simon's voice.

Lydia exhaled, her shoulders falling.

But Salome was not finished. Seizing the opportunity of distraction, she pounced on Lydia again, tangled her hands in Lydia's hair.

"Lydia!"

Simon rushed in, pulled Salome from her, and tore the two apart.

Salome hissed and scratched like a cornered cat, then eyed them both with eyes so full of malice, it seemed to fill the room.

And then she ran.

Lydia fell into Simon's arms, images, fragments of memory, of being washed ashore after a shipwreck filling her mind. She was facedown in the sand, lungs full of seawater.

≈

Simon clutched Lydia to his chest, his eyes on the doorway in case Salome returned. He would not let that—that *woman* near her again.

"What was that?" He stroked her hair, willing her to slow her breathing.

Another figure appeared at the doorway. Lydia shrieked.

"My lord—"

It was only Mariamme's eunuch, Leodes.

"I was sent to find the queen's maid. The queen has taken ill."

Lydia pulled herself from his grasp, panting. "Where is she?"

"She was carried to her own bedchamber."

"I must go."

Leodes disappeared but Simon grasped her arm. "Lydia—why—?"

"I must go! Salome may find Mariamme next!"

"Then I am coming too." And perhaps he would not leave her alone again.

In Mariamme's chamber, Alexandra sat on her bedside, mopping the queen's forehead with a cool cloth in a gesture of uncharacteristic sympathy. She rose at their entrance and handed Lydia the rag.

"It was only a faint. She had some shocking news."

Simon stayed in the doorway, watched Lydia bend over Mariamme.

The queen's eyes fluttered and her lips twitched with an attempt to smile.

"Sshh, close your eyes and rest, my lady." Lydia turned to Alexandra. "What news?"

Alexandra eyed him where he stood in the doorway, hesitated, then flicked her hand to indicate he should close the door.

He shut it firmly behind him and crossed the room to the women, his concern still focused on Lydia.

"No doubt this is Salome's doing, but we have learned that Herod left instructions. If he is executed by Rome for the murder of my son, then Mariamme is to be killed as well."

Lydia sucked in a shaky breath and Simon shook his head. Unbelievable.

"The man is a fiend, truly." Alexandra's hands were tight fists at her belly. "He is insane with jealousy over Mariamme and determined that no one but him should ever have her."

And did Alexandra regret giving her daughter to such a man? Had she even thought of her own part in the matter? Doubtful.

"We must keep her safe." Lydia smoothed damp hair from Mariamme's brow. "Her and the baby."

Alexandra paced. "Already rumors circulate in the city of Herod's death. My daughter must be removed from the palace before we know for sure." She grasped Mariamme's hand. "It must be immediate, before the baby is born and she cannot travel. And it must be far from here, where Herod's spies will not see."

Mariamme's eyes fluttered again. "Cyprus," she whispered.

Alexandra frowned.

Mariamme gave a little nod. "Cyprus. It is close to Judea, a Roman province now. The weather is fine."

Her mother nodded thoughtfully. "And a short sea voyage, which is necessary at this time of year." She patted Mariamme's hand. "It seems our storytelling this morning has done some good. When the time is right, you will return with an heir. And perhaps Marc Antony can be persuaded to—"

"Stop, Mother." Mariamme struggled to pull herself upright. "I am not going to marry Marc Antony!"

Alexandra's brows were drawn together in fury. "If Herod is not dead now, he will be one day, my dear. You can be assured that your mother is working to see that day."

Mariamme's lips parted. "Mother, what new scheme—?"

She held up a hand. "You need have no concern for that now. We must get you safe."

Lydia leaned in to help her. "How are we to get her to Cyprus, under the nose of Salome who would see her dead and Joseph who has instructions to make it happen?"

Simon stepped forward. "I will help."

The royal women turned to him, as though they had forgotten his presence.

He forced out the words that must be for the best. "But you must take Lydia to Cyprus with you."

"What?" Lydia looked from Mariamme to Simon, a question in her eyes.

"You have fallen under the wrath of Salome as well. And Mariamme will need you when the baby comes."

Lydia looked between them, as though her heart were at war with her mind.

"Yes, yes, Lydia must come." Mariamme was grabbing at her hand, her eyes wide with pleading. "I could not bear to leave alone."

Simon tightened his jaw against the overwhelming urge to take back his suggestion. To keep her here in Jerusalem. How could he let her go?

"It must be tonight." Alexandra was pacing again. "I will distract Joseph."

"Sohemus." Mariamme spoke the name quietly, as though the captain of Herod's guard was a subject off-limits. "Ask Sohemus to help as well. He can occupy Salome. She is often trying to gain his attention."

Alexandra's disapproval was evident, but she could not disagree that the captain would help. "You two"—she pointed to Simon and Lydia—"make up some pretense about having to travel for supplies, some fabrics or paints or some such nonsense. You will leave with a wagon, and we will hide Mariamme."

None of them spoke the obvious. Lydia had told him of the botched escape two months ago. They must ensure that the garrulous cupbearer Mazal was not loitering about to report what he saw.

Alexandra hurried toward the door. "I will write letters. Eudorus in Cyprus will take you in." Her voice drifted away as she opened the door and disappeared into the corridor.

Simon bowed to the queen in her bed. "And I will speak with Sohemus." His glance flicked to Lydia. The pain in her eyes took his breath away. "We will meet later."

He left the room, his words echoing. He meant that they should meet later in the day. But would they meet again after all this was over?

Or was he destined to once again lose the person he had foolishly allowed into his heart?

Twenty-Six

The day passed in a haze.

Belongings stuffed into satchels. Letters written. Crates of clothing for mother and child stowed in the back of a wagon outside the kitchen entrance.

A messenger was dispatched on swift horseback to the coast, to carry a letter to Cyprus. Another to a village six miles south of Jerusalem, where transport would be waiting for Lydia and Mariamme. Simon would get them there, but another would take them to the port of Caesarea and onto a waiting ship.

The journey to Cyprus would take a week. Would the baby wait that long?

In the midst of the confusion, Lydia avoided Simon.

To David, she whispered a few snatches. The muscles in his jaw bulged at the news of Herod's grotesque instructions.

"You must do something for me, David. The scrolls."

His back straightened. "You have found the Chakkiym?"

"No, no, I have not. And I do not know when I will return to Jerusalem. You must keep them for me—"

"No."

Her lips parted at the abrupt refusal. "You must take them to the Temple on the next Yom HaKippurim—"

"I said no." He folded his arms. "It would be an honor, of course, but it is one I will not take. I know what your friend Samuel told you with his dying breath in Egypt, and it is what I have seen since you came to Judea. The mighty hand of the One God is upon your life, and to shirk your duty, to discard your responsibility—it is a refusal in the face of HaShem!"

When had he grown into such a man of conviction and strength? Working under Simon had already changed him, and she could see the influence of the zealot on David's maturing faith.

"David, I know you believe I am somehow special, but aren't the scrolls the most important thing? Getting them into the hands of those who need them, of those who are even now preparing for the Messiah—this is much more important than who becomes the messenger."

He was shaking his head before she finished. She would not dissuade him, she could see it. She stood and paced away from him, then back again. "You leave me no choice, then, David. I must take the scrolls with me. And what if I do not return? What if I never come back to Jerusalem?"

"You will be back. It is your destiny."

"Ach!" She waved a hand. "You are arguing in circles!"

"Perhaps." He shrugged one shoulder, seemingly amused by her frustration. "But I am right."

"Very well. I will take them. And someday I will return."

He nodded once. "How can I help?"

By the time darkness fell, all was ready.

≈

In Mariamme's chamber, Alexandra embraced her daughter stiffly, then pushed her toward the door. "Go. Go quickly. I will see to Joseph."

In the corridor, Mariamme whispered something to Leodes, then gave him a quick kiss on the cheek. The sweet man flushed and nodded, then retained his post as they fled.

Lydia led the way to the lower level, Mariamme trailing. Somewhere in the upper corridors, Sohemus would be attending Salome, making certain that the king's sister did not emerge from her chamber.

Lydia motioned to Mariamme when they reached the courtyard. "We will go through the storerooms, not the kitchens." She led the queen underground, through the maze of rooms that honeycombed under the kitchen complex and then up a narrow set of stairs at the back of the palace. Stairs that opened at a back door used mainly for deliveries during the day.

They bypassed the kitchens and any servants or slaves who might be working. Hopefully their exit had been completely unseen.

A nondescript wagon, splintered and weathered, waited in the street outside the kitchen as arranged. Inside was everything they would need for the journey, including a wooden box in the bottom of a sack that had traveled from Alexandria to Rome, from Masada to Samaria to Jerusalem. Perhaps the scrolls would accompany her to the grave.

The wagon's driver was bundled in a heavy mantle and facing forward.

With whispered apologies, Lydia helped Mariamme into the back of the wagon. Awkward and unbalanced, the queen stumbled into the bed and nearly fell. Lydia jumped into the wagon with her, helped lower her to sitting and then, with more apologies, to a prone position.

"Only a few miles, my lady. We will stop and move you as soon as it is safe."

Mariamme nodded, her bloodless face pale under the cold winter moonlight. She turned on her side and curled inward on herself.

Lydia tried to smile reassuringly, then lifted the blankets over Mariamme.

In the street once more, she glanced with anxiety along the walls of the palace, but they were alone.

Except for David.

He stood outlined in the doorway of the kitchen, and she could not see his expression in the darkness. By the slant of his shoulders he was angry.

She had been strong all day. Had to be strong. She would not falter now.

A quick embrace and she pulled away. But David would have none of it. He clung to her, inhaling deeply.

No, David. Do not cling. There is no use in it.

"I will be back." She had promised the same to Caesarion. Did he watch incoming ships in the Alexandrian harbor for her, or had he forgotten even her name? How long until David forgot?

"Be safe, Lydia."

She pulled away, brittle as an overfired clay pot and just as hollow. She would crack into a thousand pieces if she did not go now. One last squeeze of his hands. A quick smile of good-bye.

Simon still said nothing, did not turn when she climbed to her place beside him on the cold wagon seat.

One flick of the reins and they were off. She did not look back.

Simon was known at the city gates, and it took only a few minutes to clear the wall and roll toward the Kidron Valley. On either side, black hills rose in barren silhouette against the purpled sky. No stars shone tonight. Heavy clouds, ominous in their intent, thickened the air.

Lydia felt every rut and crack that must have bounced against Mariamme's body, as if she were the one lying in the wagon bed. She gritted her teeth against the indignity. After this night, if Lydia could prevent it, Mariamme would never suffer such again.

Lydia counted off the minutes. She would force herself to wait until at least twenty had passed, and then they would rescue Mariamme and place her between them, warm and secure.

Simon shifted in the wagon seat, his arm pressing against hers.

Lydia moved aside, putting space between them.

Neither spoke, for there was nothing to say.

At the bottom of the Kidron Valley, Lydia cleared her throat against the tightness that threatened to choke any speech. "It seems safe to let her out now, yes?"

In response, Simon pulled the horses to the right, then handed the reins to Lydia and jumped from the wagon.

Within a few minutes, Mariamme was in the front of the wagon, sober and shivering.

Lydia wrapped an arm around the queen and pulled her close for warmth. Mariamme's head dropped to Lydia's shoulder.

As the miles rolled by, her occasional sniffling nearly broke Lydia's heart. What new mother ever dreams of being chased from her home on the eve of her child's birth? It was an atrocity, and a hatred for Herod grew in Lydia. A hatred that seemed to deaden her further rather than light a fire inside.

When the lights along the top of Jerusalem's walls extinguished in the distance behind them, Lydia took Mariamme's chilled hand in her own and leaned forward to glance at Simon's hard profile. "How much longer?"

He clucked at the horses, as if she had asked him to hurry. "Bethlehem is six miles. We should reach it within the hour."

Lydia squeezed Mariamme's fingers. "There is an inn there— it's all arranged. We'll stay the night, then in the morning leave before dawn for Caesarea."

The lights of Bethlehem were not to be compared with Jerusalem's but were welcome nonetheless. They rolled toward the village, past fields dotted with sheep pens, along a street of tombs, and into the center of town, an open square surrounded by the typical clusters of workshops and stables, an empty market, and a well-lit building that promised to be the inn they sought.

Lydia felt the pull of warm food, a fire, and a bed, but at the same time the end of this leg of their journey would mean yet another good-bye.

And this one more painful than any she had yet experienced.

No. No, there was no need to feel anything at all if she focused on the task, on Mariamme and what must be done.

Simon helped Mariamme from the wagon, bracing her arms for support and taking her unbalanced weight against himself as she half stepped, half fell to the dusty ground outside the inn.

Lydia pushed ahead and went inside. The warmth of a fire, banked at the side of the front room and glowing cheerfully, welcomed her. She shook off the chill and stamped her numb feet a few times.

At the noise, a woman appeared from the back room, apron askew and flour-covered, with cheeks reddened from the heat and a wide smile.

Lydia nodded once. "A special visitor from Jerusalem." They were the words she had been given to say.

The innkeeper's eyes sparkled as though they shared a secret. "Of course, of course. We have your room all ready. Upstairs we go."

Lydia tried to smile. "Not me. I will bring her in."

Simon was already at the door, Mariamme on his arm.

They stepped into the warm room, and anxiety seemed to roll from Mariamme's shoulders. There was a crease between her eyes and she walked stiffly, her back slightly bent.

Lydia crossed to her, braced her other arm, and between them they followed the innkeeper to the second level, where a room just as warm as the lower waited, a soft-cushioned bed in its center.

With Mariamme settled, Lydia returned downstairs to help Simon bring in the contents of the wagon, which would be transferred to their new transportation in the early morning.

They moved slowly, both of them. In spite of the cold and the late hour and the wearisome trip, to finish the task meant to say good-bye.

Too soon the wagon was empty, its stores piled in the front room of the inn. Lydia placed her own belongings in the corner. She would take them upstairs when she joined Mariamme.

When Simon was gone.

He stood near the door and she near the fire. The innkeeper had disappeared, probably to bed herself as the hour was late.

Lydia raised her hands to the fire's warmth, then rubbed her palms together. Would she ever be warm again?

She could think of nothing to say. What cool words would

effect separation between them, without useless emotion complicating the good-bye?

"We should have asked the innkeeper for something warm to fill your stomach before you leave." She looked toward the back room. "Perhaps I can—"

"I am not hungry."

She did not look at him. Could not.

The parting from David had seemed to mirror the good-bye she had given Caesarion all those years ago, heavy and suffocating. But this—this good-bye felt more like her parting from Samuel—a ripping away that was like death.

But would they not return, someday? If Herod lived, Mariamme would be safe from the executioner, but her hasty flight would give Herod another reason to destroy her. No, it would not be safe for Mariamme until Herod was dead and a new king, who cared nothing for Mariamme, had taken the throne.

Lydia braced her forehead against the mantel above the fire. What king would that be? Doris's young son? If Mariamme gave birth to a boy, her boy would forever be seen as a threat.

But Lydia had the Chakkiym to find. How could she remain outside Jerusalem forever?

"You will be back."

Had Simon heard her thoughts?

She did not turn but felt him cross the room to stand behind her.

The warmth of his hand pressed against her lower back. An intimate gesture, and it should have quickened her pulse, but she felt it as if from a distance, happening to someone else.

Simon turned her to himself, took her cold hands in his own, and lifted them to his mouth to warm them with his breath. Above their clasped hands, his dark eyes were trained on hers.

Her breath caught in her throat and she looked away. Why did he make this more difficult? Was it not better to pretend there was nothing between them, nothing to mourn when it was gone?

For the thousandth time, she chastised herself. *Foolish girl, for letting it come to this.*

"Lydia."

She pulled her hands to her sides, turned back to the fire that did nothing to melt the ice in her heart.

"I will not leave like this, Lydia."

"Like what? What is there to say?" The terse words had an air of annoyance she had not intended. But perhaps it was for the best.

Simon uttered a low growl of frustration and smacked both his hands against the blackened stone wall above the fire. "Like this! This cold parting fitting only for strangers who care nothing for each other!"

Lydia dragged in a breath, shaky but deep. "I . . . I am sorry, Simon. It is all I have."

"Truly?" He whirled on her, circled her waist with a strong arm, and pulled her to him.

The heat of his chest against her own, the feel of his breath against her hair—it burned away her resolve like the sun against the morning fog. But to yield was to feel the separation, and she could not risk the wounding.

His other arm was around her now, his lips pressed to her ear. "Lydia, there are things I must say—"

"Ly—di—a!"

The screech broke them apart like an icy drenching.

She lifted her eyes to the wood beams above them, then shot a glance toward the steps.

"Lydia, come quickly!"

Simon was on her heels as they raced up the narrow wood stairs to the room on the second level.

Mariamme stood in the center of the room, her face even paler than it had been during their journey and the whites of her eyes wide with terror.

Even in the dim light of the tiny terra-cotta oil lamp, the irregular circle of wetness on the floorboards at the queen's feet told Lydia all she needed to know.

Mariamme's labor had begun.

Twenty-Seven

"Fetch the innkeeper, Simon."

Lydia crossed the room on sure feet and guided Mariamme to a hard chair. The queen's arms trembled under her touch.

"Sshh, my lady. All will be well. Have no fear."

The queen blinked once, twice—slowly, as if she had lost her memory of where they were. "My mother, Lydia. I need my mother."

And Alexandra should be here. But that was not to be.

"We are here for you, my lady. You will have all the help you need."

The innkeeper, Hannah, already disheveled from her bed, bustled into the room, tongue clucking. "I knew she had the birthing look about her when I saw her, I did. The babies don't always cooperate, eh?"

Simon hovered in the doorway behind her, his gaze darting from Lydia to Mariamme and a deep crease between his brows.

Lydia gripped Mariamme's shoulder in reassurance and nodded to the innkeeper. "You can find the midwife?"

"Yes, yes, of course." She inclined her head toward Simon. "And your friend here will help me bring in a hard bed." She winked at Mariamme. "Don't you worry, girl. Many a babe has been born in this town, and many more to come. We may not be the big city, but we know how to do it here."

Mariamme was still shaking under Lydia's touch.

The innkeeper sent her husband into the night to bring the midwife, and within minutes she and Simon had set up a firmer bed for the birthing. Hannah covered it with a linen sheet.

The midwife arrived as they were helping Mariamme onto the bed. She clutched a birthing stool by one of its legs and in the other hand carried a large leather pouch, which she laid on the bed at Mariamme's feet. She was old enough to have born her own babies, but not so old that her wits would be dulled. She met Lydia's gaze with a confident one of her own and gave a little smile and nod. She had a long, narrow nose that hooked a bit and a chin that came to a point under narrow lips.

She opened the pouch and began removing items. "More light, Hannah. More light. And warm water."

Hannah disappeared to fetch the required items.

Lydia watched her go, then shifted her attention to Simon. "Nothing for you to do now."

"If you think I'm going back to the city—"

She half smiled. "I will find you downstairs when there is news."

He looked to Mariamme one last time, his expression grave, then nodded and headed for the stairs.

"What is your name, girl?" The midwife was still unloading her pouch—a jug of olive oil, several yellowish sea sponges, strips of wool, and bits of herbs Lydia did not recognize.

Lydia took a step forward. "Mary. Her name is Mary." She put a hand on Mariamme's leg. "And I am Lydia. She . . . she is my sister."

The midwife looked from Lydia to Mariamme, took in the difference in clothing, in coloring, and grunted. "I understand."

What she understood, Lydia could not guess. But she doubted it was the truth, and that was all that mattered.

The woman gently lifted Mariamme's feet and placed them, soles down, on the bed, so her knees jutted above her swollen belly. "I am Naomi. Is this your first birthing, Mary?"

Mariamme nodded, eyes still fearful.

Hannah reappeared, struggling with a jug in one hand and a burning lamp in the other.

Lydia crossed the room, relieved her of the jug, and placed it in a basin already sitting on a low table.

"Now, then." Naomi poured water over her hands, then a little olive oil on her fingers. "Let us see where we are."

Lydia had been present at the start of Cleopatra's birthing of Marc Antony's twins, but when the pains had come hard and fast, the Egyptian queen had banished all but the three midwives in attendance, as if she could not bear for any to see her in a state of weakness.

There would be no such direction here. Mariamme clutched Lydia's hand with a fierceness that came of having only one friend in the room.

Lydia bent to her bedside as the midwife began her examination. "I will stay with you, I promise. I will not leave."

Mariamme turned her head toward Lydia, sought out her face, and a tear ran across her temple and soaked into the linen sheet that covered what was little more than a plank of wood.

Mariamme sucked in a sharp breath at the midwife's probing, her gaze still fixed on Lydia. "This is not how it should be," she whispered.

"No." Lydia smoothed the hair from her forehead. "No, it is not. But this is what we have, and we are going to focus on the good of it." She tried to smile. "We have a warm room, an experienced midwife, and you are healthy and strong."

"Indeed." Naomi stood and wiped her hands with a woolen cloth. "All is well, Mary. The baby is in a good position, and your body will take care of the rest. You must only follow my instructions, which will not be difficult."

Her voice was soothing and quiet, and Lydia felt herself relax a bit under its spell.

"When the time is right, we will move from this bed to the birthing stool." Naomi pointed to the crescent-shaped stool, built with sturdy arms and a backing and a cutaway opening in its base. "Hannah and Lydia will be on either side of you for support, and I will be in front of you. You will watch my face, and I will bring your baby into the world. Do you understand?"

Mariamme nodded. "How long?"

Naomi chuckled. "Why, your pains haven't even begun in earnest, child. You must be patient. It will be a long night."

At first the pains were far apart and weak. In the exhaustion of their palace flight and cold journey, Mariamme dozed.

Lydia had pulled the chair close to the head of the bed, and she rested her own head there, braced on crossed arms. The midwife napped in the softer bed.

But before two hours had passed, Mariamme was awake and whimpering, a sheen of sweat glistening on her forehead as the pain bore down on her.

Lydia winced at Mariamme's crushing grip on her own hand but kept up a steady flow of reassurances and compliments on her courage and strength.

The night wore on, the baby did not come, and Mariamme grew paler, listless between the pains when before she had rested, and the midwife's pleasant chatter turned to choppy instructions. "Prop her upright. Brew these leaves and give her the tea to sip."

Lydia dared not ask if there was trouble, not in front of Mariamme. But she could see it in Naomi's face.

How many died during this, the most violent event of a woman's life?

Lydia mopped Mariamme's brow with a cool cloth and whispered silent prayers over her. Mariamme had suffered already. The One God Lydia was beginning to know would not be so cruel, would He?

And the baby—the baby must be safe as well. After the loss of her brother, the baby's birth was all that kept Mariamme from slipping into despair.

Please, HaShem, do not take Mariamme from me as well.

Was it selfish to pray for her own needs at such a time? And yet, Mariamme was more than mistress, more than queen to her. Once again, Lydia had let someone into her heart, and with that, the possibility of pain.

"Aaaahhh!" Mariamme's shoulders lifted from the bed, hair now loosed and stuck to her skin. "Something has changed!"

Naomi was there in a moment, examining.

Lydia watched the top of her head, waited for news.

"Make it stop!" Mariamme's cry ended in a sob.

Lydia wanted to sob with her. *Please, HaShem.* "Sshh, it can't be long now, my—Mary."

Naomi straightened, her expression serious but not worried. She nodded to Hannah, then inclined her head to the birthing stool. "Your sister is right, Mary. Your womb is open at last. It is time to bring this baby into the world."

Together, Hannah and Lydia helped the weakened woman to the birthing stool, eased her down to it, while the midwife covered herself with an apron, soaked more compresses in warm olive oil, and sat opposite Mariamme. Naomi wrapped thin pieces of cloth around her hands, then waved them toward Hannah and Lydia. "Each of you on a side. You'll support her arms while she bears down."

The rest of the delivery rushed past in a blur of agonized cries and determined groans. The cords of Mariamme's neck stood out like leather whips. The midwife and her conscripted helpers spoke soothing words of encouragement while the laboring mother, like all women before her, swore she would not survive.

In the small space between the pushing, Mariamme panted up at Lydia. "There is something I must tell you."

Lydia cradled Mariamme's arm between her own two arms. "Later, later. There will be time—"

"It is about the pendant. You must know—if I do not live—"

"Hush now!" Naomi's voice cut her off. "I allow none of my patients to speak such nonsense. Look at me, Mary." She waited until Mariamme shifted her breathless attention. "No more talking. You are to focus all your energy on your child now. There is nothing in this world but this. Yourself, and your baby, and my voice. Do you understand?"

Mariamme licked dry lips and nodded, the motion jerky.

"Good. Now push."

Mariamme screamed and she pushed. And in those final

moments, when all was blood and water and salty tears, they were sisters, all of them. No difference in class, no separation in wealth or upbringing or experience could outweigh the sisterhood of childbirth, of bringing life into the world. A secret no man could ever understand but every mother shared.

And Lydia was part of it, she who had yet born no children but knew in that instant when Mariamme gave a final shriek and the baby's warm body slipped into Naomi's cloth-covered hands that she would give all she had for this strange and terrible experience.

The baby's skin was a mottled, chalky gray.

Lydia looked to Naomi in concern. Was this as it should be?

But Naomi was rubbing warmth and life into the skin, clearing the mouth, drying the dark, matted hair.

Mariamme's exhaustion seemed to flee. She leaned forward, sweat running down her neck.

"You have a son, Mary."

Mariamme breathed out a sigh that was at once relief and gratitude and not a little astonishment at what she had accomplished.

Lydia knelt at her side, wrapped an arm around her. "A son, Mariamme. You have a son!"

She realized the slip of name at once—never had she called the queen by her first name, and she certainly should not have done it in front of Naomi and Hannah. But if either noticed the slight difference they did not acknowledge it.

Mariamme leaned her head against Lydia's shoulder, still breathing hard, then looked into Lydia's face. "I could not have done it without you." Her eyes shone with tears. "My sister."

Lydia smiled and kissed the new mother's forehead.

Naomi cleared her throat. She had the boy wrapped now and laid him in his mother's arms for the first time.

And Lydia wept with joy.

Sometime later, after Hannah and Lydia had helped Mariamme to the bed, with fresh blankets beneath and propped cushions, and Naomi was washing up, she spoke softly to Lydia. "If the man waiting downstairs is the baby's father, he'll be anxious for news. It would be safe to bring him up now."

Simon. Lydia had nearly forgotten the poor man, waiting in the front room of the inn all night. Leaving Naomi's implied question unanswered, she hurried down the steps.

Expecting to find him asleep on the floor before the fire, she was surprised to see him standing in the shadows near the door, speaking with someone.

He started forward at once. "We heard the babe's cry. All is well?"

Lydia smiled, then swayed on her feet, suddenly dizzy. "All is well. She has a son."

Simon caught her arm to steady her, and the man in the shadows stepped into the light.

"David!"

His face was grave, not at all what it should be after hearing the good news of the night.

"What is it? What has happened?"

"It is Herod." David glanced at Simon, then back to her. His voice was low, worried. "He is returning."

Twenty-Eight

Lydia's euphoria over the baby's birth drained away, and questions and fear poured into its place in her heart.

What to do now? The three discussed the possibilities in hushed tones.

Mariamme and the baby could not set out on the weeklong journey to Cyprus anytime soon. She could recover here in Bethlehem, until she was strong enough to travel.

But there was another possibility.

David had left on a swift horse as soon as word had been sent ahead of the royal traveling party. Alexandra had sent him, with promises to keep Mariamme's absence unknown to Herod until David should return with news.

If they could get Mariamme back into the palace before Herod realized she had fled, would she not be safe? Herod's return from Syria meant Joseph's orders to kill Mariamme would not be carried out. The only reason he would have to come against her now was the very flight she had undertaken to save herself.

It did not take long to decide what they thought best. Lydia left the two men downstairs and ran up to speak with Mariamme. Naomi and Hannah were occupied with cleaning the room and putting away supplies. Mariamme still held the baby in sleepy contentment.

Lydia hated to disturb such sweet peace. But there was no avoiding it. She sat on the edge of Mariamme's bed, leaned close to her ear, and whispered the news. Even without seeing Mariamme's face, she felt the tension jolt through the queen.

She sat back and let Mariamme think through the options Lydia had outlined.

Mariamme snuggled the baby closer, then ran a gentle finger over his cheek. "We would have to leave immediately," she whispered. "Make that cold, rough journey back to the palace."

"Yes, my lady."

Mariamme inhaled deeply, then nodded. "Send David back. Have him tell my mother about the baby. She can tell Herod that my labor has begun and he is not to disturb me until the baby is born. That will give us some time."

Lydia stood, smiled, and squeezed Mariamme's hand, and the queen returned the grasp.

"And, Lydia?" Mariamme indicated that she should bend close for another whispered word.

Lydia leaned in, as though to get a closer look at the baby.

"When we are alone, you will call me nothing but Mariamme." She grinned. "Or perhaps just Mary."

In response, Lydia kissed her on the forehead once more.

Downstairs, she gave David Mariamme's instructions, and she and Simon followed him outside into the darkness, which was beginning to lift at the eastern edge of the town. Moments later he was galloping toward Jerusalem, with the two of them watching the dust kicked into clouds behind the horse's hooves.

In the silence of David's leaving, Lydia wrapped her arms around herself. She and Simon had not been alone since last night, when things were almost said, were nearly admitted.

But now there was no need. There would be no parting.

She felt a strange disappointment, not with the canceled escape, but at the words that would not be said. "I should get Mariamme prepared for the journey."

Simon sniffed and cleared his throat. "I will take the queen home. But you should not return."

"I go where the queen goes!"

He turned on her, his eyes intense, pained. "Lydia, you forget that I saw Salome in the storerooms with you. Heard what she said. You are in as much danger as Mariamme ever was, and that has not changed."

Lydia huffed and looked northward, to where David had disappeared. "It is ludicrous. I am nothing more than a lady's maid. She has no reason to see me as an enemy."

"Salome is evil, Lydia. And you are not." He took up her hand in his own. "She sees your goodness, that you bring it wherever you go. And it angers her."

Lydia shook her head. "I have done nothing—"

"I did not say it makes sense. But I know what I saw. And you are not safe in that palace."

She thought of telling him about the scrolls. Of the "destiny" Samuel had prophesied over her. But Simon would think her deluded or self-important. And he was a man more committed to action than prophecy.

She smiled up at him, a smile of gratitude for his concern. "I am coming to believe that the One God will keep me safe, Simon, if that is what He wills. But I will not leave the queen."

Painful as it was to disturb Mariamme and the baby from their cocoon of safety and warmth, within the hour the wagon was reloaded, soft bedding placed in the back, and mother and child ensconced in as much warmth as they could manage. Hannah heated oil and filled bladders to be tucked around them.

Lydia had been given ample funds to repay Hannah and Naomi for their efforts, which the two women accepted gratefully, but neither one was pleased with the hasty departure. Wise enough to ask no questions, they simply wished the traveling party well and waved a good-bye as the wagon set off for Jerusalem.

The two-hour ride back to the palace was as cold, rutted, and fearful as their escape the night before. Simon urged the horses as quickly as he dared with the precious cargo in the back, and none of them spoke much. They reached the city gate at midmorning, with Mariamme covered again in the back of the wagon. She had exchanged her royal robes for a plain tunic donated by Hannah, but her face might still be recognized.

Simon got them through the gates without incident, to the kitchen entrance of the palace, in a strange reversal of last night's flight.

David waited at the door, nodded once, and beckoned them inward.

Lydia helped Mariamme as best she could to struggle from the wagon and walk slowly into the palace and down the steps to the storeroom chambers.

Once on the lower level, she took the baby from Mariamme. Simon swept Mariamme into his arms and carried her through the storerooms, then up the staircase that opened into the court-yard. David ran ahead, then returned to signal.

It had taken only minutes, and it did not appear that they had been spotted by anyone, miraculously.

They entered Mariamme's bedchamber as a group.

Alexandra jumped from a chair, rushed forward, and laid a hand on Mariamme's pale cheek. "Oh, my daughter, what a terrible time you have had." And then her attention was all for the baby.

Mariamme was set up in the bed, the baby returned to her arms, and the conspirators stood back and breathed.

Had they really accomplished it?

$\approx$

Marc Antony had sent Herod back from Syria with nothing more than a shrug and a grin. The Roman had ordered the death of members of his own family—it was an expedient way to handle power, he said. Why should he interfere when Herod did the same?

In the days that followed, Herod seemed taken only with the appearance of his son, and no whispered gossip betrayed them. Alexandra's vague promise that she was working to accomplish Herod's death was not mentioned among them.

Mariamme wanted to name the baby Aristobulus. Herod would not even consider it. Perhaps he feared what sort of loyalty the little namesake might provoke among the people, coming so soon after the drowning of the young High Priest.

No, he was to be Alexander, like his father and great-grandfather before him.

Lydia saw little of Salome, but the woman seemed particu-larly displeased with the turn of events. A Hasmonean son was not good news.

Within a week, somehow Herod learned of Joseph's slip—that he had told Mariamme of Herod's lethal instructions. Perhaps emboldened by Marc Antony's apathy over the death of Aristobulus, Herod seemed to think it prudent to have old Joseph executed. And Alexandra was to be kept under stricter guard—a house arrest for the queen's scheming mother.

News of the royal family hanging still buzzed in the streets the morning Lydia finally ventured into the city again to find Phineas and Ephraim, the old rabbis she had met in the synagogue, and ask them about the Chakkiym.

After a few well-placed questions, she found them in the Valley Gate, still arguing and discussing the Law. She took a seat among their listeners.

Their current conversation was about Hyrcanus, Alexandra's father and the former High Priest who had been given duties by a placating Herod but whose infirmities made him a mockery in the Temple. The rabbis seemed angry, but from what she had seen, she felt only pity for the old man.

She waited through the morning until most had drifted away before inching closer and venturing her first question about the writings of Daniel.

They seemed surprised at such a question from a woman and gave her vague and general answers. Yes, the writings were sacred with prophecies for the end of days and the Messiah to come. When would He come? It would be soon. The prophesied era was upon them, the years decreed from the end of exile until Messiah's appearance had all but elapsed. They looked for Him to appear any day now and free them from tyranny.

Did they have all of Daniel's writings intact, she asked, or were some sealed and then lost? Well, perhaps. Perhaps not.

Lydia sighed with frustration, then blurted out the question she had planned to make more subtle. "And what of the Chakkiym? Charged to guard the sealed writings of Daniel until the end?"

At this, heads jerked her direction, eyes narrowed, shoulders hunched.

"What does a servant girl know of such things?" Ephraim asked.

"I am only trying to learn as much as I can. I would very much like to speak with one of these—"

"Foolish tales." Ephraim fluttered his fingers in dismissal. "Told by fanciful old women to their sons in hopes that some secret knowledge will be our deliverance. There is nothing to these tales."

Lydia eyed Phineas, and though he did not appear to agree with Ephraim, nevertheless his eyes were hard and angry. She would learn nothing there.

She returned to the palace on slow feet. Where to go from here? Would she have no other recourse but to wait another six months for the next Yom HaKippurim?

The idea offered some measure of relief. She was tired. Tired of trying and of waiting and of feeling this constant pressure to live up to the expectations of a man no longer alive. What would it be like to simply forget the scrolls for months and then only do her duty on that one day each year?

She trudged through the palace's great arch into the central courtyard, humming with servants crisscrossing its mosaic floors and tending to the myriad flowers and trees. Was there more activity than usual?

She stopped a young slave, a Gaul, if she remembered correctly. "Are we to have important visitors?"

He nodded, eyes wide. "Visitors from Egypt. Cleopatra is coming!"

≈

The smaller of the palace courtyards, used exclusively for private family gatherings, was empty at this late hour, but the enormous iron brazier in the center still blazed, its flames only beginning to settle to black-orange embers under the chips of fuel.

Lydia leaned against the coolness of a nearby marble column, warmed enough by the fire to remain in spite of the winter air. She had wrapped a woolen mantle around her shoulders to stave off the chill. She needed to be alone.

Her eyes fluttered and closed in the drowsy warmth of the brazier, and her mind floated over facts and feelings like a butterfly flitting over a multitude of blooms.

Cleopatra would arrive by morning. Would she remember her anger toward Lydia? Would she remember Lydia at all? Most important, would Caesarion be with her?

The scrolls remained hidden in her chamber. Did she have any further responsibility to seek out the Chakkiym between the yearly holidays? Would HaShem protect her still from Salome when Lydia had done nothing for Him? Passages from Samuel's teachings returned to her. Of a God who would be her refuge and fortress, her Father. She had never had a father, and she sorely needed a refuge.

"You are exhausted."

She lifted her head from the column and searched the shadows of the courtyard for the familiar voice.

Simon emerged with a smile that looked more like pity.

"You have been attending the queen and her son at all hours. Why do you not leave it to the nursemaid?"

Lydia turned back to the fire and rested her head against the column again. "I need to be useful."

He laughed and came to stand in front of the fire, warming his hands. "This I know." He turned to her. "But it's more than fatigue. There is something else. Something around your eyes." He took a step closer. "Is it Cleopatra? Are you worried about her arrival?"

Lydia shrugged. "I did not leave under the best of circumstances. But it has been five years. She may not even remember me."

"Oh, I doubt that. You are somewhat unforgettable."

The compliment warmed her from the inside and she smiled.

"Even your smile is sad, Lydia. Tell me what is hurting you tonight."

She sighed. "I don't know. Dark memories of the past, I suppose. Thoughts of the future, which is not much brighter."

He was beside her now, leaning one shoulder against her column, close enough for her to feel the heat of his body. "Why not? What is it you want for your future that you cannot have?"

"To be needed. To belong."

"Do you not have both here in the palace?"

"Yes. Yes, you are right. I am just being—"

"No, you are not. But you are not telling the entire truth, Lydia. You want to be needed. You feel worthless unless people value you for what you can do for them. You try to remain distant, but no one can help loving you. And despite what you think, you are wonderfully able to love others. You want others to need you, but you refuse to need anyone else. Why?"

"Because it never lasts. People leave."

"What people?"

"Everyone. My parents. Before they even had a chance to

know me, they discarded me. Samuel. Caesarion. And—" The words choked in her throat.

"Who, Lydia? Who else?" He didn't touch her, didn't come any closer, but it felt as though he were inside her mind. "The one who drowned?"

The breath rushed out of her lungs, and her body sagged against the stone.

Simon's words were a whisper in the night air. "Tell me of him. Please."

She pushed herself away from the column and crossed to a bench on the other side of the brazier, still close enough to keep warm.

He joined her on the bench. "I know what it is to have lost, Lydia." He stared into the fire. "There was someone—a woman—once."

Lydia held her breath, wanting to hear it, yet not wanting to.

"I loved her. That love, it took my focus from the fight, the importance of our cause. She thought she could stand against Herod with only the strength of her convictions, and I was too distracted to see what was happening. When Herod came through Galilee years ago, she was cut down like nothing more than field grass." His voice thickened, and he said no more.

"And that was when you joined Herod, to work against him from within?" She kept her voice low, glancing to the shadows.

"We needed someone who could get information. I volunteered. And I promised not to forget, not to be a fool again. That is why it is so hard . . ." But he left off and looked away.

Lydia took a shaky breath. He had given her his story, his secrets. It was time for her own.

"He was Cleopatra's younger brother. His name was Ptolemy,

of course. All of them carried the same name." To speak his name seemed to release something in her heart. "I was abandoned as a baby in the palace, raised by the staff there. Ptolemy was five years older than I, but we were playmates. He was allowed to roam free until he was twelve and named coregent with Cleopatra. I followed him everywhere, and he never shooed me off."

"He sounds kind. Not what I would expect."

"I am not sure he was especially kind. But we did have fun together, and I loved him."

"What happened?"

"By the time he was sixteen, he and Cleopatra were at odds, fighting over the throne. Julius Caesar came to Egypt and took her side, and after the war in Alexandria, Ptolemy escaped with his troops, planning to regroup and return."

She paused, as the story was wearing her out. But she would finish it.

Simon seemed to sense she needed time and did not interrupt.

"I followed them."

"The troops?"

"Yes. I snuck onto the boat they were taking across the Nile. Halfway across the river, I showed myself to him, declared my undying loyalty."

"And you were—eleven years old?"

She nodded, studying her hands twisting in her lap. "He was so angry. Told me that a warship was no place for a girl, that I would only cause problems."

"But I would wager you were no ordinary girl, even then."

"I was a fool, and it cost him his life."

Simon wrapped her restless hands in one of his own.

"Something went wrong with the boat. I don't know. But it sank. We were too far from shore. I could not swim. He tried to save me." She broke free of Simon's hand and covered her face, finding it wet with tears. "I thought we would both drown, but in the end, somehow, it was only him on the bottom of the Nile. His men dove and dove, but when they found him, it was far too late."

"Oh, Lydia."

Simon's arm was around her shoulder now, and she hated herself for sinking into his embrace.

"It was not your fault."

"I can still feel it sometimes, that feeling of drowning—of my chest so tight, without air, without hope."

"So you had no parents, and you had lost the closest thing to a brother you had found. You have told me of Samuel and of Caesarion. It seems you continued to create family around you—a father and a younger brother. And both of them were taken from you as well."

She did not have the strength to agree. But spelled out like that, it was a sad life, indeed.

"And now others have grown to love you—you have found a sister in Mariamme and a brother in David, but you are too fearful to truly embrace either one, for fear you will again be abandoned or rejected."

She sighed again. "I suppose that is true."

"And me?"

She tensed within his embrace. "You?"

"If I have grown to love you, will you keep me at arm's length as well?"

She pulled away, studied his face. "You—I—we cannot be—"

He pounded the bench with a fist. "I know this! I have thought of little else. It is not only our positions, it is my duty. To focus on the rebellion, to leave off thoughts of my own happiness." He took up her hands in his own. "But I do not care, Lydia." His voice had grown desperate. "I will leave the palace, take a job somewhere else, if it means—"

"I cannot leave Mariamme. She needs me."

"I need you."

She pulled from his grasp and stood, shaking her head. "No, no, you only think that because I am the only person in the palace who likes you."

His eyes registered pain and he looked away. But then brought his attention back to her. "You speak the truth. I do not worry constantly what people think of me, as you do. I do not revolve my life around pleasing them, making them love me and need me. I am here for other reasons. And I suppose their dislike is well founded."

"No." Lydia bent to kneel before him, regretting her harsh words. "No, you simply don't let people know you. Everything you do comes from a place of integrity and passion. I love that about you."

"But you love your position with Mariamme more."

Did she? Did she truly want to live out her days in this palace, become an old woman serving an old queen with no family of her own? She thought of the baby, of Alexander's soft skin, his sweet smell, and the feel of his warmth pressed to her chest.

And what of her art? There would be little time for it in a life of service. Would she rather leave the palace and have the freedom to create in the way her heart longed?

The ground grew cold and she stood, with Simon still seated in front of her.

Did he sense the shift in her thoughts? Was it visible in her eyes?

His lips parted and he rose slowly, until his forehead was leaning against her own.

"No," she said. "No, I do not love my position with Mariamme more."

It was all the encouragement he needed.

His arm shot around her waist and pulled her in until they melted together. One hand was behind her head, tangled in her hair.

They had kissed once in a courtyard in Jericho. Well, twice, really.

Tonight's kiss was nothing like those.

Warm enough to set her pulse racing, deep enough to make promises, long enough to make her forget the past. She reveled in the sense of coming home that was Simon and let her heart open to the future and its breathtaking possibilities.

She pulled away at last, laughing and glancing around. "Someone will see us."

He kissed her eyelids, her forehead. "I don't care." The words were muffled against her skin.

They sat again in the dying light of the brazier and talked of his dream of a free Israel that would be their future, until it grew late and far too cold.

He kissed her again before they parted, erasing all her doubt. It could not matter that she was lady's maid to the queen and he was palace manager. If their positions kept them apart, they would simply walk away. Like he did for the palace and the orphans who lived with Jonah and Esther, Simon protected and provided for everyone. She needed him more than she had needed anyone, but it did not frighten her. She belonged with Simon.

She wandered slowly from the inner courtyard, through the palace corridors, to the front courtyard, barely noticing her surroundings. What were shadows and cold when her heart was warm and bright? She had not believed she could be so happy. Perhaps HaShem was pleased with her efforts after all.

The scrape of sandal on stone arrested her attention in the main courtyard. A young boy had wandered through the palace arch. He caught sight of her and strode toward her.

"A letter for the queen." He waved a small scroll.

She extended her hand. "I am her lady's maid. I will take it."

He seemed reluctant at first, but she clucked her tongue. "Come now, it is cold. I will deliver it at once, if she is still awake."

He made his delivery and disappeared, and Lydia crossed to the stairs. Did the letter pertain to Cleopatra's visit tomorrow? Perhaps she wrote to cancel. That would make the evening perfect.

She tiptoed to Mariamme's chamber and met Leodes at the door. He gave her a friendly wink and opened the door for her.

The new mother was awake and bent over Alexander's little bed. "Come in, Lydia."

"A message for you. Just arrived."

Mariamme frowned and took the scroll, glanced at the seal, then broke it open.

Lydia turned to go.

"Stay, Lydia. Perhaps it is about Cleopatra. I know you are concerned."

Lydia waited while Mariamme scanned the contents of the letter, but it did not appear to be good news of a cancellation. Instead, Mariamme's face paled even in the dim lamplight, and when she set the letter aside, it was with a deep breath and a determined look.

"Sit down, Lydia." She indicated a chair. "I have some things to tell you."

Twenty-Nine

Cleopatra Philopator, Queen of the Two Lands of Upper and Lower Egypt, was sick of Judea.

After nearly a week traveling southward from Syria, where she had left Antony still fighting his precious Parthians, the landscape had grown wearisome and her patience stretched taut. She came to examine her holdings and find a way to expand. If only it had been to fulfill her long-held desire to kill Herod. But alas, Antony's affections were too fickle to risk his anger over the death of a friend.

She rode alone in the finest chariot Antony could procure for her from his Roman contacts in Syria. The rest of her traveling party consisted of servants, slaves, and a few advisers who were always hanging on wherever she went. And her cook, of course. She would not travel without her personal cook. It was neither palatable nor safe to eat foreigners' food. Poisons were too easily disguised.

The hills along the western side of the Jordan River rolled past, but it was the dust, always the dust, that met her in the chariot. She took another swig of watered wine from an amphora stashed in the corner of her seat. She would be drunk by the time she reached Jericho for all this wretched dust.

She had left Caesarion and the twins in Egypt, and strange as it sounded even to her, she missed them. Caesarion had grown into a fine young man, one who could someday take the reins of both Rome and Egypt, should he ever be given his birthright. And if not, her son with Antony, Alexander Helios, would be another likely candidate.

In the meantime, she needed only to keep Antony's affections trained more on her than on Rome, a task that had been difficult the past two years as he insisted on moving with his troops. She needed to get him back to Egypt, where she could woo him with the extravagant Eastern lifestyle these staid Romans secretly craved.

She angled forward in the chariot and thrust a hand out the open side, waving for someone, anyone, to attend her.

A Nubian slave trotted to the side of the chariot. "Yes, Pharaoh?"

"Bring Anneas."

"Yes, Pharaoh."

The Nubian disappeared and she sat back, watching the Jordan River as it slid past. Water typically calmed her. Why did her nerves feel as taut as the reins of a stallion held in check?

Anneas was in the chariot in a moment, a bit breathless but smiling obsequiously. "You wanted me, my queen?"

He was a skinny man the age of her father, with a high-pitched whine of a voice, but he had served her well enough as adviser these past few years.

She pointed to the sheaf of papyrus scrolls tucked under his arm. "You brought the records?"

"Yes, yes. I assumed you would want to go over your holdings before we reached Jericho." He set the pile beside him on the seat opposite her and began unrolling the first.

She gazed out the chariot opening once more. Yes, Antony had given her enough of the wealth of Judea to fill a half-dozen scrolls. And while she loved the money, it was the *land* she wanted. Had always wanted. To restore the glory of the Ptolemaic kingdom was her greatest ambition, and she would see it fulfilled in her lifetime, even before one of her sons took the throne in Rome from that young pretender Octavian.

Octavian. She hated him nearly as much as she hated Herod. His miserable influence with the Senate, pouring poison into their ears with accusations of Antony being used by the Egyptian whore. Despite their supposed alliance, Octavian would love nothing more than to see her lover fall out of favor with Rome, even while he was off fighting their wars!

"My lady?"

Anneas's nasal whine brought her attention back to the chariot.

"Shall I begin again?"

She sighed. "Yes, Anneas. Begin again. And begin with the date-palms. They are my favorite."

Indeed, it was the sunset streaming across the date-palms of Jericho that finally eased her aggravation, hours later. At last, at last she would have a decent bath and a generous meal and a soft bed.

As for the dinner company, she had plans for Herod.

The palace loomed on the horizon, more stately and far-flung than she had imagined. "Herod has a talent for building, it would seem," she said to Anneas.

"Hmm. Apparently his workforce can barely keep up. Jericho,

293

Masada, Jerusalem. They are saying he even has plans to expand and rebuild the Jews' Temple to their One God."

Cleopatra laughed. "Why would he do such a thing? Forced conversion hardly makes for religious fervor."

Anneas shrugged.

"Well, his flair for luxury will serve us well tonight, Anneas."

The sun had dropped below the horizon by the time they reached the palace, and in the purpling twilight Cleopatra peered from the chariot. Why had the slaves who had been sent ahead not roused a welcoming party? No torches, no servants waiting to greet and unload. The front gardens of the palace lay in winter neglect, and the massive double arch at the entrance was nearly dark.

Two of her own met them at the front wall, their bare chests and white skirts dull in the gloom.

Anneas jumped from the chariot to speak with them, then returned a moment later, his chin tucked against his chest, eyes focused on the chariot's floorboards. "He is not here."

A jolt of pure hatred flowed through her veins. "What!"

Anneas swallowed, still studying the floor. "He is in Jerusalem."

"But I sent word! Did he not—?"

"Yes, he received it. The palace staff has a letter for you from Herod. Inside."

Cleopatra breathed slowly through clenched teeth, but the effort did little to calm her rage. How dare he? "Inside, then. Let us hear what the mighty king of Judea has to say."

The chariot rolled through the gate in the wall, along the bare and drooping gardens' edge, to the double arch. Anneas helped her from the chariot, and she entered the palace with all the dignity she could muster, even if only slaves saw it.

Three female slaves waited inside, one of whom took her mantle, one who put a cup of warmed wine into her hands, and another who led her into the courtyard, where at least a few torches had been lit. Somehow the promised letter ended up in Anneas's hands, and he held it to her tentatively, as if she might bite his hand.

She tore it open, blood pounding in her ears.

> *My dearest Cleopatra,*
>
> *I regret that it was inconvenient for me to attend you and your much-anticipated visit in Jericho. My wife has just given birth and it was necessary for me to remain here. Please take your ease in my magnificent palace, examine the plantations Antony has so gener-ously lent you, then make your way to Jerusalem for an audience in my throne room.*

She crumpled the letter and tossed it to the ground with a curse. One of the slaves hurried to pick it up and Cleopatra kicked her. She fell without a sound, then crawled away.

Herod's words dripped with condescension and arrogance. *Lent me?* Antony had given her Jericho's dates and balsam as a down payment on her future rule of this near wasteland.

She would kill him.

Never mind Antony. Somehow she would find a way to see Herod dead.

This latest rejection was as much a slap in her face as the night he had tossed her from his bedchamber like a slave girl who failed to satisfy.

Not even the great Julius Caesar nor Marc Antony himself had treated her thus.

"My lady—"

"What, Anneas? Will you tell me that I am a fool for thinking Herod would show anything but contempt? Fine, then I am a fool." Her face flushed like an embarrassed adolescent and she cursed again. Anneas backed away, bowing.

She took a deep breath and glanced at her surroundings. Magnificent palace—ha! How could a man who had seen the splendor that was Egypt make such an exaggerated claim?

Well, she would make the best of it. Wash the journey dust from her body, sleep for the night in his finest rooms, and examine her wealth in the morning.

And then she would go to Jerusalem.

She would have to play him with all the intelligence she had been born with, for he was a clever adversary. But she *would* play him, make no mistake. She had not come so far, seen so many rivals dead at her feet, to be bested by an Arab with a tiny, dusty kingdom.

She and Herod had business to finish.

Thirty

I have a story to tell you, Lydia."

Lydia sank into the chair Mariamme indicated, a flutter running along her nerves.

"What do you know of Cleopatra's grandfather, the ninth Ptolemy to rule?"

Lydia blinked. It was a strange beginning. "Little, my lady."

Mariamme frowned at the title.

Lydia smiled and ducked her head. "Very little. He was dead more than twenty years when I was born, I believe."

"And when *were* you born?"

"In the last year of the twelfth Ptolemy's first reign— Cleopatra's father—just before he was exiled to Rome."

Mariamme closed her eyes briefly, as if this information brought pain. "And do you know why he was exiled?"

Such strange questions. It was like her early tutoring with Samuel, though he'd been more interested in Jewish history.

"Rome took over the Egyptian-ruled island of Cyprus, where his brother was king, and Cleopatra's father did nothing to stop it. The Egyptians were angry and rebelled. He fled to Rome for protection."

"And what of Ptolemy's brother, king of Cyprus?"

Lydia studied the floor, tried to remember, then shook her head. "I remember nothing of him. Perhaps the Romans killed him? It would have been the same year I was born."

Mariamme was watching her carefully. Did she think Lydia was holding back some buried knowledge?

Mariamme seemed to make some sort of decision. "He took his own life, it would seem. He could not bear the shame of Roman annexation and wanted to die a king."

"How sad."

"He had a wife. Did you know of her?"

Lydia shook her head. "As I said, my knowledge is very limited—"

"She was the daughter of Alexander Janneus."

Lydia frowned. "Daughter? Your mother's aunt, then?"

"And my father's aunt, since my parents were the children of brothers."

"Strange. A connection between Judea and Egypt I never knew."

"Shira was with child when her husband took his life. She feared for the safety of her child, and so she fled to Egypt, to Alexandria, hoping for protection against Rome."

Lydia sighed. "Alexandria was not a place for protection in those days, I fear. Cleopatra's sister Berenice had taken her father's throne while he was exiled in Rome, and she was killing anyone who might wrest it from her, including her own mother."

"Yes. And Berenice had Shira killed as well."

"The history of the Ptolemies is much the same story, both before and after."

"My great-grandfather Alexander Janneus gave his royal seal, embossed into bronze discs, to all three of his children—my two fighting grandfathers and their sister, Shira. Hers was made into a pendant."

A strange coldness flooded through Lydia. Had the tapestries at the window been opened? Her attention drifted to the window, but they were intact.

"Are you hearing me, Lydia? Do you understand? The daughter of Alexander Janneus, married to the king of Cyprus, wore the pendant you now wear. She was killed by Berenice in Alexandria, and the child she carried was thought dead in her womb."

Lydia watched Mariamme's lips moving and somehow watched even her own self, as though she stood apart or perhaps floated above, like a spectator in the theater. A terra-cotta oil lamp flickered at some stray draft and threatened to go out. Mariamme's elegant perfume, a scent that had always marked her as royalty in Lydia's mind, was heavy in the air. She tried to focus on Mariamme's smooth voice.

She saw Mariamme stand and move to where she sat, fixed in her chair. Saw the reddish-brown hair, loosed at this late hour, hang about her shoulders as she bent her head to Lydia's. "I believe you are that child, Lydia. I believe you are the child of a Ptolemaic king and a Judean princess. You are my mother's cousin."

Lydia's cold fingers went to the string at her neck, pulled the pendant from under her tunic, clutched it inside a fist pressed against her chest.

All those childhood fancies. Daydreams of being a lost princess, torn from royal parents who still searched the world for their beloved child . . .

If it was true—if Mariamme's mad supposition was true—then they had never searched for her. They had been dead at her birth.

But while they had never searched for her as they did in her fantasies, the reality she had believed was also untrue. She had not been abandoned. Not rejected, tossed away as worthless by the very ones who should have valued her most.

The room swam and blurred. She clutched at the pendant as if it were an anchor.

Mariamme was on her knees, forcing a cup to Lydia's lips. "Drink this, Lydia. Focus on my voice."

She took a sip of the wine, studied Mariamme's sympathetic eyes, her cerulean-blue robes, the elegant curve of her neck. This was what it looked like to be a princess. Lydia was no princess.

She stood on shaky feet, needing to move, to pace.

Mariamme took the chair she vacated and did not force more questions.

Suddenly warm, Lydia went to the window, parted the tapestries, and slipped between them.

Alone in a cocoon, she looked over the city and the night sky. The winter air revived her, and she slipped the pendant from her neck and held it to the window, where a bit of moonlight filtered down.

The bronze seal was worn, but the sheaf of wheat and crown were visible. She ran a finger over its embossing. What was it Samuel had said about Cyprus as he lay dying? She could not remember. He had known, though. Samuel had known the truth and kept it from her.

She grew chilled and pulled the tapestry around her body.

She was lost, lost and confused in what could not be true,

and yet she knew it was. The truth changed not only her present circumstances, but it changed everything she had known, everything she had believed about herself. It was like knowing your life as a story, then having the first few pages ripped out and replaced.

The dizzy bewilderment swept her again, and she wrapped the tapestry tighter.

Yes, it was disorienting. But wasn't it also like being swept into the embrace of a stranger you have somehow always known?

Lydia put the pendant to her lips.

Her mother.

Giving her life in protection of her unborn child. Never getting the chance to hold that child, to love her.

But she would have loved me.

The shakiness of her limbs, her chest, grew and grew until Lydia realized she was crying.

Not merely quiet tears of release. Great sobs wracked her body, tears dripped from her chin, and her legs felt too weak to hold her upright as she wept for the mother she had never known, the mother she had condemned for abandoning her.

Mariamme slipped between the tapestries, pulled Lydia into an embrace, and whispered against her hair, "Cousin, yes. But sister first and always. You will never be without family again."

Lydia bent her forehead to the queen's shoulder as her sobs subsided, her heart hollowed out and yet filled for the first time in her life.

≈

Lydia sat on the lip of Mariamme's window, but the night had long ago fled. The warmth of a late-winter sun on her face and the tapestry at her back kept her from seeking shelter within the chamber, which was as far as Mariamme would let her go.

Not that she was Mariamme's servant any longer.

A bit of the shock had dissipated during the long night, while she and Mariamme lay side by side like sisters and talked of what all this meant. But Lydia was no closer to knowing that answer this morning.

She was a Ptolemy and a Jew and of royal blood. Both Alexandra and Cleopatra were her first cousins. But what did it *mean*?

Since the synagogue with Simon, she had been opening herself more to the Jews' One God. Remembering Samuel's teachings— that He was not a god like those of the Greeks and Romans, who cared only for their own pleasure and demanded worship and sacrifice in exchange for blessing. The Jews' One God wanted to know and protect her, to be Father to her. Was He truly *her* God now?

There was only one truth she knew as a certainty, and this she had not shared, not even with Mariamme.

Royal daughters did not get involved with palace managers.

Outside the tapestry, she heard Mariamme call her name.

"There you are." The queen smiled. "If you keep hanging about that window, I am going to start believing you wish to escape."

Lydia emerged from hiding and stood. "Did you speak with him?"

"They are in the throne room. He has put off all business and is ready to speak with us. My mother is there as well."

Lydia smoothed her plain servant's tunic. "I am sure Cleopatra is not pleased to be neglected."

Mariamme waved a hand. "She could use a few more days

of it, if you ask me. Stomping around as though it's her palace. Demanding that her own cook be allowed to take over our kitchens."

Lydia straightened, a flush of excitement running through her. "Banafrit? Has she brought Banafrit with her?"

Mariamme shrugged. "That may have been the name. Large woman, with cheeks like pink puffed pastries."

Lydia laughed and clapped her hands. "Yes, that is Banafrit!" A friendly face from home. She started forward. "I must go and greet—"

"Lydia." Disapproval edged Mariamme's voice. "You are expected in the throne room, not the kitchens."

Lydia winced. It was a distinction likely to be important now.

She inhaled a deep breath of courage and nodded. "I am ready."

They had decided in the late hours of the night that the truth of Lydia's identity should not be kept hidden from Herod, though the news would be given privately, without Cleopatra's knowledge. The Egyptian queen's constant attempts to seize Judea for herself were a source of national aggravation, and no one would have any desire to share a possible asset that Judea had suddenly gained.

In the throne room, Herod lounged on the throne and Alexandra sat in a chair nearby, a servant bent to her with a platter of figs, which she was waving away. Sohemus stood behind her, as though ready to strike her down for any misstep.

She stood at their entrance. "Finally. I was beginning to wonder if you would keep us here all day." Her gaze ran the length of Lydia. "The handmaid is to be present for this meeting you insisted be kept private?"

Mariamme caught the eye of the servant and inclined her head to dismiss him. When the room held only the four of them plus the trusted Sohemus, she slid the heavy doors closed.

"My, my." Alexandra's eyebrows lifted. "Something shocking, I presume." She tilted her head down and gave Lydia a look of derision. "Has the lady's maid gotten herself with child?"

Lydia flushed and cleared her throat, then studied the yellow and blue of the floor tiles. They had agreed that Mariamme would take the lead in explaining.

Herod spoke at last. "Mariamme, can we get this tiresome conversation finished? I have business to attend."

"Cleopatra, you mean."

He sat a bit straighter on the throne but laughed. "Oh, we have already had a scene or two since her arrival this morning, trust me. I doubt she has any more wish to see me."

Lydia's legs were a bit shaky, and she wished that the meeting were over as well.

Mariamme began at last, first with a history lesson that seemed to amuse Alexandra and bore Herod. It was the history of the Hasmoneans, after all, and besides seeing the wisdom of marrying into the family, Herod had little use for any of them.

"Mother, you told me that your grandfather gave his royal seal to each of his children, including the daughter who was married off to Cleopatra's father's brother."

Alexandra shrugged. "I have no idea what became of it, if that's what you're asking. You'll have the two upon my death, but I suppose the third is lost."

"It is not lost." Mariamme nodded to Lydia.

She pulled the pendant from under her tunic.

At this, Alexandra shot from her chair and crossed to the two of them. "What is this?" She bent to the pendant, her head brushing Lydia's chin. "You have brought us a thief, Mariamme! Where did you steal this, girl?"

"She did not steal it." Mariamme edged closer to Lydia and pushed her mother back a step. "It was her mother's."

Even Herod was standing now and took a few steps off the platform to get a closer look. "Her mother's?"

Lydia's breath held suspended in her chest while the two looked from the pendant to her face and back to the pendant.

"Her mother was your aunt Shira, married to the king of Cyprus. When Rome annexed Cyprus and the king took his own life, his wife fled to Egypt for protection. She was late in pregnancy. Cleopatra's older sister had her killed and believed the baby dead as well. I believe servants rescued the baby from the woman's womb and raised her in the palace as one of their own."

Alexandra took a step back, her eyes narrowing. "You *believe*?" She huffed. "You have no other proof than a pendant the girl could have stolen."

Herod was circling Lydia, looking her up and down, as though evaluating how he could best use this shiny new tool that had been delivered.

"Stolen from whom? Your father's sister was murdered the same year as Lydia's birth. The pendant was given to Lydia just before she left Egypt, by an old man who had known her all his life. He told her it had belonged to her mother," Mariamme said.

"Old man?" Alexandra laughed. "Let us bring this old man here, then. Let him tell us what he knows."

"He is dead." They were the first words Lydia had spoken since entering, and she delivered them with head high, looking directly into Alexandra's eyes.

"Ho! The servant girl has already acquired the bearing of a queen, I see. That did not take long."

Herod stopped circling and folded his arms over his chest. "Your mother is right, Mariamme. The information seems to fit, but we must have some sort of confirmation. But if it is true, we have been given a rare treasure—an enemy of Cleopatra's who is a friend of ours."

"I am not—"

"Not what?" Herod laughed. "An enemy of Cleopatra's?"

When Lydia said nothing he laughed again. "Yes, you know her well enough, don't you? How many family members has she killed to ensure they were no threat to her throne? Brothers? Sisters? Do you think she would hesitate at a cousin—and one who had served at her feet?"

No. She would not.

Lydia bent her head, a familiar coldness seeping in. The connection she had felt to Egypt since last night, the warm sense of belonging that came with knowing she was a Ptolemy, was smothered by the heavy truth Herod spoke. Cleopatra would never let her return to Egypt. She would never even let her live.

"Then if you are an enemy of Cleopatra's, my girl, you had better agree that you are a friend of Judea, eh?" His brow furrowed. "That is, if we can find someone else who knows the truth."

"Banafrit."

The three in the room waited, as her name meant nothing. Even Mariamme did not seem to recognize it when Lydia had spoken of her only minutes ago. Was this what it was to be part of a royal family? The names and lives of the servants no more consequential than the details of the next meal?

Lydia spoke to Mariamme. "The cook whom Cleopatra

brought with her. She has known me since birth and knew Samuel well. She may know more of the circumstances of my birth than she has told."

Herod snapped a finger at Alexandra. "Bring this cook. And Salome. My sister should hear this as well."

Alexandra's dark eyes flashed.

Was she angry at being ordered like a servant, or because the ever-present Salome was to be favored with such important information?

She left, however, without a word.

The three remaining waited in silence. Herod returned to his throne, but Mariamme stood beside Lydia and threaded her arm through hers.

The throne room door swept open a few minutes later, admitting Salome, Alexandra, and Banafrit, who waddled at their heels with eyes as wide as melons. When she saw Lydia, her face broke into joy.

Lydia gave a little cry of joy herself, escaped from Mariamme's arm, and ran to Banafrit.

She had never hugged the old woman in her life, and it had never been more inappropriate, but she did not care. She threw her arms around the woman's shoulders and embraced her and all of Egypt with her.

Banafrit gave an uncomfortable laugh and patted Lydia's shoulder twice, then pulled away. "I had hoped you would still be in service here, girl. That I would get a chance to see you." She held Lydia's arms and turned her back and forth a bit. "Ah, you have turned out fine. From a pretty girl to a beautiful woman since last I saw you. I should think you have all the male servants—"

Herod cleared his throat.

Banafrit dropped her hands and her plump cheeks reddened.

"You may visit with your old friend later, woman. Right now we have some questions for you."

Banafrit's chin quivered slightly. "My lord, she demanded I cook her favorite—"

"This is not about Cleopatra." He inclined his head. "Not directly."

The five women grouped before the throne where Herod sat forward, his arms braced on his legs. "This is about Lydia."

Banafrit glanced with concern at Lydia, and Lydia smiled in reassurance.

"We want to know the circumstances of Lydia's birth."

"Wh-what?"

Herod leaned back. "What do you know of her birth?"

Banafrit bit her lip.

"Please, Banafrit." Lydia's voice held a note of desperation. "Tell us what you know."

The old woman looked to Herod. "You will keep my girl safe? No matter what I tell you?"

Herod dipped his head in acknowledgment, a rare courtesy to a servant.

Banafrit exhaled heavily and shifted her weight from one foot to the other. "I never thought it was a good idea to keep it from her. The old man . . . the old man said she would be in danger, and I could see his point, so I kept quiet, but I always knew that *she* could be trusted with it, and she went about the palace so gloomy and sad because of the lie we had told her—"

"Woman!" Herod's voice bounced from the high ceiling and back to Banafrit.

She jumped and sucked in a breath.

"Tell us what you know."

Banafrit looked to Lydia. "I am sorry, dear. You should have known who you were."

Mariamme sighed in frustration. "Who is she?"

Banafrit seemed to find focus and courage at last. She puffed out her chest and turned to Herod. "I delivered her myself, my lord. From the womb of the Hasmonean princess Shira, just before she died at the hand of Berenice, supposed queen of Egypt."

Lydia felt the news like a blow to her chest, even though it had been expected.

The declaration rang in the air of the throne room, and only Salome's shocked intake of breath followed.

Salome took a step toward Banafrit, her brow creased. "And her father?"

Banafrit seemed surprised by the question, as though Salome should know Egyptian history. "Her father was king of Cyprus, brother to the twelfth Ptolemy."

Again there was silence.

Banafrit broke the tension with a pitying grasp of Lydia's arm. "My dear, I am sorry that we lied. He convinced me it was the only way to keep you safe. At first you were too young to understand, but as the years passed and we saw what Cleopatra was like, I came to believe that he was right. Please forgive me."

Lydia embraced Banafrit once more, buried her face in the old woman's hair that smelled of an Egyptian palace. "There is nothing to forgive, Banafrit. I owe you my life, and I thank you for it."

Alexandra stepped closer. "That will be all, Banafrit. You may go. And speak of this to no one, most especially Cleopatra."

Banafrit nodded, then shot a look at Herod. "You promised. Keep her safe."

And then she bustled from the throne room, abandoning Lydia with her equals.

Salome was already pacing, one forefinger placed against her chin and her narrow lips pursed. "I always knew something was strange about that girl. Could not discern the source." She stopped and faced her brother. "We can use this. You know that, Herod. We can use her somehow to bring down Cleopatra."

Mariamme stepped close to Lydia. "I brought her for your protection, not for you to set her up as a target for Cleopatra's paranoia."

Salome laughed, the sound derisive. "Oh, it is not paranoia. We have every intention of destroying that woman."

"You cannot—"

"Mariamme." Herod's voice was low, almost pleading. "If you understood her great hatred for our family, you would see that we must work against her. Just this morning, after arriving, she tried again to seduce me. When I refused her and left, I found her servant waiting outside the door with instructions to cry out that I had attacked and forced her!"

"I understand that she is ruthless, but must we follow in her footsteps?"

Lydia struggled to find words to add to the conversation that swirled around her, but what could she contribute that was not already known? She had no wish to leave her fate in the hands of Herod and his chief adviser, Salome, who wanted her dead, but neither did she have any idea of what should happen next.

"Listen." Salome braced her hands against her hips. "The Egyptians have no love for their queen, since she began courting Rome more than ten years ago. And Rome hates her. She has no allies but Marc Antony, who is quickly falling from favor himself.

If Rome were to put Lydia on the throne of Egypt, the people would love it. One of their own, ascended to power." She smiled, her near-black eyes sparking. "Why not?"

Mariamme faced off with Salome. "Because you might as well cover her with a lion's hide and send her into the arena for a hunt! Cleopatra would kill her before the gold cobra was ever placed on her head."

Lydia raised a hand, a slight, inconsequential movement that barely arrested attention. "I . . . I have no wish to be queen."

Salome and Herod both sighed at once.

"Lydia." Salome inclined her head as though speaking to a child. "We do not care at all what you wish."

Thirty-One

Lydia escaped the throne room while the royal family was still plotting her future.

She walked with head down, unthinking about her destination, with her new and old sense of herself bobbing in her head like driftwood in heavy surf. The true past, the untrue past, and the unknown future shifted until she could barely catch hold.

The kitchens were humming. Servants dashed past, their tunics a multicolored flash, out with trays and in with supplies. A hundred smells assaulted her, along with the chatter of a staff busy with all the preparation for an important guest. She thought of Esther, the wife of Simon's friend Jonah, who worked with her hands to feed so many children. What would Esther think of Lydia's sudden rise in status? She passed through, bumped and jostled by a few who looked at her as though she had trespassed in their domain.

She found herself at the door of Simon's private office. Perhaps she had been headed here all along.

It had to be done.

She knocked twice on the closed door, then entered at his invitation.

His smile was like a knife blade. Had it only been a few hours since their declarations in the courtyard? How had everything changed so completely?

"There you are." He stood and took her hands in his. "I've been wondering when I would see you this morning." His eyes clouded. "What is wrong?"

She pulled her hands from his grasp and seated herself in a chair. "Sit, please. I—something has happened. I have something to tell you."

He lowered himself slowly, never taking his eyes from hers.

In halting phrases and with only as much detail as she must give, she blurted the story to him. Of the rulers of Egyptian Cyprus, both dead on the eve of Rome's annexation, and of the child raised in obscurity, whom everyone believed dead.

When she was finished, she raised her eyes to meet his gaze, her soul wrung out from the telling.

Simon sat stone-faced, unmoving.

"It is hard to believe, I know—"

"It is not so hard." The words seemed to crack something apart inside him. "I have always said you had something of a princess about you. Now we know why. Royal blood will always tell." At this, he looked away.

"Simon, I—"

"I am very happy for you. You deserve all the best that life has to give." He stood. "And now, my lady, if you would excuse me—"

"Simon, please." She jumped from her chair and took his arms. "You must know how difficult this is for me."

He slipped his arms from her grasp and bowed his head. "I do flatter myself that you find it difficult, my lady. But that does not change the situation." He held a hand out toward the door, as if to escort her out.

Before either could move, the door flew open.

Cleopatra stood outlined in the light from the courtyard, her face awash with something like shock, mixed with fury.

Lydia took in the woman's features, five years older than when she had last seen the queen, but still with the arresting charisma born of power and intelligence as much as natural beauty. The years had not changed this, nor had they changed Lydia's immediate response to Cleopatra's anger. She reached out for something to steady herself and found nothing.

"So here she is." Cleopatra sidled in, looking Lydia up and down.

Surely the woman did not still hold animosity after all these years?

"*Cousin* Lydia." The words shot from her lips like daggers.

Lydia sucked in a breath and stared. "How—?"

The queen of Egypt laughed in her face. "Please. Did you think I would come to such a place without ears everywhere? That little Riva came running to me as soon as she heard."

Riva.

Lydia's shoulders fell. Somehow she felt only pity for the girl. Riva worked so hard to make herself liked, believing it was the only way to be of value. She had no idea that even those who used her felt nothing but disdain. She would always be a servant.

Not like you. At the thought, Lydia straightened.

Cleopatra stood too close, pressing in on her. "I suppose you think you'll come back to Alexandria and be hailed by all?"

Lydia stared ahead, not meeting Cleopatra's hard gaze. "I have not decided what I shall do next."

"Oh, she has not decided." Cleopatra smirked. "Well, we shall all await your decision with great excitement."

"You have nothing to fear from me, Cleopatra." The words emerged strong and steady, and with them, a measure of confidence flowed into her veins. She looked the queen in the eye.

Cleopatra shouted in Lydia's face. "You think I *fear* you? You worthless little worm-servant! You are nothing but a half-breed, raised in the sewers. You are no more to me than an insect."

"And yet here you are." Lydia kept her voice low. "Seeking me out. Attempting to intimidate me."

It felt like freedom, to speak thus to Cleopatra.

Cleopatra took a swift step toward her, arm upraised.

Simon caught the arm in mid-swing.

The queen cast a look of hatred on him and yanked her arm from his grasp.

"That will be all, Simon." Lydia nodded to him. "You may leave us now."

She had said it to remove him, to protect him from Cleopatra's wrath. But the look in his eyes at Lydia's regal dismissal pained her, perhaps more than it did him.

Simon stepped from the room and Lydia faced Cleopatra.

"Cleopatra, I have seen you charm an enemy. I have seen you cower an enemy. And I know very well how capably you dispatch those who block your desires. I am telling you that while I am no longer a worthless servant, neither am I your enemy. I am a Jewish woman, living under the protection of the king of the Jews."

Cleopatra's eyes narrowed. "Then do not forget it. Should you suddenly decide you would prefer to be a Ptolemy, be assured that I shall hear of it and send soldiers to cut off your hopes quicker than you can say 'Egyptian princess.'"

A shadow crossed the door's threshold. Mariamme.

"I heard the shouting." She looked from Cleopatra to Lydia. "Is there some problem?"

Lydia smiled at Mariamme. "The queen has received the news already, through the palace gossip. She seems to feel a bit threatened by the new addition to her family."

Mariamme paled. "Come, Lydia. I have something I need to discuss with you."

Lydia dipped her head toward Cleopatra in farewell and sailed out of Simon's chamber with her head high.

Outside the door, Simon leaned against a marble column. His gaze followed her face as she passed, but she could not read what she saw in his eyes.

In Mariamme's chamber, the queen closed the door and faced her. "They are insisting on using you as a playing piece in their games, Lydia. I cannot stop them."

"What use can Herod have for me?"

Mariamme's eyebrows rose. "You are an unmarried daughter of royal blood on both sides. You are one of the most useful things there is."

Lydia closed her eyes. Was this what she had wished for? She had a history and family and significance, and yet still belonged nowhere. Not here in Judea, the land of her mother, nor in the Egypt of her father's family.

"Herod will keep you here, and he will wait." Mariamme crossed slowly to the window and swept the drapery aside with one finger. "Wait and watch and keep his head down. Until it becomes clear who the victor will be. For Caesar has declared war against Cleopatra, and with her, Marc Antony."

"I thought Herod's loyalties—"

"His loyalty is to himself alone. If he must break with Marc Antony to retain Rome, he will do it." She turned to Lydia. "And you will be the prize for the winner."

Thirty-Two

Lydia was enduring her empty time by painting floral designs over the faded geometrics of an old pot when Simon ran past her chair in the courtyard, nearly kicking over her paints.

"What is it?" She jumped to her feet and called to his disappearing figure.

He slowed and called over his shoulder, "Trouble in the Sanhedrin!"

And then he was through the palace arch and into the city.

Lydia stood with brush in hand, staring after him. Since when did Simon get involved in the affairs of the Sanhedrin?

But then Alexandra rushed past, as fast as Lydia had ever seen her move.

Lydia gathered her supplies in a hasty pile and followed.

They reached the northern end of the Temple area, where the Sanhedrin met in the Hall of Hewn Stone, and joined the flow of citizens who must have heard the gossip as well.

Alexandra pushed through to the building's entrance, but

Lydia found Simon, straining to see over the heads of those who shouted and raised their fists outside the hall.

"There!" Simon pointed. "Jonah. I knew he'd be at the front. He's going to get himself killed."

Lydia followed Simon's raised arm. Jonah—and was that Esther with him? They were both shouting at the door, held back by Temple guards.

She tugged Simon's sleeve. "Who is on trial?"

"Hyrcanus. Treason."

The doddering old man with the mutilated ears? Even as former High Priest, how could anyone think him capable of treason?

Simon answered her unspoken question. "A letter was apprehended on its way from Hyrcanus to Malik, asking the Petran king to send troops against Herod."

Alexandra. It could only be Alexandra's plot to bring down Herod. The senile and harmless Hyrcanus could not have orchestrated such a thing. She had been willing to implicate her own father to accomplish her goals.

A shout came from the front of the crowd. "They have killed him! Hyrcanus has been strangled!"

Lydia sucked in a breath and raised wide eyes to Simon.

His face flushed with anger.

The royal entourage—Herod's advisers and Salome—were pushing out of the hall. Herod followed, turning his shoulders left and right to jostle through the crowd that pressed against him, voices mingled in hostile shouts.

Simon was forcing himself through.

Lydia followed in the wake he created. Would Esther be safe? So many innocents were relying on her.

Jonah raised a fist to a Temple guard and yelled an epithet toward Herod. The guard struck him in the face and he went down.

Lydia cried out, reached for Esther. Her hand brushed the robe of Salome instead. A coldness, strange and dark, snaked along Lydia's fingers, across her hand, and traveled the length of her arm.

Salome turned on Lydia, stared with those dead eyes.

"What have you done?" Lydia hissed the words before she could hold them back.

Salome's lips pursed slightly and she lowered her chin. "Hyrcanus has been tried and executed. His attempt to gain support from Malik against King Herod could not go unpunished."

Lydia glanced to Esther, who was helping Jonah to his feet. She was close, too close, to the king's sister. Lydia would not let Salome notice her friend.

But Esther was quiet, watching the exchange between Lydia and the king's sister with unbelieving eyes.

"Salome, you know very well that Hyrcanus is incapable of such scheming."

Herod was pulling Salome along, but the woman seemed intent on speaking to Lydia.

"Tell your friend, little Lydia, that this is what happens when she and her mother conspire. There is no one who is safe from my reach."

Lydia clenched her fists at her sides. "You will be stopped someday. The One God will not tolerate you forever."

She expected Salome to laugh at her declaration. Instead, the woman took a step backward, her chin lifting in defiance but a look of fear in her eyes. "Do you make yourself my enemy, Egyptian?"

"You are the enemy of all that is good, and you will not

succeed." Lydia did not know where the certainty came from, nor even what Salome's unsuccessful plan would be. The words poured forth as though from someone else.

Salome seemed to sense their prophetic nature. Her hands were clutched at her waist, but a slight tremor ran through them. The escorting guards prodded her toward the palace, but she did not take her eyes from Lydia's, and the unbroken stare between them had the watchful intensity of a lion stalking a sheep.

Once again Lydia had drawn Salome's dark attention. How long until the woman took steps to eliminate her, as she had Hyrcanus?

When Salome had been sucked away by the crowd, Esther came to wrap an arm around Lydia's waist.

Lydia bent her head to Esther's shoulder and wept. For Hyrcanus, for Mariamme, for herself. And for the City of God, which teetered on the edge of a destruction she had uselessly been tasked to prevent.

≈

In the days that followed, Lydia did her best to avoid Salome. She would have taken the scrolls and run if Herod had not made it clear that she was his subject, and if she disappeared, those she loved would feel the consequences. Perhaps Simon, or David. Or even Mariamme. Between brother and sister, no one was safe. Salome was feeding Herod's paranoia, his jealousy, hatred, and madness. If she had gotten him to strangle the former High Priest, a harmless old man, she could persuade him to do anything.

And so Lydia waited. Waited as news of the war between Egypt and Rome filtered to Judea. Waited through idle days, watching Mariamme try to shun Sohemus just as Lydia avoided

Simon. She watched the streets from the palace roof for the speedy approach of messengers and watched Simon from leafy corners of the courtyard for any sign that he grew more miserable with each passing day, as she did.

There were stolen glances—the occasional sideways look as he passed her at meals with the family, the head lifted at her approach before the sharp turn to other concerns. As the waiting stretched, Lydia began to live each day for only these moments, torturous as they were. She spent nights at her chamber window, overlooking the city she could not be part of and chasing away useless tears.

At least the news from the battlefronts was not good for Cleopatra. A great naval battle had been fought at Actium, with Antony's troops deserting him and leaving him a fugitive. Even Cleopatra's loyalties were in question as the queen tried to bribe Caesar Octavian. There was talk in the Senate of conferring the title of "Augustus" on Caesar.

At this information, delivered one night during a family meal by Mazal, the ingratiating cupbearer, Herod grinned in Lydia's direction. "And when that happens we shall have a fitting gift for him, shall we not?"

Mariamme patted Lydia's arm from her reclined position beside her, as if to keep her quiet. "Octavian already has a new wife, and Livia seems to please him in a way Scribonia never did."

Herod shrugged. "Not for Caesar himself, then. But he will certainly want to reward his most trusted generals."

Mariamme tried a smile in Lydia's direction. "Perhaps that handsome Agrippa who visited last year. He was very charming."

Herod's face darkened. "And do you lust after every Roman who crosses our threshold, my fickle wife?"

Lydia cringed. Herod's crazed jealousy had grown worse while they all waited, suspended with the tension of their fate decided by those outside their control. Mariamme should have known better.

Her friend scowled. "Roman, Jew, Egyptian. All but the Idumeans—they have never held much appeal."

It was Lydia's turn to quiet Mariamme with a firm pressure of the hand. While Herod seemed to grow mad with the waiting, Mariamme had grown bolder in her loathing of her husband. But under her disdain, Herod showed only more infatuation, as though the greater her scorn, the greater his passion.

But perhaps it was only the tension of the impending birth of another child. Within days, a little girl was placed into Mariamme's arms.

Herod named her Cypros, after his mother.

"She will be my last," Mariamme whispered to Lydia over the babe's fuzzy head. She had been refusing to acknowledge Herod whenever he summoned her to his bed, and had no intention of returning. The news surprised Lydia, in the face of the heightening of Herod's strange, obsessive adoration.

But they might all become mad before their futures were decided. The days stretched like dried-up threads over a loom, taut and fraying, ready to snap. She wished she could have spent an afternoon with Esther, throwing pots and speaking of ordinary things. But such an easy friendship was no longer possible. And to be near Simon, to see him every day but never speaking, never touching, was a pain worse than all the loneliness she experienced in her life. Lydia sometimes wished for it all to be over, for the course of her life to be set, even if it took her from Judea forever.

Herod traveled briefly to Rhodes to meet with Caesar

Octavian, installing the women in the fortress in Alexandrium in case any harm should come to him. While it was a respite from the daily torture of seeing Simon, the trip only aggravated the tension of waiting. And since Herod sent Sohemus along to watch over the women, the furtive moments she witnessed between Mariamme and the guard reinforced her own pain.

When they returned she tried to distract herself, and perhaps find a way back to the reason she had first come to Jerusalem, by sending for several rabbis to confer with her in a private meeting room of the palace. She asked a dozen questions about the writings of Daniel and of the Chakkiym, and yet the meetings ended with no new information gained. If the Chakkiym were more than the imaginings of her old mentor Samuel, there was no way to prove it from anything she had found in Jerusalem.

Lydia's artistic abilities were next to worthless now. Royalty did not make pots to sell at market. She was, in fact, no use to anyone. The false importance of her new name and identity had stripped her of true importance in the lives of everyone she knew.

She wandered often into the palace workshop to see what David was creating. A bench last week, a cabinet today.

He grinned at her admiration of the cabinet. "Simon says I may use the tools in my extra time and sell what I make." He blushed slightly. "I am saving for a bride-price."

"What's this?" Lydia laughed and pinched his arm. "Little David has his eye on a bride?"

"Her name is Halima. She lives south of the Temple. I cannot wait for you to meet her." His eyes sparkled.

Lydia hugged him, disguising the pain of longing his words brought. "I am certain she is wonderful."

And then the news began to pour into the palace like a river gushing from a mountain spring. Antony, defeated in one battle, was returning to Egypt to advance on Octavian's troops there. Then a victory for Antony at Alexandria, but his men were deserting. A decisive win for Octavian. Cleopatra playing both sides against each other.

And then the shock: Antony, believing Cleopatra captured, had taken his own life. But Cleopatra had struck a deal with Octavian, believing he would preserve her dignity if not her position. After learning she was to be made a mockery and paraded in chains in a Roman triumph, Cleopatra killed herself twelve days later.

Lydia received this news in the throne room, along with the rest of the royal family, and her blood raced, flushing her chest and neck and face, then draining away, leaving her dizzy. She stood alongside Mariamme before the throne and gripped her friend's hand.

"Cleopatra is dead?"

"Yes." Herod peered at her. "Surely you feel no grief, even though she was your cousin?"

"No. No, not grief. Just—shock—I suppose. She was my mistress, then my family, then my enemy for so long. I . . . I do not know what to feel."

"Well, I say the world is a better place without her." Mariamme's defiant words were born of sadness and anger, but no less true.

Lydia straightened. "What of Caesarion?"

Herod shrugged. "Caesar has been ordering executions. Antony's eldest is dead."

"And?"

"And Caesarion."

Lydia felt the blow harder than she thought she would. It

forced the air from her lungs, drained the strength from her limbs. She sank to a chair, with Mariamme easing her into it.

A numbness, heavy and solid like ice, settled in Lydia's veins while somehow her stomach flamed into turmoil.

She was going to be sick.

Mariamme held a chamber pot while she heaved. Then summoned a servant to bring wine and a rag dipped in cool water for her face.

All these years. For so long she had waited to see Caesarion again, each year imagining him as he must be, taller and stronger, smarter and more confident. He was so young.

"Why?"

It was the only word she had spoken since the news, and it rasped out of a raw throat.

Herod smirked. "He said something about one Caesar in Rome being enough."

Why had she thought it would be any different? Octavian could never allow the biological son of Julius Caesar to return, when his own sonship was a posthumous adoption, in name only.

"And you, our little mixed-blood princess." Herod's cool gaze fell on her where she sat beside Mariamme. "It would seem you are not needed to rule Egypt after all. But my suggestion has been well received by Caesar, and I am to give you to him immediately, for his general Agrippa. You will unite Egypt, Rome, and Judea with one marriage."

"Give me to him?" Did Herod think she was his to dispense, like gold plate from his treasury? "I . . . I cannot grant an answer right now."

Herod's eyes widened. "What do I care for your answer? Besides, what is here for you?"

Nothing. There was nothing here for her. Not the Chakkiym. Not Simon. And nothing for her in Egypt.

She fled the throne room, through the courtyard, past Simon's office, and then stopped.

She could not agree with Herod's plan until they had one final conversation. Simon had made it clear in his actions that she was no longer part of his life. He served her as any other palace staff would serve, with eyes downcast and a deferential voice. But she needed to hear it. To hear him speak the words.

He looked up at the sound of her sandals, then jumped to his feet, knocking a quill and some scrolls to the floor.

She tried to smile. "My apologies for startling you."

He waved a hand at the mess without taking his gaze from her. "It is nothing. Is there something I can do for you?"

She leaned against the door frame. "No. I—we have not had a moment to speak privately of late. I only wanted to see how you are."

"How I am?"

The words sounded foolish now. She took a deep breath, steadied her hand against the door. "There has been news from Rome. Antony and Cleopatra are dead. And Caesarion."

Simon was at her side in a moment. "Lydia. Oh, Lydia, I am so sorry." He reached a hand toward her, then let it drop.

A few beats of silence and Lydia felt the familiar constriction in her chest.

"Caesar and Herod want me to marry the Roman, Marcus Agrippa."

"And what do you want?"

The silence deepened. It had been an impertinent question, given their stations, and they both knew it. But she desired only to respond with truth.

"I . . . I do not know. I told Herod I could not give an answer yet. I think sometimes it would be better—"

Simon's voice was steady, even cold. "He will make a good husband, I should think. You should give an answer quickly. Soldiers are not accustomed to being patient."

"Is that what you want? Do you want me to marry him?"

He took a step back. "My lady, I am the manager of the king's Jerusalem palace. I should not think my opinion in this matter holds any weight."

She pushed forward, closing the space between them, her gaze on his face—the hard lines, the muscles twitching in his jaw. "It does hold weight with me."

His posture straightened and he trained his eyes to look over her shoulder, as though she were not a breath from him. But the cords of his neck were strained, and his hands were fisted at his sides. He swallowed hard. "Then marry him, Lydia. Marry him, and end my suffering."

The pain in his voice took her breath away. A dangerous warmth spread through her, mixed with a dawning pity. She had not known. Or perhaps she had. She touched his arm with her fingertips, but he jerked away as though burned.

"Simon." She whispered his name, but he would only look at the doorway.

"I will say this only once, Lydia. And then we must not speak again."

She nodded, silent.

"What was once between us cannot exist any longer. If you still care anything at all for me, you will marry Agrippa. It is the only way I can let you go."

As Sohemus had let go of Mariamme? What proof was

there that creating the bond of marriage would dissolve all other bonds?

"Marry Agrippa and go to Rome, Lydia." His eyes found hers at last, unshed tears sparkling on his lashes. "I am begging you to set me free."

~

When Mariamme found her in her chamber an hour later, Lydia wiped her eyes with the handkerchief her friend offered.

"What did Simon say about your impending marriage?"

Lydia glanced sideways at Mariamme, but her expression held no judgment. Only pity.

Mariamme smiled sadly. "Do you think I have not seen how much he means to you? Every day you grow nobler, more royal. But also sadder."

Lydia exhaled heavily. "He told me once that he loved me. He will not say it again."

Mariamme pulled up a chair and sat beside Lydia, clasping her hands. "You must avoid him, Lydia. You must do all you can to stay away. Trust me."

The way that she said *trust me* was an opening she had never given Lydia. "Is it still Sohemus? Do you—have you—?"

Mariamme's hands clenched involuntarily on Lydia's. "I have done nothing, nor will I. But it has only grown more difficult as the years have passed. I have urged him to marry, but he refuses." She shook her head, studying the floor. "Strangely, Herod must suspect nothing, for he continues to have Sohemus as my guard. With his jealousy, Herod never would have done so if he had any idea of Sohemus's feelings for me."

"Or your feelings for him."

Mariamme stood and paced. "We should not speak of it. It only makes it more difficult." She stopped and turned on Lydia. "That is why I tell you to trust me—you must remain distant from Simon. You know it is impossible to be together in the way that you wish, and no good will come of being near him in any other way. You will think you are only assuring yourself of his love or trying to ease his pain, but it only makes it harder, until you fear that your worst instincts will overwhelm you—"

She cut off with a sob, and Lydia went to her and embraced her.

How long she had suffered. Only her goodness and piety, and that of Sohemus, kept them both chaste and yet in pain. Herod could take as many slave girls to himself as he liked, and yet Mariamme must be denied the only man she loved.

Mariamme was right. She must remove herself from this place, from Simon.

Her time in Rome years ago had been too short, and it was an amazing city. Perhaps she could be happy there.

Nothing had turned out the way she had expected. Her destiny had not been the scrolls, nor even Jerusalem.

Perhaps it was time to let it all go.

Thirty-Three

Salome sat cross-legged on the floor with a circle of tiny oil lamps flickering around her and incense burning in the center. She swayed gently with the warmth and the spicy scent and the half-drowsed lethargy she had fallen into.

Her mind was open, her palms spread before her. Let the goddess fill her with knowledge now, for she needed answers.

For years she had not felt this oppression, this blocking of her powers to control the lives and fates of those around her, even though she had been unable to worm her way between Herod and his precious Mariamme, to open her brother's eyes to the woman's unworthiness.

But the peace had ended the day Salome faced down that servant-turned-royalty, Lydia.

Just as before, when Salome had tried to destroy the girl's mind in the storeroom, she had found Lydia protected. But not as before, for the protection was even stronger now, and it came from within the girl, not merely from without. Although she seemed yet unaware of her own power.

Salome breathed deeply of the incense and fought to keep her limbs relaxed, her hands open. What was it about the girl? Why was she important? A Ptolemy and a Hasmonean, yes. But there had to be more than this.

She whispered yet another prayer to the goddess for wisdom. For the power to defeat her enemy. For Lydia was her enemy, there could be no doubt.

A scuff at the door opened her eyes.

"What is it?"

Riva's pale face appeared in the crack of the half-opened door.

Salome growled. The girl was useful as a handmaid chiefly because she had no scruples. But she had little sense either. "You are interrupting!"

"I am sorry, my lady. I . . . I have heard something I thought you would want to know."

She sighed. "Enter. Say it."

Riva slipped into the chamber, closed the door behind her, and leaned against it as though she feared to come closer. "It is about Lydia."

Salome hid a smile. Riva was no happier than she about Lydia's elevation in status and refused to call the girl anything but her given name. "What of Lydia?"

"She sent for some men to come to the palace and speak with her. Rabbis."

Salome narrowed her eyes. "Why would she seek rabbis? I have seen little of the faithful Jewess in her."

Riva ducked her head. "When they came and met with her in a private chamber, I hid at the door and listened."

"Well done, then, Riva. And what did you discover?"

"She asked many questions, though she got few answers. They did not seem to know much about the knowledge she sought."

Salome waited, resisting the urge to get up and shake the girl.

"She asked about the writings of the prophet Daniel. About the copies that are held in the synagogues, but of other writings as well. Secret writings that have been lost."

Salome's lips parted and she scrambled to her feet.

"She also asked if they knew where to find a certain group. She called them the 'Chakkiym.'"

Salome's breath was coming short and shallow now—a mixture of surprise, elation, self-chastisement. How had she not seen it? All these years?

"Go, Riva. Go at once and search Lydia's chamber. Do not return until you have found something hidden. Scrolls, most likely."

At Riva's hesitation, she pointed. "Go!" Then called the girl back. "Be smart. If you are caught, do not expect me to take up your cause."

The girl fled, and Salome lowered herself to the lamp-lit circle once more, held her palms aloft, and closed her eyes in gratitude.

Of course. Of course it was her. Lydia had been in Egypt all those years ago when the seeker came here looking for the Chakkiym, and Salome had tortured him to reveal that the writings had been found in Alexandria. She had sent two of her best to find them and received only one message—that the first of her men was dead and the second following the scrolls to Rome. Then nothing more.

All of those years, Lydia had been in this very palace, the scrolls hidden somewhere. How could Salome not have seen it? A fiery hatred flamed through her limbs. She had focused her dark energy on Mariamme, but she had been blind. It was Lydia—the keeper of the scrolls—who was her greatest enemy.

She felt a power filling her, entering as she breathed deeply, filling her chest and her mind, running like silver down her veins to quench the fire and turn her hatred to stone.

It was time. Time to solidify the power of the Herodian family in this place. To rid themselves of the Hasmoneans for all time.

Her attack would be double pronged. She would destroy both Lydia and Mariamme.

She had been holding on to a valuable piece of information for many years, waiting for the right time to make use of it. And it would only take a few well-placed words in the ear of her jealous brother to complete her task.

In spite of his fixated jealousy, he had been a blind fool. Debasing himself before his Jewish wife, groveling for her love while the ungrateful girl kicked dust in his face. Trusting implicitly the one man who was his greatest enemy. It was time to bring it to an end.

Lydia would die. But first, Herod would soon know that his closest friend, Sohemus, was in love with his wife.

≈

Lydia spent the evening in her bedchamber. In her bed.

Perhaps she was ill. Since the encounter with Simon, nothing seemed worth rising for, not the evening meal nor Mariamme's coaxing.

And when the morning dawned with its pale winter sunlight, she rolled away from the window and wept.

By evening, Mariamme insisted that she walk with her in the courtyard for fresh air and then join the family in the dining room. Lydia complied with a few turns around the peristyle at the courtyard's perimeter, then hovered in the doorway of the still-empty dining room.

Mariamme sighed. "Would you rather have food sent to your room?"

Lydia smiled, grateful for her friend's understanding heart.

Within minutes she was in the upper corridor, walking slowly to her chamber.

Was her door ajar? Lydia drew up, a tiny flutter of her heart sending a warning. The scrolls were well hidden but were never far from her thoughts.

She took a few silent steps toward the door, then slid into the opening.

"Riva!" She blurted out the girl's name without thinking.

Riva whirled, her eyes wide and hand suspended above a near-empty basket of clothing. Its contents were piled on the floor beside it.

"I . . . I thought you were at dinner." Riva bit her lip, then began folding and replacing the clothing.

"So you thought to borrow a robe?" Lydia arched an eyebrow.

But at Riva's silence she glanced around the room and found many other things in disarray. Chairs moved, the bed slightly out of alignment. A favorite painted urn no longer in the corner.

"You have been searching for something!" The ominous heart-pounding was back. But no, Riva's hands were still empty of the scrolls.

"Thievery in the palace is a capital offense, Riva. You do know that?"

The girl's eyes widened and she stuffed the remaining clothing into the basket. "Please, my lady. I . . . I—she sent me—" Riva cut off and twisted her hands at her waist.

Salome. Salome had sent Riva to search for something. Had

she somehow learned of Lydia's hidden treasure? What did Salome know of Daniel's secret writings?

"To search for what, Riva? What were you to bring?"

Riva's eyes flicked between fear and defiance. It must have maddened her to find herself at Lydia's mercy after all these years. But Lydia would use the fear to her advantage.

"Perhaps if we had this discussion before Herod—"

"A scroll." Riva looked away. "She said to find a scroll."

Lydia would push Riva further, find out how much Salome knew. But as she opened her mouth for another question, a horrible scream tore the nighttime quiet of the palace.

She and Riva traded confused glances, then Lydia ran into the corridor and overlooked the courtyard.

Below, Mariamme was running toward the throne room.

Lydia called over the balcony, "What is it? Who is screaming?"

Mariamme glanced up but kept running. "It is Leodes. Herod is torturing him in the throne room!"

Leodes? Why would Mariamme's favorite eunuch have fallen out of favor with Herod?

Or was it only information that the king sought? Secrets that palace staff often held closely, with their royal counterparts unaware how much they knew.

Lydia pulled Riva from her room into the corridor. "If I find anything disturbed, anything missing, I promise I will tell Herod that you have stolen from me."

Riva shook her head. "I swear, my lady."

Lydia left her still shaking outside the door and ran for the throne room.

≈

Mariamme reached the throne room as yet another shriek of pain ripped through the palace air. She burst through the doors and took in the scene. Herod, standing over Leodes. Leodes, barechested and on his knees, head bent. One of Herod's guards with a Roman scourge, laced with bits of glass, hauling back for yet another strike against her poor servant's back.

"Stop!" She ran toward the three, seeing Salome in the shadows at the last moment, with a satisfied smile. "What is this?" She scowled at Herod. His face gleamed with a predatory glow of sweat. "How dare you beat my servant without my permission!"

"Ah, there she is." Herod's eyes sparked. "Stay here, my sweet wife. Perhaps you shall be next."

Mariamme took a step backward, an unfamiliar fear pounding against her chest. "What is the accusation against this man?"

Herod flicked his head toward the guard with the whip.

He raised it above his head, then cracked it against Leodes's back. The flesh tore and blood bubbled along the line of it.

Mariamme cried out and reached toward Herod. "He has done nothing. He is a good man!"

"Precisely why I chose him." Herod's brow was knit together now, in anger or suspicion, she could not tell. "If anyone should know the truth about this potion, it would be him."

Mariamme shook her head, looked to Salome and back to Herod. "What are you talking about?" Behind her, the palace doors opened again. She glanced back to see Lydia slip in, her face concerned.

"You deny it, then? Mazal has told me everything."

Mariamme faced her husband again. "Mazal? Your cupbearer?"

"Oh, you wear the face of deceit well, my Mariamme. But

Leodes will tell me, won't you, Leodes? Who was it for, this love potion that my wife asked Mazal to create?"

"Herod, you are mad!" She drew his attention from Leodes. At least then the lashing paused. "When have I ever had dealings in potions?" She eyed Salome, still skulking in the shadows. "That is more your sister's realm!"

But Herod would not hear her. "Come, Leodes." He directed the guard to bring another lash across his bleeding back, but his eyes never left Mariamme. "Surely you know everything my wife does, even in secret. You hear all her whispers and treasons. How she hates me."

She was shaking now, trembling over the horrid injustice Leodes suffered because of her. "Of course I hate you, you filthy murderer! You have drowned my brother and strangled my grandfather and chained my mother! How could I not hate you?" Tears dripped from her chin and she dashed them away with an angry hand.

Lydia took her arm with a light touch, but she shook it off.

Herod grinned, as though glad at last to have heard the truth. "But there is more, isn't there? Perhaps I am the one you hate, but there is another to whom you have given your affections, yes?" He ordered another lash, then another. "And Leodes is going to tell me."

If Lydia had not held her back, Mariamme would have thrown herself between the lash and Leodes's back.

"Please, my lord." Leodes panted, near to a faint. "I know nothing of any potion." His gaze lifted to Herod's with a hint of defiance. "But perhaps your orders to have your wife killed in Alexandrium have deadened any affection she might have for you."

No, Leodes. He should not defend her, not at the risk of his own life.

Herod blinked twice and refocused on her, his lips tight and brow furrowed. "In Alexandrium? That old fool Joseph may have told you of my instructions when I was called to Antony in Syria. But who would have told—?"

He broke off and pointed to the guard. "Take the eunuch out. And bring me Sohemus!"

"No!" Mariamme shot forward, grabbed Herod's arms. "No more should suffer! I am the one who deserves your anger!"

She felt herself being pulled backward.

Herod's face was an impassive scowl. "That's it, Lydia. Take charge of your wayward cousin before she does something she will regret."

But Mariamme would not let Lydia restrain her. She tore away and charged at Salome, blood racing. "This is you! You have done this—lies about potions— What kind of excrement—?"

Salome laughed. "Such words from a queen?" She turned her head slowly toward Herod, eyebrows raised. "You see, my brother? Have I not been telling you that she is unfit for you?"

Mariamme would strangle her. She would wrap her hands around Salome's throat the way her grandfather had been strangled in front of the entire Sanhedrin. She reached for the narrow neck, but the throne room doors swept open once more and Sohemus was prodded through at the point of one of his own men's swords.

"What is this, Herod?" His face blanched at the sight of Mariamme. Could he read the situation so easily in her eyes?

"I should be asking you the same, *my friend.*"

Sohemus batted away his guard's sword and strode to the throne. "I am your friend, Herod, and always have been. Speak your mind if you've something to say."

"Oh, I have something to say." Herod circled Sohemus. "Yes, I do."

Mariamme ran to the two men, tried to get between them.

Herod shoved her out of his way. "How is it that my wife learned of my instructions while under your guard in Alexandrium?"

Sohemus said nothing, only stared past Herod.

Mariamme's stomach roiled and her face felt as though it were on fire. She reached out to Lydia for support.

"Or perhaps I should ask a different question, eh? How many times did my wife take you to her bed before you betrayed me?"

At this, Sohemus bared his teeth and raised a fist. "You would dare insult the honor of the queen? She is guileless!"

"Oh, she has always sung your praises, my friend. That is certain. She was sure to tell me how well you looked after her in Alexandrium." He snorted. "Looked after her, indeed. I placed a eunuch at your door, Mariamme, but it appears I should have rendered your mother's guard half a man as well, eh?"

Mariamme regained her strength and got between the two men again. She drew Herod's attention to her face, pushed Sohemus away. "It is a false accusation, husband. I have been a faithful wife to you."

Herod smacked her face with the back of his hand and sent her reeling. "Then explain how you knew of my orders, when only Sohemus had such information!"

Mariamme breathed heavily, hand across her stinging cheek.

"My wife and my friend. Is there no one loyal to me in this wasteland?" Herod waved them all away. "Enough. I have no wish to see any of you now." To the guard who had brought Sohemus, he inclined his head. "Take him. Have him executed."

"No!" Mariamme threw herself at Herod once more. "You defy the law to condemn a man without a trial!"

Herod held her off with one arm and nodded toward the guard. "She is right." He shrugged. "Make it look like an accident."

Mariamme tried to gouge at his eyes, but he was too strong.

Instead, he laughed. "You only condemn him further with your outrage, my dear. I know you will grieve to lose your lover. But you must see that I cannot allow—"

"I fought as hard for Leodes! Do you believe I have also taken the eunuch to my bed?"

But Herod was not listening and Lydia was dragging her backward.

She caught a last glimpse of Sohemus as he was being shoved from the throne room. He turned to look at her over his shoulder, then planted his feet against the injustice. "Hear me, Herod." His voice echoed from the throne room walls. "Your wife is innocent. I have loved her only from afar." He met Mariamme's eyes. "Though I have loved her well."

The guards dragged him out, and Herod and Salome strolled from the throne room as if nothing more than the usual palace business had been transacted.

Mariamme crumpled against Lydia.

The end was coming. This could not go on much longer.

Thirty-Four

Lydia's blood was pounding in fury by the time Salome and Herod left the throne room, but it was not the time to commiserate with Mariamme. The queen must be taken to the safety of her chamber before she did herself harm by attacking her husband.

Mariamme's new lady's maid, a mouse of a girl named Tikva, peeked into the room and saw her lady huddled on the floor, arms wrapped around her knees, leaning against Lydia.

"Bring Simon!" Lydia barked the command to the girl's astonished face.

Tikva looked between them as though deaf.

"The palace manager! Fetch Simon and tell him his queen needs him here."

The girl ran, and Lydia smoothed Mariamme's hair back from her head. Memories of that night in Bethlehem flashed across her spirit. It was not a birth they awaited today, but a death.

Mariamme's teeth were tapping against each other in spasms that also shook her body. "My fault."

"Sshh." Lydia knew this pain, and it was not going to end for a long time. But she would stand by Mariamme and fight.

Fight Salome.

Certainly this was Salome's doing, from Mazal's ridiculous lies about love potions to the torture of Leodes. And Riva's search of her room, looking for a scroll.

Lydia exhaled, still holding Mariamme to herself. Salome was aligned against them both now, and there was more than their own lives to think about. The scrolls represented the hope of a nation against tyrants like Herod and his sister. Thoughts of conceding, of giving up on the scrolls, fled before a new resolve. She would not fail her people. Not ever.

Simon ran into the room as though someone needed pulling from a fire.

Lydia gave him a quick, grateful smile. "She will not rise. I need to get her to her chamber."

He took three swift steps across the throne room floor, bent, and swept Mariamme into his arms as he had done the night they returned from Bethlehem. "Is she ill?"

Lydia followed behind. "Have you not heard what has happened tonight?" She would have thought Leodes's high-pitched screams could be heard to the Dung Gate.

"I . . . I have been—unwell—since yesterday."

Yes, she could understand that. She caught up with him in the corridor, walking shoulder to shoulder. "Let us get her safely to her bed."

A glance from Simon said that he understood she would speak more of it out of Mariamme's hearing. And when she had closed the door to her chamber, with promises to return with any news, she met Simon in the hall.

Her own strength, holding until now, failed her and she leaned against the wall and covered her face with her hands.

"What is it?"

She felt the heavy warmth of his hand on her shoulder for a moment, only a moment before he drew it away.

She lifted her head and surveyed the corridor, but it was empty. At a time like this, when Herod's wrath was running high, staff and family alike knew it was best to remain unseen.

"Sohemus," she whispered.

Simon's glance of concern toward Mariamme's chamber spoke much. Did all the palace know of her affections for the captain of Herod's guard?

"Salome has no doubt bribed Herod's cupbearer, that loathsome Mazal, to tell the king lies. He has accused Mariamme of asking for his help with a love potion. Herod beat Leodes until he let it slip that Sohemus had told Mariamme secrets while Herod was gone and the women at Alexandrium. Herod assumed that the two are lovers."

Simon exhaled heavily, paced away from Lydia, and back again. His face was a mask of anger. "What now?"

"Herod is having Sohemus executed. No trial."

Simon's hands were white-knuckled fists, and he pounded one against the stone wall beside Lydia's head.

She flinched and closed her eyes.

"You see, Lydia?" His voice rasped in her ear. "Do you see how vile a man—?" He was pacing again. "Nearly ten years I have served at the feet of this man, ensuring that he wanted for no luxury, all to provide information to those who could use it against him. I have sacrificed everything to bring this land back to the people. And for what?" He slammed a fist against a palm this time. "For what? What use have I been?"

Lydia caught his arm and halted his pacing, her palms slick with dread. "Simon, I fear for Mariamme—that in her anger and shock she will push Herod beyond even his love for her. But please, he has no love for you that would stay his hand should he learn of your disloyalty! You must control this anger."

He shook off her hand and faced her, a savage look in his eye. "Why? What more can I lose?"

"Your life, Simon!"

She would have said more, but Alexandra suddenly appeared, breaking the two apart. She eyed their sudden movement with suspicion, but her focus was on her daughter's door. "Where is she?"

Lydia nodded. "Inside. She is not taking it well."

Alexandra disappeared into the room.

Lydia felt some relief. The woman was a scheming manipulator, but Mariamme relied upon her and Alexandra would rise to the occasion to comfort her daughter.

"You are a fool!"

Alexandra's harsh accusation pierced even the closed door. Lydia's mouth dropped open.

Simon only shook his head. "I will find out what is happening with Sohemus." He glanced in each direction of the balcony and leaned closer. "Perhaps his men will have enough loyalty to help with an escape."

He left Lydia standing outside the door, her hand on the wood. Should she interrupt Alexandra's tirade?

"How many times have I warned you about that man? And now your foolishness is going to cost us everything!"

Lydia could hear no reply. She pushed the door open and faced Alexandra's indignant scowl at the intrusion. So be it. There were plans to be made.

How many times had Lydia been involved with an escape from this palace? Alexandra and Aristobulus wheeled away in coffins. Mariamme on the eve of her first child's birth. Herself, even, wanting to run from Salome and from her destiny.

She would not run, not from the fight. But first she would plan yet another escape. It would be harder this time. With Mariamme's young children and probably Alexandra, they would need help and supplies. But she would make it happen.

She must.

≈

Lydia spent the night making arrangements. She would not involve Simon. His position in the palace was too vital to jeopardize. Instead, she ventured into the city to procure wagons and supplies, drivers and townswomen willing to make a journey for a promised payment of twenty shekels.

For the first time, the strange irony of her own position as a penniless child of royalty struck her. She had nothing of her own with which to pay anyone and lived at the generosity of her bene-factors. If she were to leave the palace, disappear into the city with the scrolls until she somehow found the Chakkiym, she would have to support herself.

How many years had it been since she dreamed of opening her own pottery shop? Secreted her meager obols under her bed-roll with hopes of breaking free? She was no freer than she had been as a servant in Cleopatra's palace.

There could be no shop here in Jerusalem. She would need to remain unknown, hidden. Perhaps Simon's political friends would hide her. Should she tell them of the scrolls? She had been so guarded with them all these years, never even trusting the relationship with Simon enough to share the secret with him. Perhaps it was time. Until then, however, she removed the scrolls from her bedchamber and hid them in the deepest recess of the storerooms, hopefully safe from Salome.

Mariamme slept late into the morning, and Lydia did not wake her. They would not leave until nightfall, when they had a chance of gaining distance before their escape was noticed. The palace was quiet again in the morning, though a few odd visitors were trickling in, supporters of Herod's from the Sanhedrin. Each new face soon disappeared into the throne room. Was there some military or political threat to distract Herod from his anger toward Mariamme? That would be a blessing.

She tracked down Simon in his office chamber and asked about Sohemus. His body had been found earlier this morning, throat slit by bandits in an alley. She braced a hand against the door frame and fought to use the anger and sadness as fuel for what must be done.

"I must keep Mariamme in her chamber today. No risk of more hateful spewing at Herod, especially if he is entertaining supporters."

She turned to go, but the sound of marching boots rooted her to the floor.

A cadre of four soldiers marched in two pairs across the courtyard, toward the front palace stairs.

Panic raced along her veins, propelled her forward. She was at their backs in a moment, passed them on the stairs, ran ahead down the corridor, and burst into Mariamme's room.

The queen was holding little Cypros, with her maid Tikva standing by. Mariamme's head shot up at Lydia's forceful entrance and her red-rimmed eyes widened.

"Soldiers, sister." Lydia crossed the room as Mariamme stood. "They may be coming for you."

Mariamme quickly lowered the baby into Tikva's arms, kissed the little forehead, and grabbed Tikva's shoulders. "Take her to your own chamber. Keep her safe. Promise me!"

The young girl's face was as pale as the moon, but she nodded. There was no more time.

The soldiers were at the door, and then they were in the chamber. One of them shoved Lydia aside as though she were still a servant while another grabbed at Mariamme's arm. Simon's anxious face appeared in the doorway, but the soldiers shoved him back.

"She is the queen!" Lydia pushed between the men. "She can walk unassisted!"

Mariamme took a deep breath, raised her chin, and preceded the soldiers out of the room.

Lydia followed, her stomach in knots. She brushed Simon's outstretched hand as she passed him, but their escorts would not allow him to follow, perhaps fearing his interference more than they feared Lydia's.

They should have escaped last night. Why had she waited, trying to make everything perfect, trying to prove her competency to arrange the challenge?

The tight group marched to the throne room, through its doors, and into the center, where a seated group of men to the right of Herod's throne did not bode well.

Lydia spotted Alexandra to the left, also seated but clearly not of her own free will. Salome stood behind Herod's throne.

The soldiers marched Mariamme to the center of the room to stand before her husband, who looked as though he had not slept nor shaved nor eaten since the incident with Sohemus the previous night.

Lydia slipped to the windowed wall, stood beside one of the tapestries that blocked both the chill and the sun. A razor-thin line of morning light etched the floor in front of her feet, like a boundary she should not cross.

Herod nodded majestically, first to Mariamme and then to the sycophants arrayed on his left.

"Gentlemen, as you may have heard, there is news from Rome this morning. Egypt has officially become a province of the Roman Republic, under the rule of Princeps and First Citizen, Caesar Octavian. The groves and gardens of the Jordan Valley, which Marc Antony stole from us to give to his Egyptian whore, have been restored."

He smiled on the men, who were nodding gleefully in return. "In addition, our generous benefactor, Caesar Octavian, has given us new territories of more than ten cities to expand our kingdom and is sending Cleopatra's personal bodyguard of four hundred Galatians to us." He spread his hands to the men. "As you can see, it is a good day to be in favor with your king, who has fallen into great favor with the First Citizen of Rome, Caesar Octavian."

He sighed heavily, as though the recitation had exhausted him. "And now, let the trial begin."

Trial? What sort of mockery was this? In Herod's palace rather than before the full Sanhedrin in the Hall of Hewn Stone, with no public hearing? And who would sit as judge?

As if in answer, Herod stood. "I shall serve as both the prosecution and the judge."

Lydia gaped and looked to Alexandra. Surely something

could be done! But the woman's face was stony, her gaze fixed straight ahead.

Herod was circling Mariamme, as he had done last night, the wild look in his eyes running up and down her body.

This morning she stood stoically, without emotion.

"The queen is accused of unfaithfulness to her husband." He waved a hand and Mazal hustled out of the shadows. "As proof, we offer Mazal, cupbearer to the king, whose help she tried to procure for making a potion that would bind her lover to herself for all time."

Mazal nodded energetically, but it did not appear any actual questions were to be directed toward him.

Herod waved him off.

Lydia watched the faces of the little court Herod had assembled. They were appropriately aghast, and the only sympathy seemed directed at the king himself.

"As for her lover, unfortunately he cannot appear before us to admit his wrongdoing as he was tragically overtaken by criminals early this morning and his life cut short."

At this, Mariamme's knees buckled.

Lydia pushed from the wall. But the queen was rallying. *That's it, Mariamme. Show no weakness.*

"Ah, you see by her reaction that she is overcome with grief over the loss of her lover."

Herod returned to his throne and took his seat slowly. "The prosecution has ended its argument, and as there is no defense, I would ask that the court render its verdict, whether the queen is innocent or guilty of crimes to be paid for with her life."

What? Lydia stepped across the slash of light at her feet. No defense? Not even a witness against her? The heads of Herod's supporters were bent to each other in mock deliberation. As though any of them would dare contradict the king.

"I will speak in my own defense, husband."

Lydia silently cheered Mariamme.

Herod raised his eyebrows. "Speak, then. I would have the court hear your lies."

She turned her head slightly to face the seated men. "I know of no such potion, for Mazal does not speak the truth. But even if there were such a thing, how does the king know it was not prepared for him?"

Herod's face flushed. He opened his mouth, then closed it again, as though weighing his choices. He fixed his gaze on Mariamme, and the look was one of pain and betrayal. For all his cruelty and growing madness, his compulsive love for Mariamme still burned in his eyes—the look of a man so at the mercy of a woman who despised him, who wanted to somehow be free of him.

When he spoke, the words were measured and cold. "As the queen has refused to come to the king's bed for nearly a year, this idea is preposterous."

It cost him, this admission. To refuse a king in anything was a direct affront to his authority. The eyes of the men flicked between Herod and Mariamme.

And in that moment, she was condemned.

Whether she had taken Sohemus to herself or not, it mattered little. She had refused the king, and this was reason enough to call for her death.

Again, heads bent as if it were necessary. The head of the Sanhedrin stood and bowed his head briefly toward the king.

"My lord, the court has reached its verdict. The queen is declared guilty of these crimes and sentenced to death."

Lydia felt her own limbs weaken. How could this be happening? She grabbed at the tapestry, twisted it between tight fingers.

Herod slumped against the back of his throne, and from behind Salome put a hand to his shoulder. He looked on his wife and his voice became pleading. "You see, Mariamme? You see? Even they are in agreement. You have done me wrong. Not been a proper wife to me." His gaze flicked to Alexandra, who had not moved or spoken during the proceedings. "You and your mother have done nothing but conspire against me since we were wed."

The words were angry, but Herod seemed to have no anger left. He sagged on his throne like a deflated wineskin, like a child whose tantrum has been successful but left him exhausted.

"I am a generous king, as you all know. The sentence of death shall be commuted to imprisonment."

Lydia's fingers loosened slightly on the tapestry and she found her breath again.

But Salome jolted forward, her face white. "Brother! Think what you are doing! This woman—and her mother—they are both determined to see you removed from power. As long as she lives, your life is in danger. Who knows but that this potion she was concocting was not actually a poison meant to kill you?"

Lydia huffed. Either Mariamme was unfaithful or she was a murderer—Salome could not have it both ways. But Herod seemed disinclined to think logically.

"She would tear this country apart, my brother. Incite the people to rise up against you. There will be riots! Riots and civil war!" Salome's face was red with rage now. She gripped Herod's shoulder like a vise. "She conspires with the zealotry, I have heard. Even here in your own palace there are traitors!"

Lydia's body went cold. Would Salome condemn everyone Lydia loved in one morning?

Herod's fatigue had fled, and his sister's words were like a bellows to the fire of his rage. He sat forward on the throne, a look of fury thrown down on Mariamme. "Is this true? Do you work against my kingship?"

Grovel, Mariamme, Lydia begged her silently, even as her eyes filled with tears because she knew her friend and cousin and sister well enough. She would not give Herod what he wanted. Not even to save her own life.

True to her noble birth and her family name, Mariamme raised her chin and looked Herod in the eye, a calm and settled dignity in the carriage of her shoulders.

"You have no kingship, Idumean. You are a Roman puppet, just as your father was before you. Those of us who truly belong to Israel"—she gave a pointed glance to the flatterers on his left— "those of us who know that the One God has given us this land as a possession forever, we also know that your reign will end."

Lydia clutched at her robe with one hand, the other arm wrapped about her waist. She could do nothing, say nothing, to stop this now.

"I curse you, Herod the Idumean. In the name of the One God, Righteous and True, I curse you to die a painful death, removed of your pride, shamed before this nation. May your name ring out over the ages to come as a byword for cruelty and madness."

Herod fell back once more, his arms resting limply on the arms of the throne. He was superstitious enough to find Mariamme's curse the most frightening thing he'd ever heard.

Good. Let him suffer.

Salome was petting his shoulder now, a soothing motion, and whispering in his ear.

Herod nodded, then waved a weak hand without lifting his arm. "Take her to the gallows."

Lydia was panting. She must keep her head.

"No!" She shot forward, past the still-silent Alexandra. "This is not justice! Mariamme has done nothing wrong! She has been faithful—"

Another whispered word from Salome, whose gaze pierced Lydia with a frightening hatred.

Herod sighed. "The court suspects both Mariamme's mother and the Ptolemy Lydia of conspiring against the king as well—"

At this, Alexandra jumped to her feet with a shriek. "Lies! I have known nothing of her plots, my king!"

Lydia whirled on Alexandra, shock rendering her speechless.

The guards were grabbing at Mariamme, pulling her backward.

Coming for Alexandra. Coming for her.

Alexandra tore at her hair and turned on Mariamme. "You ungrateful wretch! Foul and traitorous!" She spit at her daughter's feet. "You have treated our benefactor Herod in the vilest ways. Your punishment is just retribution!"

A stunned and heavy silence fell upon the chamber.

Mariamme was being prodded toward the door now. She paused for a long look at her mother but said not a word. And then she set her face for the door and led the soldiers out.

Herod was shaking his head at Salome. "Enough sentences for one day." He rose, at which each of those seated also rose, then he crossed to the narrow door at the head of the throne room on heavy feet and disappeared.

Salome paused as she passed Lydia and leaned to hiss in her ear, "You are next, Egyptian." And then they were gone.

The room erupted at once in the chatter that followed a shocking drama.

Lydia cast a look of disgust on Alexandra, but she would not stop to berate the odious woman now.

There was no time.

Thirty-Five

Jerusalem kept its gallows at the ready.

There was no telling when a public execution might be called for—to quell unrest, to rid the kingdom of agitators.

To hang a queen.

It seemed the entire palace followed in the wake of the soldiers. Lydia fought her way through the crowd that gathered citizens as it flowed through the street—citizens on their way to shops and markets who clotted the streets and alleys for a look at whatever traitor was being led to his death today.

Somewhere behind her, Simon and Jonah worked through the crowd, using their influence to keep the tenuous peace. There could easily be more bloodshed when the people realized it was their Hasmonean princess being led away. Simon had tried to hold Lydia back as well, but she left him to his important work and pushed through to her own.

Lydia shoved and jostled those ahead, taller than she. Dodged between shoulders and elbows to get a glimpse of Mariamme. She could not think of Salome's threat to herself. Not until she saved Mariamme.

Only the back of the queen's head, with her honey-red hair flowing loose and uncovered down her back, appeared between the heads of the crowd.

The gallows loomed, weather-blackened and ominous. A rudely constructed platform, two poles and a crosspiece like an artificial doorway that led only to Hades. A twisted rope with a single loop barely wide enough to fit over a head.

Every part of Lydia's body felt numb and on fire at once. She stumbled forward, fighting not to retch, ears ringing with the shouts of the crowd.

Did they cry for Mariamme's blood or for her vindication?

Would no one speak for her innocence?

Up, up the stairs.

No, it was too soon.

Mariamme's thin frame did not waver, her spine did not bend.

Lydia pushed forward, jammed her body between those who clamored for a better look at the spectacle. A woman about her age turned a nasty eye on her and scowled with blackened teeth.

"Stop this madness!"

Her scream was lost in the din.

The sun beat down on their heads from a cloudless, pitiless sky.

They were stretching that hideous loop around her head.

HaShem, have mercy.

She barely felt her chest heaving for breath, sucking in air, choking on sobs. "Mariamme!"

The queen's gaze met hers at last. The first flicker of emotion Lydia had seen since the throne room passed over her face.

Mariamme nodded, wordless, to Lydia. All the love of the years they had spent together passed between them in that moment. Mariamme reached her right hand out across the open space of the platform.

Lydia shoved to the front of the crowd, to the base of the gallows and reached, reached for her friend, as though the reaching could save her, could connect them in ways that would span the afterlife, outlast death.

Her eyes were blinded with hot tears and Lydia shook them away. She would keep this fragile contact, not let it go. She was still reaching across the empty air when the floor beneath Mariamme released.

Her own breath ceased with the jolt of the platform. Her chest was stone, her lungs solid, her throat sealed.

Mariamme hung from the rope, her head tilted playfully. Had Lydia not seen her stand in the nursery doorway just so, her head inclined in mock disapproval of her children's antics?

It was all a farce. It must be.

Herod loved Mariamme. Loved her obsessively. How could he have let it come to this?

Lydia clamored up the steps onto the platform, reaching for Mariamme's dangling legs.

The executioner pulled her back.

The drop had rendered her unconscious, but strangulation took minutes.

There was still time.

She scrabbled for her legs, would have lain across that opening and forced Mariamme's body upward if they would let her. But the grip of soldiers was so tight, it cut off the blood to her arms, and her screams went unheeded.

They were replacing the floorboard. Cutting her down.

The guards released Lydia at last, and she fell forward in time to catch Mariamme. Her body crumpled into Lydia's arms, the neck horribly loose and rope-scraped.

The blue sky above the gallows wavered and grew dim. Blackness pushed in from the crowd. An undulating blackness that reached out for her.

Lydia's body gave up its refusal to breathe, and she dragged in a harsh gulp of air that slashed at her throat and chest like it had teeth. That terrible suffocation, like a drowning in the Nile, that always clutched at her chest when she got too close, when love was ripped away. She sucked in a breath, then another and another and another.

But it was not enough. The water would take her too.

The sky and ground and crowd melted together and she fell across Mariamme's body. Sisters in life, they would be so in death.

Thirty-Six

She became aware slowly. A bouncing rhythm and a beating heart.

Carried.

Her eyes fluttered open.

Simon's stubbled jaw, set in an angry line, jutted across her vision. His arms braced beneath her back and knees. He angled her body, feet first, against the flow of the crowd.

"I can walk," Lydia whispered, the sound jagged.

He did not acknowledge her words or even that she was conscious.

She closed her eyes and let it be.

She felt the change in atmosphere, from the street, through the palace arch. Across the fountained courtyard. Through shadowy corridors.

When he laid her on a bed, she opened her eyes, expecting her own chamber. But the room was unfamiliar.

He closed the door, poured water from a jug, and brought it to the bedside.

She struggled to sit. "Where—what is this?"

"I brought you to my bedchamber."

She was too far spent to even feel a jolt at the inappropriateness. She sipped the water obediently, as though water could quench the sting.

Simon perched on the edge of the bed and brushed the hair from her eyes. "Salome is hunting you. You must remain here until we can get you out of the city."

"She is dead." The words dropped like stones from her lips.

Simon laid a warm hand on her cheek. "I know. I am so sorry."

"He killed her."

"Yes."

"I did not think he ever would. Not really. He loved her."

Simon smiled sadly. "That was not love, Lydia. *You* loved her."

His words brought a fresh wave of grief, rising in her chest and spilling from her eyes. "I did love her, Simon. She was my family."

He pulled her into an embrace, but she pushed him away. "But what purpose did it serve, my love for her? Did it save her? Did it save any of them? What use was I to any of them? Ptolemy. Samuel. Aristobulus." The overwhelming sadness pressed in on her like a crushing weight, and she dropped her head into her hands. "Caesarion."

Was this how it would always be? Those she was foolish enough to love would be taken from her, leave her bereft and trampled?

Simon had backed away and was pacing, hands braced against his hips. His empathy was giving way to righteous anger. "And how many will die before the battle is won? How many more will I fail to protect?"

Lydia set the cup aside and curled herself on the bed. "You could not have stopped him, Simon. It was not your fault."

"Nor yours."

She nodded, her tears dampening the pillow. "I know. But I see now that it is hopeless to try to love, for life is the enemy of love."

"Not true." Simon was at her side again, kneeling beside the bed. "Not true, Lydia. You must not let this loss erase what you have learned. You put too much of yourself into the value others place on you. When they are taken, you think there is nothing of you left. But you are more than your skills or your talent or your kindness. You have value apart from all that."

She tried to smile. "You sound like Samuel. He always said that the One God's love for me gave me worth, even if I was rejected and abandoned by all others."

He took her hand in his. "I know too little of HaShem, I fear. I have spent many years angry that He has not freed His people from tyranny. But I suspect your Samuel was right. If you could see your value as the One God sees, you would find a solid foundation on which to build your life. On which to build love."

"And you, Simon? Was it not you who told me that love and the fight could not coexist? Can't you see that the fight will never be finished? If there is ever to be love, it must happen alongside the fight."

His face was so close to hers, but he looked away. "I—the last time—my distraction led only to pain—"

She nodded. There was no need to repeat the pain that the failure to keep her heart closed had brought.

Simon took several deep breaths, then seemed to come to a decision. He squeezed her fingers. "I am taking you from here. I do not understand Salome's hatred, but she has ordered guards to seize you on sight, to bring you for trial and certain execution."

"It appears I have become completely worthless, then."

"As a political tool, perhaps, and that is a blessing. But as a woman—" His words caught in his throat. "I know I have no right to ask you to trust my protection—"

"I would trust no one more than you, Simon."

He brought her hand to his lips. "Thank you for that."

"But I cannot leave Jerusalem."

He exhaled. "I will not argue with you now. But at least we are leaving the palace. And we are not coming back."

She pushed herself to sitting, swung her legs over the side of the bed. "What about your position here? You have worked long and hard to gain favor so you could give information to those who would—"

"My work here is finished."

She shook her head. "You have done nothing to bring Herod's wrath on you, Simon. You can still fight—"

"Lydia." His eyes were on hers, the barriers of status and position forgotten. "The only fight I care about now is keeping you safe."

That he would find her worth this sacrifice, the giving up of everything he had struggled to gain, was like a healing ointment applied to her raw heart.

"And I will keep you safe, Lydia. Not only from Salome, but from gossip. Wherever we go, nothing of impropriety shall reach the ears of Rome. If Marcus Agrippa will still have you—"

"There is no Agrippa, Simon." She touched his cheek with her fingertips. "There is only you."

He clutched at her hand, still against his face, and closed his eyes. "I would take you out of this city, out of this country, even, if it would keep you safe."

She smiled, the cold grief of Mariamme's death thawing in

the warmth of Simon's words, but also in the fire of the battle that she still needed to wage, one that Simon knew nothing of. "There is fighting still to be done, Simon." She breathed in courage. "Stay here. I have something to show you."

He shook his head. "There is no time. We must leave at once while the palace is still in chaos."

"I must gather my things."

"It is not safe to be about the palace. We can purchase—"

She touched his arm. "There is something I cannot leave behind." She wore her mother's pendant. Only the scrolls were necessary. She started for the door, but he caught her arm and pulled her back.

His left arm went around her waist and his right hand tipped her chin. His kiss was urgent, determined.

She responded, but only for a moment. There would be time later.

"Hurry." He whispered the word at her back as she left the room.

≈

How many hiding places had the scrolls seen in the ten years since Samuel's death?

Lydia gathered a few clothes for their escape from the servant Tikva's room—plain tunics and robes that did not bespeak royalty. They would not be leaving the city, only hiding, and they could get more if needed. If Simon had money, that is.

In a dark storeroom, she slid a shelf from its position, pried up a large floor tile usually pinned by one of its legs, and reached into the dark hole she had painstakingly dug into the dirt below.

Her fingers closed around its squared edges and she brought

it into the light, then sat back on her heels and brushed the dust from its lid, as she had done when she pulled it from the hole in the corner of Samuel's house.

Samuel. Would he approve of what she was about to do? Simon was not a rabbi, not a priest. But he could be trusted, just as she had trusted David with the knowledge of the scrolls years ago, though they had made a pact not to speak of them.

Simon would give up his fight for her sake. She could risk the opening of her secrets, to show him why that fight must continue.

She reached into the hole once more, pulled out the familiar sack, dingier and more ragged than it had been years ago but still serviceable. She thrust the wooden box to the bottom and piled in the few articles of clothing she had taken.

She would not even go to her own bedchamber. It was not her home. She had no home. Not yet.

A trickle of doubt slid into her thoughts. How could she leave without completing Samuel's task for her? But she had failed to find the Chakkiym, regardless of her efforts. How would leaving the palace make any difference? Perhaps Simon would have a better plan.

She hurried back the way she had come, to Simon's chamber on the lower level. She tapped on the door, then pushed it open.

Simon had a wooden crate set on the bed and was tossing possessions into it. He exhaled at her return and eyed the dirty sack. "This was so important?"

She held up her treasure. "Yes, this is everything. Simon, I— there is something I must tell you, show you—"

He nodded but continued his packing. "There will be time for talking soon, Lydia. I must get you out of here without delay."

Her fingers tightened around the sack. Yes, perhaps it would be better to wait until they were in hiding. It was a long story, after all.

She set the sack by the door and crossed to his bed. "Can I help?"

"I am nearly finished." He bent to a chest along the wall and drew a folded piece of cloth from the bottom. Sharp creases and faded colors marked it as both old and long unused. He ran light fingers over the fabric and sighed. "It has been many years since I even thought of this."

She bent for a closer look. It was white with red stripes.

He shook it out.

The folds fell away. Red and blue tassels quivered at the corners.

Lydia sucked in a disbelieving breath and a tremor passed through her, as though angels had run their fingers down her spine.

Simon glanced at her, then turned fully, his lips parting in concern. "What is it, Lydia? You are so pale!"

"Wh— Is that . . . is that a tallit?"

He held it up. "A family heirloom, you could say. Passed down from my father— Lydia, you are shaking!"

"Finish. Finish, Simon. Why did your father give you this covering?"

He hung his head. "Another failure on my part, I'm afraid. My father came to Jerusalem when he was only a boy, with his father who had been a scholar in Persia. My grandfather, and then my father, went every year to the Temple in a fruitless tradition that left them disappointed every year."

"Waiting on the steps of the Temple. Waiting for one who never came."

His eyes flickered with confusion. "You know of their duty?"

But she could not speak more, not until she heard it all.

He swallowed, still watching her face. "When my father died, I was a very young man. At first I too went every year. But as the years passed, I grew to disbelieve that any answers were to be found there. If Judea and our people were to be free, it would be in the strength of our fighting arm, not the scribblings of an old prophet." He exhaled and shook his head. "Lydia, I—you must tell me—"

In answer, she stumbled to the door, picked up her sack, and returned. With trembling hands she reached in and pulled the wooden box from under the jumble of clothing.

Simon's gaze was on the box, but without recognition.

She dropped the sack of clothing at their feet. Lifted the tiny latch on the box and opened the lid.

The unmarred wax seemed to glow where it sealed the scrolls.

"What are they?" Simon's words sounded reverent, as if he somehow sensed the truth.

Lydia found her voice at last. "The scribblings of an old prophet."

His eyes went to hers, then back to the scrolls. "I do not understand."

"Every year on the Day of Atonement, Samuel told me. Just before he died. Wait on the steps of the Temple for the one who will come wearing a red-striped tallit with red and blue corded tassels." She took a shallow breath. "Wait for the Chakkiym."

Simon's jaw was slack, his eyes glassy. He eased the box from her hands, then sank onto the edge of his bed. "And were you there, all these years?"

She swallowed, her throat dry. "Except when I could not be. I would never have missed, except that I thought it was hopeless. I thought perhaps he—you—had been killed when Herod took the city on Yom HaKippurim all those years ago."

Simon ran a light finger over the surface of the scrolls, and when he looked up, tears were in his eyes. "How I wish my father and grandfather were here to see this day."

She nodded, smiling through her own tears. "Samuel too. He spent his life searching. Gave his life protecting them."

At this reminder, she inhaled sharply. "Simon, do not ask me to explain now, but it was Salome who sent the men who killed Samuel in Alexandria. She knows now that I have the scrolls."

He jumped to his feet, closed the box, and returned it to her, then pointed to her sack. "We are leaving."

She twisted the sack between her fingers, the box hidden once more.

Simon took up his crate and headed for the door. He paused and turned, looking over the crate at her. "Everything is changed now, Lydia."

"I know."

"You have done your duty. Delivered the scrolls. From here, there is no need for you to incur more danger. And if you leave with me, you will likely never be known as a Hasmonean, nor a Ptolemy, again. I know what it means to you, to have discovered your birthright. I cannot ask you to give it up—"

"My life, my identity, is not built upon my birthright, Simon. It matters little who my parents were, nor even if they willingly gave me up, or had me snatched from them, or died protecting me. I am a child of the One God, and that is all that matters. And I will stay with you, whether in Jerusalem, or Judea, or farther."

He smiled over the crate. "Then farther we shall go."

Thirty-Seven

S imon had people everywhere.

Lydia had never realized the extent of his network, the number of palace staff in place for when the time was right. The men who worked through the city under cover of darkness, striking at Israel's enemies. If she had known, she would have been terrified for Simon.

For Simon, and for David.

As she suspected, David had become one of Simon's followers. And in the darkness of an underground storage room once more, Lydia and Simon shared everything with him, showed him the tallit, given by Simon's father. And in spite of the horror of the day, Lydia found herself smiling at his outright joy.

How he had grown since she first met him at the rail of the cursed ship sailing out of Alexandria. He had been an awkward boy, shy and at odds with his body. Now David stood before her a man, ready to assume the mantle of responsibility that Simon was passing to him, as a father to a son. He nodded at each of Simon's instructions, sober and focused on names and places and objectives.

Jonah and Esther came, brought somehow by Simon's messengers. Simon shared his joy over the scrolls, but there were many tears at the parting that must be. In a solemn moment, Simon took the hand of David and the hand of Jonah and joined them together.

Simon was leaving the fight behind, but he was leaving it in good hands.

And then their friends were gone, leaving them to wait in the darkness while the threads of Simon's influence were pulled to arrange safe passage not only from the palace but from Jerusalem as well.

For they were going to Persia. Though held by the Parthians now, those who had lived there for generations since the exile still clung to the old ways, to the old names.

This was the charge laid upon Simon by his father and grandfather. *"When the scrolls are found, they must be returned."* The Chakkiym still lived and studied, they had promised. Back in Persia they were waiting for news of the Messiah, of the coming of the kingdom. The scrolls must be there when the time of the end was come.

They would travel north, through Samaria and on to Damascus, then across to take the Persian Royal Road southward. And within two months, Lydia would see the Persian Empire.

The afternoon of waiting in the storeroom passed swiftly, with whispered conversation about the future, sad remembrances of Mariamme, shared concerns over what would become of her children, left here in the palace with their wicked grandmother and aunt to raise them. Lydia would have to leave all of that in the hands of HaShem, whom she had learned to trust in the journey from Alexandria to this moment.

In a sense, she had been right. A life built on pleasing others to be loved, worrying whether people accepted her, loved her, were faithful to her, would never work. People would abandon and reject, be taken from her, leaving her feeling guilty and worthless or resentful. She must decide that who she is must be grounded elsewhere, in the confidence born of being God's. A life built on *this* truth would allow her to reach out and risk, to love others joyfully and without fear, with a hope built on the secure love of a God who would never forsake her.

When David came at last with promises that all was ready, she stood eagerly, stretching her stiff legs.

Simon caught her hand in his own. "You are not sad to leave Jerusalem?"

She frowned. "Though I have spent years here, I have seen little of it. This palace has been something between a home and a prison. I have not come to think of Jerusalem as my city. I have barely come to think of myself as a Jew." She smiled at David. "There is only one thing I will miss in Judea."

David held his arms out to her, and she went to him and let him wrap strong arms around her.

"Thank you, my friend." She whispered the words against his chest. "I should have been lost without you. You have done me nothing but good from the moment we met on that ship, and I am so proud of the man you have become."

He sniffed and pulled away.

"No sadness. We go to fulfill what was always meant to be." She squeezed his hands. "And we will write. When it is safe, we will send letters with news, and you will send letters of your bride, and your house full of children, and the amazing things you will build with these hands."

He smiled through tears and nodded, then turned to Simon for a clasping of arms, a slapping of backs.

"Be careful," David said. "Herod is beside himself with grief and rage. He staggers from room to room, crying out for Mariamme as if she lives."

Lydia closed her eyes, the words of Mariamme's curse in her ears. She nodded once. *Let him go mad, then. Let him drown in his madness.*

And then they were off, running up the stairs to the side entrance. Outside in the darkness, a figure shifted from the palace wall.

"Riva!" Lydia's heart lurched. They were so close.

But Riva's pale face was tear-streaked and she held out a package to Lydia. "Her jewels." She swiped at her tears. "She would have wanted you to have them."

Lydia took the package from the girl's outstretched hand, then pulled her into an embrace. "Get free of this place, Riva. Find yourself in the One God. He will love you like no other."

And then Simon tugged her toward the darkness, and they were vaulting to the wagon bed as it rolled away.

They rounded the corner of the palace, kept close to the wall as they crossed the front, where the wide square of paving stones marked the beginning of the royal fortress. Past the massive arch, the Temple behind them. The stars were blotted out tonight, masked by heavy clouds that threatened rain.

The horses' hooves echoed off the paving stones and the walls of the palace, a rapid click that beat in time with Lydia's pulse.

And then it was more than the clouds that held a threat. The very air around them seemed to grow thick with menace.

A shout from the palace roof drew their eyes upward. There at the lip of the roof, a dark blot against the gray-black sky.

Salome. Arms upraised and yelling.

Their driver slowed, not because of the spectacle on the roof, but because of the swarm of guards that had appeared before and behind, pouring like insects into the paved front court of the palace.

Above Salome, the very clouds seemed to swirl with the blackness of her rage. The words of her ranting fell upon those below like hailstones.

"Lydia, Daughter of Ptolemies. Lydia, Daughter of Maccabees. You are nothing!"

Lydia rose to her feet in the bed of the wagon. Simon pulled at her hand, but she slipped from his grasp.

"Goddess, hear my cry!" Salome raised her voice to the wind. "Al-Uzzá, goddess of my people, come to my aid. Destroy this one who would rip power from your favored ones!"

A darkness that could not be seen with the eye but only felt with the spirit pressed upon Lydia, a presence of the darkness that had forever set itself up against the people of God.

She raised her eyes to Salome's wrath, to the powers of the air she implored. "Drive on, Reuben."

She felt the driver look back at her in question, but she did not break the connection with Salome, only held up her hands to the guards who approached. Held them outstretched, like Moses did as the people fought the Amalekites. She had forgotten that story until this moment, but the words of Samuel were as fresh as if he told it yesterday. The Amalekites, whose descendant now stood upon the palace roof and tried once more to wage war against the plan of God.

Lydia kept her arms raised, her feet spread wide for balance, as they passed through the clot of guards untouched, and Salome shrieked futile curses down upon their heads.

Lydia had been raised in a Greek palace in the capital of Egypt. She had seen royalty in the power circles of Rome and been claimed as family in Jerusalem, City of God. But not until this moment did she truly understand herself, truly see who she was meant to be. Her childhood fancies of a royal birth had become truth, but the truth of her birth did not define her. Did not give her any more worth than she'd already possessed as a child of God.

Greek or Egyptian, Roman or Jew—one day they would all bow before the One God. All peoples, nations, and men of every language, as the prophet Daniel had said. His dominion was an everlasting dominion that would not pass away. His kingdom was a kingdom that would never be destroyed.

And as part of that kingdom, Lydia could not be shaken.

Salome's screaming curses ceased. The guards closed ranks behind them and they rolled on, through the streets toward the Valley Gate. Lydia lowered herself to sit beside Simon, who wrapped a tight arm around her waist.

But Salome would not be defeated. She was there suddenly, flying out of the darkness astride an ebony stallion, like some sort of avenging demon, black hair streaming backward from white eyes and bared teeth.

The horse galloped alongside the wagon on Lydia's side.

Simon stood, one foot braced against the wagon bed.

Salome reached for Lydia, grabbed at her robes, and yanked.

A yell from Simon and the wagon rumbled to a stop, but not before horse and ground and Salome blurred into one.

Lydia fell to the hard-packed dirt, tangled in the clawing arms of the woman who had sworn to see her dead.

Salome's face appeared above hers, a wicked grin creasing the taut skin. "Worthless servant. Did you think—?"

And then she was gone, jerked backward by Simon's strong arms.

Lydia struggled to her feet, every joint bruised.

Salome writhed in Simon's grasp and spit at Lydia. "You cannot get away. Not from me."

Lydia tilted her head to study the woman. A strange peace enveloped her. "Let her go, Simon."

Simon held her tighter. "She is fueled by the fires of Hades."

"Let her go." She did not take her gaze from Salome, though she felt Simon's hesitation and then his trust.

He dropped his arms and took a step backward.

Salome hurtled toward her, then straightened as though slapped.

Lydia walked a slow circle around the woman. The futility of her dark magic hung like a visible shroud, and Lydia could see its vain efforts stretching back into the past and even into the future somehow.

"What have you done to me?" Salome struggled as though still in Simon's grip, though he had stepped away from them both. "What magic do you use against me, servant?"

"No magic, Salome. It is not I who holds your life in His hand." She stopped her circling to stand and speak before the king's sister. "You would destroy the hopes of our Messiah, but I have been given a role as well. And no opinion of man, neither condemnation nor praise, bears any consequence in the face of this great destiny. It is a destiny offered to every man and every woman who would take it up, who would live a life of courage and risk because our future is secure in the hands of the One God."

Yes, risk. Like the scrolls, Lydia had kept her heart buried for ten years. And like the scrolls, her heart would never change the world as long as she kept it hidden.

Still trapped in unseen bonds, Salome's expression passed from hatred to fury to something else—something almost pitiful in its despair. Her face lowered and her chest heaved.

"Kill me, then, servant girl. You would strip my power and leave me at your mercy. Why stop there?" The words were raw and hopeless, almost tearful. "Strike me down and end my humiliation."

"It is not for me to name the time and the season of your judgment, Salome." Lydia crossed the space between them. Simon helped her back into the wagon, and once seated, she looked down on the woman, small and defeated and cowering in the dirt. "But know this. The One God sees you, as He sees us all. And you will never win."

Salome's eyes were dead in their blackness, her arms limp at her sides, her tirades silenced at last.

The goodness of the One God to give her this moment to see His victory swept over Lydia and brought healing tears as the wagon rolled to the Valley Gate, leaving Salome in the darkness behind.

The gate opened with a salute to Simon from its keeper, and Lydia fell into Simon's arms at last, exhausted. She bent her head to his and set her eyes eastward.

A long journey awaited, a journey certain to come with hardships.

But somewhere in Persia, a group of men awaited their arrival, living in faith that someone would come bearing the scrolls of promise, sealed until the time of the end.

The *Chakkiym*. Strange Aramaic word. Here in Judea and around the world, it was spoken only in secret, passed down from father to son.

But in Persia . . .

In Persia, they would find this proud and ancient group thriving.

The Chakkiym.

Wise men.

Watching the horizon from the east, for a sign that the Messiah was come at last.

The Story Behind the Story . . . and Beyond

Thank you for reading *The Queen's Handmaid*. I hope you enjoyed Lydia's tale. The story you have just finished has been my most ambitious to date, both in scope and in the amount of historical fact wedged between the lines of fiction.

The idea for this book really began with my lifelong curiosity about the magi who came to Bethlehem at the birth of Jesus. Where did they come from? How did they know they sought a king? These are questions I still plan to address in another book, but I found myself wanting to take a step backward in time from that pivotal moment in history, to understand the religious and political climate in which it took place. When I happened upon the little-known fact that Herod the Great was a close friend of Marc Antony's, and that he made an enemy of Cleopatra by refusing her manipulative advances, I had an episode for fiction that was too good to pass up.

The meeting of Cleopatra and Herod the Great, both incredibly powerful world leaders, became a natural opening for the story. I traveled the length of their relationship, watched empire-shaking events take place over the course of a decade, and arrived at an ending point for my story with the death of Herod's wife. Now I needed a pair of eyes through which to see these events. Casting about, it soon became clear that most of the major players in this drama were corrupt or dead by the end of it, so it became necessary to invent a character as my "witness." I wanted to begin in Egypt, to meet the future Caesar Augustus in Rome, and to travel to Judea to focus on Herod, and thus Lydia was born as a servant in the palace of Alexandria, Egypt. I decided to make Lydia an orphan because I wanted to examine some issues of identity. What is it that makes us worthwhile and valued? Is it our parentage? Our own efforts at pleasing others and making ourselves needed? Our achievements? Or is it something else, a firmer foundation on which we can truly build a life?

So I had lots of history and a sympathetic character through whom to witness it, but my character herself had no story. All of the considerable and factual excitement was happening *around* her. She needed something to be busy about herself. It was not long after this point in the story development that a closer reading of the book of Daniel showed me something I had never seen before. The last few chapters of the book are concerned chiefly with "the time of the end" and in chapter 12, verses 4 and 9, the angel Michael, speaking to Daniel, tells him to "roll up and seal" the words of the scroll until the time of the end. What were these words, I wondered. If only the book of Daniel itself, then it was apparently unsealed before the time of the end. Is it possible that *other* words, other scrolls, exist somewhere still sealed with unknown prophecies? It was enough of an intriguing idea that I decided to place these scrolls in Lydia's hands, and charge her with returning them to the guardians who had lost them generations before.

With the major elements in place, it was time to decide which historical events and characters to include. As I mentioned, this story relies more heavily on true events, of which there were many. The Maccabean revolt that placed the Hasmonean family on the throne occurred 120 years before the start of *The Queen's Handmaid*, and eventually that feuding family invited Rome into the conflict in hopes of settling it. Instead, in 63 BC, the Roman general Pompey nearly destroyed Jerusalem and made Israel a client kingdom of the Roman Republic. Pompey restored the Hasmonean Hyrcanus (Alexandra's father) as High Priest, but placed the Idumean Antipater (Herod's father) on the throne as king. The Idumeans had been forced to convert and incorporated into Judaism years before but were still resented.

Antipater was a shrewd politician, a friend to Julius Caesar, and he paved the way for his son Herod to eventually become king. Factions within Jerusalem were still supporting the dethroned Hasmoneans, in the person of Hyrcanus's nephew Antigonus. In 37 BC, with the help of the Romans who had already declared him king, Herod defeated Antigonus in Jerusalem and took Judea for himself, hated by nearly everyone but his close friend Marc Antony.

Meanwhile, back in Rome, Marc Antony and Octavian, two of the three members of the Second Triumvirate, were falling out. The marriages and divorces outlined in my story are factual, but in the end these alliances solved nothing, and Marc Antony's growing allegiance to Cleopatra alienated him from Octavian and from Rome. By the summer of 30 BC, he and Cleopatra were both dead at their own hands.

There are too many incidents of history woven through *The Queen's Handmaid* to detail here. Suffice it to say that much of the story, like the attempted escape of Aristobolus and Alexandra in coffins, the drowning of Aristobolus in Herod's swimming pool, the murder of Cleopatra's various family members, the murder of the Sanhedrin members, the deaths of Cleopatra, Marc Antony, Hyrcanus, Joseph, Sohemus, Caesarion, and Mariamme are all factual. The circumstances of the death of Ptolemy's brother, king of Cyprus, is factual, but details of his wife's identity are unknown, and I fictionalized her connection with Judea.

I have taken one liberty, which I hope my readers will forgive for the sake of the story. It concerns the timeline. From the start of the story in 39 BC, through to the point where Lydia's identity becomes known, the story follows a strict timeline. At that point, however, I needed to account for four years until the death of Mariamme. Originally, I wrote a chapter to cover this span, in which Lydia hides out in Rome with Antony's wife Octavia, biding her time while the major players battle it out. But my editors and I agreed that it slowed the story too much, and needed to be trimmed. So in that section you will find Lydia impatiently waiting for history to unfold, with the amount of passing time unspecified, but nothing like four years implied. During these four years a major earthquake occurred in Judea, but I needed to skip that event as well. By the time of her death, Mariamme had given Herod four children, but in my truncated version, I was only able to fit in two.

I have been privileged to travel to most of the locations in this story—Alexandria, Rome, Jerusalem, Masada. I hope you'll join me on my website, www.TracyHigley.com, to read more about the locations of the book, to see travel photos, and to read stories of my adventures. There is also a place for you to check up on my next story and even give input to what you'd like to see included!

And what of the story beyond the story? As hinted in the

final pages, after Mariamme's execution, Herod's obsession with her led to increasing insanity. Historians tell us that Herod had been a master politician, charming, and well-liked. The madness we see in him twenty-five years later at the birth of Jesus apparently began in this moment, at the death of Mariamme. Not long after, he has Mariamme's mother, Alexandra, executed as well. Herod will continue to terrorize Judea for many years to come, his sister, Salome, at his side, and come to be known as "Herod the Great," mostly due to his extensive building projects in Judea, including the Temple Mount that still stands today. Octavian becomes Caesar Augustus, the first emperor of the newly forming Roman Empire. The New Testament contains a confusing mix of Herodians, but of highest interest are probably one of Herod's sons (by a wife after Mariamme), Herod Antipas, who kills John the Baptist; Herod Agrippa, his grandson, who arrests Peter; and Herod's great-grandson, Agrippa II, who listens to Paul's defense in Acts.

So I leave this story in 29 BC with the Pharisees, Sadducees, and zealots arguing and the city in poverty under the reign of a madman. With the prophets silent for centuries and the rabbis despairing that their Redeemer will ever come to break their bondage. With a star, rising unknown on the horizon and the Chakkiym watching in the East. There will still be two decades of sorrow, suffering, and questions. But the darkness will not last forever.

Even so, come, Lord Jesus!

Reading Group Guide

1. This story contains a wealth of historical anecdotes and facts. Did you enjoy learning some of the history of Cleopatra, Marc Antony, Octavian, and Herod as you read? What were some new things you learned?

2. Lydia struggles throughout the book with issues of identity and feelings of worthlessness. Do you relate to her struggle? In what way?

3. The story references the scrolls of Daniel mentioned in Daniel 12, which the angel told Daniel to seal up until the "time of the end." Had you ever considered what this passage might mean? What did you think of the author's speculation that these scrolls may still have been sealed hundreds of years later? Do you think it's possible they still exist somewhere?

4. This story spans the globe, taking in Egypt, Rome, and Israel. What did you learn about these locations?

5. In what ways do you feel the author's travels through these countries and other ancient lands have informed her writing? Which of these locations would you most like to visit? Why?

6. How did you feel about the relationship between Simon and Lydia, which took years to develop?

7. With what character did you most identify? Why?

8. The story did not end happily for everyone. How do you feel about this? Did the ending leave you thinking about the coming of the Messiah not many years later?

9. How do you feel about the author's portrayal of spiritual darkness in the story? Do you believe that people like Salome may have been in touch with evil powers at this time in history? How about now?

10. Lydia enjoys feeling needed by others in her life, but she also learns that she can't center her life around what others think. Is this a struggle in your life?

Acknowledgments

Once again, an idea has made its way from a tiny seed in my often-strange brain to the story you hold in your hands. And once again, the evolution of that first idea did not happen without the help, support, and encouragement of many.

First, a thank you to my readers. Many of you joined me on my website to give input into this book as it was taking shape—asking questions and inspiring me with ideas. I am, of course, hard at work on something new, so please visit again and share!

The fiction team at Thomas Nelson has been a joy. Thank you to Ami McConnell for such wise guidance in the writing and editing phases. Thanks to Kristen Vasgaard for the fabulous cover, and for all the folks there that work so hard to bring a book to print and get it out to readers.

Julee Schwarzburg, you are amazing. As I read the final product I know that it is my story and my voice, somehow made much better by your skillful editing.

To my agent, Steve Laube, the dedication of this book is heartfelt. I have loved having you in my corner on this publishing journey. Thank you.

And as always, my family continues to support, cheer, roll their eyes at my insecurities, and make me feel they are proud of the work I do. Ron, Rachel, Sarah, Jake, and Noah—I'd probably be a crazy person without all of you to keep me sane. I love you all very much.

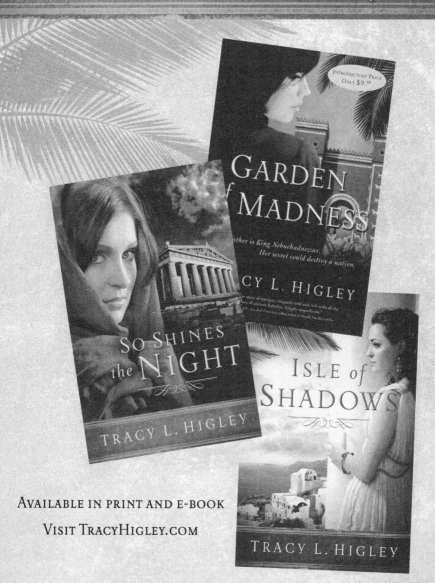

About the Author

Photo courtesy of Mary DeMuth

Tracy L. Higley started her first novel at the age of eight and has been hooked on writing ever since. She has authored nine novels, including *Garden of Madness* and *So Shines the Night*. Tracy is currently pursuing a graduate degree in Ancient History and has traveled through Greece, Turkey, Egypt, Israel, Jordan, and Italy, researching her novels and falling into adventures. See her travel journals and more at TracyHigley.com.